OTHER TITLES BY STEPHANIE WROBEL

Darling Rose Gold

This Might Hurt

THE
HITCHCOCK
HOTEL

STEPHANIE WROBEL

BERKLEY
NEW YORK

BERKLEY
An imprint of Penguin Random House LLC
penguinrandomhouse.com

Copyright © 2024 by Stephanie Wrobel
Penguin Random House supports copyright. Copyright fuels creativity, encourages diverse voices,
promotes free speech, and creates a vibrant culture. Thank you for buying an authorized edition of this
book and for complying with copyright laws by not reproducing, scanning, or distributing any part
of it in any form without permission. You are supporting writers and allowing Penguin Random House
to continue to publish books for every reader.

BERKLEY and the BERKLEY & B colophon are registered trademarks of
Penguin Random House LLC.

Library of Congress Cataloging-in-Publication Data

Names: Wrobel, Stephanie, author.
Title: The Hitchcock hotel / Stephanie Wrobel.
Description: New York : Berkley, 2024.
Identifiers: LCCN 2024002315 (print) | LCCN 2024002316 (ebook) |
ISBN 9780593547113 (hardcover) | ISBN 9780593547120 (ebook)
Subjects: LCGFT: Thrillers (Fiction). | Novels.
Classification: LCC PS3623.R628 H58 2024 (print) | LCC PS3623.R628
(ebook) | DDC 813/.6--dc23/eng/20240117
LC record available at https://lccn.loc.gov/2024002315
LC ebook record available at https://lccn.loc.gov/2024002316

Printed in the United States of America
1st Printing

Book design by George Towne
Interior art: Tree silhouette © Ihnatovich Maryia/Shutterstock.com

For Ali

My theory is that everyone is a potential murderer.

—*Strangers on a Train*

Which is the cat, and which is the mouse?

—*Rope*

We all go a little mad sometimes.

—*Psycho*

THE
HITCHCOCK
HOTEL

PROLOGUE

The crow waits until the guilty one disappears; then he flies down the hallway. How he wound up in this part of the hotel, he cannot recall. He has no memory of the tartan wallpaper, the dim flicker of the sconces. He does not know which humans lie behind which doors.

He knows only to obey the scream of his instincts.

Leave.

Now.

Go.

Danger hangs over this place like a blackening cloud. The people inside are not to be trusted. The crow rests for a moment on the horse hanging from the sky. He dares not wait long. Soon they will all rise again. Soon there will be much commotion.

He did not catch more than a glimpse, but a glimpse was all he needed. Such an ugly shape the limbs made, the neck contorted. The thing hardly looked human at all.

The crow takes to the air again, finds himself ever more eager to return home to his kin. What will the rest of the murder think? He flies around and around, yet still he cannot locate the path back to the aviary.

It's no use. He's trapped like the rest of them.

ACT
ONE

Always make the audience

suffer as much as possible.

—Alfred Hitchcock

THURSDAY
OCTOBER 12

ONE

Alfred

Let us begin with an establishing shot. A three-story Victorian house stands alone on a hill in the White Mountains. The house boasts a wrap-around porch, mansard roof, and bay windows. Despite the building's age, her shingles gleam, shutters sparkle. In other words, she is beloved.

We swoop in through an open window on the third floor to reveal a handsome hotel room. A woman with a face of cracked earth leans against a four-poster bed, watching a man in his thirties survey himself in a pedestal floor mirror.

I twist away from the mirror to face my housekeeper.

"How do I look?"

Danny takes her time considering me. "Like Norman Bates," she jokes.

I scowl. "I meant my outfit."

"Not many men can pull off a turtleneck, particularly with a suit," she says. "You look good, Alfred."

"Too much?" I ask, holding the pocket square to my chest.

She scrunches her nose and nods. I toss the silk square back on my desk, then hand her my stack of note cards. "Quiz me."

"You've been over these a hundred times."

"Go on." I turn back to the mirror.

Danny sighs and pulls one from the deck. "What are Samira's children's names?"

"Aditi and Shivam." Got that from Facebook.

"TJ's official title?"

"Freelance security specialist." LinkedIn.

"Zoe's drink of choice?"

"Lagavulin with one ice cube." This detail took some effort. I started by calling Saint Vincent, pretending to be a devoted fan who wanted to send a celebratory bottle the head chef's way. Imagine my surprise when I was told Zoe was on indefinite leave from the restaurant she opened. From there I turned to Instagram and tallied all her photos with alcohol in them. In twelve percent she held a glass of red wine, in thirty-six percent she gripped a pint, and in a solid fifty-two percent a glass of scotch sat by her place setting. In the scotch photos, a bottle of Lagavulin appeared in the background nine times out of ten. I've stocked half a dozen bottles, to be safe.

"You're ready, honey." Danny crosses the room and palms my cheek. "If you knew any more, they'd think you're a stalker."

I look once more in the mirror and finger the soft cuff cloaking my neck. They will comment on my turtleneck—I know they will—but what choice do I have? I haven't bared my neck in years, and I'm not about to start today of all days.

Never mind. No one has even arrived yet, and already I'm falling into old routines, getting defensive. I have much more important things to do today than hide in my room.

"Staff meeting," I say. "Shall we?"

I hold the door for Danny. I was skeptical when she interviewed for the job—she's the fittest senior I've met, but she has to be pushing eighty. Happily, she's proven my doubts unfounded. She's my hardest-working employee and rarely complains, unlike the younger ones. She's also become my trusted lieutenant.

Danny pauses at the threshold and meets my gaze. "I won't let them hurt you," she vows.

The old widow is overprotective of me, which I grumble about but adore. In this case, she need not fret. They'll be dolls in my dollhouse. I am the child at play.

We walk down the third-floor hallway in quiet companionship. I note with pride the vacuum lines on the plush navy carpet. Sometimes I still can't believe I own a hotel. Technically it's an inn, but "hotelier" sounds grander than "innkeeper."

The house has three floors, excluding the attic. On the first floor are the lobby, restaurant, bar, home theater, parlor, and aviary—probably the sole hotel that has one in the country, a real feather in our cap. The second and third floors host six guest rooms each. This weekend's guests will take the rooms on the third floor. Only the best for my former best friends.

In the lobby I wait with my hands clasped behind my back for the rest of the staff. I try to see the space as a guest would, searching for dust bunnies in corners, shoe prints on tiles. I've styled the hotel like a Scottish hunting lodge—low lighting, dark rugs, upholstered furniture, heavy drapes. Moody portraits of women hang on the walls because Hitch surrounded his heroines with them on set. The reception desk to the left of the staircase took me weeks to find: an antique piece with a matching chair that would fit perfectly inside a medieval castle.

And what of the staircase? Devotees will know that harrowing things happen on Hitch's staircases. Ours is T shaped with two landings, one halfway up the central section and another at the top. Mahogany steps jut out from both sides of the landings. These steps lead to the guest rooms.

Suspended from the ceiling above the staircase is our pièce de résistance: one of the original carousel horses from *Strangers on a Train*. It wasn't cheap, but can you put a price on owning a piece of one of the most iconic scenes in cinema? The horse's mouth is agape, eyes distressed. I swear, on occasion I've seen it sway ever so slightly, giving a ghoulish feeling to an otherwise refined space, which was the effect our set designer was going for.

(It's me. I'm the set designer.)

I greet each staff member as they arrive, wait patiently until all have gathered. "Okay, folks," I say. "We're giving up a high-season weekend of leaf peepers for this free stay. Let's make it worth the lost revenue."

For the next few days I'm hosting my five closest friends from college. We met at Reville, took a film studies class together, then went on to found the campus film club. I haven't seen them in well over a decade, so this is an informal reunion.

I carry on. "I know how hard you've all worked lately. As a thank-you, I have a surprise." I pause. "You can take Saturday and Sunday off."

The twentysomething bartender gasps. A brief commotion ensues. The staff is surprised and confused after the fuss I've made this week. I laugh off their concern, say my friends and I would like some privacy.

"Let's get these folks settled in. I'll take care of the rest."

Danny, of course, will stay. I can't do this without her.

I remind the concierge that we'll have no late reservations or walk-ins. The staff disperses as I move to the round table in the middle of the lobby. I tip my nose into the autumnal floral arrangement, then fan out the half dozen copies of *Travel + Leisure*. I glance at one of the headlines: 14 MOST UNIQUE STAYS IN NEW ENGLAND. With any luck, my hotel will make that list next year.

I glance at the wall mirror and tug on my turtleneck. My temples glisten. I wipe my forehead.

"I'm going to wait for Zoe," I call over my shoulder. The concierge waves in response.

Outside, I breathe easier. Though it's supposed to rain the rest of the weekend, today the sun is shining. New England is at her best in the fall. The mountains surrounding our region are aflame with color—trees painted crimson and gold. From our hilly perch we have a clear view of the valley that houses my small college town. There I spent some of my happiest days—and also the worst of my life.

October is a month crafted for Hitchcock. This is the lone time of year when villains don't have to hide in the shadows, when frights are welcomed, even begged for. The cooling weather sends people indoors, to their sofas, to their television sets—to cherished films. Autumn is the perfect season to commemorate the Master of Suspense. Here we are, celebrating our second fall in business. One year ago today was the hotel's opening. At times I worried we wouldn't make it to year two.

The parking lot has twenty spots over two rows. I squint and notice a small wad of gum stuck to the blacktop. From my pocket I pull a Swiss Army knife and scrape at the gum until it comes free. I toss it into the stone receptacle near the front door, then survey the lot again. *Better.*

I run through my greeting with Zoe. Do I give her a hug? Shake her hand? Wave? Hitchcock used to introduce himself as "Hitch without the cock," but only geniuses get to be that crude. I check my watch: ten minutes after two. Zoe has never been known for her punctuality.

Just then a Wrangler speeds up my quiet lane. My breath quickens, heart pounds.

What I've done, what I'm doing, is a risk.

The tires screech as the SUV rips around the corner. I swallow, mouth bone-dry. I catch a glimpse of Zoe as she does a sloppy parking job in the second to farthest spot from the building. Still that same blond pixie haircut and enough eyeliner to pass for a raccoon. She climbs out of her Jeep, dressed in all black and combat boots.

People don't change—not much, anyway. The thought calms me. I know these people. I can predict what they'll do.

I breathe onto my palm and sniff. It doesn't smell, but I put two Altoids in my mouth anyway. I watch Zoe hoist a duffel bag out of the back seat of her vehicle, then head toward me. She waves. From this far away I can't tell whether she's smiling. I wave back.

"Welcome to the Hitchcock Hotel," I call.

And . . . action.

Hitchcock was never concerned with plausibility in his films. That was the easiest part, he said, so why bother? Call the police, and the story is over. He was much more interested in evoking a mood, in creating suspense.

—*Excerpt from Essay #18,*
"The Suspension of Disbelief in Film"

TWO

Zoe

Zoe can't believe Alfred actually fucking owns the fucking house at the top of the hill.

"You bought the *Psycho* house," she calls, relieved when her voice doesn't shake.

Alfred waits for her with long arms extended. He's still lanky and pale with a full head of hair—always neatly combed, like a little boy's. (Cringe.) His ears are slightly too big, adding to that boyishness, but his jaw is sharp. He smiles, revealing two rows of perfect teeth, canines gleaming. His dark eyes are set even deeper than Zoe remembered, as if, hiding beneath thick brows, they're being slowly sucked into his skull. The last thing she wants to do is hug him, but she does it anyway.

Alfred steps back to inspect her. "Zoe."

"Alfred."

"You look the same."

"So do you. Still rocking those turtlenecks." Zoe had once overheard students at a house party in college theorizing as to why Alfred wore turtlenecks exclusively. One kid guessed Alfred had been burned with cigarettes by a violent father. Another claimed that when Alfred was a toddler his mother had taken a razor blade to his neck before using it on herself. They were all curious what scars Alfred Smettle was trying to cover. To her knowledge, none of them ever asked him.

Zoe turns her attention to the house. It resembles the Bates family home, which Hitchcock modeled after Hopper's *House by the Railroad* painting. (More useless trivia she's never forgotten. Thanks, Alfred.) The film club had had a lot of fun back in the day, dreaming up rumors about the house's occupants while munching on French fries at Eggy's. Alfred would keep the storytelling going for hours if the others didn't shut him up.

"Let me take your bag," he says. His voice is soft and airy, in a way Zoe once thought comforting but now finds eerie.

She hands it to him, then peeks over her shoulder. Is she the first one here?

Alfred leads her up the balustraded front stairway, which is lined on both sides with pumpkins and baskets of mums. Iron lanterns hold ivory candles, lit though it's the middle of the day. Two black rocking chairs stand at the ready under the portico. Alfred pauses at the front door. "Do you feel like poor, doomed Arbogast?" He raises an eyebrow. "Waiting for one of the Bateses to answer the door?"

He's talking about the cop in the movie, Zoe realizes. "I hope that's where the similarities end," she says.

Alfred pushes open the door and gestures for her to lead the way. Zoe hesitates for a moment before stepping through the entrance. The lighting is dim after being in broad daylight. She has to squint to make out the receptionist sitting behind the desk at the far end of the lobby. She waits for her eyes to adjust.

"Whoa," she says under her breath when they do. "This is awesome." She has to admit that Alfred always had good taste—in material things, anyway—but she half expected (hoped?) the hotel would be a catastrophe. He was never ambitious in college, never showed passion for anything but old movies. He could be resourceful when he set his mind to something, though. Zoe grimaces. She feels Alfred standing behind her. Where did he get the cash to buy and renovate this place? According to Samira, he'd been working at La Quinta Inn for most of the time since school, and Zoe knows he didn't grow up with money.

A tall old woman with abnormally straight posture awaits them. Alfred gives her Zoe's bag.

"This is my housekeeper, Danny," he says.

"Zoe. Nice to meet you." Zoe sticks out her hand, but the woman makes no move to shake it. She holds Zoe's duffel with both hands instead.

The elderly woman's face is gaunt, with piercing eyes and a nose long enough to serve as a bird's perch. Her silver hair is pulled back into a tidy bun, not a strand out of place. She wears a shapeless black dress, tea length, with a white Peter Pan collar, and white cuffs on the short sleeves. On her feet are sensible Mary Jane slip-ons. Zoe wonders whether this uniform was her idea or Alfred's. Danny bows her head, then walks away. Weirdo.

Alfred gestures to the room on their left. "Want to have a look around?"

The floorboards creak under Zoe's feet. She follows Alfred.

"This is the parlor," he says.

She takes it in—the grand piano, the homey fire, the cozy scents of leather and smoke. Gathered around the hearth are two velvet armchairs and a sofa. There are vases on pedestals; from them grand arrangements of dried flowers fan out like peacocks' tails. An antique wooden chest serves as a coffee table. On the chest is a British-looking arrangement—a three-tiered china tray with sandwiches, scones, and cakes, plus a silver pot of tea and several delicate teacups. A shout-out to Alfred's revered director, no doubt. He is waiting for Zoe's reaction. She will not give him the satisfaction of impressing her twice.

Zoe wanders toward one of the walls. Identical shadow boxes are lined up in a row, each one holding the call sheet for a Hitchcock production. *Topaz, Torn Curtain, Marnie, Frenzy.*

She turns back to Alfred. "These real?"

He thrusts out his chest. "All originals."

Not for the first time, Zoe wonders why he invited them here. Is it to show off his hotel and success? Or does he want something from them? If so, why now?

Alfred's invitation came via group email on a Sunday night one month ago. No one responded for a full twenty-four hours. Zoe presumed everyone else was as shocked and reluctant as she was. She decided to wait for someone else to decline first, then follow suit. On Tuesday morning a reply landed in her inbox from grace.liu@whelan.com.

> Thank you for the invitation, Alfred. A reunion in the mountains
> sounds wonderful. A Hitchcock-themed hotel—how original!
> Looking forward to catching up with you guys.

Zoe had been surprised. Samira said Grace was a bigwig hedge fund manager at a company called Whelan Management, married with two kids. Surely she had better ways to pass a weekend.

Then again, Grace had owed Alfred one for a long time.

Minutes after Grace's first email arrived, Zoe received a second one from her, addressed to Zoe alone. When was the last time she'd spoken to Grace? Zo, it implored, I know you won't want to go, but I also think you know why we should.

For days Zoe agonized over the decision, long after the rest of the group had said yes. She dreaded seeing Alfred again and wasn't eager to see Grace either. In the end, Zoe agreed to attend anyway. Two months on the wagon, but she was still out of a job—banished from her own kitchen—so fuck it. Maybe this weekend could give her something years of drinking, overwork, and therapy had not: closure.

Alfred glances at the food spread. "The staff has set out sandwiches and tea, but I assume you'd like something stronger?" He heads for the doorway. "Lagavulin?"

She blinks. How does he know her drink?

"You always liked whiskey in college," he explains, "but I figure you've upgraded from Jack and Cokes by now. Unless you'd like a return to your Reville glory days this weekend?"

You smug dick.

"Sparkling water if you have it. Otherwise tap is fine."

Alfred raises an eyebrow.

"I'm sober," Zoe adds, not that her recovery is any of his business.

"Are you?" He leans against the parlor doorframe. "Good for you, Zoe."

She hasn't drunk Jack Daniel's since college, but now that he's brought it up, she can taste the dry spice and smoke. Her hands fidget, so she jams them into the pockets of her bomber jacket. Drinking gave her something to do with her hands. Cooking too, but she hasn't done that in weeks. She wonders what the Hitchcock Hotel's kitchen looks like, whether Alfred would let her prepare a meal one night. It'd be weird to ask, and she doesn't want to give him the upper hand ever again. Zoe misses the weight of the Zwilling in her palm, the mania of the Saturday night shift—the sole time her feet outpaced her thoughts.

"How's Saint Vincent?" Alfred asks. Zoe startles again. "I read that piece about you in the *Times* a few years back. Your own restaurant! I was so impressed."

She swallows. "Yeah, it's good."

"I want to hear all about it. Let me get you that water first." He leaves the room.

Zoe sinks into the couch and pinches the bridge of her nose, eyes closed. Why had she lied when she could so easily be found out? One quick google and her friends would see the news. No way will she be able to keep it quiet.

This weekend is going to be a fucking nightmare.

"Look who I found," Alfred calls, his voice preceding him into the room. A second later he appears alongside an apple-cheeked woman. Both of them grin at Zoe.

"Samira!" Zoe rushes across the room and envelops her friend in a hug. "I'm so glad you're here." She means it too. Zoe has had more than enough one-on-one time with their host.

"This get-together couldn't come fast enough," Samira gushes. "If I'd had to sing 'The Itsy Bitsy Spider' one more time this week . . ."

Alfred hands Zoe a glass of sparkling water, then turns to Samira. "Something to drink?"

"A bottle of tequila." Samira winks. "That tea over there has my name on it."

They all move toward the hearth. Samira takes off her camel coat and collapses onto the couch with a sigh. "I think I live here now."

Zoe nestles into her, resting her head on Samira's shoulder. Samira hooks an arm around Zoe. They used to sit like this while watching TV on Sunday nights in college. Zoe feels a pang for the shared bowls of popcorn, their matching fuzzy socks.

"How are Henry and . . . the little ones?" Zoe asks without lifting her head. She winces. She should know their names; she's the worst. She had lunch with Samira, what was it, a few months back? No, wait—that was almost a year ago.

"Yes, how are Aditi and Shivam?" Alfred asks.

Zoe glances at Samira, whose eyebrows shoot up. Samira sips her tea to cover her surprise.

Alfred smiles. "I love when photos of your family outings pop up on Facebook."

"They're much cuter in 2D. Promise," Samira says with a laugh. "Please don't feel obligated to ask more. I'm using this weekend to pretend I have no responsibilities whatsoever."

Something Zoe loves about Samira: her kids are the least interesting thing about her. She loves them fiercely but doesn't bring them up unless you ask, would much rather discuss the shit show of American politics or her vibrator startup, an award-winning business she funded with her own savings. Zoe was surprised when Samira told her about the company— her modest friend had never struck her as erotic or entrepreneurial in college. Then again, Samira has always wanted to help people. She may not be the flashiest person in the room, but she's never shied away from topics that make others uncomfortable either. Zoe recently watched a YouTube clip of Samira delivering an impassioned speech to college students about the importance of female pleasure—with a child on each hip, no less. That's the badass type of mom Zoe would like to be, but she would never subject an innocent child to her messy life.

Samira lights up. "Wasn't it such a trip driving along Greet Street? I was this close to grabbing Bagel and Deli."

Zoe had almost stopped at their favorite campus haunt too. Greet Street is Reville's main drag. Some of it, like the bagel shop, the hanging flower baskets, and the blue-and-white-striped awning of the ice cream parlor, remains the same. But a lot has changed in sixteen years too. There's an Insomnia Cookies next to the Jimmy John's now, plus a new (to Zoe, anyway) gift shop across the street. "Was that Starbucks there when we were students?" she asks.

Samira shakes her head and laughs. "That's where Stadium used to be. Tell me you haven't forgotten Stadium." Now Zoe remembers the bar that exclusively freshmen frequented, because of its shitty plumbing, pun very much intended. Not knowing any better, she'd taken her mom and dad there for parents' weekend her first year, only to discover standing water in the bathrooms. She'd almost gotten into a fistfight with a guy who knocked into her mom that night. Health-code-violating dive bar aside, Greet Street is a slice of classic small-town Americana. The entire Reville campus is. Its quad had once been voted the most beautiful in the country by a publication that took the time to rank such things.

"What was the bagel sandwich you guys loved?" Alfred asks. "With the Doritos?"

"The Crunch and Munch," Samira squeals. "I passed the bookstore too. Bet they're selling the same Reville hoodies. I should've worn mine this weekend as an homage. Do you think the Crazy Taco still does dollar margaritas? Maybe we can stop in."

Alfred frowns. Without taking a breath, Samira continues. "Okay, tell us everything. What made you decide to open a hotel? When did you buy this place? I can't believe you own the house on the hill."

Another thing Zoe loves about Samira: she carries the conversation, so Zoe doesn't have to.

"I needed a bigger warehouse for my collectibles," Alfred jests, then clears his throat. "Well, I've worked in hospitality since college. A decade or so at La Quinta. I think I held every position they had, from house-keeping to cook to reception. Hotel work is the only kind I've ever done. My one area of expertise." He chews his lip, debating something. "You know, when storytellers are asked where their ideas come from"—Zoe struggles not to roll her eyes—"they often say they wanted to read a book about X but it didn't exist, so they wrote it themselves. That's how I felt about the Hitchcock Hotel. During slow shifts, I'd fantasize about living during Hitch's time, being able to immerse myself in his worlds and sets. One day, on my lunch break, I thought, why not?"

Zoe had forgotten Alfred's pet name for Hitchcock, like they were best friends. Of course he would idolize a sadist with a fragile ego.

"I think you taught me more about Hitchcock than Dr. Scott did," Samira says.

An ache forms in the back of Zoe's throat.

"How could a boy not be curious about his namesake?" Alfred says.

Alfred's mom must have been a nutjob, Zoe thinks for the hundredth time. Her focus returns to Jack Daniel's. She could handle one drink.

"Tell us the story of the house," Samira pushes. "How long have you owned this place?"

"Four years," Alfred says. "Renovations took two and a half. Today is the anniversary of our grand opening."

"Congratulations! God, this place was falling apart when we were at Reville, but you'd never know it now. You must have put so much work in here," Samira says.

Alfred lifts his chin—*Great, here comes a never-ending monologue,*

Zoe thinks—but before he can begin gloating, a broad-shouldered man fills the entryway.

"Knock, knock," TJ says.

"Teej," Samira shrieks, spilling some of her tea as she rushes over to pull him into a bear hug. How she manages to get her arms around him is a mystery to Zoe. TJ is jacked now, a far cry from the scrawny boy she went to school with. At least he still wears those black-framed glasses.

"Samira," he says warmly.

"You're somehow even more of a beefcake than the last time we got together," Samira says. "Your biceps look like they're ready to burst. What are you taking?"

Samira is the only one who still keeps in touch with everyone in the group—except Alfred, apparently, since she hadn't even known he'd opened a hotel.

"Lots of eggs and regular workouts," TJ says. "You know I don't mess with steroids. Thanks for having me, Alfred. Nice turtleneck." Alfred goes in for a hug while TJ extends a hand. The exchange is painful to watch.

Zoe lets TJ make his way to her. To her disappointment—and then surprise at said disappointment—there's no longer any heat in his gaze. Well, what was she expecting? That he'd harbor a crush for someone he hasn't spoken to in ten years? After one measly hookup—and that was before she fell apart.

"Hi, Zoe," TJ says.

She gives him a hug and murmurs, "I can't believe you showed."

"Wouldn't miss it," he says nervously.

She pulls back and studies him. TJ doesn't meet her eye.

"What can I get you, man?" Alfred asks. Zoe flinches at his attempt at brotherliness. A certain type of guy can pull off "man" or "dude" or "bro." Alfred is not that type. Is she going to spend the next four days squirming with discomfort? She returns to her seat, gripping her glass of sparkling water. All these old faces remind her of a Zoe she hates. She knows what her friends thought of her senior year, what some of them said behind her back, maybe still do. She's determined not to make an ass of herself this weekend.

"A beer would be great," TJ says. Alfred shoots Zoe a sympathetic glance, and she has an urge to poke out his eyeballs. *I'll take a scotch* is on the tip of her tongue. She wets her lips.

Alfred leaves, while TJ and Samira plop onto the couch. Samira's hand settles on TJ's forearm. "Today's the day you tell us who your big fancy client is." She turns to Zoe. "TJ is a bodyguard for some VIP in DC, but he won't tell me who."

"And never will," TJ says. "A confidentiality clause is written into my contract. I could get fired."

Zoe almost laughs. She can't think of a job the TJ she knew would be less suited for. The kid who majored in English, who wanted to be an editor at a big publishing house, who wrote his senior thesis on Shirley Jackson, for Christ's sake? The only conflict he could tolerate in college was the fictional kind. Although he certainly looks the part of a security guard.

"Blink once if he's a Democrat. Twice if he's a Republican," Samira says.

TJ stares at her, unblinking.

"Maybe they're not in politics," Zoe says, getting into it. "Maybe they're a celebrity."

"What kind of celebrity lives in DC?" Samira asks.

Zoe shrugs. TJ shakes his head. Alfred returns with a pint for TJ, making sad eyes at Zoe all the while. She feels like they're two gunslingers in a duel, each sizing up their opponent. A rematch sixteen years too late. Half of her is afraid of Alfred and wants to leave the past in the past. The other half wants to dig it up, then bury him.

"How long you think until Julius shows up?" TJ asks.

"Smooth change of subject," Zoe says. TJ wiggles his eyebrows.

"Julius runs on JST," Samira says. An old joke from college—Julius Standard Time. His perpetual lateness was in no way fashionable. "The show starts when he feels like it."

"Listen to you little shit talkers. If I had feelings, they might be hurt."

Four heads turn to find Julius Thénardier in the doorway. In college Julius's wardrobe tended to turn heads. Apparently nothing had changed in the intervening years, as today he's wearing a neon orange satin blouse with white trousers. Zoe often wondered if he dressed big to make up for his height—five feet six inches if she was being generous.

Samira hurries over, Zoe and TJ close behind her. Samira ruffles Julius's blond hair. "Come on, now. You feel plenty."

"That's true. Greed, anger, emptiness." Julius laughs, and the two hug. When Samira lets him go, Zoe sees tears in his eyes.

"Are you crying?" she asks, shocked, as she moves in for her own hug. She's never seen his eyes so much as well up before.

He chuckles and wipes his eyes self-consciously, then shakes hands with TJ. "I'm just happy to see you guys. I've missed you." This is, by a long shot, the sappiest thing that Zoe has ever heard come out of Julius's mouth. She cocks her head.

Alfred makes his way over reluctantly, a child waiting for punishment. Julius focuses his attention on their host and clucks his tongue. "Alfred, I swear to God, I'm going to cut the necks off all your turtlenecks while you sleep." Alfred tenses. "I had no idea what to expect this weekend, but one thing I knew for sure: Alfred would be standing there, stiff as cardboard, covered up to his chin like a nun."

Everyone but Alfred laughs. There's the old Julius they know and love. Alfred tilts his head, watching him. "Sixteen years wasn't long enough for you to come up with new jokes?"

The room quiets, and the silence is strained. Zoe finds it odd that Julius, the king of banter, has no comeback at the ready. She studies him. He appears tired, thin. Then again, she hasn't seen him in a long, long time. Maybe this is his normal weight when he isn't drinking six nights a week.

"I didn't mean—" Julius protests.

Alfred claps Julius on the back harder than necessary, and the smaller man coughs. "I'm kidding. Good to see you."

Julius pulls Alfred into a hug. "Congratulations, my friend. The hotel is exquisite. I mean it."

"How about a drink?"

"I thought you'd never ask. I'll take two shots of vodka; hold the judgment." With that, their routine is reestablished.

"Coming right up," Alfred says. If Zoe had ordered two shots, they all would've clutched their pearls, but when Julius does it, no one says a word. "Once Grace is here, I'll give you all a tour," he adds.

"She got held up at work," Samira says at the same time TJ declares, "She'll be late."

"In that case, everyone, follow me," Alfred says. Back in the lobby, he introduces his staff of five: the concierge, the chef, the bartender, the groundskeeper, and the housekeeper, Danny.

"More like the crypt keeper," Julius snickers as he loops his arm through Zoe's. She's too busy watching the concierge—a stooped man with a greasy complexion—to respond. He's trying to catch the eye of the mulleted groundskeeper, who's staring intently at Samira. Eventually the concierge gives up.

Zoe focuses on the chef next. He's middle-aged but looks older, skin-and-bones thin, with a huge tattoo of a rose on the side of his neck. How good can he be, working in a tiny hotel in the middle of nowhere? She'll wait to pass a verdict until the group has had their first meal, but she's sure she can beat whatever he has planned.

The bartender hands Julius his requested shots. He rips them in quick succession, puts the glasses back on her tray, and thanks her with a wink.

Alfred guides the group to a room off the right of the lobby. The home theater has three rows of seating, four plush recliners per row. The room smells like old books, and no wonder. Three of the walls are filled from floor to ceiling with built-in bookshelves crammed with every biography, analysis, and criticism ever printed about Hitchcock, even ancient stuff that Zoe doubts is still in print. On the wall closest to them is a projector screen, where Alfred says Hitchcock films play twenty-four hours a day. "If you have trouble sleeping," he adds, "you can sit back on one of the recliners and occupy the night hours with Hitch. Right now *The Lodger* is playing. I've put the viewing schedule there on the table, so

you don't miss your favorite movie." Black speakers hang in the corners
of the room. On the floor beneath the screen is a subwoofer. Alfred gestures across the lobby into the parlor. "If the films are too distracting, feel
free to take any books in there and close the door. Make yourselves at
home."

Hard pass.

They move through the theater into the game room, where Alfred has
set up chess, checkers, and a poker table. In a back corner of the house is
the restaurant. Here Zoe relaxes a little. An oversized chandelier, a dozen
tables on overlapping oriental rugs, trendy wallpaper, tasteful sconces.
Riedel glassware and Tiffany candlesticks on the tables—the same ones
Saint Vincent has. The scents of bacon and thyme drift from the kitchen.
The room oozes luxury, encourages idleness. This scene is a world away
from the paper oatmeal packets, stale bagels, and shrink-wrapped plas-
ticware of what Zoe imagines was Alfred's previous job. She wonders
again what shifty shit he did to secure the money for this place. Alfred
isn't afraid to get his hands dirty.

He's standing by a buffet table against the wall, pointing at an old-
fashioned black telephone inside a glass case. "This is a prop—*the* prop—
from *Dial M for Murder*. You'll remember that Grace Kelly was using this
telephone when a hit man emerged from behind the curtain to strangle her."

A cursory glance around the group confirms to Zoe that no one but
Alfred has seen the movie.

"Breakfast is served seven to ten," he continues. "If you'd like to eat
at a different time, let me know, and I'll have the chef adjust." She's sure
Chef loves that. "Lunch is between noon and two, and dinner starts at
seven."

TJ moves to the windows at the back of the dining room, hands in
his pockets, and stares at the courtyard.

"How could I forget the aviary?" Alfred makes his way to TJ's side.
The rest of the group joins them. The geodesic dome is eight feet tall and
huge. "The sanctuary is large enough to house a hundred birds, though
I only have fifty crows for now."

"Only?" Julius snorts, in brighter spirits now that he has some booze in him.

Inside the aviary are palms, eucalyptus, and bamboo. Birdhouses hang from the ceiling at varying heights. Alfred says his groundskeeper installed the accent lighting, plus the bubbling fountain and statuary. The space is colorful and cheerful, save for the long faces of the several dozen crows watching them. Zoe thinks of the baby bird from senior year and shudders.

Alfred concludes his tour at the bar. The bar itself is made of one long plank of wood, with stools to match. A hundred bottles of liquor stand on display. A quick glance at the menu tells Zoe that Alfred has an excellent wine list, plus a few solid beers on tap. She focuses on the bubbles in her sparkling water. She's drunk barely anything. The tremor in her hands revs up again.

The bar walls are filled with portraits of women in varying states of distress—probably thanks to the bird shrine next door, Zoe thinks. A great horned owl hangs above the bar, its wings outstretched—the span has to be at least four feet—with yellow eyes boring into the group.

"Rest easy knowing the owl only *looks* real," Alfred says. "Norman Bates can have his taxidermy, but I couldn't bear to keep dead animals on my property."

The owl is incredibly lifelike. Zoe can't stand to gaze into its spooky eyes despite knowing they're made of plastic.

"That isn't the actual prop from *Psycho*?" Samira asks.

Alfred shakes his head. "I have yet to convince Universal to sell me that one. Pretty good replica, isn't it?"

He gestures at the young bartender, who stands with a smile behind the bar. "Jenna will be happy to get you another drink. Otherwise, my concierge will show you to your rooms. We'll have dinner in the private dining room this evening." He points to his left, at enormous rustic doors with faux antlers for handles. "I'll see you all later." Alfred glides out of the room. Could he be any more pleased with himself?

"Will you settle a bet for us, Jenna?" Julius asks the bartender as he sidles up to the bar. She's blond and pretty, so Zoe assumes he'll try to sleep with her.

Jenna nods gamely. Julius gestures at TJ. "My friend says you wouldn't have a drink with me in a million years."

TJ shakes his head but is smiling. He served as Julius's wingman countless times in college. "I never said that."

"She's on the clock," Zoe ribs Julius. "Leave the poor woman alone."

Julius ignores them, focusing instead on Jenna. "On one hand, look at you. Clearly out of my league." The bartender bites back a smile. "On the other, did I mention I can play 'Mambo No. 5' on the xylophone? I believe that technically makes me a musician."

Jenna's laughing now. She pulls two rocks glasses from behind the bar and gets busy making cocktails. Zoe steals glances at the rest of her friends. TJ is studying the paintings on the wall. Samira is texting on her phone. Zoe pulls out her own phone for something to do, somewhere to train her gaze on. She feels weirdly shy around these people who used to be her closest friends. She once knew their strengths and flaws, their obsessions, their cruelties. Her stomach fizzes, teeth grind.

It's just three nights, she tells herself. As long as she keeps her wits about her, she has no reason to worry.

THREE

Alfred

A proprietor has few places to turn when he wants privacy. For me, one space is the attic. Neither my guests nor my staff knows about it, making it the perfect spot to clear my head. Up here my mind runs wild. I let myself dwell in the past.

The most common question I get from guests is where my love of Hitchcock comes from. I always give them the abridged answer: my mother was a fan, and we watched his movies together. The longer story is sadder, but they don't want to hear all that.

She was born the same year Hitch released *To Catch a Thief* (1955) and grew up watching *Alfred Hitchcock Presents* alongside her father—the only twenty-five minutes a week she was allowed in his study. By the time she reached her teenage years, Mom had big dreams of becoming the next Tippi Hedren. Like the *Birds* actress, Mom vowed to give herself over to Hitch. She would let him train her in acting, elocution, and fashion, remake her in his own ideal. True, she was a brunette, not one of the icy blondes Hitch preferred, but she would convince him to make an exception.

Then she went and did the one thing her father warned her not to:

she met a boy. A man, actually. Fifteen years older than her and from the "wrong side of the tracks," as my grandfather put it. Determined to prove her father wrong, Mom married this man. My grandfather cut them both off, but Mom didn't care. Her new husband would provide for her, loved her so much that he wanted her all to himself—no wife of his was going to be on television or in movies. Her hope of becoming a Hitchcock actress faded, but she figured she was trading one dream for another. This new one was equally shiny, even more exciting—until her husband left without a word on a Friday afternoon. The divorce was finalized two years after the wedding. My grandfather offered nothing but a *Told you so*, so at twenty-two Mom got her first job, selling tickets at a movie theater. A few months later she sold one to my father. She took things slow this time, dating for seven years before agreeing to his proposal. She still dreamt of life as an actress but took no steps to make it happen. She was always more dreamer than doer.

Mom and Dad married, and a year later I made my debut. Mom said the next five years were the happiest of her life, right up until Dad drove his car off the cliff. No inclement weather, no traces of alcohol on the toxicology report, no swerving to avoid another vehicle, yet Mom insisted it was an accident. *A deer in the road,* she said. *Your father loved us.* I hardly remember the man, so I can't weigh in.

Dad's death was Mom's breaking point. Twice she had been robbed of love—three times if you counted my grandfather. She said it was more than one heart could bear. The men in her life were always leaving her. *Not me,* I promised.

Mom had been able to quit the movie theater job when Dad came on the scene, but now she begged to get her old job back. I helped out as soon as I was old enough, mowing lawns and babysitting neighbor kids a few years younger than me. Every morning Mom trudged to work while I trudged to school. I paid enough attention to keep my grades up but was too busy worrying about my mother to enjoy recess.

I learned that I could return some of the lightness to Mom's eyes if I put on Hitch's movies. She owned every single one on VHS. Night after night, as soon as my homework was done (on bad nights, even before then) we'd work our way through Hitch's fifty-three films. Once we finished them all, we'd start again. I'm not sure she even followed the plots—she never chuckled or squealed when she was supposed to—preferring to sit slack-jawed, a glass of wine in one hand, a cigarette in the other, getting lost in the leading ladies.

Those first few years of watching, I wanted only to please her, to give her a warm body to cuddle up to because she couldn't stand to be alone. As I matured, though, I began to see what she saw. The stories held me on edge. The dialogue was a tennis match, repartee swatted back and forth, rhythmic, at ease. Hitch was a master of comedy as much as suspense. His movies took you by the throat and refused to let go. After college, I went to Mom's house every Sunday afternoon to continue our tradition. I don't think I missed a single week until her brain aneurysm in 2017, an aberration no one saw coming. Fade to black.

I have told her story as a tragedy, but she was a firecracker, my mother. She loved puns and laughed generously when she was well. She posted me a birthday card every year of my childhood because I loved the ritual of mail: walking to the mailbox, slitting open the envelope, scanning the contents before poring over them in detail. At least once a week we had dance parties to Mariah Carey or Shania Twain. Our favorite meal was breakfast for dinner. She made the best blueberry waffles.

Some people escape their troubles via books or video games, but I lost myself in Hitch's films. After Mom passed, it wasn't enough to watch. I wanted to contribute somehow, partake. I began bidding for things on eBay. Small items at first. Replicas of movie posters and film stills. Shot glasses and other tchotchkes. I didn't have enough money then to collect anything of actual value.

Now my love for Hitch is less about my mother and more about propriety. In Hitch's world the hero saves the day or wins the girl—often both—and the villain is always brought to his knees. This tidy ordering of fictional universes was a relief to a boy who learned too early that the real world didn't play by the same rules. In the real world a good man could drive off a cliff; a grandfather could refuse to forgive; a mother could be struck down at random. In the real world a college student could watch as his life fell to pieces, powerless to put them back together.

What kind of a place is that? Where is the fairness? Who wouldn't prefer to live in Hitch's universe?

After thirty minutes in the attic, I make my way toward the door to the left of the staircase on the third floor. Room 304 is my bedroom. On the desk is one of the most valuable pieces in my collection, a beat-up olive green Olympia typewriter. Joseph Stefano used it to write the *Psycho* screenplay.

I run through the afternoon. As anticipated, everyone but Samira teased me about my turtleneck. That's okay. I held my own and maintained control of the room. All is well.

Phase one is about decisions. I need to choose who in the group is going to help me with the task at hand. Phase two is execution. Until then, I will be at their beck and call, as I am with every guest who passes through my doors. White-glove service is a necessity if you want to grace the pages of *Travel + Leisure*.

Someone knocks on my door. I open it.

"How are you doing?" Danny asks, eyebrows knitted together.

"Fine, all things considered."

"I think it should be the boy in the garish clothing," she says. "I don't like the way he speaks to you."

"Julius has always had a big mouth."

"Maybe he should pick on someone his own size," she sniffs. "Like Jiminy Cricket."

I snort and tuck away the dig for future use.

"Keep your chin up," Danny says. "Your last guest just arrived."

My mind stills. Grace.

I rush to the lobby and find Grace Liu standing at the reception desk, hand on her hip, appearing irritated with the concierge. The mere sight of her used to make me weak-kneed.

"Alfred." Her body language changes as soon as she sees me. She caves in on herself. Her voice is strained, more high-pitched than I remember. "Look what you've done."

I step toward her until we're close enough to touch. I expect the sweet perfume of our youth—Fantasy by Britney Spears—but am greeted with something unfamiliar in its place. Woodsy, almost masculine. Judging by her corpselike rigidity, she would not return a hug, so I keep my arms by my sides. No one benefits if I lose my composure.

I study this new, older Grace. Her hair is shorter, brushes her collarbones now. In college she dyed the tips turquoise one month, hot pink the next. She used to wear a silver stud in her nose too, but those small rebellions have been replaced by a cool professionalism. Now she wears a uniform befitting Wall Street: sharp navy suit and heels.

In all the time we spent together during college, never once did Grace's cheeks flush or tongue tie. She was somehow incapable of embarrassment, laughed off acne and flubbed presentations with equal ease. She had her entire life planned out by senior year. After graduating, she'd move to New York City, get a job with a hedge fund, marry by thirty, make partner by thirty-five, and have two kids by forty. Over the years, I've watched from afar on social media as she's ticked every box.

"Sorry I'm late," she says.

"You haven't missed anything."

She takes me in. "We good, Alfred?"

Electric shock is often portrayed in movies as painful, even deadly, but the voltage zipping through every inch of me right now is an exquisite torture. The way I pined over this woman in college, how deferential I was to her. We had a real connection, Grace and I. Even now I sense it. But there are more heady pursuits than infatuation. Power, for instance.

"You tell me," I say.

"I'm here, aren't I?" I catch the flicker of defiance, the real Grace struggling to stay hidden. "I did as you asked. Now what?"

"You're an excellent deputy." She bristles, as I knew she would. "We're about to have dinner. You'll join us?"

She forces a smile. "Do I have a choice?"

No. She doesn't.

Cut to me sitting at the head of a long table in the private dining room. I arrive first, ridiculously early, so no one can gossip about me in my absence. Before long, my guests have assembled and are prattling to one another. I've seated Zoe on my right and Grace on my left, Samira and TJ in the middle, Julius at the end.

Samira is first to comment on the seating arrangement. "This is how we sat during poker nights at the blue house."

Zoe laughs. "Because you were superstitious as shit and demanded we keep the same seats once you won."

Samira winks. "Worked, didn't it?" That's true—she won more hands than not in college. I wonder if good luck will find her this weekend.

At seven, Jenna and Danny enter with bottles of sparkling wine. "Champagne, anyone?" Jenna asks.

Zoe hesitates, then shakes her head. Samira says, "None for me, thanks." Has Zoe told her about her latest attempt at sobriety? Samira is the type of person who would join her in solidarity. Everyone else accepts a glass.

Grace sips her champagne and studies the dining room. "This is supposed to be Manderley, isn't it?"

She misses nothing, Grace.

I've indeed copied the famous hall from *Rebecca* as best I could: high-backed chairs around an elegant table, candelabra on the buffet, enormous mantel with roaring fire. Even the dishes and silverware are the same.

The first course is a potato leek soup with crème fraîche and smoked bacon, perfect for the dropping temperature. Jenna and Danny place a bowl before each guest, serving me last. I unfold the thick cloth napkin at my place setting. Its weight rests on my lap.

I tap my spoon against my champagne flute and wait for the others to quiet. "I want to thank you all for coming, for sharing this exciting chapter of my life. After what happened in college, maybe you all thought I'd never recover." I study each face. Samira smiles encouragingly, TJ wears a blank expression, Zoe refuses to look at me, Julius purses his lips, and Grace is wide-eyed, hand at her throat.

"At times I didn't think I would either," I carry on. "Getting here has been a long road. I'm thrilled to have some of my dearest friends and fellow film lovers with me to celebrate the anniversary of the hotel's opening."

"We couldn't be prouder, Alfred." Grace lifts her glass. "To the Hitchcock Hotel."

The others hurrah and clink. Julius downs half his glass in one gulp. Zoe watches him with a growing restlessness. She'll fall off the wagon by the end of the night.

I sip my champagne and relish the tickle of the bubbles on my tongue.

FOUR

Zoe

The dining room is quiet as Zoe and the others dig into their soup.

Samira breaks the silence. "Gosh, I still can't believe you wound up buying this house, Alfred. Remember the first time we drove by it freshman year?"

"Oh yeah," TJ says. "It was on the way to that old bowling alley we liked, the real cheap one. Is that place still in business?"

"No," Alfred says. "It was torn down years ago."

"Bummer," Zoe says, and she means it. She likes bowling. The game is straightforward, and she usually wins when she plays.

"Two elderly people were in rocking chairs on the porch." Julius gestures toward the front of the house. "They looked like brother and sister, but people on campus said they were married."

"What did we used to call them?" Samira asks.

"The Olds," Alfred says at the same time Zoe thinks it.

"Young people are the worst," Samira groans.

Zoe was the one to come up with the nickname. She chews the inside of her cheek.

"Remember how they stared us down?" TJ asks. "Never said hi or waved or even smiled?"

"Their lawn was always so patchy," Zoe adds.

"Anytime we went bowling, we had to pass their house," Julius says.

"Must have been half a dozen times, at least," TJ says.

"No matter the time of day, they were always in those chairs, not saying a word."

"Until that one time junior year, we drove by—"

"And it was only her!"

Everyone but Zoe got sick of bowling around then, so they quit going to the alley. Still, their imaginations ran wild. They passed hours at the campus diner inventing ever more elaborate theories about what the old woman had done to her husband.

"I still think she buried him alive," Julius says. They all chuckle, a little uneasily.

"Have you found any bodies yet, Alfred?" Samira jokes.

"No . . ." Alfred trails off.

"That wasn't very confident," Samira says.

Danny refills the champagne glasses while everyone waits, enraptured. Zoe can tell Alfred is enjoying watching them hang on his every word. He lowers his voice, so they're forced to lean in.

"Well, from what I was told, the old man was constantly after her about the state of their yard. Keeping the house in order was Mrs. Old's job. That included mowing the lawn and weeding—the two chores she loathed most. Early in their marriage, she wanted to make him happy, so their lawn was flawless. But as the years wore on, he treated her worse and worse. She neglected her duties, especially the yard. This became a point of contention between them. One day he calls her a pig, an embarrassment."

What an asshole, Zoe thinks.

Alfred lowers his voice even more. "By this point, the old man had been sick for months. I'm not sure what he had, but it left him bedridden.

Mrs. Old had to wait on him hand and foot. He depended on her to survive." Alfred pauses. "Guess what she fed him."

"Cockroaches," TJ says.

"IKEA's Swedish meatballs," Julius says.

"The organs of their grown children," Zoe says.

"Jesus, Zo," Samira says.

"Grass," Alfred murmurs.

"What did you say?"

"Day after day, she shoved fistfuls of grass down his throat."

There's no way this is true, Zoe thinks.

"You may be aware the human stomach can't digest grass. He died a week later."

"Dude, are you serious?" Julius says.

Zoe narrows her eyes. *Fucking liar.* "How could you know all that?"

"The Realtor was chatty, so we got to talking," Alfred says. "She's lived in the area her entire life, went to school with the Olds' children. One of the kids is a teacher now, and the other's a police officer here in town. The son told her everything."

"She volunteered this information to you?" Zoe says, still skeptical. "Not at all worried it might tank her sale?"

"This was after I'd already bought the house—which was in tatters, by the way," Alfred says. "The process was long, what with all the inspections and stuff. I befriended her along the way. She said this was a lot of house for a single man, so I explained my hotel idea. She loved it, was a big Hitchcock fan herself. I said I could use a good urban legend or two about the house if she had any, even better if the story was true. She hesitated at first, but once I told her what we'd seen as college students, she opened up. At the end of the day, people are dying to share their stories. Especially the creepy ones." He smiles.

Maybe it is true, Zoe thinks. *Their grass was super uneven.*

She shudders.

"That story didn't make you second-guess your purchase?" TJ asks.

"It made me want the house even more," Alfred says. "What better Hitchcockian history could I ask for?"

"You're a freak," Zoe blurts. Alfred rolls his head around on his neck. She glimpses the tension in his jaw.

"No," Julius says. "He's like those people who visit haunted places hunting for ghosts."

"But who buys a house they think could be haunted?" Zoe pushes.

"There's no such thing as ghosts," Alfred says. "The spirit of the old man is not roaming through my walls."

"As far as you know," Samira mutters.

Grace speaks up. "Which room did she keep her husband in?"

A perfect disquiet settles over the table.

Holy shit, what if he's actually telling the truth? What if the old man died in my room?

"Who knows?" Alfred gives a cavalier wave. "Anyway, I've always loved this region. Plus, the house evokes fond memories with you all."

Fond memories? Zoe exchanges a dubious glance with the others.

Julius lets out a whistle. "What a story."

"I can already see the movie," Samira says, clearly ready for a new topic. "Remember how many Hitchcock movies you screened in film club? We should've called it the Hitchcock Club."

"Did I ever steer you wrong?" Alfred asks.

"Yeah, what's the one with the uncle and niece both named Charlie?" TJ says.

"*Shadow of a Doubt.*"

"Has there ever been a less convincing murderer?" TJ asks with a laugh. "He goes on this crazy rant about widows—while detectives are searching for a widow killer! We're supposed to believe this dude is a mastermind?"

"But there's that wonderful interplay of the father and his neighbor discussing the perfect murder, while an actual murderer is living under the father's roof," Alfred protests. He rubs his chin. "It makes you wonder—"

Makes you wonder what, Alfred?

Zoe's leg bobs under the table. She needs a drink. Fast.

"Oh boy. Here we go with another one of Alfred's hypotheticals," Samira interrupts. "If you could force your worst enemy to trade lives with a movie character, who would you pick?"

"Would you rather be Norman Bates or his mother?" Julius adds.

Zoe still remembers the lively conversation the latter question had spurred. *Uh, well, his mother is dead,* she had pointed out. *Yeah, but Norman's a psychopath,* Samira had countered. In the end, Samira and Alfred had voted to be the mother. Everyone else wanted to be the killer.

Alfred throws up his hands in a mea culpa. "They may seem silly, but there's always a reason behind my hypotheticals." He pauses. "Besides, I think you're going to like this one." Zoe takes a big gulp of water, wishing dinner were already over.

"If you had to commit the perfect murder, how would you do it?" Alfred asks.

Zoe chokes on the water and slams down her glass.

FIVE

Alfred

The others flash Zoe looks of concern while she coughs and struggles to breathe. I rise from my chair. "You okay, Zo?"

She waves me off. "I'm fine," she manages. "Wrong pipe."

By the time she settles down, Jenna and Danny enter with the mains. "For those who chose the meat entrée," Jenna says, "we have a tenderloin prepared in a red wine sauce with caramelized shallots, accompanied by hash browns cooked in duck fat." She delivers the plates to the carnivores—TJ, Zoe, Grace, and me. Grace gazes at her dish without pleasure. She should be making more of an effort.

"For those having fish tonight," Danny says, "we have a pan-roasted Dover sole with toasted almonds, green olives, and an aged-sherry wine emulsion. Bon appétit."

"Thank you both," I say.

"I'll be right back," Jenna says. Danny steps to a corner of the room, awaiting any guest requests. I've asked her to be my eyes and ears for the weekend. She already knows so much about these people; I wonder what she makes of them now that they're here in the flesh. Does she find my depictions accurate—or clouded by bias?

For a while there's only the sound of forks clinking against plates, knives tearing into animal flesh. Then TJ speaks. "The most important thing is to make sure there's no body," he says. "No body, no murder. Get the person near water and shove them overboard on a cruise ship in the middle of the ocean." He stops to think. "Better yet, take them to a swamp in Florida. Alligators would get the job done."

"Vicious." Samira laughs and flicks the back of TJ's hand.

He smiles, then spears a piece of beef. Jenna reenters with two bottles of wine. Zoe avoids all our gazes as she raises a finger to ask for a glass. That didn't take long.

"What if you're landlocked?" I say as Zoe chugs her wine like the planet is running out of grapes. I peer at TJ.

"Then I would stage it to look like a suicide," he says. Cheater—he's stolen the plot of *Vertigo*. (I should mention now: expect spoilers of Hitch's movies in this story. You've had fifty years to watch his later films and a hundred to watch the early stuff. If you haven't gotten around to *Vertigo* by AD 2024, that's on you.)

"Fooling the cops is a lot harder these days," Julius counters.

"He says with the confidence of someone who's tried," Samira teases.

Zoe glowers at me. I meet her scowl calmly.

She breaks eye contact first and refills her glass. "I always thought the most important thing was to make sure no one finds the weapon."

"That's why Hitchcock loved strangulation so much," Grace says. "No weapon."

"Those were the days before DNA testing," TJ points out.

"Not to mention," Zoe says, "you'd need to be stronger than the person you're trying to strangle to hold them down long enough. I'd stab the victim with an icicle. That way my weapon melts."

"What would you use, Grace?" I prod.

"I don't know," she says. "This game is creepy."

"You can't think of anything at all?" I raise an eyebrow, relishing the awkward silence that falls over the room.

"What you want is to make it seem like an accident," Julius says.

"Maybe you'd get an old bear trap," Samira says, "then hide it and lead the victim into it."

Everyone bursts out laughing.

"Are there even bears around here?" Zoe asks.

"Sure, black bears. Besides, Alfred didn't say the murder had to happen locally." Samira looks at me. "Is the murder happening here?"

All five faces turn toward me. No one's laughing anymore. Zoe polishes off her second glass.

"Jenna," I say, "another bottle of wine, please. My friends are thirsty." Zoe fixes me with a homicidal glare.

"I was thinking you'd get the victim good and shit-faced," Julius says, "then push them off a cliff."

I watch Grace while Julius thinks. I can tell by the way she fidgets that she feels my eyes on her.

"Or down a flight of stairs," he goes on. "Splay the body at an odd angle at the bottom of the staircase. Maybe knock off a shoe. Imply that they fell."

"Splat," I say.

"Isn't that what you did?" Zoe says flatly.

"Excuse me?" I say.

"I said, isn't that what you'd do?" she says.

But that's not what she said; I'm sure of it.

"I agree, an accident is the way to go," I say. "What do you think, Grace?"

She nods but doesn't look up from her lap. I almost sigh. Why does she have to be so difficult?

"What about you, Danny?" I ask.

Everyone at the table turns to ogle the housekeeper, still standing with her hands behind her back in the corner of the room. I'm sure they'd all forgotten she was even there.

Danny turns her head and addresses me. "The method doesn't matter. The getaway is most important." She considers. "A gunshot to the head would be the most efficient and least painful."

"Christ," Zoe mumbles.

"What if you want to inflict pain?" I ask.

"Passion clouds reason," Danny says. "A process can't be perfect if led by emotion." She's right, though I don't admit as much.

"Who's ready for dessert?" I ask.

TJ opens his mouth to answer, but a ringing phone cuts him off. He reaches into his pocket, peeks at the screen, then frowns. He sets down his wineglass and pushes back from the table. "Excuse me," he says as he hurries from the room.

"What was that about?" Julius asks.

Danny brings out a mouthwatering Sacher torte, while Jenna refills wineglasses. Zoe drinks more slowly now that she knows she's being watched.

I can't help showing off a little. I ask Grace whether she's seen the necktie—aka murder weapon—of Barry Foster from *Frenzy* hanging behind the bar, or the signed Bates Motel key in the home theater. Both behind thick Plexiglas.

"Signed by whom?" she asks.

"Hitch."

Grace brightens. I should've known money talk would bring her out of her shell. "Those couldn't have been cheap."

"Compared to the typewriter in my room, they were."

Samira cocks her head. "Which typewriter is that?"

"The one *Psycho* was written on." I imagine myself a rooster, chest puffed out.

Grace appraises me. "That must be worth at least twenty thousand."

"Thereabouts."

"What's worth twenty thousand?" TJ says as he reenters the room. He appears shaken.

"Everything okay?" Samira asks. He nods and returns to his seat, then pulls a roll of TUMS from his pocket and pops one into his mouth.

"Some old-ass typewriter Alfred bought." Julius shakes his head. "Next time you have money to burn, come to me and I'll show you how it's done."

Zoe snorts. I tug at my turtleneck. Julius may be the sole heir of the 49.2-billion-dollar Thénardier luxury brand founded by his shoe-making grandfather, but to me he is little more than acid reflux with arms and legs, a burning in my chest.

"I hardly think you're a voice of financial wisdom," Grace says to him before I can come up with my own retort. I'm glad to see our arrangement stands for the time being—I protect her; she protects me.

Julius's nostrils flare. "Maybe not," he says. "No one pounces on financial opportunity like you do, Gracey, casualties be damned."

My breath catches in my chest. What a thrill to watch them turn on one another. I can use this.

"That's enough, Julius," TJ says. Grace won't like that. She hates when men try to play the white knight, which TJ did all the time in college. As I said, people rarely change.

"I can fight my own battles," Grace barks.

"I'm trying to help," TJ says. He once called Grace a raging bitch behind her back.

"No one asked you to," Grace says.

"You think you're hot shit, Teej, 'cause you look like the Hulk now." Julius slurs his words, the shots and wine catching up to him. Now that they're liquored up, maybe they'll be in the mood for a little hand-wringing.

Bless me, Alfred, for I have sinned. My last confession was sixteen years ago.

(Hitch's biographers say he loved the spectacle of his religion, Catholicism. I imagine he relished the drama of the sacraments while fearing the punishments promised for sinners. Torture and suffering galore—no wonder he was capable of such dark thoughts. I like to think he'd approve of what I'm doing here.)

TJ stiffens. "Muscles have nothing to do with the size of a man, Julius."

"Guys, come on," Samira protests.

"Spare me your aphorisms," Julius says. "You sound like a shitty motivational poster."

Based on the expression on TJ's face, I worry that he's going to flip my table. He runs a hand over his head. "What do you have to show for yourself since college? What have you done with the last decade and a half besides get wasted with the cast of *Real Housewives* and plant mentions of yourself in *Page Six*?"

Zoe snickers into her wineglass.

Julius blinks in shock but quickly recovers. "I'm a philanthropist," he says haughtily.

"You're pathetic." TJ rises from the table. "I'm going to bed."

SIX

Samira

Samira bites her lip as TJ strides out of the dining room without a backward glance. This is not how the weekend was supposed to go. First that horrific story about the Olds, and now her friends are squabbling like teenagers.

Alfred's face falls. "I was going to propose a nightcap at the bar." As tired as Samira is from the long drive, she feels too guilty to say no. She can give him this much, at least.

"Sounds good to me." Zoe tips her glass to catch the dregs of her red wine. *So much for staying sober.*

"Me too," Julius says, unconcerned about the mess he's made a whopping four hours into their reunion. He could be such a jerk sometimes.

Samira is torn. Should she chase after TJ to smooth things over? Or watch out for Zoe like she used to? *How about neither?* she hears Henry reproach. *You went away this weekend so you could take a break, not mother your grown friends.*

"I'll talk to him," Grace says. Samira gives her a grateful smile as Grace marches out of the room, muttering about infantile men. Grace was unusually quiet at dinner, and Samira is glad to see her vigor return.

Grace and Samira were the first two in the group to meet. For weeks before move-in freshman year, Samira had worried what her roommate might be like. All she had was a name: Grace Liu. Facebook was not yet a thing—God, she's old—so all she could do was wait, imagine, worry. What if Grace Liu played her music too loud or didn't want to be friends or literally stank? She remembers arriving at Anderson Hall that first day and walking into her room with bated breath to find Grace kneeling on the top bunk, sticking a poster on the wall with Blu Tack. Samira had been disappointed, not because she wanted the top bunk but because she wanted to live with a girl who asked, not assumed. She would soon find out Grace didn't ask for anything—not forgiveness and certainly not permission. Still, Samira had hope. The poster was from a Third Eye Blind concert; they were Samira's second-favorite band, after Blink-182. Samira had thought of the "poster" folded up in her own suitcase—the side that she'd cut out of an Abercrombie & Fitch bag, a black-and-white photo of a couple making out topless in the sand. The photo had seemed edgy when she'd packed it but now mortified her.

Grace had glanced over her shoulder, looked Samira up and down. Then: "A chick in the bathroom told me the girl across the hall is addicted to caffeine pills. They went to high school together."

Since Grace had made the first move, this initial gesture toward friendship, she would later consider herself the founder and heart of the group. Samira didn't mind. She was even grateful—all too happy to flop onto the bottom bunk and dive into an icebreaker far less painful than hometowns and how they'd spent their summers.

Samira had surveyed Grace's belongings. A milk crate full of snacks and drinks, plus a trio of hot sauces on one of the school-issued desks: Cholula, sriracha, and Valentina. When Grace saw Samira observing them, she launched into a tirade about how gross Tabasco is. (Too much vinegar.) Grace had those überpopular sheets with the Eiffel Tower and blossoming cherry trees on them, plus a throw pillow that said *PARIS* in all caps. The effect was effortlessly cool, like everything else about her new roommate. Meanwhile, Samira had stood in the bedding aisle of

Bed Bath & Beyond for over an hour, paralyzed by the fear of making the wrong choice. In the end, she'd opted for *Finding Nemo* sheets, half ironically but also because she loved the movie. Now, seeing Grace's choice, she saw she'd picked wrong. She hoped Grace wouldn't think she was a dork.

Samira had braced herself for a polar-opposite roommate because that's how it was in the movies, but she and Grace were refreshingly alike. Both loved *Friends* reruns. (They agreed Ross was in the clear; he and Rachel had been on a break.) Both were business majors, both good students, though Samira would learn she had to work much harder than Grace to achieve the same results. Both had gotten drunk around ten times in high school—primarily in their own homes after their parents had gone to bed. Both were eager to make friends. They agreed to keep their door propped open those first few weeks of school. Where they differed, they tended to balance out. Grace was better at makeup, but Samira had already lost her virginity. Grace was more confident, but Samira had a cousin on campus who invited them to his house parties. Within a few hours, Samira felt like she'd known Grace her whole life.

Their open-door policy proved successful when, later that afternoon, Zoe Allen entered the picture. She appeared in their doorway, one hand buried in a bag of Doritos. "My roommate's addicted to caffeine pills," she announced as she munched. Grace shot Samira a triumphant smirk. "She's bouncing off the walls. Want a chip?"

Zoe sat on their carpet and folded her legs pretzel-style. Samira accepted the chip. She was sorry for the roommate but too anxious about making friends to take on anyone else's problems. Samira needed these friendships. The summer after high school graduation was supposed to have been epic; instead, her best friend since fourth grade, Rosa, had more or less dumped her for a new boyfriend. Samira had other friends, but none as close as Rosa. She wasn't comfortable going to the popular kids' parties—or any parties, really—without Rosa by her side. Instead, she sat home, grinding her teeth as her parents nagged and chided her all summer long. *Why aren't you researching internships?* they wanted to know. *You spend too much time thinking about socializing. Focus on your studies. Why can't you choose a respectable career like your brother?* (He was a pediatric oncologist.) Samira had never been close with her family. She felt inferior in their eyes. Rosa had been her support system, but now Rosa was MIA. Samira had counted down the days until summer was over. When she arrived at Reville, she was desperate for friends. She would fashion her own newer, better family. A chosen family.

On that first day in the dorms, she, Grace, and Zoe debated and ranked chip flavors—to this day they can't agree on the superiority of Nacho Cheese versus Cool Ranch—until an implicit understanding was reached: *We will stick together.* They went to the dining hall for dinner and never looked back.

Zoe was different from the two roommates, and therefore more interesting. Grace might've had colored tips in her hair—which Samira's parents would never let her do—but Zoe had a pixie cut, like an actual rock star. Zoe's family was also poorer than hers and Grace's were. Not that it was something they discussed. Samira and Grace could tell by the way she worried about money. (Samira felt guilty, as she had no idea how much tuition even cost at Reville.) Zoe had no filter and was full of wisecracks. Unlike every other student, including Samira and Grace, she didn't want to get hammered but wouldn't say why. This was perhaps the most alluring thing about her. The first few weeks of college, when Zoe wasn't a drinker, almost seem a chimera now. If you'd asked baby-freshman Samira who in her crew would wind up abusing alcohol, Zoe would've been the last person she'd have guessed.

Alfred leads the rest of the group to the bar. Samira puts a hand on Zoe's arm and signals for her to hang back. "What's going on?" she asks.

"What do you mean?" Zoe says. Samira can't tell if she's drunk.

"You told me you weren't drinking anymore," Samira says gently.

Zoe pulls her arm away. "I changed my mind. How can anyone stand a whole weekend with this crew stone-cold sober?"

Samira is about to find out.

"I swear to God, Samira, if you say you're worried about me, I won't talk to you the rest of the goddamn night," Zoe adds cheerfully.

Samira racks her brain for something to say that she hasn't already said a hundred times. Sober Zoe is driven, mischievous, and fun. But her friend doesn't know how to do anything in moderation: work, sleep, booze. Since senior year, when Zoe drinks, she keeps going until she can't tie her own shoes, until she picks stupid fights. More than once Samira has questioned how she wound up with such a hotheaded group of friends. None of them have asked what's going on with her yet. She's not sure she'll tell the truth if they do.

Samira grins. "You must be mistaking me for someone else. I'm as laid-back as they come."

Both women laugh. Zoe puts her arm around Samira's waist as they make their way to the bar.

Julius is already halfway through a gin and tonic by the time they reach him. Alfred is tending the bar. Zoe orders a scotch with one ice cube.

"You mad at me too?" Julius asks, bumping shoulders with Zoe.

She shakes her head. "He and Grace can both be so high and mighty."

Samira is surprised to hear Zoe pick Julius's side over TJ's on anything. The former was obviously the instigator.

"I know," Julius mumbles. "But I was also kind of a dick."

Samira butts in. "Kind of?"

"Okay, Mom." Julius pulls a face. "I'll apologize."

Samira nods, satisfied. One small concern checked off her list. These days all she does is worry, despite her bounty of good fortune. She's the founder and CEO of Babe, a super-successful sex toy company. She has two bright little spark plugs for children. She has more friends than she has free time to spend with them. Multiple colleagues have described Samira as "having it all." Yet she feels a constant pressure on her chest, like a dozen encyclopedias are stacked there. When was the last time Samira felt bold and juicy joy? Unbridled, full throttled. Lately Samira has found herself nostalgic for a simpler time, an era of her life free of responsibilities and commitments. Like the four years she spent in this small college town with the group of people gathered here, for example.

Zoe sips her scotch. "So, Mr. Philanthropist, what causes do you donate to?"

Julius becomes absorbed by the wood grain of the bar. "Nobody wants to hear about that."

"You have no idea, do you?" Samira smiles. "Must be nice to have so much money you're not even sure where it all goes."

Alfred tsks, then turns to put away clean glassware.

"I do too," Julius protests. "We do . . . film grants and other stuff." Samira watches him struggle to recall any specifics. His eyes light up. "As a matter of fact, we just funded a female filmmaker who's going to remake *Dracula*."

"Just what the world needs," Alfred grumbles.

"We watched *Dracula* in Dr. Scott's class, didn't we?" Samira asks. American Film as Communication was the first class they'd all taken together sophomore year. Grace had convinced the others to sign up.

"With Bela Lugosi in the starring role. The original, from 1931," Alfred says, his back still to the group. He's probably right. Alfred has always had a good memory.

"To be nineteen again," Samira says. "When all we had to do was sit around discussing old movies."

"Nineteen was a heck of a lot more fun than twenty-two—that's for sure." Alfred turns to face her.

Samira flinches. She's come to Alfred's hotel this weekend to clear her head, but she also said yes out of guilt. Alfred deserved better than they gave him way back when. All afternoon and evening, she has been keeping an eye on him, searching for signs that he's nursing an old wound but finding none. Is he referring to the senior year debacle, or is it something else? She glances at Julius and Zoe, but they're both swaying on their barstools, oblivious. Should she speak up? Put a hand on Alfred's arm? She doesn't want to touch him. The guilt deepens.

"Life only goes downhill from here," Julius says.

"That's not true," Samira objects, though she's had the same thought from time to time.

"What do I have to look forward to?" Julius stares at his drink. "Our bodies are breaking down little by little every day."

When did you become introspective? Samira thinks, then feels bad for the thought. Julius puts on the snarky shtick to make people laugh, but his outlook is typically sunny. Samira studies her friend slouching on his barstool. He appears tired, depressed.

She nudges him. "What's going on with you?"

"A whole lotta nothing. What's new in the world of vibrators?"

Samira smiles. In 2013 she quit her job as a sex therapist to start Babe with twenty-five thousand dollars of her own savings. Her company mission was and still is to make sex as pleasurable for women as it is for men. Her first vibrator won a CES Innovation Award, which led to a six-month waiting list. Today Babe sells seven vibrator models, a line of massage oils, and arousal gummies. Samira recently raised three million dollars in seed funding, which she plans to use for research and to assemble a clinical advisory board. She devotes half her time to speaking engagements at universities around the country. She wants the next generation to be bolder, more empowered. This is her life's work.

Usually, though, people just want to hear about the vibrators.

"We released one for couples last month." Samira pulls a silicone egg from her purse and drops it into Julius's hand. She flicks the switch. "It has three intensities. This is the lowest."

Alfred, wide-eyed, pours Zoe another scotch. Samira has lost track of how many drinks Zoe's had tonight. *Quit counting,* she scolds herself.

The egg buzzes in Julius's hand. He giggles, glum mood forgotten. "This is the most action I've had in a while."

"What's a while? Twenty-four hours?" Zoe teases.

Samira turns off the vibrator and tosses it back into her purse. "Come on. Spill the beans. Whose heart was broken this week?"

"I only go for heartless women. You guys know that." He winks. "I've been working my way through the cougar circuit of Manhattan."

Zoe clinks glasses with Julius, sloshing her drink.

"I don't know—rich people are boring." Julius chews his lip. "I might be sick of myself."

"That makes two of us," Alfred says. "Do any of you ever think about senior year?"

Samira's mouth falls open before she can stop it.

"Fuck you?" Julius says, more puzzled than angered by Alfred's putting him in his place twice in one day.

"I think about senior year all the time, Alfred," Zoe says. Samira recognizes the old looseness in her vowels, the slight increase in volume. Zoe is wasted and glaring at their host.

Samira squints back and forth between Alfred and Zoe. Neither of them has blinked.

"If you have something to say," Alfred says, "go ahead and say it."

Zoe holds his gaze for another moment, then backs down. "You're not the only one who had a shitty time in school," she mutters. "Get over it."

"Zoe!" Samira chastises.

Alfred keeps his smile pasted on, but it's false; Samira can see that. His cheeks don't move.

Zoe shoves her empty glass at Alfred. He doesn't reach for it. "He blames us for every bad thing that's ever happened to him."

"He never said that," Samira says, though she notices Alfred doesn't deny Zoe's point. He leans back against the counter with his arms folded, lips a tight line.

Samira doesn't even have to fake her yawn—she's been up since five a.m. "It's getting late. I think we better go to bed, Zoe."

Julius thumps the bar, affects an old-timey accent. "Another round, barkeep."

"Bar's closed, I'm afraid," Alfred says without taking his eyes off Zoe. The ice in his glare makes Samira's spine twitch.

Julius and Zoe boo him in unison.

"The things you've done . . ." Zoe trails off.

"Zoe!" Samira says again, glancing apologetically at Alfred. "Let's go."

Zoe slides off her barstool, trips, and falls to her knees. She sits there, laughing. Samira gestures for Alfred to help her. He comes around the bar. They hoist Zoe by her armpits.

"What about me?" Julius calls.

They ignore him and more or less carry Zoe to the lobby. The housekeeper is there, watering the flowers on the table. Samira wonders when her shift ends. The older woman puts down her watering can and hurries to Alfred's side.

"What can I do?" she asks.

"Press the elevator button," Alfred grunts. "Thank you, Danny."

The elevator is tiny and old, paneled in cherrywood. It hasn't been renovated along with the rest of the hotel. Samira imagines Mrs. Old clenching fistfuls of grass in this same box.

Samira and Alfred have to stand with their shoulders touching to squeeze all three of them inside. By the time they haul Zoe into the carriage, she's passed out. Danny leans inside the elevator and presses the 3 button. She stands in the lobby, watching them, as the doors close. Music starts to play. Samira recognizes the screechy notes from the *Psycho* shower scene. The elevator shudders into movement, lurches upward. Samira swallows.

She glances at Alfred out of the corner of her eye. He's good-looking if you're into the intense, brooding sort.

Alfred is composed despite Zoe's outburst. "She says the strangest things sometimes."

"Don't give it another thought." Samira feels his edginess filling the small space. She flicks her gaze to the ceiling and notes the round black eye watching them. So the elevator has seen at least one renovation.

The door opens on the third floor. They stop in front of room 303. Samira fishes in the pockets of Zoe's jeans for her room key, then unlocks the door. Alfred supports Zoe's weight while Samira plumps the pillows and pulls back the comforter. They put her gently in bed. Samira makes sure Zoe lies on her side, then places a trash can next to the bed. Alfred sets a glass of water on the nightstand.

The two leave and head to their respective rooms.

"You're a good sport, Alfred," Samira says.

"That's me," he says, eyes flinty. "Always the good sport."

SEVEN

Alfred

I make my way down the hallway to my room. Once inside, I slump in the desk chair and massage my temples. These old faces and memories are bringing on a migraine. I force myself to wander further back in time, to when my college years held promise, evoked optimism.

I still remember the seventeen-hour drive to Reville from my childhood home in the Chicago suburbs freshman year. I was snappy and twitchy the whole way—I couldn't decide whether I was more excited or nervous. Mom tried to distract me with silly car games, but I could tell she was as anxious as I was. Once she returned home, she'd be living alone for the first time.

One overnight stay in a motel, four stops for Taco Bell, and countless gas fill-ups later, we made it to my dormitory, Leigh Hall. I checked my reflection in the car's side mirror, then pulled our beat-up suitcase from the back seat. Mom trailed behind me with a laundry basket of odds and ends, talking too long to every parent we passed on the way to my room. I let her put the sheets on the bed and hang my clothes in the closet, then walked her back to her car. Part of me wanted to jump in beside her, but

I also wanted her gone, didn't want to be the guy whose mother lingered longer than the others. She cried when she hugged me goodbye. Later she'd tell me she bawled the entire drive home. I assumed she was exaggerating. Could anyone cry for seventeen hours straight? *Whatever*, I thought at the time. *I have more important things to worry about.* (The callousness of youth!)

My primary worry was my social life, or lack thereof. Though I'd requested a roommate, Reville had, for reasons unknown, assigned me a single. To this day, I believe the room mix-up was what set me on the wrong path. I suspected my floor mates thought I'd opted for the arrangement. I worried that they were whispering wild theories about rare and contagious diseases, creepy hobbies, antisocial behavior. Someone once asked whether it was true that I was born in the woods. Needless to say, I was mortified.

Despite the abundance of warm bodies, college is one of the loneliest places on the planet until you find your people. Everyone in Leigh Hall was a semiliterate gamer or a knucklehead preparing to rush a fraternity or a nice guy who spent most weekends visiting his long-distance girlfriend. I wasn't interested in video games and knew a frat house would not be a welcoming environment for a guy like me.

I tried going by Fred, then Smettie—anything to make me more approachable, less of an outsider. The names didn't stick. To be honest, I never could identify what stood out about me. I've often been described as intense, but why is that a good trait in some people and an unnerving one in others? Over the years I've learned that people bring their own preconceived notions and biases to the table, which is another way of saying *It's them, not me.*

But what about when it's all of them? What about when they all have the same bias against the same person? What conclusion can a young man draw when he's the only one who has a hard time making friendships that last? Maybe they stay away for a reason. Maybe his core is rotten. Maybe they all know something he keeps hidden from himself.

After a full hour of pacing my room, I still haven't calmed down. Meanwhile, Zoe sleeps across the hall, not a care in her muddled head. On a loop I hear the way they all laughed when Julius threatened to cut the necks off my turtlenecks.

The day's events speak for themselves. Not only do these people lack remorse for our college years, but they still see me as the butt of their joke. Everything I do is grounds for criticism. I'm a creep for buying a hotel with a sordid history. My housekeeper is too old, my posture too stiff. My movie choices are lame, my birds unnerving. My very existence is wrong, other.

Never mind that I bought the house on the hill, that I created my business from scratch. Or that I invited them all for a free stay and have been working my tail off to ensure their experience is nothing short of perfection. I've given them the best cuts of meat, the freshest fish, and the highest-rated wines that I can afford. My clothes are from respected brands. I invest in good tailoring. I have striking memorabilia displayed on my walls. I ask incisive questions, demonstrate my interest in their lives. I never make the first dig. I grin until my cheeks quiver from the effort. I give and they take, take, take, like greedy, grubby children.

I'm not saying I'm perfect. Far from it. As Zoe pointed out this evening, I've made mistakes that haunt me, irreversible choices made in the rage of a moment. But that was a long time ago. I've moved past the past, tried to become a better person. Can any of them say the same?

Though it would've thrown my plans into disarray, some small part of me hoped they had, in fact, changed over the years. Occasionally I allowed myself to daydream that five compassionate souls would show up at my front door, apologies at the ready. What would I have done then?

Better for them to be as horrible as I knew they would be. This way the plan is bulletproof. I put my hand in my pocket and rub my thumb over the casing of my Swiss Army knife.

The past year has been rocky. The Hitchcock Hotel had steady bookings our first months in business, thanks to discounted stays and mentions on local radio. The new and shiny attracts attention, but by the time we hit our sixth month of operation, community interest had moved on. Save for a solid few weeks in July, summer was a disappointment. Autumn is turning out much the same. Whenever we hit a dry spell, I keep the hotel afloat with my own funds, but those funds aren't endless. I need a stable influx of guests if this hotel is going to survive. Families and couples aren't interested, and who can blame them? The concept doesn't scream *wholesome fun* or *romantic getaway*. What my business needs is a pivot.

People can't resist a mystery—to do so is against human nature. *How might I create a buzz around this hotel?* I mused night after night. *A buzz that's uniquely Hitchcockian?* When the solution came to me, I grinned at its brilliance. By this time next week, the entire country will have heard of the Hitchcock Hotel.

FRIDAY
OCTOBER 13

EIGHT

Alfred

Six hours of sleep works wonders. Whistling, I make my way down to the kitchen. The space is spotless, a mix of industrial and homey: stainless steel appliances and prep table, blue tiled floor, a bowl of fruit on the counter in case the staff gets hungry. Every whisk, every colander, every toothpick, has its place. On one wall is a trio of photos of Hitch. My favorite is the one in the middle—Hitch standing in his kitchen, donning a green chef's hat and his quintessential suit. On the table in front of him are half a dozen blocks of cheese. He holds a long saber cheese knife in one hand, a sharpener in the other, arms crossed, with a deadpan expression. The director was a noted gourmand, a great lover of food. My hotel's menu has to live up to his standards.

I ask Chef what he's serving this morning. Eggs Benedict for the savory option, lemon-and-poppy-seed pancakes for the sweet, he says. My guests are in for a treat. Chef used to work at a nice restaurant in Portland, Maine, but relocated when his wife landed an administrative position at Reville. I scooped him up right away.

While he bustles around the kitchen, he thanks me again for giving the staff the day off tomorrow and Sunday. I pat him on the back before returning to the dining room, where Danny is setting up the space for breakfast. She checks that the silverware is gleaming and that each place setting has a mug. Though meal service isn't part of a housekeeper's duties, Danny takes care of breakfast here, since she spends the night at the hotel half the time anyway. She claims this is because she doesn't want to bother with the thirty-minute commute late at night, but I suspect the real reason has less to do with the drive and more to do with the empty house awaiting her.

I sit at one of the dining tables, drinking black coffee and flipping through the news on my tablet. One by one, the crew trickles in. Grace is first, in designer yoga clothes. Her shoulders sink when she sees I'm here alone.

"Everything okay with TJ?" I ask by way of a greeting.

Her gaze flicks upward. "You would think he'd have thicker skin by now. Some things never change." She bites her lip. "Alfred, can we talk?"

Speak of the devil—TJ walks in and cuts our tête-à-tête short. Clad from head to toe in Nike, he apologizes for last night's outburst. "Julius can get under anyone's skin," I sympathize.

"I was being shortsighted," TJ murmurs. I don't know what he means by that.

Grace clears her throat. "The milk and cookies on the desk last night were genius."

I warm despite myself. A staff member delivers them while guests are at dinner. "I hoped someone would get the reference." TJ looks confused.

"Milk is big in Hitchcock movies," Grace explains.

She's playing nice because she has no other option.

TJ's phone buzzes on the table. He glances at the screen, declines the call, then returns the phone to its facedown position.

"Everything okay?" Grace asks.

He nods and pulls a TUMS from his pocket. I note his fingers quivering but don't comment. The room is hushed enough to hear the disk crunching between his teeth.

Samira arrives next. "You two missed out on Reville reminiscing last night." She yawns and rests a palm on Grace's shoulder. "How's your mom, by the way?"

"She's out of the hospital now. Thanks for asking." Grace squeezes Samira's hand.

Julius comes down sometime after that. We sit around the table, sipping coffee and tea. I like seeing everyone in a vulnerable state—unshowered, with stale breath, rubbing the sleep from their eyes. The tableau reminds me of mornings in the blue house senior year before everything fell apart.

TJ clears his throat. "Sorry about last night, man," he says to Julius. "I was cranky from the long travel day and took it out on you. I don't even know if you know any Real Housewives."

"I do," Julius reassures him. "The burn was accurate. I'm sorry too. To both of you," he says, glancing at Grace.

She waves him off. "This wouldn't be a true reunion without us getting in a silly argument, right?" Grace winks. "Glad we got it out of the way early." Julius bobs his head with obvious relief.

The conversation flows from there. When an hour has passed and Julius has mentioned three times that he's starving, I speak up. "I was hoping to wait for everyone, but maybe we should eat without Zoe?"

They all nod.

"What was her deal last night?" Grace raises an eyebrow. "I thought you said she's sober now."

Samira shrugs, trying to impart facts without gossiping about a friend. Always the Girl Scout.

Grace searches for a more willing accomplice. "Did she get drunk last night?" she asks Julius.

"Oh yeah." He yawns. "Alfred had to carry her to her room."

Off TJ's piercing stare, I add, "Samira helped." Danny comes over then to take everyone's order. Fifteen minutes later, breakfast is served. Danny retreats to the kitchen to eat her own meal, and Chef pokes his head out of the door, watching us. I give him a thumbs-up.

Julius has finished his food and is in the process of choosing a second meal—"You eat like a teenaged boy," Samira marvels—when Zoe makes an appearance. She has showered, her hair wet, face bare, but is moving slowly and avoiding eye contact. If she wanted a discreet entrance, Julius doesn't let her have it. He slow-claps as she makes her way to our table.

"How are we feeling this morning?" he asks with a grin the size of the moon.

She gestures at his face. "Less of this."

Samira pulls out the chair next to her. "Are you all right?"

Zoe nods and slumps in her seat. "Didn't even need the trash can. Thanks for that, by the way. The water too."

"Alfred got you the water."

Zoe studies me, doesn't say anything. Of course she wouldn't. There's a saying in our trade: *The customer is always right.* We say it, we preach and profess it, but show me a single person who has worked in the service industry for more than a year who actually believes it. The key to longevity in this business is the ability to keep your mouth shut. That, and well-honed acting skills. The better an actor you are, the nicer the hotel you get to work in. Staff at the ritziest places could rival any Oscar winner; I promise you that.

I make sure to keep the cheer in my voice. "What can I get you, Zoe?"

"I'll take toast and an apple juice. Please," she adds without feeling.

"I'll grab it right now." I speed walk until I'm out of the group's sight, then slow to a relaxed pace. I tell the chef to take a break. Danny pops two pieces of bread into the toaster while I pour a glass of juice. A few minutes later I deliver the items to Zoe, who mumbles a thank-you.

I address the rest of the group. "Normally I suggest our guests get out and see the area. There's plenty of hiking and mountain biking trails around here, plus a tennis court and disc golf in the backyard. We have vendors for white-water rafting in the summer and snowmobiling in the winter." I glance at the window. Rain beats against it. "But since the weather isn't cooperating, I thought you might want to spend the day lounging around the hotel. Tonight I thought we could"—I mimic a drumroll—"resurrect the film club! We can all watch a movie together, this time with cocktails." I glance at Zoe.

"I love that," Samira says. The rest of them nod with less enthusiasm.

"Does seven o'clock work for everyone? If no one objects to a slightly later dinner, we can eat after the movie. Say around eight thirty?"

"Sure," Grace says. "I'm going to put in a few hours of work until then."

"I'm heading out for a run." TJ pulls his earbuds from his pocket.

"In this weather?" Samira says. "You'll be soaked."

"No big deal," he says. "I'll dry."

The three of them say goodbye to us, then make for the lobby.

"Can I talk to you for a minute, Alfred?" Julius asks—it can't be—nervously? I almost say *Me?* But he's already leading me by the elbow across the room, away from Zoe, who stares at her toast as if she's vacated her body.

I put my hotelier voice back on. "Has everything been to your expectations thus far?"

Julius appears puzzled. "What? Yes. Listen. I'm a big fan of what you've set up here."

Part of me is thrilled, filled with pride. Another part is skeptical. Julius is hardly a movie fan. He took film studies because he heard it was easy, and he joined the film club for fear of missing out. "I'd like to invest," he adds.

I chuckle politely. Another stupid prank.

He scowls. "I'm serious."

"As in an angel investment?"

Julius fusses with the silk scarf tied around his neck. "More like a grant."

"A grant?" I repeat. "You mean a donation?"

"Call it what you want. I'm no savant, but I've heard money is key to the success of small businesses."

My brain struggles to compute this new reality. I've never received an investment offer from anyone. Why am I getting one now? Does he know I'm struggling? Since when does he care? In little but ghastly ways, Julius bullied me through all four years at Reville. Never once has he apologized for the way he treated me. Could he feel bad for his behavior? Is he trying to show me he's a better man?

"You're not pulling my leg?" I ask.

He tousles a blond curl, borderline offended. "Of course not."

I make a noise in the back of my throat. An infusion of cash is exactly what we need right now. Plus, if Julius invested, he'd be incentivized to help the hotel succeed. Maybe he'd tell all of his famous friends about us—or, better yet, bring them here to stay.

There'd be no need for my plan, for the rest of this weekend.

"Is that a yes?" he asks impatiently.

"Let me, um, er," I stutter.

Julius crosses his arms. I study the arrogance in his posture, the condescension in his expression, and find myself suddenly furious. After all this time, *now* he wants to lend a hand? What about his betrayal, the way he stood by idly while my dream of becoming a film studies professor went up in flames? What about the decade I spent struggling to make ends meet, never hearing a single word from him, from any of them? He swans in now, wanting to save the day? The utter nerve of this guy. It's too late to turn back. The window for making amends has closed.

"How generous of you, but we're doing quite well here," I lie.

"My grandpa used to say the bottom line can always be topped."

Why am I not surprised?

"We're not talking about a life-changing sum," Julius continues. "Just a few million."

Zoe's silverware clatters off the table. Our eyes meet across the room.

Julius glances at her, then at me, and corrects himself. "I mean, I know that's a lot. I'm saying it wouldn't be missed from the family coffers."

"That's extremely thoughtful," I say. "But I can't."

He bewilders me by pushing. "Why not?"

"I don't like to mix the professional with the personal."

"I don't care what you do with the money. Use it on strippers and blow for a staff party if you want." He laughs, undoubtedly tickled by the image of me receiving a lap dance.

"Why are you doing this?"

He pulls out his phone. "I'll wire it to you. My lawyer can get the transfer started today."

"Julius, stop. I don't want your money."

His chin juts out. "What's wrong with my money?"

"I want to succeed because of my own hard work, not thanks to a handout." By the bitter expression on his face, I can tell he's correctly interpreted my comment as a dig at him.

"Got it." His tone is clipped. "Forget I said anything." He turns on his heel and stalks off.

"Smooth," Zoe says.

Are you still here? I almost yell. Instead: "Can I get you anything else?"

"I'll take a coffee. The juice was too sweet for me."

Fruit juice too sweet? You don't say. This is almost on par with last week's guest who complained that the ice in his glass melted too quickly.

"Did you know some juices contain as much sugar as a can of Coke?" I smile apologetically. "Be right back with the coffee."

I take my time fetching a mug and filling it; pulling a gallon of milk from the refrigerator, a creamer pitcher from a cabinet. I'm in the middle of pouring the milk into the pitcher when a chair shrieks as it's pushed away from a table. The chairback bangs against the floor. Boots pound tile. I peer into the restaurant and catch Zoe clutching her stomach before she disappears around the corner.

Hangovers are such a pest.

NINE

Zoe

Zoe reaches her guest room just in time and runs straight for the toilet. She has suffered more hangovers than most, can predict her symptoms like clockwork. A poor night of sleep followed by a day of exhaustion, pounding headache, guilt, and a lack of appetite. Typically it takes her until the evening to feel better—or until she has her next drink, whichever comes first.

She throws up. The last and only other time she's vomited after drinking was senior year at Reville. Weeks before graduation, she'd passed out on a random lawn. Samira had shaken her awake and forced her fingers down Zoe's throat for fear that she'd need her stomach pumped otherwise. Zoe flushes the toilet and leans her head against the wall.

She feels dizzy and slow minded, though last night was nothing compared to her usual night out. Her tolerance couldn't have fallen off that much in two months, could it? Then again, she'd never gone that long without drinking, so this is uncharted territory.

Addiction runs in Zoe's family, the worst hand-me-down of all time. Her dad hasn't had a drink in twenty-five years. Her grandfather wasn't so lucky, drinking himself to death before Zoe was even born. Her mom had been a social drinker but quit once her dad went to rehab. Zoe's older brother had never started drinking, not after a childhood spent watching their dad struggle. Zoe had intended to follow her brother's plan—until she arrived at college.

Those first weeks of school stressed her out. She loved Samira and Grace, but like every other student, they wanted to spend the weekends getting wasted. As long as the three stayed in the dorms, things were okay. To their credit, Samira and Grace didn't pressure or pry. They guzzled vodka out of Gatorade bottles while Zoe drank actual Gatorade. Grace had made a *Friends* power hour—sixty minute-long clips from various episodes. Every time the clip changed, she and Samira took a shot of vodka-Gatorade mix. They had Zoe take shots of plain Gatorade so she could play too. She had never been more touched or hydrated.

After a couple of weeks, though, the allure of dorm drinking had worn off. Samira and Grace grew antsy, wanted to get out and about. "My cousin's having a house party," Samira offered. "We're going," Grace said. She wanted to invite this guy Julius whom she'd met at orientation, a big partier, lots of fun. Zoe knew that spelled trouble but was too scared of being left behind to bow out. Nothing was more terrifying in college than having no friends.

When they showed up, Samira's cousin was cool. He offered them drinks but didn't push when Zoe declined. The three friends floated for a while, trying not to geek out over the fact that they, mere freshmen, were socializing in a sea of juniors. Zoe couldn't believe how much college resembled high school sometimes. Was life going to be one long popularity contest?

Then Julius arrived in his flashy outfit and his sunglasses at night, two bottles of liquor in each hand. He may have had more money than their peers, but Zoe knew his type—the kind of guy who wouldn't rest until every person in the room agreed to a shot, who made drinking a sport, a battle. He was witty and persistent, but Zoe managed to hold her ground. Until they made their way to the basement.

A karaoke machine had been set up down there. Two guys in polo shirts were belting "Sweet Caroline." Zoe froze. "What song should we do?" Grace asked her and Samira, not *Should we do this at all?* Zoe had never sung karaoke for a reason. More than a few pairs of eyes on her made her skin crawl, but Grace was already pulling each of them by the sleeves to the song book. Zoe glanced at Samira, hoping for strength in numbers, but Samira was cackling and letting herself be pulled along. When Zoe scanned the room for a sympathetic face, she landed on TJ. Later, he'd come over and introduce himself as the friend of a girl who was dating one of the guys who lived there. Later, he'd explain the difference between "shy" and "quiet." Later, he'd slot seamlessly into the group. Now he gave Zoe a lopsided smile.

Oh shit, she thought. *I'm gonna do this.* She asked Julius to pour her a shot.

Zoe wanted to solidify these tenuous new connections. She wanted to be as fearless as Grace, as cheerful as Samira. So she took the shot and belted "I Wanna Dance with Somebody" with her two new friends. Another round of shots, another Whitney classic. Hours in, Zoe realized she didn't care how bad she sounded, that she was incapable of embarrassment, a feeling that normally trailed her like a shadow. Was this what booze granted you? Invincibility? Everyone in the basement cheered her on. She and her friends cried, they were laughing so hard. This was the life of a rock star.

She set rules for herself to ensure that things didn't get out of hand. She drank only Thursday through Sunday, and never more than four drinks in a night. Zoe was already struggling to keep up with her course work; she didn't need booze to set her back further. She was the first person in her family to go to college, a point of pride her parents share with shining eyes to this day. Her dad was a line cook; her mom worked in construction. They never would have forgiven her if she'd failed out of school, especially if the reason had anything to do with alcohol. She found ways to compensate for her academic shortcomings, namely study groups and better students who helped write her papers. She wasn't thriving, but she was surviving.

Then came the shitstorm with Alfred senior year.

She saw what she saw and couldn't forget it. Zoe abandoned her rules. Her drinking escalated. Those last few months of college, she didn't recognize herself, peeing in crushes' beds and narrowly avoiding ER visits. She told herself it was senior freaking year, that everyone else was blacking out too, though she knew she was more out of hand than her friends. All these years later, she still goes scarlet with shame when she thinks about what a mess she was.

After Zoe graduated, she needed a reset, an industry that matched her work-hard, play-hard credo. She was never going to sit behind a desk or dress in business casual every day. She wanted an environment that was fast paced, barely under control. Zoe operated best when bedlam was simmering.

She would become a chef.

Her dad was against it. The whole point of a degree is so you don't have to spend all day on your feet, he argued. But she saw the easy camaraderie between him and the other cooks. She hated mornings, came alive late at night, was enthralled by the idea of going to sleep at four and waking up at noon. This industry was exactly what she needed.

Zoe didn't want to work at just any restaurant; she wanted to work for the best. She moved to New York City and lived with five roommates. Her bedroom was an actual closet. Julius helped her get a foot in the industry door—his dad was friends with the owner of the hottest French place in the Village. For years and years she worked her ass off, starting as a line cook like her dad, climbing to better kitchens, better gigs. Her goal was to open her own restaurant. She found a space in Brooklyn Heights with pricey rent but excellent foot traffic. Securing the money was tough, but Zoe got it done.

She still remembers the soft opening, a trial run for friends and family. Saint Vincent's menu was a love letter to her parents, comprising dishes they had cooked throughout her childhood—plus a sprinkle of Zoe's flair. Her beef stroganoff used crème fraîche, fresh dill, and cognac. Her meat loaf had a brown-sugar-and-apple-cider-vinegar glaze and was topped with a peppered bacon crumble. Her s'mores were served in a smoking glass box. The kitchen was slammed all night, but Zoe found time to keep peeking through the window, breath held as she watched her waitstaff present each course to her parents. Mom clapped a hand over her mouth at the meat loaf, which was served in the shape of a cursive *V* for "Vincent." Dad threw back his head and laughed with delight at the s'mores box. While her parents held hands across their table, Zoe quickly wiped away a tear. (Everyone on her team—and outside it, frankly—thought Zoe was a hard-ass. She saw no reason to disabuse them of that impression.) After the meal, Zoe walked her parents to their car. Dad had his arm slung around Zoe's shoulders. He told her how proud he was of her, that he wished Grandpa could have seen all this. (Grandpa being the eponymous Vincent, the "saint" bit tongue-in-cheek. The stories she had grown up hearing about her grandfather! Before his tragic ending, he had been one of those jolly, larger-than-life rascals everyone loved. When asked which dead person she'd most like to meet, she chose Vincent every time.) She can still remember Mom's words verbatim: *We always knew you would do great things.* That was the single best day of Zoe's life.

She hasn't told her parents she's on a forced leave of absence. Before she left, she made a deal with the GM. If Mom and Dad come in, he's to say Zoe is tied up in the kitchen, but *thank you for coming, and your meal is on the house.* Zoe will pay back the GM after the fact. (Mom and Dad have never gone in. They can't afford the prices, and they wouldn't ask for a comped meal in a million years.)

Nor do her parents know that Zoe has an addiction. What little drinking she's allowed them to see, they've chalked up to college shenanigans and then the hard-partying ethos of the restaurant industry. The more out of control Zoe's habits get, the more she steers clear of her family. Her job is an evergreen excuse. She cannot let her parents know they were wrong about her, that their forty years of twelve-hour shifts and chronic back pain were for nothing. Some days she believes she is not beyond redemption, that she can still be the Zoe in her parents' minds.

Today is not one of those days.

She throws up in the toilet again, then lies down on the tiled floor and cries. How proud she was of this plan, of her commitment to find closure instead of boozing away her problems. The stress of facing Alfred is what did her in. His dark gaze, the sneer he flashes when no one else is looking. Alfred Smettle is a reminder of her cowardice, her inability—no, refusal—to do the right thing. The first glass of wine had felt like an inevitability more than a choice. She had picked up the drink to avoid Alfred's glare, to task her hands with something other than jittering.

Her friends had all expected her to fall off the wagon anyway, hadn't they? No matter how many accolades Zoe stacks up as a chef, no matter how many years she puts between her current and college selves, she can't help believing that college Zoe is the real Zoe. The fuckup, the mess, the chick with the squirrelly morals. How badly she had wanted to prove herself wrong this weekend. To show her friends she had changed. Already she has failed. A bone-trembling rage descends upon her.

A knock at the door makes Zoe wipe her mouth and sit up. She shuffles over, swings it open. The elderly housekeeper stands there, clutching a bottle of Pepto-Bismol.

"Alfred said you weren't feeling well." Danny extends the bottle. Zoe takes it from her. "I liked your icicle idea," Danny adds.

Zoe squints at the woman, thanks her for the medicine, and closes the door. For a moment, she has no clue what Danny was talking about. Then she remembers last night's "perfect murder" conversation. Zoe had suggested a weapon that melts. Julius mentioned something about making it look like an accident. Then, wine bold, she added something snarky.

Isn't that what you did?

Zoe startles at the memory. The storm on Alfred's face, his barely concealed wrath. He might be able to fool the others with his manners and hospitality, but Zoe knows the real Alfred.

He looked like he wanted to poison her.

"Fuck," she says, feeling a sudden need to lie down. She stops short when she reaches the end of the foyer and the bed comes into view. A shriek sticks in her throat. A strangled cry comes out instead.

On Zoe's pillow is a clump of grass.

TEN

Alfred

For the first month of school, I rarely spoke to anyone who wasn't a TA or an RA. That changed in Introduction to Speech Communications. For fifty minutes, three times a week, I sat behind a girl named Grace Liu. The class was hideously boring. To pass the time, I sometimes watched as she doodled on her notebook cover. When I saw she was sketching famous film quotes, I had to say something.

We became fast friends. After class we'd sit on the south quad. Sidewalks crisscrossed the lawn, which was surrounded by uniform redbrick dorms and the school chapel. If I close my eyes, I can still smell the mowed grass, feel the cobblestones under my feet, hear the thumps of students dropping their backpacks to the ground. We had no idea how small our world was then. We wouldn't have cared had anyone told us. Everything we needed lived inside that bubble.

Grace and I discovered we were planning to sign up for the same film studies course sophomore year, once our core classes were out of the way. She said her friends were going to take it too. Countless times I plucked blades of grass and listened to her talk about her favorite movies, what she adored about them, how she would've shot them were she the director. She said I was the first person to truly care about her artistic ideas. Her high school friends had spent their free time babbling about the football team, and her family saw little value in analyzing old movies.

She told me about her childhood in Albany. Her father was Chinese American, her mother white. She had a brother she wasn't close with, for no reason other than pure incompatibility. Grace couldn't decide whether she wanted to devote her life to doing what she loved or to making an ungodly amount of money. That's the exact phrase she used—"an ungodly amount of money." "Should I direct movies or manage a hedge fund?" she asked me. I told her she'd excel at either. I knew her parents were pushing the latter, though she craved the former. "No one has ever called me creative," she said. "You give passion as much weight as reason."

We grew closer, taking turns scratching provocative quotes we loved onto the invisible parts of each other: crooks of elbows, backs of necks, once along her rib cage—the boldness of which, some twenty years later, is alien to me, the smooth moves of a James Dean type that I assure you I have never been. Still, she kept following me to the quad after every class, and I was sure that was a sign of something. One Thursday night in December we went to an art house screening of *Rear Window*. When the villain Thorwald went hunting for an incapacitated James Stewart, Grace grabbed my left hand and squeezed. I vowed never to wash that hand again. The following week she invited me to a house party that the cousin of her roommate, Samira, was throwing.

I was nervous to meet Grace's friends. While I made my way from the dorm to off-campus housing, I questioned how much their bonds might have solidified over the course of a semester, whether they had room for one more. I tried not to worry, focused on the slick ice patches, my ears ringing with cold. By the time I arrived, my face was numb. I couldn't tell whether snot was dripping from my nose, checked three times before entering through the back door of the house like Grace had instructed. The kitchen was a mess—the sink full of empty cans, counters buried beneath discarded pizza boxes. The house smelled like stale cigarette smoke commingled with popcorn and beer. The tiled floor was sticky. I smiled.

I pushed through the noisy crowd, searching for a lone familiar face. I found her in one of the bedrooms. She and four of her friends were seated in a circle on the rug, playing a drinking game with cards. When I called her name they all turned, like a five-headed monster.

Grace moved to make space between herself and a glossy-haired girl who turned out to be Samira. Grace patted the floor. "Come play."

I sat. Grace explained that they were playing—excuse my language—Fuck the Dealer, which I had never heard of, let alone played. They went around the circle introducing themselves with a wave.

"Welcome," the blond boy with the ridiculous wardrobe said. "If you screw over any of these girls, I will haunt you for the rest of your life."

My eyes widened.

"Jesus Christ, Julius. Give it a rest," said the balding kid named TJ. "Let's do a bottle race."

Grace sized me up. "Can you drink fast?"

"Not well," I admitted. She grinned, not discouraged in the least.

The rules were simple: first pair to finish their bottle of liquor won. *As in 750 milliliters?* I almost asked, but I had my answer based on the bottles in their hands. Teams were decided: TJ and Zoe would drink the Captain Morgan, Julius and Samira the Goldschläger (a questionable choice, in my humble opinion). In the freezer Grace found the two of us a bottle of Burnett's cherry vodka that Samira's cousin said she could take if she paid him back. She whistled with her fingers to signal the start of the race.

Mixers sloshed after liquor into red plastic cups. The group chatted and laughed, drinking all the while. I loved the easy shorthand they had with one another, the inside joke I didn't understand—something about a stoner geology teacher living in the woods—that had Samira doubled over with laughter. I listened more than I spoke, slipped in *Family Guy* references where appropriate. (I had made a point the summer before college to expand my pop culture repertoire to include TV made this century.) The vodka burned at first, but I was determined to keep up, not to let Grace down. It felt like an audition.

No more than forty-five minutes after we started, Grace finished the last of our bottle, mere seconds before TJ and Zoe emptied theirs. We whooped and high-fived while Julius groaned at Samira—they hadn't even come close, still had one-third of their bottle left. The room spun as the others clapped me on the back. TJ started a chant that spread down the hallway. "Al-fred! Al-fred! Al-fred!" I was both embarrassed and thrilled. I'd be laid low the next day, but I had never been happier.

To my delight, our first night together wasn't a fluke. I went out with Grace and her friends the following night, and the one after that too. (Ah, college, the days when going out three nights in a row was the norm, not grounds for a week of sick leave.) Every outing was more fun than the last. These people asked me questions and wanted to know my answers.

TJ and I chatted about books. We both loved horror and exchanged recommendations. He introduced me to *We Have Always Lived in the Castle* while I lent him *American Psycho*. (Some wouldn't classify that as horror, but if you've read it, you know they should.) We both had attempted *House of Leaves* once but struggled with its density and sophistication. Sophomore year we did a buddy read of the book together—not only did we finish; we adored it. For a solid week we talked about little else.

With Zoe I discussed food. Her dad was a cook at a Mexican restaurant, nowhere fancy, a divey place that served burritos on paper plates. She advised me that when it came to Mexican food, the divey places were always the best. I had grown up eating the beigest of meals. Overcooked meat with a potato, maybe a green vegetable if Mom was feeling fancy; milk with dinner no matter the spread. (I later learned from the gang that this is a Midwestern custom.) Zoe helped me understand that food is more than just fuel. Food can be art; cooking is a craft. The first time she cooked for me—mac and cheese; my mouth waters at the memory—I remember thinking, *You should devote your life to this.* When I said as much, she demurred, but I caught the corners of her lips turning up before she moved away.

Samira and I debated politics. I had never paid much attention to the news and I thought politics was boring, something for real adults to worry about—until I talked to Samira. She had opinions on gun violence, the war on drugs, and especially women's rights. But she was also undecided about issues like the death penalty and immigration. She wanted to hear my thoughts on the best ways forward (as if I had any idea). Discussions with Samira made me yearn to be smarter, better informed. She helped me register to vote. By senior year we were having weekly lunch dates, just the two of us, during which we'd spend an hour debating whatever policies were in the news.

Not all friendships have such depth. There's nothing wrong with that. Some bonds are built on little more than a shared commitment to getting drunk or a mutual love of the Chicago Cubs. You meet a fellow fan of *The Office* or someone who, like you, can quote every line of *Parks and Rec*. That was Julius and me. One night junior year we came close to a drunken discussion of our wayward mothers, but for the most part we stuck to safe topics, like funny videos on the Internet and the best brands of cereal. "Shallow" doesn't mean "meaningless"; "shallow" means "light." When he wasn't picking on me, no one made me laugh harder than Julius. Given the choice, I think most people most of the time will choose sidesplitting laughs over deep heart-to-hearts. As a species we can handle only so much darkness.

I sometimes ponder what might have happened had I not taken the same class as Grace or if I'd skipped Samira's cousin's party. What if I had never met this group at all? On one hand, they were the cause of my eventual ruin. On the other, these people were fundamental to the man I've become. For four years we were family. They shaped my beliefs and sense of humor. They cheered me on. They accepted me. Right up until they didn't.

Film theorist Laura Mulvey introduced
the concept of the "male gaze" in her 1975 essay
"Visual Pleasure and Narrative Cinema." To
support her position, Mulvey cites
three Hitchcock movies: *Vertigo*, *Marnie*, and
Rear Window. In this paper I will
argue that these are merely the most
flagrant examples, as many more Hitchcock films
involve the surveillance of women. The director
himself was a self-confessed voyeur and quite
likely a predator.

—*Excerpt from Essay #65,*
"Hitchcock: Genius or Monster?"

ELEVEN

Samira

Samira tries to distract herself by studying the black-and-white pictures on the walls of her room. Each frame holds a photo of Hitchcock on one set or another. There he is getting a haircut from Grace Kelly. In the next he shoots the breeze with Ingrid Bergman and Cary Grant. In a third he demonstrates to Jimmy Stewart how he wants him to hold a gun.

The diversion doesn't work. Every time she sees the bed, she pictures Mr. Old moaning in agony. She wonders if hers is the room where he died.

Someone pounds on the door. Samira startles. She glances down to make sure her robe is covering what it needs to, then shuffles to the door in white hotel slippers. She opens it to find Zoe, panicked and gray-faced, clinging to the doorframe.

"What's going on?" Samira asks.

"Someone left grass on my pillow," Zoe says.

"Huh?"

"Someone left a fucking pile of grass on my fucking pillow," Zoe repeats, more loudly this time. When Samira squints in response, Zoe adds, "The story about the Olds? The wife feeding her husband grass 'til he croaked?"

Samira's eyes widen. "Come see," Zoe says as she grabs her by the arm and drags her into the hallway. The housekeeper is pulling a vacuum out of a closet. Zoe's hand shakes as she jams the key into the lock. She pushes the door open, gestures for Samira to go first. "After you."

Nervously, Samira creeps along the foyer. The foot of the bed comes into view first. The sheet and comforter are rumpled, the bed unmade. She can't remember a single day in four years of college that Zoe made her bed—not that Samira should talk. She holds her breath.

The pillow is white, pristine.

Samira turns back to Zoe with a questioning look. "Where's the grass?"

Zoe blinks dumbly. "It was here a minute ago."

Samira examines her friend. *Is this some kind of practical joke?* But no, pranks were more Julius's thing, not Zoe's. Samira comes up with a sadder solution. *Is Zoe already drunk again?* She looks around the room, opens the small refrigerator. The minibar is untouched.

Zoe checks beneath the pillows, tossing them off the mattress. She falls to her knees to search the carpet, then under the bed. Samira watches Zoe's growing desperation with discomfort.

"I swear to God, Samira," Zoe says without looking at her, "I'm not making this up."

"Maybe Julius was having fun with you," Samira offers. She likes this solution because it would mean Zoe isn't losing her mind.

"I guess." Zoe sits on the bed. "There's something else. I've been puking all morning."

Samira wants to be a good friend, to rub Zoe's back and restore her to good health, but a not-small part of her screeches, *What did you expect? I have seventy-two hours to get my head on straight, and I am not your mother!*

"I'm sorry," she says instead. "Can I get you something?"

Zoe stares at the ceiling. "I don't think this is a hangover."

Samira is glad her friend isn't looking at her, so she doesn't catch the incredulous expression on her face. "What do you mean? You think it was something you ate?" Samira doesn't see how that's possible. Everyone else is fine.

"I think I was poisoned." This time Zoe does glance at Samira to gauge her reaction.

"By the Shiraz or the scotch?"

Zoe frowns. "I'm serious. I never vomit after drinking. You know that."

"Maybe you do when you stop for two months and then suddenly start up again."

Zoe shakes her head. "I was fine this morning." Samira raises an eyebrow. "Nothing unusual, anyway. Headache, dry mouth, tired. The nausea didn't begin until after breakfast."

"So you're saying, what? Someone tampered with your food?" Samira tries hard to keep the disdain from her voice but isn't sure she succeeds.

Zoe locks eyes with her. "I'm saying Alfred poisoned my food."

"Don't be absurd." Samira thinks back to last night, the loathing in Alfred's eyes when he glared at Zoe across the bar.

"He hates me, Samira."

"Well, you could stand to be nicer to him." Samira feels herself slipping into mom mode. "You were pretty rude yesterday. Do you remember that?"

Zoe picks at her black nail polish, chipping it.

"Even if he doesn't like you, why on earth would he poison you? Do you hear how crazy that sounds?"

"Because I know shit," Zoe says.

This is like a bad episode of *CSI*. "What shit is that, Zoe?"

Her friend stays quiet.

"Hello?"

Still nothing. Is she referring to the trouble Alfred got into senior year? Samira feels that slinking sense of guilt return. What could Zoe know that the rest of them don't?

"I love you, Zo, but I think you need a good hard look in the mirror. You can't blame other people for your screwups. Alfred has been nothing but a wonderful host to us."

Samira can tell by Zoe's roving eyes that she's no longer listening. "Have you had anything to drink today?" she asks.

Zoe's face hardens. Without a word she marches across the room and holds open the door, waiting for Samira to leave.

Samira takes that as a yes.

TWELVE

Alfred

The hotel is quiet. My friends have all retreated to their rooms. "Anything interesting thus far?" I murmur to Danny in the lobby.

"I heard Zoe, Grace, and Julius discussing where you got the money for the hotel." Danny twirls the feather duster she's been using. "Zoe was trying to convince them this place is a front for a scam you're running."

I sigh. The truth is far less interesting, as truths tend to be. My grandfather died in 2019, two years after Mom. Mom's dad left most of his fortune to his siblings, but a small piece of it went to me. I didn't even know said fortune existed until his executor called. Mom had mentioned that her father was an oil executive, but I'd never spent any time with him. My inheritance was big enough to buy this house, turn it into a hotel, and operate it for a couple of years. Danny knows all this, so I don't bother dispelling the rumor.

"Anything else?"

"Don't be angry, but"—Danny's eyes flick to her shoes—"I might've rifled through a bag or two while you all were having breakfast."

I keep my voice level. "And?"

"TJ's packing."

My jaw drops. "As in, a gun?"

She nods.

"Why would he need a gun at a reunion weekend?"

"My thought exactly."

I crack my knuckles. "Although he is a security guard."

Danny grips my hands to stop my cracking. "That'll give you terrible arthritis, honey."

I tuck my hands under my arms. "Maybe he takes it everywhere."

She raises an eyebrow, and she's not wrong. TJ has become a more viable candidate than I would've thought.

I tell Danny I'm going to rest for a while, then climb the stairs to the third floor. I walk to the end of the hallway. My hand is on the doorknob of the storage closet when a guest room door opens behind me. I spin around.

Samira stands on the threshold of 301, the room next to the closet. She's bundled up in a raincoat, scarf, and boots. Keys dangle from one hand, an umbrella from the other. "I left my book in the car." She holds up the keys, then glances behind me. "Where are you off to?"

I swing open the door and grab some rolls of toilet paper off a shelf. "Restocking. Do you need any toiletries?"

She shakes her head.

I bow mine. "Enjoy your book." I move into the storage closet, wait until Samira walks away, then grab the metal rod from the corner. I use it to unlatch the hatch door in the ceiling and pull down the ladder that leads to the attic.

The attic runs the full length of the third floor below. Overhead are exposed wooden beams, pipes, and wiring, plus an exposed light bulb with a pull chain. My mother's rickety rocking chair sits in a corner. Most of the boxes and bags on the right side of the attic are full of her stuff. These items are worthless but remind me of my childhood home. Three chipped frames lean against a wall, bearing regal portraits of Hitch's leading ladies. Grace, Joan, and Ingrid got prime real estate above our staircase at home, where most people put photos of their family. A stack of old newspaper clippings balances on the rocking chair. The same stack once sat on the hutch in our living room—Mom saved her favorite reviews of Hitch's movies. The attic smells like old books, insulation, and rotten fabric, owing to the three large garbage bags of Mom's clothes.

Lest you think I've built a shrine, it's not only her things up here. Lining the left wall of the attic are ten storage tubs of memorabilia, cheap trinkets that made up my Hitchcock collection before I received my inheritance. Blu-ray discs and refrigerator magnets and stamps and jigsaw puzzles and action figures and board games. In the corner opposite the rocking chair is a rejected idea for guest room decor—a mannequin wearing the same long-sleeved housedress as Norma Bates, plus the blond wig Mom used to don on Halloween. (Every year my mother put on the same costume: a cheap replica of Grace Kelly's powder blue gown from *To Catch a Thief.*) An antique dresser holds moth-eaten sweaters and a dusty pair of men's glasses. Strangest of all the odds and ends up here is the stuffed crow atop the dresser. A delighted guest sent it to me in the mail as a thank-you after staying here. He said he saw the aviary in the courtyard and the owl in the bar and thought I might like to add to my compendium. Unlike my owl, however, this bird was once alive. I'm too disturbed to display it in the hotel but would feel guilty if I threw it away—the guest must have gone to great lengths to acquire it for me—so the crow lives in the attic with the rest of my secrets.

Rain beats the roof. The attic ceiling is six feet high where the roof pitches, five feet everywhere else. I move around with a stooped back, stepping carefully near the vents. From the closest windowsill I pick up a dead fly and squeeze it between my fingers until it turns to paste, then peer out the dormer window with a view of the back of the house. From here you can see the aviary and tennis court. Farther out, my grounds-keeper skims the pond, his last task before heading home for the weekend. I've installed a few benches by the water, bought pedal boats and paddleboards. Mountains loom beyond my property.

I move to the opposite side of the attic to peek out the other dormer window, the one that overlooks the front of the house. I catch Samira crossing the parking lot. Her head disappears into the back seat of an Acura SUV. She emerges with her book in hand. I scan beyond the parking lot to Reville's campus in the distance. Manicured quads separate identical brick Georgian buildings with white window shutters. My beloved Carroll Hall, where we took our film classes, looms over the others. Students swarm the sidewalks. Class must have just let out.

Odd to regard a place with equal parts love and hate. I thought long and hard before buying this house. How would it feel to live within sight of the school, to risk encounters with people I knew in town, to face daily the place where my so-called friends betrayed me? Did I want an ever-present reminder of what had happened? Any normal person would struggle to put the past behind them when it was right in front of them. Wounds don't always heal. Sometimes they fester and chafe.

Eventually I decided that if I bought the house on the hill, I'd be the one on top—literally and metaphorically. I also happen to believe it builds character to keep reminders of one's failures in view, to have a visual memory of how far one has come. No matter how bad a day I have at the Hitchcock Hotel, it couldn't be worse than that last year at Reville.

I listen to the wind rustle the leaves of the nearby trees. If I can see the students in the valley below, it stands to reason they could spot me lurking up here by the window. But no one at Reville has ever paid my hotel any attention. Why would they start now?

Oblivious, every last one of them. I am the only one watching.

THIRTEEN

Samira

Samira sits on the hotel bed, fifteen pages into Nora Ephron's *Heartburn* when Henry FaceTimes her. She uses a CVS receipt as a bookmark and answers. Her children's faces fill the screen, and her body aches with love for them. They shout over each other to be heard. Samira has to remind them, "One at a time. Aditi, you first."

Her daughter sticks out her tongue at her brother, which Samira pretends not to catch. Aditi is learning to read and insists on a dramatic page-by-page performance of *Go, Dog. Go!*, her current favorite book. Once story time is finished, Aditi flips the phone toward Shivam, who clutches a PAW Patrol toy in each hand. Her boy can't form sentences yet, but he yells "Mama" every time he sees her. When Shiv was an infant, she used to let him nap on her chest, the world's best weighted blanket. The kids are both so manageable and sweet from afar.

With Henry she keeps the conversation brief, guilt nagging her all the while. Samira has always hated keeping secrets—from him, from anyone. She makes up a white lie to get off the phone, then slumps against the headboard.

She and Henry had six happy years, followed by six crappy ones.

They'd both held on those last six, knew marriage has its peaks and valleys. At what point do you admit the valley is a desert, that there are no more peaks? At what point do you call it quits?

Their relationship was born of passion and possession—not in an unhealthy way. At least Samira didn't think so. More like, in the beginning, she could peek over at his arm and sense it was hers to rub or kiss, to drape over her shoulders. His limbs were an extension of hers—the thought of them, their closeness, was enough to make her tingle. Years of cohabitation eroded that perception slowly, steadily, until one day she glanced over and no longer felt she possessed him. She asked before she touched, as did he. Somewhere along the way, he had become individual again.

For a time, friendship was enough. They helped each other run their companies—an advertising agency for him, sex products for women for her. They were equal partners, "cofounders of their family," as Henry liked to call them. (She found the phrase embarrassing but went along with it.) They tried fantasy boxes, couples therapy, trips away. All the stuff you're supposed to do to stave off the facing of facts: this person whose every neurosis you knew, whom you heard take a dump daily while you did your makeup, who had become like a brother more than a lover—this was the final person with whom you'd have sex. The guy who almost always chose sleeping over sleeping with you (and you chose the same).

What's so noble about sticking it out, anyway? they asked each other on the sofa late one night. Funny how when you're dating someone, your friends encourage you to leave if he so much as sneezes wrong, but once you're married, anything short of violence can and should be worked through.

Samira and Henry decided they weren't going to stay together just because society said they should. They were a modern couple, capable of co-parenting. For months they fretted about the effect on the kids. Then again, so many parents worry how their children will suffer if they split up—but how many consider the impact of sticking it out? What would eighteen formative years spent observing a bitter, loveless marriage do to their daughter and son? Wasn't it better to get out now—before someone cheated, before they hated each other? Practically everyone divorced these days. Henry himself was the product of divorced parents, and he had turned out fine. They weren't going to feel guilty or deem themselves failures or hush up the split. The day the papers arrived in the mail, they threw a party with all their closest friends (which didn't include anyone from the film club, Samira noted after the fact). It wasn't a divorce party but a celebration of their marriage. Just because the union was ending didn't mean it hadn't been a success. This chapter was closing. It was one of Samira's most treasured.

As the party wound down and Henry washed dishes, Samira felt that old stirring of possession. It was about to slip through her fingers for good. Eventually someone else would lay claim to Henry's shoulders and back and legs, stroke them without asking at any time of day she wanted. Samira longed to leave her print on him once more, right there on the kitchen counter. Even as it was happening, she thought, *What a cliché!* It was the best sex of her life. They signed the papers the next day. Samira was at peace, ready for a fresh start.

That was three weeks ago. And now, no matter how many sticks she pees on, they keep telling her the same thing. She is furious with both Henry and herself for letting this happen. *I'm thirty-eight!* she objects. *I had to take Clomid to get pregnant with the first two!* she protests. Still, the fact remains: she, a former sex therapist, had sex without protection, and now she is pregnant.

She hasn't told a soul. Samira knows Henry should be the first to find out, but given the circumstances, she's tempted to reach out to a friend and ask for advice. She thinks of Grace across the hall, Zoe next door. At one time they were her two best friends in the world, but now they wouldn't even make the top-five list of people to whom she'd turn. Samira sees them once a year, maybe twice if she's lucky. It's been ages since they had the familiarity of a quick call, a few moments to check in during a commute or between loads of laundry. Any conversation now is a marathon by necessity, because of the infrequency.

Samira longs for the easy intimacy they once shared. She remembers a monthlong obsession junior year when they planned their weddings—despite all three of them being single at the time. Samira chose a beach wedding in Mexico, Grace wanted a lavish production somewhere like the Plaza or the Carlyle, and Zoe opted to run off to Vegas and hire one of those Elvis officiants. That they'd be one another's bridesmaids was a given. The reality? Samira married in her hometown of Columbus, Ohio. By the time Henry proposed, she was closer with other women, whom she asked to stand by her side instead. The following fall, Samira attended Grace's wedding (which actually was at the Carlyle, because Grace was Grace and did whatever she damn well pleased). Samira was no more significant to the day's proceedings than Grace's uncle or a distant family friend. Grace too had found other women on whom to lean.

Their last night in the blue house is a memory Samira replays often. After graduation, all the furniture had been packed, so she, Grace, and Zoe sat on the carpet in Grace's room. Samira presented both women with scrapbooks she'd made—remember scrapbooks?—that catalogued their four years together. Even Zoe was reduced to tears. They vowed to coordinate visits to their new cities at least once a month. How naïve they were, how hopeful. Samira would miss TJ, Julius, and Alfred too, but not in the same way.

She hates these life transitions, the slow unraveling of relationships that once meant everything to you. First you leave behind your elementary school friends, then high school, then college. The pattern continues if you move jobs or cities. Every time she relocated, she left behind another set of wonderful friends. It became overwhelming, then impossible, to keep in close touch with everyone; the task would have been a full-time job. Once she had a partner and children, forget about it. With distance comes distance.

These past few years, Samira has prioritized work friends and couple friends and parent friends. Relationships born of circumstance, not bone-deep connections. She wonders idly if that's what adulthood comes down to—convenience and proximity. She considers herself an extrovert, but the cycle of new friends is exhausting. Occasionally she fantasizes about living in a small town and staying put, surrounding herself with the same warm faces from cradle to grave.

Samira tosses her book on the bed. Maybe a shower will clear her mind. She closes the drapes, cloaking the bedroom in darkness, and pads to the bathroom. Everything inside is black or white. On the wall opposite the sink is a framed photo of Hitchcock, his head and arms sticking out of an enormous cannon. Matching soap and lotion dispensers sit atop the counter alongside glass jars with Q-tips and cotton balls. Samira wipes a fingerprint off the mirror. She doesn't remember touching it.

The bathroom tile is ice-cold on the bottoms of Samira's feet. Goose bumps scurry up and down her body. She hums to herself as she undresses, then yanks open the sheer shower curtain, the metal rings clinking against the rod. Scalding water cascades from the rainfall head. Samira leaves the bathroom door ajar so the mirror doesn't fog. She examines the fancy little bottles of shampoo and conditioner. Eucalyptus with a hint of mint. She climbs into the shower and tries to focus on the soap and hot water streaming down her back.

She's going to keep the baby. What will Henry say when she tells him? Will he want to get back together or stick with the current plan? Which is she herself leaning toward? On one hand, she's finally free, and loath to give up that freedom. On the other, the prospect of running a business while keeping a newborn plus two other children alive makes her knees shake.

Samira rinses conditioner from her hair, then shaves her legs, enjoying the scrape of the razor blade across her skin. She had planned to decline Alfred's invitation, to explain to Grace and the others that she had a product launch coming up, and the timing just wasn't going to work. But then she found out she was pregnant. Her first impulse was to flee, to head elsewhere, ideally backward in time, to before life was so complicated. She thought of Alfred's email in her inbox and decided the Hitchcock Hotel would be her place of escape. She would turn to these old friends for a distraction. These people knew her before Henry, before the kids.

They weren't invested in or affected by the decisions she made now. A weekend of laughs and reminiscing about youthful antics was exactly what Samira wanted—though so far there's been more tension than she'd hoped.

"Shit," Samira hisses when the razor blade snags. She feels the sting of the cut before any drops of blood appear. Does she have Band-Aids in her toiletry bag? She wipes the water from her face, peers at the kit hanging from the towel rod, and chokes on a scream. Someone is standing in the dark of her bedroom.

FOURTEEN

Samira

Samira watches the intruder's head swivel owlishly on their neck to look at her.

"Who's there?" she croaks.

In the darkness she can make out no features, just a shadowy figure. She feels paralyzed. The earth seems to slow, then freezes on its axis.

When it picks up again, everything moves too fast.

She finally gets the shriek out and grabs wildly for a towel, tries to wrap it around her body at the same time she leaps out of the shower, water still running. Samira slips on the wet tile and comes down hard on her left wrist. She winces, and when she looks up, the figure has disappeared. Samira scrambles to her feet, grips the bathroom doorframe, flicks on the nearest nightstand lamp, then throws open the drapes. The room floods with light.

She is alone. Samira glances at the door, firmly closed. The intruder must have straight up vanished, but no, that can't be right. This is the real world, ruled by the laws of physics. She runs to the closet, searches under the bed. Nothing. Samira realizes she's still screaming. She stops.

She trades the towel for gray sweatpants and a sweatshirt, then stands at the door, working up the nerve to poke her head into the hallway. When she does, heart in her throat, she sees no one but Alfred and Danny. They stand near the staircase with their backs to her, huddled around Danny's housekeeping cart and deep in conversation. Samira doesn't want to bother them. They seem busy.

She closes the door and paces the room. Who was in here, and what had they wanted? She thinks of the supposed grass on Zoe's pillow. Samira told her it must've been a prank, someone looking for a laugh. Could Julius be behind this? Maybe he was trying to scare them all, keep Alfred on his toes.

But how had he gotten away so quickly? Could she even be sure she actually saw someone? Maybe Alfred's story of the Olds got to her. Maybe she was seeing things, making monsters out of shadows. Samira shakes her head, frustrated by her uncertainty.

But I did see someone, she thinks.

Samira returns to the hallway, steps tentatively toward Alfred and Danny. Only when she reaches them does she realize how crazy she must look—barefoot, hair dripping and uncombed. Alfred looks her up and down, concerned. "Is everything all right, Samira?"

She pushes her hair off her face with a shaking hand. "I—I was in the shower when I saw someone in my bedroom." She blinks away tears as she recounts the rest of the story. "Could it have been someone on your staff, do you think?"

Alfred stares at her. "Danny's the sole employee with room keys."

"I swear I'm not one of those degenerates you see on the news," Danny adds.

Alfred puts a hand on his heart. "I promise you no one on my staff would ever do something so unprofessional."

What about you, then? Samira thinks but doesn't say.

"And I've been in the shed with the groundskeeper for the past hour," Alfred says, reading her mind. "I only came up a minute ago." He hesitates. "To be honest, this reeks of Julius. You know he loves a good prank."

Samira shakes her head, thinking more clearly now. "He went for a walk on one of the trails."

Alfred scoffs. "Julius? In nature? Voluntarily? I thought his idea of enjoying the great outdoors was poolside margaritas at the Four Seasons." He glances out the window, and Samira follows his gaze. A steady drizzle is still coming down. "Not exactly ideal hiking weather," he notes.

Samira starts to shiver. Alfred puts an arm around her. "You must be freezing. Why don't you get back to your room and dry off?" He glances at Danny. "Will you fetch a pot of tea for Samira right away?"

The housekeeper heads for the stairs.

Alfred steers Samira back toward her room. "I'm so sorry this happened," he murmurs. "I'll talk to the group."

"It's just, I don't think our friends would do this," Samira says. They're not nineteen anymore—juvenile pranks no longer appeal. Not to her, anyway.

"I should hope not." Alfred takes a deep breath. "But a lot can change over the years. How well do we know one another at this point?"

Samira frowns and pulls away from him as she steps into her room.

"Don't worry," Alfred says brightly from the other side of the threshold. "I promise I'll get to the bottom of this."

His smile remains firmly in place as she closes the door.

FIFTEEN

Alfred

I stand outside Samira's door until I hear the dead bolt turn; then I make my way up to the attic. The wind rattles the windows in their frames. I peer out the back one, then the front, reassured by the quietude. Nothing to see but the rain.

I shift my attention to the louvered vents in the floor. I'm not going to apologize for them. How can a proprietor serve at a guest's pleasure if he doesn't know what that pleasure is? You can't rely on the guests themselves to tell you—they won't be honest with a stranger about their predilections and peccadilloes. This platform is strictly in the name of exquisite customer service.

I'm no Peeping Tom, but I do like to observe people—their gestures and emotions, the way they talk, the way they think. So many times I have ridden in a train or sat in a lobby wishing I could watch a scene unfold without being part of it, without any awareness of my own corporeality—the need to focus my stare elsewhere, to fake absorption in a magazine or phone, to keep my face still when something surprising happens. People behave differently when a stranger is nearby. They sense when they're being watched. Most of us don't like the feeling if the attention is unsolicited.

Up here I observe without intrusion. I believe that, were Hitch not so famous or so busy, he would have constructed something like my viewing platform in his lifetime. After all, the man was an undisputed voyeur. He believed everyone had something to hide. During shifts at La Quinta, I used to daydream about what my Reville friends were up to while I was mopping floors or cleaning toilets. Now I don't have to imagine. I can watch.

I check the north-side rooms first. In 301 Samira is biting her nails in bed, watching the door. In 303 Zoe palms a minibar bottle—debating whether to crack it open, no doubt. 305 is empty. TJ must be out on his run, although he left breakfast well over two hours ago.

I cross over to the south side of the third floor. 306 is also empty. Apparently Julius is still "hiking in the rain." 304 is my room. I've saved the best for last—in 302 is Grace. I peer through her vent and barely stifle a gasp.

Grace is in bed, on her back, topless. Back arched, eyes closed. Someone's head is between her legs, but I can't tell whose because the bedsheet is covering them. Based on the size of the feet and the hairiness of the calves hanging off the mattress, it appears to be a man.

I wait, frozen, for the adulterer to appear, though I have a sinking feeling I know who it is. I don't want to watch but I have no choice. This isn't her husband paying a surprise visit. I pull up the Voice Memos app on my phone and record audio.

For what feels like two lifetimes Grace moans, getting louder and louder until she convulses. She claps a hand over her mouth, which does little to muffle the noise. When she stills at last, the snake slithers its way up the bed. He lies on his side facing her, profile turned toward me.

In all my research and stakeouts, not once did I catch these two together. My entire body trembles, palms slick with sweat. I watch him speak softly into her ear. I hear only static.

One of Hitchcock's favorite methods to
illustrate the difference between
surprise and suspense was the "bomb under the
table" example. If two people sit in a café
talking for fifteen minutes, and at the end
we the audience discover a bomb is under the
table, that's surprise. But if we the audience
know from the beginning of their conversation
that there's a bomb while they don't, that's suspense.

—*Excerpt from Essay #39,*
"Surprise vs. Suspense in Hitchcock's Oeuvre"

SIXTEEN

TJ

TJ gazes at the woman lying in bed beside him. "I love you, Grace Liu," he says. Grace smiles with her eyes closed.

Something thumps overhead. TJ bolts up in bed and scopes the ceiling. "What was that?" he says.

Grace's lids flutter open. "What was what?"

He climbs out of bed. "That bang. Like something fell." He walks the room, studies the ceiling, stops at a vent in the middle. "Is there another floor above us?"

"I don't know, Teej." She pulls the comforter up to her neck. "I told you we shouldn't be doing this here. Someone could catch us."

Would that be such a bad thing? he thinks.

TJ isn't proud to be sleeping with another man's wife, to play a part in jeopardizing their family. He reminds himself that he isn't responsible and shouldn't worry—Grace has told him as much a hundred times. Once he and Grace began hooking up, after a chance encounter at a French restaurant in SoHo, TJ broke things off with the woman he'd been casually dating. He's never said so to Grace, but he has no clue how she's looked her husband in the eye every day for six months and divulged nothing. The secret would eat him alive.

His own secret already is.

Grace pulls on her underwear, then clasps her bra. TJ goes to the window and opens the curtains a sliver. He scans the parking lot. No one there. The rain is coming down in sheets.

"Get away from the window," Grace says. "Someone could see you."

TJ sits in the desk chair. "Have you given any more thought to telling Rob?"

She sighs. "I don't want to talk about the future right now."

Grace never wants to talk about the future. TJ hates when she dismisses him this way, gives him the verbal equivalent of a pat on the head. She's not the only one with something to lose here. You don't have to rake in a million plus a year and birth two kids to understand risk.

If you'd told twenty-year-old TJ that he would someday wind up in love with Grace Liu, he would've laughed in your face. Did he even find her hot back then? He remembers the afternoons they spent on the quad arguing over stories like "The Lottery" and "The Yellow Wallpaper." Truth be told, he had been more intrigued by Zoe. She was fun, a little mysterious, and offered the right amount of instability. Grace was always so capable, even at Reville. That's exactly what he finds attractive about her now. Give him a woman who knows what she wants and gets it over one who's constantly flailing. The hot mess isn't so hot after college. Grace doesn't need him; she wants him. The distinction is important.

"Isn't it nice having a whole weekend together?" she says.

What difference does it make if we're peeking over our shoulders the entire time?

"I'm only here 'cause you asked," TJ says. "Over my dead body would I set foot in Alfred's hotel otherwise."

TJ wants Grace to believe that she's the sole reason he's here, but TJ has his own aim for the weekend, one he can't tell Grace about. Coming to Alfred's hotel is the perfect solution to his problems. When you're trying to avoid people who wish you harm, there are places you don't want to hide: (1) A regular hotel. They will blend in, and they will find you. (2) Your childhood home. You will risk putting your family in harm's way. (3) Anywhere alone. You need the right-sized crowd for protection. Which is how he wound up saying yes to Alfred's random invite. Even if they found him here, they wouldn't dare trespass in a place of business with a closed guest list (would they?). Too many witnesses, too small a crowd. TJ knows putting his old friends in potential danger is unkind, but he needs human shields. A familiar burning sensation spreads across his chest. He reaches for the roll of TUMS on the desk and pops one.

Grace stares. "You're eating those things like candy this weekend."

TJ forces lightness into his tone as he gestures at the walls, which are papered in old movie posters. "We could've had ourselves a nice little weekend in Atlantic City, but no, you wanted to come to this bizarro shrine to a director who's been dead for forty years."

"Don't you feel the least bit guilty about what happened to Alfred?" Grace asks. She's in a strange mood this weekend. Regret isn't her thing. Nor, as illustrated by the double-crossing of her husband, is guilt.

"No, and you shouldn't either. He was in the wrong, not us." A vein in TJ's forehead twitches. "Did Alfred threaten you?"

"What? No."

"Has he said anything at all?"

Grace shakes her head. He's not sure he believes her.

"Then where is this coming from?"

"You don't know what you don't know," she says.

He wrinkles his nose. "What's that supposed to mean?"

"It means I don't think there's anything wrong with supporting a friend who went through a rough time," she snaps.

TJ rolls his eyes. "Have you seen this place? Alfred's doing fine. All I'm saying is, you know how obsessed he was with you. Probably still is. What's that book about giving a mouse a cookie?"

"Don't patronize me," Grace says. Despite the fact that she's now pissed at him, he's glad to see the fight back in her eyes.

He throws up his hands in surrender. The pill TJ cannot swallow:

Grace doesn't love him back. Their affair (God, he detests that word) is escapism for her, an adventure. TJ hates hearing about her family and their sweet plans—it makes him feel worse about this arrangement. More than once he's opened his mouth to break things off, but then he glimpses the dimple on Grace's left cheek or the curve of her shoulders, imagines never brushing his lips over those parts of her body again, and he can't bring himself to do it. He's given her more and more space in his life, and now it feels like she's the whole story, not a chapter. Panic tap-dances in his chest.

He crosses the room to her. "I'm sorry," he murmurs. Then, to change the subject: "Samira asked three times yesterday who my client is."

Grace sighs again, but this time the sound is halfhearted, one that means she's not that irritated. "Tell her it's someone she's never heard of. She'll lose interest."

Maybe he doesn't want Samira to lose interest, but TJ won't admit that to Grace. Back when he had dreams of being an editor at a publishing house, his friends raved about how cool the job sounded. No one ever says that now besides Samira, and that's only because she thinks he works with someone famous.

TJ had come close to living that other life. He'd made it to the final round of interviews for an editorial assistant position with one of what were then the Big Six publishers in New York. That was mere months before the Great Recession. The company froze all hiring, and by then no one else was bringing on new employees either. TJ moved back in with his folks and picked up a job at an electronics store near their house—the same place he'd worked at in high school.

He spent the year after graduation bitter, an emotion previously foreign to him. Here he'd done everything he was supposed to: took out the crippling student loans, earned the grades, worked at the same bar as Zoe to cover books and food. He'd finished school magna cum laude, but no one gave a shit. He understood that Reville wasn't Harvard, but it was a decent university. He had taken the steps the powers that be told him to take, and now he was literally in the same frigging place he'd been in high school—except he had six figures of debt this time around. The resentment coursing through his body worried him. He needed an outlet.

TJ had never been an athlete, hadn't bothered setting foot in a weight room in high school or college for fear the other guys would bag on his skinny frame, but now he didn't care what douchebags from his hometown thought. Every day before work he hit the local gym: treadmill, free weights, abs. He couldn't believe the way exercise lifted his mood; he'd always assumed those claims about endorphins were horseshit. He also couldn't believe how quickly his body changed. He liked the way women noticed him now, men regarded him. He was no longer ignored.

After six months of working out religiously, he'd gotten friendly with a couple of the other gym members. One of them offered him a security gig at a concert—a one-time thing because the kid was attending said concert—and TJ said, "Sure, why not?" One job led to another. More responsibilities, higher pay. TJ didn't want to start back at the bottom of the ladder in the publishing industry, so he stuck with the security work.

His current job is not as sexy as Samira imagines. He's providing detail for a paranoid member of Maryland's house of delegates, a former businessman with a track record of screwing over powerful people. Still, until recently, the job had its perks. Ravens tickets and a free round of golf at a prestigious country club. Most important, TJ had finally paid off the last of his student loans a few weeks ago. He shudders.

"Can you believe Zoe is drinking again?" he says.

"Real talk—I'm more surprised that she tried to stop. She has no willpower whatsoever."

TJ winces, though he knows Grace is right.

She gets out of bed and puts her hands on her hips. "I wouldn't be surprised if she made up the whole two-months-sober thing. You remember the way she used to lie in college. She did whatever she had to do to keep herself out of trouble."

Hey, pot, you're black, TJ thinks, then feels bad for thinking it.

Grace gives him a queer look. "You want to join me in the shower?"

"Does that mean you're not mad anymore?" He follows her into the bathroom.

She glances back at him. "Depends how good the shower is."

SEVENTEEN

Alfred

It's TJ. Grace is having an affair with TJ.

I hurry down the attic ladder and out of the storage closet, then lean against the door, working the meat of my palm like a stress cushion. I've never used my viewing platform to watch my guests engage in coitus, except for just now, and that was because I needed to know who was in bed with Grace. I'm not up there to polish the banister, is what I'm saying.

Under ordinary circumstances I'd be thrilled to hear that Grace feels regret and guilt over my mistreatment. But instead of me, she confided in TJ, nearly giving me up in the process.

You don't know what you don't know.

Grace is playing with fire.

I'm tempted to barge into her room, can see the scene now. Me holding my phone overhead. The recording playing at maximum volume. The blood draining from Grace's face. Grace plugging her ears when her moans won't cease. Burying her head in her arms. Me reminding her I'm in charge here.

I glance at the framed portrait of Hitch on the wall. The photo was taken for a *Harper's Bazaar* shoot. The magazine had asked him to share his recipe for a Christmas goose. To give the photo a Hitchcockian twist, Hitch holds a dead and plucked goose by the throat, a bow tied around its neck. He gestures at the goose with his free hand, a hollow gaze in his eyes.

How would he have handled this new development? (Hitch, not the goose.) More strategically than kicking down Grace's door—that's for sure. I wait for my fury to settle, for logic to take over.

This development actually works in my favor, I realize. An affair means zeal, muddied thinking, unwise risks, motive. Crimes of passion. Hitch didn't give a whit about believability, but I don't have that same luxury. I can use this.

Danny appears with a broom in hand at the other end of the hallway. When she sees me, she traipses over. "Everything okay, dear?"

"Not now," I say. She nods and makes herself scarce.

For twenty minutes I stand there, waiting, until at last TJ peeks into the hallway. I don't bother to pretend I've been doing something else. I watch with amusement as he jumps, startled.

He emerges from Grace's room, dressed in the Nike running outfit. He nods at me, then moves down the hallway toward his own room. *He's not going to address me at all.*

"Last I checked, Grace's room doesn't have a running track," I say.

He turns. "I was helping her with a work thing."

"Really?" I say, not moving off the door. "Is there a lot of overlap between bodyguarding and hedge funds?"

A flicker of irritation crosses his face. "Her firm wants to hire a couple security guards. I was giving her the contact info of a few guys I know."

"How considerate of you."

Over my dead body would I set foot in Alfred's hotel, TJ had said. I envision my head spinning off my neck, pinging off the ceiling, and administering swift but fatal blunt force trauma upon him. He skulks into his room.

I stand there like a sentinel. Two minutes later, he reappears, now with earbuds in. He glances down the hallway, sees me still waiting here, and makes for the staircase. "I know what happens if you give a mouse a cookie," I call after him.

I shouldn't have said that, but a man can bite his tongue for only so long before it bleeds.

TJ stops, pulls out an earbud, and peers over his shoulder at me. "What did you say?"

"Why, he's going to want a glass of milk."

EIGHTEEN

TJ

TJ's worries follow him as he pounds the pavement.

If you give a mouse a cookie . . . he's going to want a glass of milk.

That's what Alfred said, meaning he was eavesdropping on their conversation and heard TJ talking shit about him. Not only that, but he wanted TJ to know he'd heard. TJ would not soon forget Alfred's expression during the confrontation. The clenched jaw, the flared nostrils, the hard coal black eyes. For the first time ever, TJ finds himself afraid of Alfred. It doesn't matter that TJ has at least fifty pounds on the guy, that he could likely bench-press Alfred if he wanted to. This isn't a question of strength. Strength has little advantage against insanity. When people hear the word "insane," they tend to think of chaos and confusion. TJ knows better. Sometimes insanity lurks, stalks, grins. Insanity can simmer. It can be quiet.

TJ tries to focus on his surroundings, on the fresh air filling his lungs. It feels good to run outside again. Lately he's been too nervous, has stuck to the crappy old treadmill in his building's gym. Even now, though, he imagines nosy eyes watching him. TJ tells himself he's being paranoid. No one knows where he is. This place is making him irrational.

Eager for a distraction, TJ thinks back to the first day of class sophomore year. The whole gang had signed up for the ten a.m. Tuesday/Thursday section of Dr. Scott's film class, though Alfred and Grace were the only serious movie buffs among them. The six of them shuffled, hungover, through the double doors at the back of the lecture hall that morning. (Did they really used to get drunk on Mondays, then function all day Tuesday?) Samira, Alfred, and Grace found seats in the front row. TJ slumped between Julius and Zoe in the back row. His eyes itched from too little sleep.

No one talked much while they waited for class to begin. Someone repeatedly clicked a pen. TJ flashed dirty looks around the room but couldn't find the culprit. Another student popped open a can of soda. A third wrestled with a granola bar wrapper. Was everyone always this annoying? TJ pulled up the hood of his sweatshirt and rested his head on his flimsy desk.

At nine fifty-nine a fiftysomething man in loafers and ill-fitting jeans swept into the room. "Why the long faces?" the professor boomed, bespectacled and cheery. "You folks are getting college credit to watch movies."

A few people laughed. TJ sat up straight. Alfred was scribbling notes up front—about what, TJ had no idea.

"Hello to my film lovers, as well as to those of you who are here to fill an elective." *Guilty as charged,* TJ thought. The professor grinned. "I hope to make film lovers out of you too. I'm Dr. Scott, and I've been a professor of media and communication at Reville for eighteen years, as long as some of you have been alive. Every year you all keep getting younger, and I stay the ripe old age of thirty-two." More students chuckled. "If you're not a fan of dad jokes, I suggest you drop the class. Now," he rumbled, "let's get down to brass tacks."

Dr. Scott lowered the projector screen, then brought up a PowerPoint deck from his laptop. He clicked past the title slide. The next one was a photo of two golden retrievers sitting in a red Radio Flyer wagon. Dr. Scott crouched between them, an arm around each. The professor used a laser pointer to indicate the dog on the left. "This here is Charlie, and the other one is his brother, Buster. They are the best dogs in the world, and I won't hear any different. On movie days I bring them in with me, so not only do you get to watch movies in class, but you get to do it while petting my pups. Tell me college isn't a dream come true."

By now several of the students were cooing over the dogs, and everyone was awake. Dr. Scott stood back, reveling in the chatter and enthusiasm.

"A little more about me, now that you've met my fur babies, as my godson calls them. My house is in Portland, where my wife works, so I spend weekdays here and weekends there. I think *The Aviator* should have beaten *Million Dollar Baby* for best picture this year. I take my lunch break every day on the roof of this building. You will not find a better view of the White Mountains on campus. I dig watching the seasons change little by little." He paused. "Note that I am in no way suggesting you do the same. Don't want y'all getting yourselves—or me—in hot water."

He clicked to the next slide.

"On a more serious note, let's discuss the syllabus. This class is thirteen weeks, which means I get to show you thirteen films. I'm going to do my level best to introduce you to or reacquaint you with some of the best directors of all time. At the end of the semester, I'll expect you to write a ten-page paper—double-spaced; don't worry—on your favorite of these directors. That will be your final. After every film we watch, you'll also write a three- or four-page analysis. Bring those to class, and we'll discuss the themes you bring up in your papers. Additionally, there will be a five-page midterm paper, but we'll get into that when the time comes."

TJ heard Julius curse next to him. "I thought this class was supposed to be an easy A," he muttered.

"The first film we'll watch is *Casablanca*. How many of you have seen it?"

Half a dozen people raised their hands, including Grace.

"For those who haven't had the pleasure, this is the story of an American expatriate, played by Humphrey Bogart, who's forced to choose between his love for Ingrid Bergman and helping her resistance-leader husband escape the city of Casablanca so he can continue his fight against the Nazis. Did you know a number of the actors who played Nazis in the movie were Jews who escaped Germany?"

Rather than stand at the podium, Dr. Scott walked back and forth across the room, gesticulating as he talked, like he couldn't contain his excitement. TJ liked him immediately. He took the class through the rest of the syllabus, concluding with the section on plagiarism. "Reville has a zero-tolerance policy," he reminded the students. "Don't be dummies, folks. See you Thursday." With that, the first class of the semester was dismissed.

TJ watched Alfred, Grace, and Samira gather their things while Julius and Zoe did the same on either side of him. Despite the occasional squabble, the six of them were tight back then. TJ had assumed they'd be close for life. Who could have guessed, as they sat at their desks with pounding headaches, that this class would change the trajectory of their friendship? Who could have known Dr. Scott's course was the beginning of the end?

ACT
TWO

"The more successful the villain,
the more successful the picture.
That's a cardinal rule."

—*Alfred Hitchcock*

NINETEEN

Alfred

Once TJ is gone, I knock on Grace's door. She opens it, scrapes a hand through her hair. "What's up, Alfred?"

I put on my hotelier smile. "Have you had lunch yet?"

She shakes her head. "I haven't had a chance." Grace points to the desk in her room. Three or four gadgets and a yellow legal pad clutter the surface.

"You've got a whole Apple Store in here," I chide. "All you do is work, work, work. What kind of host would I be if I let you skip a meal? Come on." I offer her my arm, and she takes it without smiling.

We make our way down the hallway and staircase. I keep the conversation going since Grace is decidedly unchatty. I tell her which movie I've picked for this afternoon and ask if she approves. All film fans appreciate the technical sophistication of *Rope*. More than sixty years before the likes of *Birdman* or *1917*, Hitch was stitching together long takes to tell a story in real time. I change the topic to a *Vertigo* remake that a Hollywood A-lister has in the works. Grace agrees that the reboot is pointless. Why redo something that was done right the first time?

Our conversation reminds me of film club. The club was my idea, as was asking Dr. Scott to be our advisor. For two years we screened a movie in the basement of Carroll Hall every other Thursday night, then spent an hour discussing it, sometimes as one big group, sometimes in smaller circles. Since I was the club's founder, I got to pick the movie for the inaugural meeting. I chose *Psycho*—predictable, yes, and not even my favorite Hitch film, but I knew I wouldn't get as many attendees with *The Lady Vanishes* or *The Trouble with Harry*. What a joy to pay attention to and dissect a film instead of brainlessly munching on popcorn while scrolling through our phones. Art is meant to be poked and prodded, talked about, fought over. To take it in with no reflection is missing the point.

Not until we're seated with turkey club sandwiches in front of us does Grace ask, "Why are we here, Alfred?"

"I told you last night. I wanted to celebrate the anniversary of the hotel with old friends who would appreciate its theme."

"Why did I get a separate email from the rest of the group?" Grace twists her hands into a knot. She hasn't touched her sandwich.

I bite a hunk off my pickle spear. "You wouldn't have prioritized the reunion without a nudge."

She tucks her hands under her legs and leans forward. "Nudge received. I convinced each and every one of them to come." She meets my eye for the first time all weekend. "I need to know we're good."

"You should eat." I dig into my own sandwich. "Don't want those fries to get cold."

She scowls. I make the motion of zipping my lips, but she doesn't appear any less on edge.

"What can I do for you, Alfred?" When I say nothing, she prods. "One of your staff mentioned business has been slow. Do you want me to take a look at your books? Figure out where you can cut expenses?"

I cock my head. "Grace, your servitude won't buy my silence."

"That's not what this is," she insists. "I'm trying to help."

I finish my sandwich, then wipe my mouth with my cloth napkin and fold it the way I learned at La Quinta. "You know how you can help? By not making allusions to the past that might raise other people's suspicions."

"I haven't," she protests. "I wouldn't."

"Not even to TJ?"

She squints. "Why would I tell him of all people?"

"You two seem close," I say. "I wish you'd eat."

She picks up her sandwich and takes a small bite. "We're not. Close, I mean."

"One thing I always liked about you, Grace, is that you never played dumb. That sort of thing was beneath you. Do you think that still holds true?"

Her expression darkens. She puts down her sandwich. "Where is this going?"

Don't say another word.

But I need to remind her who's in charge.

Don't do it.

In the end, I can't help myself. I place my beautifully folded napkin on my fry-littered plate. Calmly, quietly, I say, "I hadn't heard you moan like that in years and years."

Her face loses all color.

I glance at my phone clock. "Shoot, look at the time. I have errands to do before our big screening. You won't think me rude for leaving you to finish alone?"

Grace shakes her head, speechless.

"I didn't think so. Make sure you're in the theater at seven sharp. Don't go getting distracted by any rendezvous!"

I take my leave without waiting to see her reaction.

TWENTY

Samira

Samira sits at the desk in her hotel room, heart racing. Every time she closes her eyes, she sees the stranger in the dark. How long was the intruder standing there? What were they searching for? The idea of their eyes crawling up and down her naked body makes her sick.

What if they come back?

She rises from the chair, double-checks that the door is chained and dead bolted, then pulls the drapes across both windows again. The last thing she wants is to sit here alone. Then again, she'd be more exposed in one of the common areas. Anyone could watch her out there. She wraps her arms around herself. This weekend is supposed to be fun and uncomplicated. So far it's been neither. She considers marching straight to her car and driving home without stopping.

Who was in her room? Who has a key? She thinks of the elderly housekeeper first. Maybe Danny came in to clean the room, not realizing Samira was in the bathroom, then fled. But why wouldn't she admit the mistake in the hallway earlier? Was she afraid of getting in trouble with Alfred? Something doesn't add up there. Besides, the intruder seemed bigger than Danny, more menacing.

One of the other employees must have a key they shouldn't have. Samira has seen the groundskeeper, a pale man with a mullet, around the property. When she went to the car earlier to get her book, he'd glanced up from his weeding and watched her walk across the parking lot and back. Or what about the slick-smiled concierge? Samira checks the hotel's Tripadvisor reviews to see if guests have mentioned anything odd but finds nothing more than a dozen four- and five-star ratings, plus a single two-star that reads, "The place was nice enough, but I prefer Poe." Everyone raves about the cookies and milk at bedtime. Nothing about shadows in the rooms, lurkers near the showers. She considers that she might've imagined the whole thing.

Samira has a hard time believing her friends would find such a creepy act entertaining. Yes, Julius loves pranks—or at least he used to—but he would've announced himself right away, eager to claim glory. Could it have been Alfred? He's never shown the slightest interest in her. If he were to lurk outside anyone's shower, it'd be Grace's. Samira still remembers the night she met Alfred at her cousin's house party, the way he followed Grace around like a puppy. Grace has a penchant for collecting followers. Samira has always thought she'd make a great cult leader.

Before this weekend, Samira hadn't spoken to or seen Alfred in a long time. He's been off the past couple of days, in a way she can't put her finger on. The daggers he shoots when he thinks no one's paying attention, the grins at inappropriate times—again, when he thinks no one will notice. The problem isn't that this is unusual behavior for him. It's unusual for anyone. Shouldn't he be worried by Samira's room break-in? Not to mention the number of times Zoe has vomited today. True, she drank a lot last night, and there's no love lost between her and Alfred, for reasons Samira doesn't understand, but if Alfred is as obsessive about his hotel's reputation as he purports to be, he should want to ensure that no one leaves unhappy.

Samira changes into black jeans, a marigold sweater, and high-top sneakers. For once, because she's kid-free (kind of), she takes her time doing her makeup, spreading out tubes, pencils, and compacts across the desk. While reaching for an eye shadow brush, she knocks over a jar of foundation. The liquid coats everything—the desk, her book, her phone. "Shit," she cries, wiping it all down with her palm. The makeup has stained the cream rug too. She hurries to the bathroom, grabs a snow-white face towel off the rack. Samira would hate to ruin the linen, but either that or the rug has to be sacrificed. Her frantic thoughts are interrupted by a knock on the door. She freezes.

Samira grips the bathroom counter so hard her knuckles hurt. *What if that's him?* She moves to the middle of the bedroom, wringing the towel with both hands, vaguely aware of the stain settling into the rug. She holds her breath, feeling like she might pass out.

"Who is it?" she squeaks.

The person doesn't answer but knocks again. They're not going away. *Why won't they go away?* Samira tiptoes to the desk, opens the drawer, finds nothing but a hotel-branded notepad and ballpoint pen. She uncaps the pen and presses her thumb into its point. *Is this thing even sharp enough to puncture skin?*

She figures if she stabs hard enough, it will.

Samira puts her ear to the door and listens. She imagines the intruder's ear inches from hers, resting against the other side of the wood. Revolted, she pulls back. She wishes the door had a peephole. The pen is slippery in her sweaty palm.

"I said, who is it?" she says, more loudly this time. Nothing.

Should she open it?

Samira looks down at her stomach and takes a deep breath. Leaving the chain lock in place, she reaches for the doorknob with one hand and brandishes the pen with the other. She opens the door an inch or two. She doesn't intend to scream, but she's so scared that the sound comes out anyway.

Standing in the hallway, waiting with a room service cart full of tea things, is the housekeeper.

Samira stares, confused until she remembers. Alfred asked Danny to bring Samira tea. That was a couple of hours ago. She lets out the longest breath of her life, and drops the pen when she clocks Danny gawking at it with wide eyes. "One second. Sorry," Samira says. She closes the door, undoes the chain, then throws the door open.

"Shall I put this on the desk?" Danny asks as she loads the tea set onto a tray.

"That would be great. Thanks, Danny." Samira makes sure to use the housekeeper's name, so Danny knows she's one of the good guests, someone who takes the time to speak to and thank the staff, doesn't bark orders or ignore their existence altogether.

Danny leaves the cart in the hall, then sets the tray on the desk. Samira watches the old woman's eagle eyes roam the room and feels embarrassed by the mess she's made—piles of clothes on the floor, hair products littered across the bathroom counter, balled-up tissues on the nightstand. Danny's gaze stops at the foundation stain on the rug. The housekeeper's lips pucker with disapproval, spurring Samira to action. She grabs the bathroom towel off the bed where she dropped it and hurries toward the rug. "I was about to—"

Danny howls and grabs Samira by the arm. The old woman is surprisingly strong. "Don't!" Samira jerks away from her. "You'll ruin both the rug and the towel. Leave it. I'll be right back."

Without waiting for a response, Danny rushes for the door with the ease of someone twenty years her junior. Her arms are ropy, calves taut. If you saw her from behind, only the silver hair would give away her age. Danny flicks open the swing-bar lock so the door doesn't shut behind her when she exits. Then she's gone. Samira can still feel the old woman's grip on her bicep.

Danny returns seconds later with a dingy dishrag and a spray bottle of carpet cleaner. Samira stands in the middle of the room, unsure what to do, as Danny moves around without acknowledging her. The housekeeper sprays foamy liquid onto the rug. She checks her watch, sits back on her Mary Janes, and glares at Samira.

"I'm s-sorry," Samira stutters.

Danny mutters something unintelligible in response.

Samira crouches by her side. "I didn't catch that. What'd you say?"

"I said I'm not the one to whom you should be apologizing," Danny says.

"Excuse me?" Samira says, because she can think of nothing else to say.

Danny dabs angrily at the foam. "That's Samira for you. Always the polite one."

Samira backs away. What has Alfred told her? She sits on the bed, watching Danny work. "If I've offended you somehow . . ." She trails off, not wanting to apologize again and incur Danny's wrath a second time. Maybe the housekeeper is upset about what Samira suggested earlier, that the staff broke into her room. She didn't act upset at the time. In fact, this is a total one-eighty from the affable person she met in the hall hours ago.

Could Danny have been the one in her room?

The old woman finishes scrubbing and stands to survey her handiwork from farther away. The stain is gone. Samira would be impressed if she weren't so intimidated. Danny gathers her tools and heads once more for the door. On her way, she scoops up the forgotten pen, then spins around to face Samira. Danny hands her the pen with the tip sticking out.

"In case you need to fight off any other intruders," she says. Samira accepts the pen without a word.

Danny opens the door, then pauses. "Alfred worked his tail off to make this weekend perfect for you all. How do you repay him? With jokes at his expense and accusations of misconduct."

"I haven't—" Samira starts, but Danny puts up a hand, silencing her.

"If you're searching for boogeymen, you leave my boy alone. Maybe you should take a closer look at your so-called friends instead. There are things they've done that they're not telling you. Of that you can be sure."

TWENTY-ONE

Alfred

In the kitchen I ask Chef to cook some plain rice and make toast for Zoe. Then I carry the tray of food up the two flights of stairs to her room. Carefully, I balance the tray on one hand, knock on her door with the other.

When she opens it, she appears less ghoulish than she did this morning. "Feeling better?" I ask.

Zoe eyes the tray. "What's this?"

"I figured you might not be up for a trip to the restaurant this afternoon, so I've brought lunch to you. I stuck with the BRAT diet because it's supposed to settle an upset stomach, but I can bring you something else if you'd like." She says nothing, so I add, "'BRAT' stands for 'bananas, rice, applesauce, and toast.'"

"I know what it stands for."

A beacon of cheerfulness, as usual.

"May I come in? Set the tray down?"

She examines the food like it's been poisoned. "No, I'll take it."

I hand the tray over. "Is there anything else you need? I have a mini pharmacy in my room."

"I'm good." If she weren't holding the tray, I know she'd cross her arms right now.

"Can we expect you for the movie later?" I ask hopefully.

She searches my face. "Yeah," she says. "I think I'll be okay."

"Fantastic. The others will be happy to hear it." I wait for her to do something—crack a smile, nod, add some pleasantry—but no, she stares at the tray of food she's holding. "Listen, Zoe. I feel awful about last night. I never meant for my festivities to get in the way of your sobriety." I try to squeeze her shoulder, but she backs away.

"Are you trying to get rid of me?" Zoe asks.

"Hmm?" I say.

Her jaw works back and forth. "Because I know what you did?"

Classic delusional Zoe. "I'm sorry, but I have no idea what you're talking about. Have you been drinking this morning?"

"Fuck you, Alfred," she spits. "You're the goddamn reason I have a problem."

"I'm sorry you feel that way, but you did this all on your own, Zo. If anyone here is a victim, it's me."

She sneers. "If you don't take responsibility for your actions—"

"That's rich, coming from you," I say.

"—I'll set things right my own way. You don't scare me." The tremble of her chin gives her away, though.

"Ooh, a vigilante." I put my hands in my pockets and squeeze the Swiss Army knife. "How heroic."

Danny steps out of the storage closet, holding a stack of hand towels and washcloths. "What's heroic?"

"Zoe here is in pursuit of justice," I tell Danny.

"Aren't we all?" the housekeeper says agreeably.

Zoe glowers back and forth between us, then closes the door with her foot. Danny raises an eyebrow and gestures at Zoe's door with her head. I put my finger to my lips and nod. Danny smiles, then takes the fresh linens to my room. She disappears inside without another word.

I wait for a minute, then make my way toward the staircase. What a shame we've become estranged, Zoe and I. As I said, we used to be close. Food wasn't all that bonded us.

We had just finished fall-semester midterms junior year when I stumbled upon Zoe in the library one afternoon. I had come straight from my last exam, for a marketing class on consumer behavior, and planned to reward myself by checking out a new book on Hitch. What were the odds that Zoe would choose that same biography aisle to sink to the carpet and have a meltdown? Sometimes I wonder if it was a cry for help. Maybe she was hoping I would find her there.

Her head was buried in her arms, knees pulled up to her chest. I could tell by her heaving shoulders that she was crying.

I sat next to her and spoke discreetly. "What's wrong, Zo?"

She lifted her head to reveal tear-stained cheeks. "I'm failing half of my classes."

I tried not to react. Perhaps I shouldn't have been shocked. We hadn't taken any courses together since Dr. Scott's class the year before, but I'd heard from the others that she was struggling to keep up. Her work schedule wasn't helping. By this point she was bartending five or six nights a week at a popular bar on Greet Street. Her shifts often lasted until three a.m.

The idea of failing a single class, let alone half of them, shook me. I wasn't as smart as Grace, but I was a diligent student who managed mostly A's. What I lack in talent I have always compensated for with discipline. If you can't outsmart them, outwork them.

I could tell Zoe was ashamed, so I stared straight ahead at the bookshelf across from us. "What can I do?"

"My parents are going to be crushed if I get kicked out."

I noted that she didn't say they'd kill her, said only that they'd be disappointed, yet the prospect of disappointing them was enough to devastate her. I doubted my own mother would even notice had I flunked out of school. The resolve within me hardened. I became desperate to help.

"My classes are pretty easy this semester," I lied. "I could help you get back on track with yours."

"Really?" She peeked at me for the first time since I'd sat down.

"Why don't we meet here for a couple hours every afternoon? Which class are you doing the worst in?"

"Microeconomics," she said.

I pulled a face. "You have Calthrop?" She nodded. "He lectures like he's speaking to a roomful of economists. I had no idea what he was talking about half the time."

This appeared to cheer her. She wiped her nose on her sleeve, pulled herself to standing, then helped me up. "Thanks, Alfred. You're a good guy."

I beamed. That was the nicest thing she'd ever said to me.

True to my word, I tutored her every day for the rest of that semester. I helped her study for tests, rewrote her papers—she is not a skilled writer—and she wound up with four B's and a C. (Econ was a lost cause.) She came back to me for help spring semester, then senior year as well. To say I single-handedly stopped Zoe Allen from failing out of Reville is not a stretch. Under two years of my tutelage, she flunked only one class, and by then I didn't have time to worry about Zoe's academic success. I was busy learning the hard way that there are fates worse than failed classes.

TWENTY-TWO

TJ

After his run, TJ trudges, dripping wet from the rain, through the lobby. Alfred's words about the mouse and the milk linger as he does ten sets of twenty push-ups in his room, followed by a thousand bicycle crunches.

Originally TJ thought the point of this weekend was for Alfred to show off to his old friends, to prove what a dynamo he's become—although Grace overheard the concierge say the hotel is struggling. Now he wonders if Alfred's motives are more sinister. What does he want from them? TJ lies on the carpet and stares at the ceiling, letting his gaze roam. He notes a louvered vent above the bed, same as the one in Grace's room.

TJ wouldn't care if Alfred opened a hundred hotels—there's something off about the guy. He liked Alfred a lot when they were freshmen, but things shifted as the semesters went by. Something about the way Alfred watches people when he thinks no one is looking—overly intent, almost leering. Some people get your hackles up, make you feel unsafe without ever opening their mouths. They enter your train car and you're compelled to move to the next one, an animal instinct alerting you to the possibility of danger. By the end of senior year, TJ hoped never to see Alfred Smettle again.

How had Alfred even heard him and Grace talking in the first place? Was he lurking outside her room with his ear to the door? Goddamn creep. Grace is right—they need to be more careful.

TJ sometimes wishes he could tell Grace's husband about the affair himself. He can't stand sneaking around, grew up in a family that prided themselves on their morals and passed those values on to TJ. His relationship with Grace makes him feel like a lowlife, though he's done nothing but fall in love. Grace may not return his exact feelings yet, but she's not in love with Rob either, so there's hope. TJ just has to clear up mistakes from his past, and then he and Grace can be together. After all, the only thing her marriage offers her is stability. How many people wade through life unhappy because of their unwillingness to challenge the status quo? When did the prospect of misery become more palatable than the prospect of change?

Once his abs are exhausted, TJ sits cross-legged, sets his watch timer for ten minutes, and closes his eyes. Normally he's good at meditating, but today his head is all over the place. One worry after another stacks up. Alfred's creepiness. The situation with Grace. The threatening calls. TJ needs to talk to Julius, and soon. What a bonehead move it was to insult him last night.

At minute seven of the meditation, he gives up. Oh well. There's always tomorrow. That's why they call it a practice.

TJ pulls himself to his feet, then grabs his loofah and dopp kit from his suitcase. He's used to life on the road. Where his client goes, he goes. Mostly that means trips between Maryland, New York, and DC. While his client wines and dines campaign donors, TJ sits at the next table over or stands on the outskirts of the room, scanning, always scanning. Often he wishes his job had more intellectual heft, but sometimes he appreciates its straightforwardness, his caveman-ish reliance on his five senses. "Straightforward" doesn't mean "easy." Not many people can be still nowadays. They fidget and seek distractions, unable to focus. Their radar is tuned inward, not outward. Most human beings in the twenty-first century would make terrible security personnel. When TJ is at work, he has to compartmentalize. He puts his worries and dreams and to-do lists in a bucket, then tucks that bucket away in the back of his head. For eight, ten, sometimes twelve hours a day, he does nothing but take in the world around him. Does anyone live in the present more than a bodyguard?

He used to, anyway. Lately all he does is worry about the future and relitigate choices from his past.

TJ goes to the bathroom. Shits, showers, shaves. Plucks a stray nose hair. Runs a hand over his head. He needs a haircut. If he lets it get any longer, people will be able to see his receding hairline. TJ fishes a black baseball cap from his bag and pulls it onto his head. He studies himself in the mirror. Sometimes he still expects to see a scrawny kid staring back at him. Isn't that who he is beneath the six percent body fat? The college student who had a crush on Hermione, who preferred losing himself in a book over playing Edward Fortyhands with his friends? How has he lost his way?

TJ throws on jeans and a black T-shirt, then slips the half-eaten roll of TUMS into his pocket. *I should have brought another pack,* he thinks. He hoped this weekend would be a reprieve from the stress, not an addition to it.

He hears a door down the hallway open at the same time he opens his. TJ steps out to see who's there. Grace. He lifts a hand to wave, then notices her head is peeking out of the wrong room. She's supposed to be in 302, not 304.

Grace is standing in Alfred's room.

She leaves the room, then closes the door behind her while TJ hurries over. "What were you doing in there?" he asks.

"Alfred asked me to get something."

Liar, TJ thinks as he observes her empty hands. "Is he in there?"

Grace shakes her head. "He's setting up for the screening."

"Speaking of," a voice at the top of the stairs says, "you'd better get down there, or you'll be late."

TJ whirls around to find the old housekeeper with ramrod posture and her hands behind her back. How long has she been standing there? Did she see Grace leave Alfred's room?

"He'd be devastated if you were missing," Danny continues.

TJ gestures for her to lead the way, then exchanges a look with Grace. She mouths *What the fuck?* as they follow the housekeeper down the stairs. In the lobby, Danny holds the door to the screening room open for them. She slinks off without a word.

Everyone except Alfred is inside the theater. TJ chooses the same row of seats as Grace but sits on the opposite side of the room. "Can you believe he roped us into this?" TJ plops onto a recliner. "I feel like I'm nineteen again."

"Same old Alfred," Julius says. "Still intense about old movies and turtlenecks." TJ studies Julius. He has a nervous, twitchy energy, unlike the confident kid he knew in college.

"He's not the only intense one around here," Samira murmurs.

"How are you feeling, Zo?" Grace asks.

"A little better," Zoe says. "I think I have mild food poisoning."

Grace peeks at TJ and shakes her head, but he's too preoccupied to acknowledge her. He thinks back to Alfred leaning against the closet door earlier. TJ assumed he'd timed his exit poorly, that pure bad luck accounted for why Alfred happened to be standing in the hallway at the same moment TJ stuck his head out of Grace's room. But Alfred wasn't doing anything in the hall, was he? He stood there like he was waiting, like he knew what was coming. How was that?

The memories come in flashes now. The sound of metal clanging overhead in Grace's room. The vent above his own bed. *If you give a mouse a cookie, he's going to want a glass of milk.* What if Alfred hadn't been listening at Grace's door? What if . . . ? TJ jerks in his chair.

Alfred is spying on us.

"Do you guys have vents in your room ceilings?" TJ asks, pulse racing.

The others shrug. TJ feels exasperation at their lack of observational skills, further proving his earlier point that people today are too inwardly focused. Rarely does he enter a room without taking in its details—cataloguing exits, threats, opportunities. Hazards of the job.

"Why?" Julius asks.

"My room has a bit of a draft," TJ says.

"More likely to be from a window than a vent," Julius says, as if he's ever performed an hour of manual labor in his entire life, as though he has any clue about home building. Like he's the one who spent every summer of his teenage years alternating shifts between construction and the electronics store.

TJ nods, distracted. *There must be another floor above our rooms. Maybe an attic or something?*

He closes his eyes, runs through his afternoon with Grace. Was Alfred watching them in bed? Has he observed his friends undressing, talking on the phone to their loved ones, performing all the little tasks and rituals you do when you think no one's watching? TJ's insides burn. He chews a TUMS.

We should leave.

He almost says it aloud, then considers the consequences of doing so.

"I wonder where Alfred is." Samira checks her phone clock. "He never used to be late."

Zoe props up her feet on the recliner in front of her. "I'd rather take a nap than watch this stupid movie anyway. Why are we even here?"

TJ wonders if the theater is bugged, if Alfred is watching them on a monitoring system right this minute.

Grace scowls at Zoe. No one answers her.

Julius speaks up. "We're here because we feel guilty. Right?"

"I don't," TJ says.

"Me neither," Zoe says.

"Well, I do," Julius counters.

"Let's just get through the weekend," Grace says with a shudder.

Samira says nothing, chewing her lip.

If TJ tells them about the vents, they'll run for the door, and then there go his hiding place and human shields. He can't return home, in case the unsmiling man is staking out his apartment again. What if the man followed TJ here to the hotel? What if he's crouching in the back of TJ's rental car right now? As much as TJ would like to involve the cops, it's out of the question.

TJ knows he can't outrun the man forever, but he reassures himself that the man won't hurt him as long as the others are around. Too many witnesses. TJ has no choice, then. He has to stay put, and he needs his friends to stick around too. If they go home, he'll need a new plan.

He does some calculations in his head. He can play dumb a bit longer, buy himself more time. Let Alfred get his rocks off by spying on them. Let him have the world's most pathetic power trip. They're not in real danger here. Not compared to what TJ is facing beyond these walls. The Hitchcock Hotel is the safest place for him.

In the majority of Hitchcock's films,
the viewer knows something important
that the characters don't.
That's why *Rope* keeps us on the edge of our
seat. We know that body is lying in the chest,
waiting to be discovered. Meanwhile, every
partygoer except the two murderers is oblivious.
Will they be found out, or won't they?

—Excerpt from Essay #117,
"Defining the Term 'Hitchcockian'"

TWENTY-THREE

Alfred

I walk into the home theater exactly twenty minutes late. All my guests are seated, looking edgy and annoyed. Good.

"Sorry to keep you waiting." I carry the velvet drawstring pouches to the last row, where Julius and Zoe sit. Julius wears red-and-white-checked pants and a white collared shirt, sleeves rolled up, tattoos peeking out. I hold up a pouch. "Your phone?"

He gapes at me like I'm nuts.

"Come on." I drop the pouch into his hand. "For old times' sake."

Before screenings, Dr. Scott used to hand around a basket to collect our phones, then keep it on the podium at the front of the room. He wanted us absorbed in the movie experience, he said. I wonder if that practice would be allowed on college campuses now. Maybe not, given all the school shootings. But this is my hotel, my rules.

"That was the worst part of the class," Julius grumbles, but he puts his phone in the bag and hands it over.

"Not for me, it wasn't," I say. He opens and closes his mouth like one of those singing bass that uncouth people hang on their walls. "How was your hike?" I ask.

"Wet," he says. "But good to get some fresh air."

Since when? I almost say. "I'm glad to hear it. Now, should we go ahead and get your dig at today's turtleneck out of the way?" I toy with the cuff of my charcoal sweater.

Julius's eyes bug out a little. "No, thanks," he manages.

"The good news continues," I say.

I know what my classmates used to say about me, that I wore turtlenecks all the time because my dad once tried to strangle me, or my mom had a habit of stubbing out cigarettes on my neck. How macabre these guesses were, how hopeful of violence. My peers would have been underwhelmed, even disappointed, had they known the truth: I have an enormous purple birthmark on the left side of my neck. It has always made me self-conscious, never more so than when Julius pointed it out to the group and dubbed it Herbert. The name stuck. I tried to laugh it off and make jests along with them, terrified that they would know by my flushed face that I didn't find the nickname funny at all. I didn't want them to think me weak, the guy who couldn't take a joke, though I guess I am. I began wearing scarves and turtlenecks no matter the season. When summer rolled around, I sought out lightweight fabrics and shorter sleeves. Out of sight, out of mind. To this day, if I catch sight of the mark I think, *Herbert.* You will not be surprised to hear that Julius has never apologized for his taunts.

I move on with the phone collection. The others protest like Julius did, but I stand firm. In the front row, Samira sits alone. "I talked to my staff," I say in a low voice so the others can't hear. "No one has been in your room today."

She appears unconvinced as she pulls her phone out of her back pocket. "Can't we just silence them? What if my kids need me?"

"I'll give them back in a few hours," I promise. "They'll be under lock and key in the concierge's desk." On cue, Jeff sweeps into the room to gather the pouches from me. He leaves without a word. They all watch him go.

Danny and Chef come in next with a cart full of goodies. "What can I get you to drink?" Danny asks, pen and notepad at the ready.

Chef prepares an individual tray for each guest—a big bowl of popcorn, plus smaller bowls of melted butter, and salt and other seasonings. He passes them out, and my guests become less distressed about their absent phones. How easily distracted they are, like children.

I stand in front of the projector screen and clear my throat. "Today we're going to watch a film that expands on last night's dinner conversation." I pause. "Hitch made the movie in 1948. He called it *Rope*." Again I pause for dramatic effect, waiting for the gasps and excited nods, but get nothing. What a bunch of drags. They deserve what's coming. "The story is about two friends who decide to commit the perfect murder." I press a button on the projector remote. The opening shot appears onscreen—a bird's-eye view of a peaceful street in Manhattan.

"Thank God it's not black and white," Julius murmurs.

I poke my tongue into my cheek. "I don't want to spoil anything, so let's go ahead and watch. Run time is an hour and twenty minutes. If you need the restroom, there's one in the game room next door." I take a seat beside Samira, who's buttering her popcorn. "All your chairs recline, so please kick back and relax."

I press play on the remote. The camera pans to a high-rise building, rests awhile on a window with closed curtains. We hear a scream, then cut inside the apartment. Gloved hands hold a rope tightly around a man's neck. Three seconds later, he is dead. Killed by two of his friends.

A sense of calm washes over me. This must be how day care providers feel when all the kids go down for a nap. Here I'm in my element—a dark room illuminated by story, a world that transports me to someone else's problems, struggles that can be resolved within two hours. I try not to get irritated every time someone leaves to use the bathroom (how can they stand to miss even a second of the action?), and I focus on the positives instead. After this weekend, interest in the hotel will peak. There might be a lull at first, shock over what transpired. But then a Reddit thread here, a podcast episode there, and the ghouls will descend in no time.

The wait list will be a mile long. Revenue will pour in, and we'll be back in the black. Soon the Hitchcock Hotel will be an objective success.

I haven't felt this accomplished since I turned Zoe's grades around in college.

My success with Zoe fall semester of junior year got me thinking that Christmas break: why couldn't I help other students the way I'd helped her? I couldn't take their exams, but I could assist them with their papers—especially when it came to Dr. Scott's classes. I had no shortage of opinions on the movies we viewed. Genre, structure, theme, plot, character development, symbolism, red herrings—you name it, I've thought about it.

Every semester Dr. Scott taught two courses, COM205 and COM206. Each course had two sections of fifty students. I charged thirty dollars for a three-pager, fifty for a midterm, and one hundred for a final essay. Students had to write a paper after every single movie we watched throughout the entire semester. You could do the math, or I can tell you I made roughly six thousand dollars. That was just my share.

The business was digital, conducted via a dummy email account and PayPal. I kept my business a secret from my friends, but the group had heard rumblings around campus about the Easy A essay writer. I was never more popular than in my days as Easy A, though no one knew my identity. I'd hear the name mentioned at parties, whispered in libraries, shared among students who were stretched too thin. Some small part of me felt guilty for cheating, but I reassured myself that I wasn't stealing someone else's intellectual property. In fact, this was the ultimate extra-credit assignment. Who had reflected upon Dr. Scott's syllabus more than I had?

Senior year I pushed my friends to sign up for COM206, Diversity and Culture in American Film. I'd grown to love Dr. Scott, even if he never quite took to me. He had this way of empathizing with any character in any movie—especially the rotten ones that everyone else hated. He liked to bring a Snuggie from home to wear while we watched films. He sat in the last row, laughing and clapping more loudly than anyone else in the audience, though he must have seen every movie two dozen times. You could disagree with his stance on something but, by the end of class, find yourself nodding along at his point without any sense of having been manipulated. He made me believe it was possible to have a career in movies—maybe as a critic or a professor, or even a filmmaker.

I peer around the dark room at the faces illuminated by the screen. I would have done anything for these people back then, and did, in fact. I was much more loyal than I should have been.

But it's never too late to rectify the past. My guests are gathered; the staff has gone home. The fun is finally starting. I turn back to the movie and settle into my chair.

TWENTY-FOUR

Zoe

The movie ends with police sirens wailing. Grace claps. Julius and Samira join her. Alfred stands and faces the group with a self-important smile.

"Wow," TJ says. "Two sickos kill their friend, hide his body in a trunk, then throw a dinner party atop the trunk, with his family and girlfriend nearby. This is your idea of a masterpiece?"

Zoe smirks. *TJ's not wrong.*

"Hitch will be Hitch," Alfred says. "This isn't the Disney Hotel."

TJ snorts, then rises from his chair. "I gotta take a leak."

"Philistine," Alfred mumbles as TJ leaves the room.

"One thing about the movie didn't make sense to me," Julius says. "Brandon goes on and on about committing the perfect murder, but isn't the perfect murder one you get away with? They might've committed the ballsiest murder, but no one would argue it's the smartest one. Leaving a body at the crime scene, then inviting a bunch of people to hang around?"

"What's with Hitchcock's murder fascination, anyway?" Zoe asks.

"A number of Hitch's plots came from real news, you know," Alfred says. "He had his finger on the pulse of human obsession long before podcasts and Netflix existed."

An itchy urge nags at Zoe—the need to get under Alfred's skin, to knock him off his perch. "I don't understand why you adore this guy so much, considering the way he abused women," she says. "He was like the Weinstein of his era."

"Oh shit," Julius says. He, Samira, and Grace whip their heads toward Alfred, waiting for his reaction.

"Not true," he says calmly.

"Tippi Hedren said he tried to kiss and grope her a number of times," Zoe pushes. "When she turned him down, he vowed to ruin her career. Which is exactly what he did."

"Allegedly," Alfred says. "Hitch was never arrested for misconduct of any kind."

"Powerful men rarely were," Zoe snaps. Maybe she should be more cautious, but she's too pissed to be scared right now.

"I had no idea you'd taken such an interest in Hitch's life," he says.

Zoe never gave much of a shit about the star director, but when she found out Alfred had opened a hotel in his honor, she did some googling. What made this guy so compelling? He was talented, sure, even visionary at times. But didn't his flaws overshadow his gifts? She still doesn't understand Alfred's fascination.

"Tippi isn't the only one who made those accusations. He assaulted multiple young women."

"What's your point, Zoe?"

"My point is, you've created this altar of hero worship for a sex offender."

Alfred takes a deep breath. "I don't deny that Hitch sometimes behaved badly." He pauses. "Why can't I acknowledge his misbehavior while also admiring his art? Can we not separate the art from the artist?"

"No," Zoe says. "I don't think we can."

"You're not still listening to Michael Jackson, then, I take it? If I remember correctly, you spent most of junior year blasting the *Thriller* album on repeat in your room."

She frowns.

"We each have to decide which monster we're willing to make hypocrites of ourselves for. Mine is Hitch. Yours is Jackson."

"Condescending prick," she mutters, scooting lower in her seat, enraged by the smug expression on Alfred's face. She can practically see him thinking, *I win.*

The room quiets. Alfred glances at the others, whose heads had been ping-ponging back and forth, watching their argument.

Julius speaks up. "I liked the movie. It was funnier than I expected."

"*Rope* is a guest favorite." Alfred pats his legs. "Duty calls. Excuse me." He lopes out of the theater.

TWENTY-FIVE

TJ

TJ looks both ways down the third-floor hall, steps out of his guest room, and sneaks toward the storage closet. His hand is on the knob when the door to room 302—Grace's room—opens. He flies back from the closet as Danny emerges. She holds a plastic tub of cookies, the same kind that were left on his nightstand during turndown service last night.

"Can I help you with something?" she asks.

He slides his hands into his back pockets and shakes his head.

"Your room is at the other end of the hallway." She points to his door like he's an idiot.

"Bad sense of direction," TJ says apologetically. He heads for the stairs and nearly collides with Alfred.

"Where did you go?" Alfred asks.

"I told you," TJ says. "The bathroom."

"There's one in the game room."

"I didn't know that. I went back up to my room." TJ slides the roll of TUMS from his pocket and tosses one into his mouth.

"You're eating an awful lot of those this weekend," Alfred observes.

"Heartburn." TJ presses his chest.

"You should see a doctor."

"I'll take that under consideration," he snips.

"Unless you think the pain is stress induced? Poor life choices catching up with you?" Alfred winks. "I told you at the beginning of the movie that the game room has a bathroom."

TJ scowls. "I must not have heard you."

"You nodded at me, though," Alfred says coolly. "I watched you."

"You do plenty of that, don't you?"

Alfred blinks several times but seems unfazed. "We're all discussing the movie in the theater."

Danny approaches from behind. "I'd better escort him, Alfred. This one has a bad sense of direction."

"Back off," TJ grunts at Alfred before following the housekeeper. As he and Danny make their way down the stairs, TJ glances over his shoulder. Alfred stands stone still, watching him.

In the movie theater, twenty minutes crawl by. Danny stands guard at the door, watching the group with crossed arms. The more time passes without word from Alfred, the more restless everyone gets. Samira paces the front of the room. Grace jiggles her leg. TJ shifts from foot to foot.

He's about to go looking for Alfred when the door bounces open. Their host enters with clasped hands. "What have I missed?" he booms.

Samira stills. "This blast from the past has been fun, Alfred, but can we have our phones back now?"

"Of course," he says. "Jeff has gone home for the day, but I'll get them for you. Be back in a minute."

TJ heads toward him. "We'll come with you."

"Don't trouble yourselves," he says. "I'll bring them here."

"I'm ready for a change of scenery." Samira worries the sleeve of her sweater.

"This room is getting claustrophobic," Zoe adds.

"I could stretch my legs," Julius says.

"Fair enough," Alfred says. They all march out of the theater behind Alfred. TJ tries to sneak a peek at his face but can't. Alfred is walking too fast.

The group crosses the lobby to the reception desk. Alfred pulls on the top drawer, which is locked. He grabs a ring of keys from his pocket and sits in the reception chair, humming the overture to *North by Northwest* under his breath. The group gathers around the desk. Zoe wrings her hands. Julius clears his throat. Alfred takes his sweet time sifting through the keys. Seconds before TJ blows a gasket, Alfred holds up a small silver key in triumph.

"Aha. Here we are." He studies the anxious faces surrounding him. "I do appreciate you all indulging my nostalgia. Wasn't it nice to disconnect from the outside world for a few hours? Focus on being present—"

"The phones, Alfred," Samira barks. TJ glances at her in surprise. Samira rarely loses her cool.

"Right, right." He puts the key in the lock and turns it. With a flourish he pulls open the drawer. "Ta-da."

They all peer inside.

"I don't get it," Julius says.

The drawer is empty.

TWENTY-SIX

Samira

Samira could kill someone.

"What's going on, Alfred? Some of us have kids. We need to be able to check in with them."

Alfred wears an uneasy expression. He smooths his already-smooth hair. "Where else would Jeff have put them?" he mutters. He rises from the chair and opens the cabinet behind the desk, rifles through file folders and office supplies. Samira's and Grace's eyes meet.

Say something, Samira tries to urge her with the tilt of her head. Grace wraps her arms around her body and tucks her chin to her collarbone, throwing Samira off. Since when is Grace a passive bystander? Normally she would've shoved Alfred aside and found the damn phones herself. Why isn't she trying to control the situation now?

Samira studies Grace. The tendons in her neck strain, veins beating a visible pulse under her skin. Every time Alfred glances in her direction, Grace averts her eyes.

Is Grace afraid of Alfred?

Samira can't recall Grace ever being scared of anything. Not before final exams, not when they got lost in Rome during a summer-abroad program, not even when she had a breast cancer scare last year. In college Grace wielded total control over Alfred. For the most part she was kind to him, but a few times Grace took advantage of Alfred's feelings for her in a manipulative way. Why is she recoiling from him now like he's going to reach out and throttle her?

Alfred pulls the cabinet apart until all of its contents are strewn about the floor. One thing is clear: their phones aren't in there.

He turns to face his friends. "Sorry about this. There must have been a misunderstanding with my staff. I'll call Jeff right now." He sifts through the pile of detritus and locates a small address book.

"Why am I not surprised you still have one of those?" Zoe chips black polish off her fingernails.

Alfred lifts the receiver of the phone on the desk and dials. Samira listens to the phone ring and ring, her hopes sinking further the longer the call goes unanswered. Her own body tenses in response to Grace's as she ticks off the weekend's oddities, which feel increasingly ominous. The shower intruder. Zoe getting sick, plus the supposed grass on the pillow. Grace's unusual behavior. The missing phones. The housekeeper's warning.

Samira had intended to say something about Danny's rebuke to Alfred after the movie, but now she's not sure she should. The old woman is protective of Alfred. Maybe she's blind to his flaws, and he to hers. What has Alfred told Danny about the rest of them? What did Danny mean when she said Samira's friends weren't telling her everything? Is there any merit to the claim—or has the housekeeper gone senile?

The concierge doesn't answer his phone. Alfred lets the voice mail recording play until the beep, hangs up, then dials again. This time he leaves a message.

"Danny," he calls, his voice ringing out through the lobby.

The housekeeper pokes her head out of the game room. "Yes, Alfred?"

"Do me a favor and check whether Jeff's car is in the lot."

"Pretty sure he headed out a while ago." She moves slowly toward the front door of the hotel, much more slowly than Samira observed her moving earlier.

"Great. We should have our phones back by 2025," Julius mutters.

"Why don't you pick on someone your own size?" Alfred says coldly. "Like Jiminy Cricket?"

"Damn," Zoe says under her breath, stifling a laugh. Samira is surprised when Julius doesn't fight back. All weekend his performance as comic relief has been halfhearted, distracted. She watches him sink into a chair nearby. He flinches when he changes the cross of his legs.

Danny returns minutes later. "He's gone. Charlie and Chef too. Just you and I are left."

How are they supposed to function without their phones? What if something happens to the landline? They're out here in the middle of nowhere. Reville's campus is the closest sign of civilization, and even that's a bit of a hike. What if they have an emergency? How will they get help?

Samira doesn't want to connect the dots. She has tried to hold off the thought, but here it comes anyway: what if the guy who spied on her in the shower also took their phones? What if he's more than a Peeping Tom? Maybe their own Norman Bates is loose in the hotel. What if it's Alfred?

"I'm so sorry," Alfred is saying to the group. "Maybe Jeff took the phones home with him by mistake. But how on earth would that have happened?"

"How do we know you haven't hidden them somewhere?" TJ says.

Alfred bristles. "My phone is in one of those pouches too."

Grace cuts in. "Alfred, what if we try calling our phones from the reception phone? Maybe we can locate them that way."

Alfred turns his head from TJ to Grace. For a terrifying moment, Samira thinks he will rip the landline from the wall and bash Grace over the head with the phone. Instead, he pushes the phone across the desk. "Be my guest."

They each take a turn dialing their own cell phone number, then waiting in strained silence. They try spreading out, moving from room to room to listen for muffled ringing. This exercise yields nothing but wastes plenty of time.

"Did anyone bring a laptop or tablet with them this weekend? We could use the Find My iPhone app," Julius suggests.

Grace pulls an iPad from her purse. "Already tried," she says, "but my phone didn't show up anywhere."

"Someone must have powered it down, then," Julius says.

Grace eyes Alfred. "I only had two percent battery before the movie. It probably died. Anyone else have another device here with them?"

They all shake their heads. "Didn't think I'd need it," TJ says.

Samira can't take much more of this. "Um, Alfred, can we please call our families now?" she asks. "If that's not too much trouble."

"Absolutely," Alfred says, flustered. "Good idea, Samira. I'll check a few other places around the hotel in the meantime."

Danny steps forward. "You all can use my phone too, if you want. I'll get it from my room."

"Thank you, Danny." Alfred and the housekeeper head up the stairs together. Samira overhears him say, "When they're finished, keep trying Jeff, will you?"

"He's probably at the bar by now," Danny says.

"Let's hope not," Alfred murmurs, and then they're too far away for Samira to hear what comes next.

She lets Grace call her family first. Grace tucks her shiny brown hair behind her ears and takes a deep breath before dialing.

Samira paces the lobby. "Do you guys believe the concierge took our phones home with him? Something isn't right."

"Maybe we should leave," Julius says.

"How are we going to get our phones back then, genius?" Zoe asks.

Julius works at an imaginary smudge on his sneaker. "I'll buy you all new ones."

Samira is about to ask whether he's serious when Danny reappears at the top of the staircase. She holds her cell phone aloft like the Statue of Liberty. "Who needs a phone?"

Samira raises her hand. Danny makes her way down the stairs with a grimace. When Samira reaches for the phone, Danny grips it more tightly. Samira's about to say something when the old woman lets go.

Thank God Samira knows Henry's number by heart. She feels better hearing the sound of his voice. Samira does her best to explain the missing phones without insulting Alfred or the hotel, since Danny is watching her. She doesn't want the housekeeper jumping down her throat again.

"They lost your phones?" Henry says loudly. "What kind of incompetents are running this place?"

Samira winces. Danny works her jaw back and forth.

"They'll turn up soon," Samira says in a tone that convinces no one, not even herself. "In the meantime, I wanted to let you know I'm safe and sound."

Julius arches an eyebrow at her.

By the time Samira gets off the phone with her kids, Alfred has returned to the lobby too.

"No sign of them yet." He checks his watch. "My God, it's ten o'clock! You all must be starving. Why don't you sit down to dinner? Danny and I will serve your meals, then continue scouring the hotel." He glances at his housekeeper, who nods.

Alfred heads toward the restaurant and gestures for the others to follow. The group eyes one another, hesitant.

Grace fingers the thin gold chain around her neck. "We have to eat." She's the first to follow Alfred.

"She's right," Zoe says as she takes off after Grace. Before Samira falls in step with Zoe, she catches TJ tapping Julius on the arm.

"Can I talk to you about something?" he asks in a low voice.

"Later, Teej." Julius sounds irritated.

In the end, everyone trails Alfred and Danny into the dining room.

No sooner has Samira taken her seat than TJ asks if he can switch spots with her. He obviously wants to sit next to Julius, though Samira's unsure why. Weren't they quarreling last night? She has a panicky feeling, like the walls are closing in on her.

Samira rises and wanders over to the sliding glass door that leads to the courtyard. She gazes outside. The rain is coming down hard again. The crows stare sullenly at her from the aviary. She grips the door handle and glances back at Alfred, who is watching her.

"Okay if I open this? Let in a little fresh air?"

"Why not?" he says.

Samira holds her breath, half convinced the door won't budge. It slides open easily. A cold gust of wind flies into the dining room, hinting at the winter to come. The weather is too chilly to leave the door ajar, but Samira feels better this way, knowing she has an escape route. She returns to her chair.

Alfred fusses over them more than usual, trying to make up for the phone debacle. He triple-checks that everyone has the type of water they like, gives generous pours of wine. Samira would kill for a stiff drink right now. She has told everyone she's not drinking this weekend to support Zoe. Apparently the rest of them don't care enough to change their behavior.

Once food orders have been placed, Alfred excuses himself. "Danny will bring out your dinners. I'll be back with your phones." The housekeeper floats silently into the kitchen.

As soon as Alfred's gone, Julius picks up his campaign. "Maybe we should leave after dinner."

"No one's stopping you. We're not a family," Zoe says. "We don't function as a single unit."

Why does she want to stay if she thinks Alfred is poisoning her? She should already have her bags packed.

"You don't function at all," TJ mutters.

"Hey," Samira barks at him as Zoe slams down her glass. "Totally unnecessary." TJ glances away sulkily.

"W-we have to stay," Grace stutters. "Don't overreact, Julius. They're just some misplaced phones." Again, something doesn't add up. Why does Grace want to stick around when she's clearly uncomfortable? Samira tries to catch her gaze, but Grace stares at her plate, blank behind the eyes. Danny's words ring in Samira's ears.

There are things they've done that they're not telling you.

"Let's at least stay the night," TJ interrupts. "My phone is brand-new, and I'm not looking to fork over another thousand bucks to replace it. Not to mention, Alfred weighs a hundred and sixty pounds soaking wet. If he tries anything, I'll put him in his place."

The kitchen door swings open. Danny appears with plates of food stacked up her arms. "Two shrimp scampi, three venison." She slides the dishes onto the table.

"Sorry to keep you working late tonight," Samira says.

"I'm staying the night anyway, so I don't have to drive home in the dark," the housekeeper says. "Alfred gave the rest of the staff the weekend off."

"Why not you?" Grace asks.

A tiny smile crosses Danny's face. "I'm indispensable. Enjoy your dinner." She heads back toward the kitchen.

"Hey, Danny?" TJ calls. She spins around. "What's the chef's name?"

She studies TJ suspiciously. "Tony. Wendice."

"I heard his wife works at Reville," TJ says.

"That's right. Where'd you hear that?"

"We all went to school there." TJ gestures at the five of them around the table.

"So I've been told," Danny says.

"How long has she been at Reville?"

"You'd have to ask Tony." Danny disappears behind the kitchen door.

Zoe squints at TJ. "Do you always do recon on hotel staff, or do you have something to share with the group?"

"Why would Alfred send his staff home for the weekend?" Julius asks. TJ cuts a piece of shrimp in half and frowns. Samira notes that he didn't answer Zoe's question.

"He could be trying to minimize costs," Grace says. "We're all staying for free, so he'll take a loss for this weekend."

Everyone but Zoe is digging into their meal. She eyes her meat as she sips her wine. Samira grinds her teeth.

"Can we close the door?" Julius shivers. "I'm freezing."

"I'd feel better keeping it open," Samira says.

"Me too," TJ and Zoe both say.

"Fine." Julius elbows TJ. "What did you want to talk to me about?"

TJ peers around the table and mutters, "Something private."

Grace stops eating. "Why can't you talk about it in front of us?"

"I just said it's private," TJ retorts.

"Are you talking shit?" Grace asks.

"Not everything's about you, Grace," TJ says. Grace blinks, obviously stunned.

Samira ignores their arguing. She could get home without her phone. Her car has a built-in GPS. But New York is five hours away, and she doesn't feel safe driving in the middle of the night, especially with the pregnancy leaving her so drained. God forbid that she should nod off at the wheel. She could ask to catch a ride with one of the others, but they're all behaving almost as strangely as Alfred. She's not sure she wants to be a passenger in any of their cars right now.

"Everyone, get ahold of yourselves," Julius says. "There's room for one drama king in a group, and long have I reigned."

The joke does little to dispel the tension. Grace has almost cleaned her plate, while Zoe is pushing green beans around her mashed potatoes. Samira doesn't know why this, of all things, sets her off, but it does. She's sick and tired of caring for a grown woman.

"You need to eat, Zoe," she says. "You haven't had anything since breakfast this morning."

Zoe opens her mouth to lash back but clearly thinks better of it when she sees the expression of motherly warning on Samira's face. Zoe cuts off a piece of the venison. She chews cautiously, then closes her eyes as she swallows. Samira exhales and nods.

Dinner wears on in tense silence. Samira is ready for this day to be over. She wants to retire to her room and try to get some sleep. She decides to head home tomorrow, phone or no phone. Maybe during the long drive she'll get some clarity on what to do about Henry.

"Um," Zoe says, staring at the open courtyard door.

Samira turns to see what she's gawking at, when something big and black rushes past her face. She screams, shoving her chair back from the table.

A crow is loose in the dining room.

It flies around in circles, soaring and plunging like it's being hunted. Grace bends in half and protects her head with her hands. Zoe darts out of the room to the parlor. TJ stands to try to shoo the thing back outside, sending the bird into a greater frenzy. It dive-bombs straight into Julius's face.

"What the shit?" he shrieks, batting at the bird as it pecks his skin.

"Get it off of him!" Samira screeches, frozen to her chair, watching the scene between her fingers.

Grace waves her cloth napkin at the bird until it flies away. Samira gapes as the crow glides into the parlor, then around the corner into the lobby. Julius is chalk white, save for the scratches on his cheek. A cut on his nose bleeds a little.

"Great. So now we have to fight off killer birds too," Zoe grumbles as she returns to the dining room. "Fun at the Hitchcock House of Horrors never stops."

"You okay, Jules?" Grace asks.

Julius blinks a few times, then wipes the blood from his cut. They all watch him, waiting.

He clears his throat and shakes his head. "I'll tell you what's getting one star on Hotels.com," he quips, but the quaver in his voice gives him away.

Everyone laughs. Samira watches Julius relax, his position as group jester restored. The rest of them loosen up some too. Zoe picks up her fork and continues eating. The others follow suit.

Grace refills her wineglass. "If this isn't a story for the kids . . ."

"Remember that time I visited Uncle Alfred's hotel?" Samira says.

"Remember when Uncle Alfred lost all our phones?" Zoe adds.

"Remember when Uncle Alfred sicced his bird assassin on me?" Julius says. "I'm not crazy, right?" He dabs at the cut with his napkin. "That bird came at me like it was on a mission." Zoe nods. "Can you train a bird to attack?"

"How did it get out of the aviary in the first place?" Grace asks.

TJ walks toward the courtyard, closing the sliding glass door behind him. He moves around the geodesic dome, disappearing in the clutter of trees, fountains, and birds. When he returns to the dining room, his clothes are sopping wet from the rain.

"The aviary door was open a crack," he says. "I shut it."

"The groundskeeper is going to be in trouble when Alfred finds out he left it open," Grace says.

"You think that was an accident?" Zoe says.

"I don't," Julius says.

Samira's head spins. She isn't sure what to believe.

"Listen to yourselves," Grace scoffs. "Not everything is a conspiracy. Wild animals get loose from their pens all the time. Let's just hope that crow isn't shitting all over the hotel right now."

"How is Alfred going to catch it?" Zoe wonders. "The lobby ceilings are, like, twenty feet tall."

"I have Neosporin and bandages in my purse," Samira offers Julius.

He waves her off. "I'm barely bleeding. Besides, chicks dig battle scars, right?"

"They'll be falling all over you when they hear your tale of valor," Grace teases.

Zoe examines the green bean speared on her fork. "Do anyone else's beans taste funny?" Jesus Christ, this day is going to be the death of Samira.

"Green beans are nature's punishment. The way they squeak between your teeth . . ." Julius blanches.

"Funny how?" Samira asks.

"Sweet?" Zoe says.

The others stare at her. Zoe extends her fork across the table to Grace. "Try this."

Grace shakes her head. "I already had a bunch. They were fine."

Zoe sets her fork down and looks at her mostly empty plate.

This reunion was a bad idea. Samira doesn't want to share her pregnancy news with anyone here, given their weird behavior, nor are any of them providing a decent distraction from her worries. She approached this weekend full of nostalgia for a simpler time with these people she once loved, but that time feels unreachable now, nonexistent. Instead, everyone's been at one another's throat, she's spent the whole time refereeing, and she feels no closer to a resolution on Henry and the baby. Not to mention Alfred still hasn't figured out who broke into her room—and doesn't seem to be trying all that hard to find the answer. Why did Samira let Grace convince her to come?

Zoe rests her forehead on the table, pulling Samira out of her reverie. "Zo, you okay?" she asks.

Zoe groans. "I don't feel good." Her wineglass is empty.

Grace fills Zoe's water glass from the crystal pitcher. "Here. Maybe you're dehydrated."

Zoe rocks her head from side to side. "None of you ever believe me," she moans to the floor. "Not every alcoholic is unreliable." Without warning, she shoots out of her chair and runs from the room.

In a low voice Julius says, "She didn't exactly prove her point just now."

TWENTY-SEVEN

TJ

Danny glides back into the dining room.

"Zoe seemed to be in an awful hurry," she comments.

"She's not feeling well," TJ says.

"Pity."

"Any sign of the phones?" Julius asks.

Danny shakes her head. She clears the table, carrying plates and utensils to the kitchen.

The group moves to the lobby and stands in a circle, waiting for an update. The crow is nowhere to be found, much to Julius's obvious relief.

"What if we drive to Reville?" Julius says. "One or two of those inns must still be in business. We can come back to the hotel in the morning to get our phones. Assuming they ever turn up."

TJ checks his watch and tries to keep his voice level. "By the time we get there it'll be midnight. Are we going to waltz up to reception and request a room for five people?"

"Yeah, you think small hotels like those even have twenty-four seven reception?" Grace asks. "This one doesn't."

Julius sighs. "Then let's sit in their lobby until morning. Seriously, are none of you worried?"

Grace frowns. "Sure, but your ideas are impractical and irrational. The best course of action is to spend the night here."

TJ should take Julius aside right now and come clean, beg for his help. He shouldn't have even waited this long to say something. But once he does, there's no turning back. The reputation for morality and forthrightness that TJ has spent a lifetime molding will be destroyed. Julius will never regard him the same way again. Alfred's juvenile spying is trivial by comparison. TJ reasons that keeping the vents hush-hush for a little longer is okay. What choice does he have? He pictures the unsmiling man sneaking into his apartment, waiting patiently on TJ's bed with a gun in his lap. TJ wishes he could call the police, but that'd be even worse than facing his pursuer.

Alfred appears at the top of the staircase. He plods his way toward them. When he reaches the bottom step, he says, "I've searched high and low. No one can get ahold of Jeff." He swallows and presses his thumbs into his eyelids. "I'm so sorry about all of this. I just wanted to get the group back together, to host the perfect weekend for you. Something like this has never happened under my roof."

The lobby is quiet. TJ doesn't buy Alfred's "woe is me" act for a second.

"One of your birds is loose in the hotel," Julius says.

Alfred nods, worried. "He was flying around the second floor a few minutes ago. He's on the carousel horse now." He gestures to the prop hanging from the ceiling. Sure enough, the crow is perched on the horse's saddle. "I don't know how that happened. Someone on staff was in a rush, I guess. I'll try to catch him after you all go to bed. He didn't bother you, did he?"

"Look at my face," Julius says.

Alfred's eyes widen when he takes in the cut and scratches. Is it TJ's imagination, or do Alfred's lips curl upward ever so slightly?

"Let's go to bed," Samira says. "We'll resolve things tomorrow."

"You have my word," Alfred says.

Which counts for how much?

Samira heads up the stairs. "I'll see you all in the morning."

"Anyone up for a nightcap?" TJ peeks at Julius.

"Read the room, Teej," Julius says, not unkindly, before following Samira. Grace follows too, without so much as a glance in TJ's direction. She must be pissed at him for the *not everything's about you* jab.

TJ and Alfred stand alone in the lobby, side by side, not looking at each other.

"Can I get you anything before you head to bed?" Alfred asks. "A glass of milk, perhaps?"

TJ lingers in the lobby for a while. First he locks the front door of the hotel; then he double-checks that the door to the courtyard is also locked. These precautions do little to reassure him.

Monsters are both inside and outside the house.

TJ trudges up the stairs like the others before him, focuses his thoughts on something he can control—getting back into Grace's good graces. He screwed up with that dig at her. He was punishing Grace for shutting down the conversation about coming clean to her husband. That was unfair of him. She told him from day one that she was never going to break up her family. He has always known the limits of their potential.

TJ considers going to Grace's room right now to set things straight but decides this is not the time or place, particularly if Alfred is spying on them. Tomorrow he'll convince her to move to a different hotel with him, after he speaks to Julius. *This weekend is salvageable,* he tells himself.

He's about to step onto the third-floor landing when he hears the creak of a guest room door opening. Out of instinct more than reason, he hides behind the stairwell wall, waits a few seconds, then peers around the corner in time to see Grace tiptoe out of her room and into the storage closet. She closes the door behind her.

What the hell is she doing?

TJ waits five minutes, then ten. Grace doesn't emerge. She's been in the closet much longer than it would take to grab a spare roll of toilet paper or an extra face towel. What else would she be doing in there? Maybe the entrance to the attic is in that closet. Is Grace upstairs now? He steps into the hallway to follow her, then hesitates. Grace might already know about the attic and the vents. She was in Alfred's room earlier; plus, she's the one who begged TJ to come for the reunion weekend. Maybe she and Alfred are tighter than TJ thought. What might he find if he marched into the closet right now? His need for information, to gain some control over his surroundings, tempts him. Still, TJ doesn't want to stir up more shit than he already has. If Alfred kicks him out of the hotel, TJ will lose both his hiding place and his chance to talk to Julius. He's better off observing from afar for now.

He goes to his room, leaving the door cracked open so he can hear any activity in the hallway. The space has been tidied, the towels replaced—by Danny, he supposes. He washes his face and brushes his teeth, packs his bag and puts it next to the door. TJ will get up early tomorrow, go downstairs and wait in the parlor, observe any comings and goings, ensure that everyone is behaving as they should be. He pokes his head into the hallway, though he's heard not so much as a peep for the past thirty minutes. TJ is tempted to knock on Grace's door, to check if she's returned to her room. Does it matter? She's doing something shady, and he's already up to his eyeballs in shadiness. The last thing he needs is more trouble. He closes the door all the way this time.

TJ climbs into bed, puts his hands behind his head, and stares at the ceiling. His gaze settles on the vent. *Abso-frigging-lutely not.* He pads to the desk, then rips a few pages from the issue of *Travel + Leisure* displayed there. He pulls a roll of tape from the emergency kit he always keeps in his bag when he's on the road. He stands on the bed and tapes the magazine pages over the vent until it's covered, until there's no way that pervert can see into his room. Afterward, he feels better, more in control of his surroundings. No one can watch him now.

TJ turns off the lamp on his nightstand. He lies in the dark for a minute, thinking. Something feels off. Something looked off when he went to the desk. He turns the light back on and peers around the room, logging every detail. His stomach flips when he reaches the window. Peeking out beneath the curtains is a pair of boots.

TWENTY-EIGHT

Alfred

A vicious wind blows through my bedroom. I close the window. Through the fog and rain the moon glows gloomily. I check the time on my phone. Eleven thirty, and the hotel is still. My friends have retired to their respective rooms. No pitter-patter of snooping feet, no sleepovers tonight. The hallway is morguelike. I scarf down peanut butter on toast, the first chance I've had to eat since lunch with Grace.

Any good director must keep firm control of his production. When Danny told me TJ was poking around on the third floor, I sensed my grip on the reins loosening. While Danny stood guard in the theater, I did two things. First I checked to make sure the closet hadn't been disturbed. Then I took the phones to my room. I searched TJ's phone for photos or videos of the attic—specifically the views of the guest rooms through the louvered vents. He has no proof of anything, has nothing to take to the police. All his bluster about me watching them is based on no more than suspicion.

You're wondering how I broke into TJ's phone, whether I possess advanced hacking skills that I forgot to mention prior to now. What I have is even better: an unwilling accomplice with two bad options. Before our movie screening, I presented Grace with a choice. Either she could tell me TJ's phone passcode or I could text her husband about her new relationship. She hesitated, but only until I showed her that the text was ready to go, her husband's number typed into the To box. All I had to do was press send. My thumb hovered over the button. When her eyes widened with fear, I knew I had her.

"One-one-one-two-eight-five," she'd blurted.

"Copycat," I'd mumbled.

TJ too had chosen Grace's birthday as his passcode, though that date has been my passcode since college. In case it wasn't already obvious, this is much more than a fling for TJ. For Grace? Maybe not, given how easily she gave him up.

After all that, she must know their phones aren't with the concierge, that I'm the one who has them. She hasn't confronted me, though. As far as I can tell, she hasn't said anything to the others either. Now, that's loyalty.

After turning off the phones, I hid them in the attic. The next twelve hours will run better without them. The phone on the reception desk is still available, but not for long. Soon that will go missing as well. I prickle at the possibilities. The puzzle pieces are falling into place.

At one a.m. I reason it's late enough. Even those riddled with insomnia will have settled into bed in a half-conscious stupor. The moon is gone, hidden behind thick clouds. My room door groans on its hinges when I open it. I wince, wait. No one stirs. I eye the closet at the end of the hallway. I want to check on my charges one more time before the games begin.

The wall sconces cast long shadows along the carpet. I tiptoe down the corridor, avoiding the creaky spots. I'm struck by how well I know this hotel that's come to feel like home. I pray that the closet door doesn't squeak, then thank my lucky stars when it keeps my passage secret. I close the door behind me.

The trapdoor ladder is down.

A rock sits heavy in my throat. Moths beat their wings inside my stomach. For as long as I can bear it, I stand stock-still in the night-black closet, peering at the hatch in the ceiling. No sound comes from above. No infinitesimal shift of weight or intake of breath. I exhale, though I can't say I'm comforted. I may be alone now, but someone has been in my attic. I have never left the ladder down. I would never.

I reach into my pocket for the Swiss Army knife and grip it in my damp right palm—just in case. I put my left hand on a wooden rung and climb. With each step I vacillate between fear and fury. Who was up there? Have they left anything behind? Did they see the vents? How will I explain?

I cling to the railing. A splinter plunges into my finger, and I bite my tongue hard to stop myself from crying out. The metallic tang of blood fills my mouth. I climb up, up, up, until all of me is in the attic. I take a few cautious steps, then reach for the lightbulb string in the dark.

I hold my breath and pull. Light doesn't spread to the farthest corners of the attic, but it's bright enough to illuminate what's in front of me.

My legs nearly give out. I think of the poster. How could I not?

I'm seeing things. This can't be happening.

I squeeze my eyes shut, count to ten, then dare a second peek. This is not a mirage. It's still there. I bite my knuckles.

In the middle of the attic floor, atop a silver platter, is a tall glass of milk.

SATURDAY

OCTOBER 14

TWENTY-NINE

Julius

Julius wakes up wired, despite getting only a few hours of sleep. He flips the nightstand clock toward him. Seven a.m. He decides to shower and head downstairs. Maybe the others didn't sleep well either, given all that happened last night.

Thirty minutes later, he's dressed in wide-legged jeans, a white T-shirt, and a brown cardigan with yellow ducks. He slips on white Vans and surveys himself in the mirror.

"Missing something," he muses. He throws on a beaded necklace and checks again. "Better."

Julius slides on the Rolex Submariner that *Pépère* handed down to him. He misses his grandfather. Even if *Pépère* never quite understood Julius's style—the man wore a custom suit and loafers every day, even while on holiday in the Riviera—he appreciated his grandson's risk-taking. The two of them shared a love of fashion, which Julius's father has never appreciated, despite being CEO of the family luxury-goods brand. Julius knows his father believes he dresses too flamboyantly, wishes his son would stick to classic French tailoring like the rest of the family. Which is why when Julius throws on his Rolex, he also adds a beaded necklace. He doesn't want to twin with his dad, who is an insufferable jackass and, even worse, boring. Julius finds the idea that men should be interested in their wardrobes but not too interested regressive and pedestrian, especially coming from a man in charge of one of the biggest fashion conglomerates in the world. On the rare occasion when his father deigns to see him, Julius makes sure to paint his nails beforehand, solely to piss him off.

He sticks his head into the hallway and finds Grace leaving her room in silk pajamas and Birkenstocks. She waves.

"Who do you think won last night's battle?" Julius asks in a low voice. At Grace's confused expression, he adds, "Alfred or the crow?"

Grace chuckles. "What I would give to watch footage of that face-off."

Julius feels an urge to hook his arm through Grace's, to walk with his head huddled with hers like he used to. He misses that closeness.

When they get to the dining room TJ is already there, pacing between the tables. He turns when he hears them approach. "Someone stuck a pair of men's boots in my room last night."

"Good morning, Grace. Good morning, Julius. How did you guys sleep?" Julius jokes.

TJ ignores him. "They positioned them so it looked like a prowler was hiding behind the curtain. I thought someone was going to jump me."

"What type of boots?" Julius asks.

"Nice ones. Brown leather. Does it matter?" TJ pulls a necktie from his pocket. "This was on the floor next to them."

"I don't get it," Julius says. "Someone half disrobed in your room, then took off? Why?"

Grace chews her lip. "I think that's a reference to *Dial M for Murder.*" Julius and TJ wait for her to elaborate. "There's a scene where a hit man hides behind a curtain, waiting for the right moment to strangle Grace Kelly. He tries to do it with a necktie."

"What the actual . . ." Julius mumbles.

Grace gazes at the telephone prop in the middle of the room. Didn't Alfred say that was from the same movie? Maybe now the others will listen to Julius about leaving. This hotel gives him the willies. Frankly, he's relieved that Alfred didn't take him up on his investment offer.

"It had to be Alfred, right?" TJ asks.

"What about the housekeeper?" Grace says. "Maybe this is part of the hotel's shtick. They might prank guests to create a spooky ambience."

"A prank?" TJ repeats. "I thought I was about to be hacked to pieces."

Grace scratches her jaw. "Where'd you get the coffee?" she asks TJ.

"In the kitchen. I made it myself. Staff has the weekend off, remember?"

"You still take yours black?" Grace asks Julius. He nods, incredulous that she can think of caffeine after all that's transpired.

He and TJ sit in silence once Grace leaves. TJ cracks his knuckles, scanning the room with a jumpy energy. Julius is pretty sure he knows what TJ wants to speak to him about, but he's not going to be the one to broach the topic.

By the time Grace returns with two coffees, Zoe has joined the group. Julius asks how she's feeling. Zoe says she stopped puking around one in the morning, is doing better now. Before long, Samira comes down as well. None of them appear rested, but Samira's eyes are especially puffy, like she spent the night crying. Julius considers asking if she's okay but doesn't want her to interpret the question to mean *You look like hell.*

The five of them sit around the table, swallowing from their mugs. The atmosphere is less energetic than yesterday morning. Without their phones, they're forced to make conversation that no one wants to have. Julius steals a glance at Grace. Why did she insist that he come this weekend?

By nine o'clock neither Alfred nor his creep-show housekeeper has made an appearance. All topics of small talk have been exhausted—weather, jobs, kids, spouses, travel, even the books they've most recently read. (Julius kept quiet for that one, since his was *Fifty Shades of Grey,* ten years ago.) They all keep glancing between their watches and the wall clock.

"I swear to God," Julius says, "if Alfred doesn't walk through the door with a tray of Bloody Marys in the next forty-five seconds . . ."

No one laughs, which makes Julius want to die a little. *Dickhead,* he chastises himself. He lives in fear of seeming needy, of being perceived as trying too hard. It takes a lot of effort to act like you don't give a shit.

His stomach growls. "Should we run and get breakfast?"

"I don't think we should leave," Grace says. "I can make us something."

Zoe rises. "Let me," she says, with such authority that no one argues. She disappears into the kitchen. Julius would've thought the last thing a chef would want to do on her day off is cook. Maybe this is what (annoying) people mean when they say you should do what you love.

"You think Alfred is still searching for our phones?" Samira asks.

"Or he has them and doesn't want to give them back," TJ says. "I think he's hiding from us."

Samira stares at him, wide-eyed. "Inside the hotel or out of it?"

"We could check the parking lot, see if his car is here," Julius suggests.

"Do you know what he drives?" Grace asks. No one does.

Twenty minutes later Zoe delivers five plates to the table. She's made jalapeño omelets filled with bacon and cream cheese, plus an arugula salad, which she serves with a baguette on the side. Everyone gushes about the beautiful presentation and delicious smell while Zoe stands there with her head bowed. Grace tells her to join the rest of them, but Zoe steps back from the table, chewing her lip, refusing to sit until they've all taken a bite and told her what they think.

"I've never heard of putting cream cheese in an omelet," Julius says with his mouth full, "but this is one of the best things I've ever eaten."

"Oh my God, same," Grace says.

"I don't even like eggs," Samira raves. "You've got to give us this recipe."

Zoe breaks out into an enormous grin. This is the first time she's smiled—truly smiled—all weekend. Julius had forgotten how lovely she can be when she isn't scowling. How nice, for a minute, to sit with old friends and enjoy a meal. This moment is what he'd been hoping for when he came to the Hitchcock Hotel. Zoe says she's going to get started on the dishes, then heads back to the kitchen.

TJ finishes his omelet twice as fast as everyone else. He wipes his mouth with his napkin. "Alfred's not coming, guys."

Samira glances up, startled.

"Have you ever known him to be a late sleeper?" TJ says. "He told me yesterday he has to get up at five thirty every morning, even on the weekends, in order to run this place."

Alfred always woke before the rest of them in college. He's one of those infuriating people who can function on four or five hours of sleep.

"If you want to see your phones again, we need to find him," TJ continues.

"Or we can stick with my original suggestion and get the hell out of here," Julius says.

"Where should we check first?" Samira asks.

"His room," TJ says.

"You think he's staked out in there?" Grace asks skeptically.

TJ narrows his eyes. "There's an easy way to find out."

The dining room quiets until Zoe bursts out of the kitchen. "Look what I found!" she hollers, carrying a plastic bottle. "I told you guys. I told you. I told you!"

She holds up a bottle of antifreeze for everyone to see.

THIRTY

Zoe

Zoe is going to murder Alfred when she finds him. That's one way to get closure.

"I was looking for dish soap and found this tucked in the back of the cabinet," she says. "Give me one good reason why any hotel would store antifreeze in the kitchen."

She'll wait. She knew that motherfucker was poisoning her.

Samira's mouth drops open. Julius whistles. TJ shakes his head.

"Weird," Grace says.

"*Weird?*" Zoe screeches. "I'd say this goes well beyond weird, Grace."

Grace shifts on her chair. "I mean, I agree, it looks bad, but it doesn't prove anything, does it? How do we know Alfred's the one who put it there?"

"The fastest way to find out is to ask him," TJ says. "I'm done sitting around. Let's go."

"I'll come with you," Zoe says.

Julius hops to his feet. "Me too."

"We should split up," Grace says. "If Alfred comes in through the front or back doors, Samira and I will see him."

TJ nods and gestures for Zoe and Julius to follow him to the lobby.

Zoe's talking a big game, but she's panicked at the thought of coming face-to-face with their host. She knows Alfred is dangerous, but she never thought he'd stoop to hurting one of them. For the dozenth time, she wonders why he invited them here.

"Since when is Grace Alfred's number one fan?" TJ asks as the trio climbs the stairs.

"What do you mean?" Julius says.

"She's been defending him all weekend," TJ says.

"She probably feels like she owes him," Julius says.

"Owes him for what?" TJ asks.

Zoe exchanges a look with Julius. Does TJ really not know? She assumed they all did by now. Julius catches up with TJ, then explains quietly. Zoe watches TJ do a double take. His mouth opens, closes, opens again. No words come out.

The closer they get to Alfred's room, the less sure Zoe feels about this plan. She imagines what they'll find in there. Women's jewelry, locks of hair, a former girlfriend's head in the closet. What if Alfred himself is inside, waiting with a gun or knife? Zoe thinks back to what he said when he brought the tray of food to her room yesterday afternoon. *If anyone here is a victim, it's me.* The entire hotel could be a booby trap. None of them know this building, these rooms, as well as he does. Alfred has the home-court advantage. He could be hiding anywhere, watching them right this second.

Zoe's hands take up their familiar tremble. She clenches and unclenches them, trying to regain control of her body. The first and last thing she needs is a drink. It would calm her nerves, but she's got to keep her wits about her. She glances over at Julius as they climb the last few stairs. He clutches his stomach, seems more exhausted than alarmed.

"You okay?" she asks him. He nods and lets go of his belly.

Zoe peers around the third-floor hallway, at the frames on the walls. One image features a Daliesque eye. Another is an overhead shot of a spiral staircase. A third shows Hitchcock gripping a dead goose by the throat. That one gives her the creeps.

Zoe, TJ, and Julius stop in front of room 304. "Are you sure this is the right one?" Julius asks.

TJ doesn't answer. The crease between his eyebrows deepens.

"Teej?" Julius says.

TJ snaps out of it and nods. He clears his throat, then lifts a fist to the door and knocks. "Alfred?" he calls, then takes a step back.

They all wait, breath held. Zoe isn't sure whether she wants him to be in there or not. She can't hear any movement on the other side of the door. She swallows.

TJ leans forward and pounds again. "Alfred, open up."

Nothing.

"He's not in there," Julius says, clearly relieved. Swaying on his feet, he grips the doorframe to steady himself.

"Dude, are you sure you're okay?" Zoe asks.

"I need a minute." He sinks to the floor.

TJ crouches next to him. "What's the deal? You've been off all weekend."

"I'm fine." Julius leans his head against the wall, eyes closed. "Just get inside Alfred's room. There's gotta be something in there that can tell us where he went."

"Not to mention our phones," TJ says. He tries the door handle. Locked. "Now what?"

"Can we kick the door down?" Julius asks.

TJ flashes him an amused expression. "We?"

Julius rolls his eyes. "You."

TJ sizes up the door.

"I can get us in," Zoe says. "I need some scissors."

"I have a small pair for facial hair in my dopp kit," TJ offers.

"That'll work." When TJ leaves, she sits next to Julius on the carpet. "Tell me."

"Zoe, drop it," Julius says.

"I'm not getting off this floor until you tell me." She crosses her arms and gives him her best resting bitch face, so he knows she means it.

THE HITCHCOCK HOTEL   183

Julius sighs in defeat. "You can't say anything to the others." Zoe holds out her pinkie for a pinkie promise. Julius hooks his finger around hers, looks her straight in the eye, and says, "I have testicular cancer."

A whoosh of breath goes out of Zoe. She wraps her arms around her friend and squeezes him. "I'm so sorry," she says over and over into his shoulder. She hears Julius sniffle.

"I'm having surgery next week," he says. "I'm scared shitless. No one else knows."

Zoe holds Julius tightly, unsure what to say. *Not even your parents?* she thinks, though she's pretty sure she knows the answer. If his mother and father were neglectful for the first twenty-two years of Julius's life, relations are unlikely to have improved in the decades since.

When TJ's door opens, Julius springs back from Zoe's embrace. Zoe scrambles to her feet, then helps Julius up.

TJ peers between the two of them. "What'd I miss?"

Julius makes big eyes at Zoe when TJ isn't looking.

"Not a damn thing," she says as she slides her key into the lock of her own room. The second the door is closed behind her, Zoe puts her face in her hands. She tries to imagine herself in Julius's position but finds she can't. She cannot fathom what he's been going through. All alone too.

Zoe clocks the minibar. Her mouth waters, brain crowded with thoughts of dry spice and smoke. She grabs one of the complimentary bottles of water from the desk instead and finishes what little is left. She brings the bottle into the hallway and uses TJ's grooming scissors to cut a palm-sized panel of plastic out of it.

The redness in Julius's eyes is already gone. No heaviness in his limbs or terror on his face. He's going to pretend their conversation never happened. "How do you know how to do this?" he asks.

Zoe can pretend too, if that's what he wants. She scoffs. "You guys grew up with too much money."

"Don't lump us together," TJ says.

"Apologies." TJ's family wasn't as poor as Zoe's was, but they weren't well-off like the others'. Alfred grew up with a single mom and was middle-class, so he had a bit more awareness, but Samira, Grace, and Julius could be so clueless. Money, or lack thereof, was one of the things that Zoe and TJ bonded over in the early days. Zoe didn't begrudge her friends' mommies' and daddies' limitless credit cards (okay, maybe she did a tiny bit), but it was nice to have someone who understood that her budget had no wiggle room, that it was not a suggestion.

Zoe shimmies the piece of plastic between the doorframe and the door. So many contractors install these door locks incorrectly, failing to double-check that the dead-locking plunger on the latch is engaged before they finish the job. When Zoe was a kid, her mom would come home from a shift at whatever construction site and deliver long lectures about things like dead-locking plungers or thermal bridging, topics eight-year-old Zoe found beyond boring. The older she got, however, the more useful Mom's lessons became—though her mother didn't intend for Zoe to use said lessons to break into locked rooms. Zoe never stole anything or committed serious crimes. Mostly she snuck into her brother's bedroom and went through his stuff. Dad says her rebellious streak comes from him.

Zoe hears the click of the lock giving way. She glances over her shoulder at TJ and Julius, which is as close to a *Ready?* as she's going to give them. TJ shifts his weight while Julius toys with his necklace.

Zoe braces herself, then pushes open the door.

THIRTY-ONE

Julius

Julius lets the other two enter Alfred's room first. *(Coward.)* When no poltergeist flies out of the drapery to snatch TJ's and Zoe's bodies, he goes in too.

"He's not in here," TJ says, disappointed.

The room is clean and shipshape, like Alfred. The tree wallpaper is a bit tacky, in Julius's opinion. *(Are you honestly criticizing his interior design choices right now?)* Julius glances at the tidy bed.

While Zoe and TJ pull Alfred's desk apart like vultures, Julius opens the doors of the armoire. Hanging on the left side of the rack are several pairs of pressed trousers. The middle is for suit jackets. The right side holds a dozen turtlenecks in a variety of shades and fabrics. Julius feels a twinge of guilt. He shouldn't have made that turtleneck dig the other day, especially within five minutes of arriving at the hotel. He sees that now, but Julius doesn't excel at thinking before he speaks. He's put his foot in his mouth so many times over the years, he could open a shoe store in there.

Julius knows the turtlenecks are a defense mechanism, one Alfred adopted because of him. Alfred began wearing them after Julius razzed him about the birthmark on his neck. What was the nickname he'd given it? Herbert. Julius feels another spike of regret. He had bagged on Alfred for no reason other than getting cheap laughs from the rest of the crew. How many times had he turned Alfred—the others too, but especially Alfred—into a joke so that he could feel good about himself? Julius is the funny one; that was his function in this group. He knows he's not particularly smart or driven or kind, not compared with the others. But he could always be counted on for a laugh. If he's not the comic relief, then his sole purpose is to be a piggy bank. For a long, long time, he has worried that people want to be friends with him only because of his wealth.

Julius intends to apologize to Alfred for those years of teasing, not to mention the senior-year betrayal that Alfred doesn't even know about. Making amends is why he showed up to the reunion this weekend. That, and the push from Grace. Yet what did Julius do as soon as he walked through the door? Fell into his old role, making jabs at Alfred and the rest of them. Can he blame Alfred for despising him? For believing himself the underdog?

Here is what Julius has come to understand about people: we all like to think of ourselves as underdogs. No one wants to be Goliath. Everyone wants to be David. Some of us *are* David; some of us will find a way to contort ourselves into him. Every privilege can find a disadvantage. Take beauty, for example—the beautiful are objectified and assumed to lack depth. The famous live in golden cages. The rich are villainized for their success. Children of the beautiful, famous, and/or rich are believed to possess no merits of their own. (As a nepo baby himself, Julius would know.) There's your height or your weight or your toxic family or your unbearable grief. No matter how fortunate your position in this world, you can find a way to conclude that you are lesser, lacking. You can list the ways the world has knocked you down, the times you got back up. The world is full of Davids searching for their Goliaths. If we were honest with ourselves, Julius thinks, we would admit that to someone somewhere, *we* are Goliaths. Julius has many, many flaws, but fancying himself an innocent or a victim is not one of them. He has more in common with the villains than with the heroes of most movies. No one should be sorry for him. Few are.

Yet no amount of money can prevent a cancer diagnosis. True, his diagnosis came more quickly, and his doctors are better, and his treatment will commence sooner than most patients', but at the end of the day he's still about to have his left ball removed. Health is the great equalizer.

Julius is surprised that he hasn't shed a single tear until this weekend, not even on the day he received the news. Then again, he can count on one hand the number of times he's cried in his life. *Thénardier men don't cry*, his father likes to remind him, including at *Pépère*'s funeral, after Julius broke down mid-eulogy. Julius has numbed himself to every hardship with booze, drugs, and sex—or, in his more responsible phases, therapy. Sometimes he worries that something is wrong with him, that he's not regulating his emotions. His father would call that psychobabble.

Julius crosses the room to Alfred's bed and opens a nightstand drawer. Inside are a black satin sleeping mask, a handful of lozenges, and an inhaler. Does Alfred have asthma? Julius feels bad for not remembering.

He watches Zoe examine the typewriter atop the desk. That must be the valuable one Alfred mentioned at dinner. TJ sits in the desk chair and opens Alfred's laptop. A password request pops up. TJ types, waits, types some more.

"I've tried *Hitchcock* and *Hitchcock Hotel*." TJ drums his fingers on the keyboard. "I have one log-in attempt left."

"Try *Grace Liu*," Grace says from the doorway, tapping her foot. Julius glances at Zoe, who shakes her head.

"*Aaand* I'm locked out." TJ sits back, defeated.

"What happened to divide and conquer?" Zoe asks.

Grace shrugs. "I got curious. Find anything interesting?"

No one answers. Julius moves to the other nightstand, which holds a bunch of chargers and an old retainer case. He'd like to say he can't believe how boring Alfred is, but he absolutely can. *(What if I'm geneti-cally incapable of dropping the snark?)* He kneels to check under the bed. Not so much as a dust bunny.

"Try the mattress," Grace suggests.

Julius makes a big show of sighing loudly. "We're not your worker bees."

"I would never hire you." Grace laughs. "You'd make an awful em-ployee."

There's the Grace we're used to.

Julius huffs but runs his hand between the mattress and the box spring anyway, feeling for God knows what. TJ moves to the opposite side of the bed, does the same. He lifts a pillow sham and tosses it on the floor. The bed has no fewer than eight pillows, and TJ works his way through them methodically, flipping one after another off the bed. When he gets to the last one, he sighs before flinging it. After that, he doesn't gasp or yelp or make any noise at all. Julius knows he found something only by his sudden stillness, the lack of breath.

He pops up from his side of the bed and follows TJ's gaze. Their eyes meet. Sitting on the snow-white comforter is Alfred's iPhone.

THIRTY-TWO

TJ

TJ picks up the phone and taps the screen. The background is a photo of Hitchcock. "Definitely Alfred's."

"He was lying to us all along, then? About the concierge taking our phones home by mistake?" Julius says.

"I knew it," Zoe says.

"Asshole," Julius mumbles.

Grace is at TJ's side in an instant, letting the room door close behind her. She puts out her hand. "Give it to me," she says, like she's talking to one of her kids. He raises an eyebrow. "Please," she adds.

Now that TJ knows what he knows, Grace seems strange to him, unknown. Zoe didn't seem surprised by Julius's reveal on the stairs. Had everyone but TJ been clued in? Why hasn't Grace told him? *It's not a big deal,* TJ tells himself. *College was a long time ago.*

He hands the phone over to Grace. She taps out six digits, gaining access on the first attempt. "How'd you know his passcode?" TJ asks.

"I tried my birthday." She walks away with the device.

"What the hell, Grace?" Zoe says.

"We want to see what's on it too," Julius adds. They both stand there with crossed arms. Grace ignores them.

TJ follows Grace, hanging near her shoulder as she clicks on the Messages app. Grace glowers at him, but he doesn't care. He's the one who found the damn phone.

Alfred has zero existing chats. TJ hopes that's because he deletes his texts. The alternative is too pitiful to consider. Grace moves on to his email inbox. She scrolls through his Sent folder, his drafts, each labeled subfolder. Almost everything pertains to the hotel—business documents and guest requests and employee payroll reports. She finds receipts for some of Alfred's memorabilia, a few discussions with fellow Hitchcock fans and eBay bidders. After ten minutes of searching in vain, she stamps her foot and navigates back to the phone's home screen. Her finger hovers over the Photos app. She hesitates.

"What?" TJ says in a low voice.

"Can you give me some space?" she asks.

What is she hiding?

Out of nowhere, a crow squawks as it zooms past Alfred's window. Grace startles and drops the phone. TJ scoops it up.

"Praise be. The murderous bird is free," Julius says.

"How do you think it got outside?" Zoe asks.

"Open window?" Julius guesses.

"Or Alfred let it out," TJ says.

"He wouldn't do that," Grace says. "Alfred would return the crow to the aviary."

"Maybe it's a warning," TJ says. Grace shakes her head.

Julius turns a slow circle. "Have none of you considered that Alfred might not be hiding because he's afraid?"

"Why else would he?" Grace says.

Zoe clears her throat. "Because he has something planned."

TJ thinks of the boots peeking out from under his curtains. He doesn't buy Grace's prank theory at all. The four of them stand in the room, uneasy.

Zoe breaks the silence. "Well, he's not in here. Neither are our phones."

"Is it possible Alfred gave them to the concierge but held on to his own?" Julius asks.

"Possible," Grace says, "but not probable. I think they're somewhere in the hotel. He's too controlling to hand them off to someone else." TJ, Zoe, and Julius give her pointed looks. "Takes one to know one," she says, with a strained smile.

"Why steal our phones in the first place?" Julius says.

"Maybe to see if we were talking about him," Zoe says. "Or to keep us here longer."

Or he thought I'd been up to the attic and taken photos of the vents, TJ thinks, *and wanted to delete them off my phone before I could show the cops.* Maybe the boots and necktie were an intimidation tactic. Maybe Alfred wanted to scare TJ away from his property. Too bad. As much as he'd like to, TJ can't leave until he speaks to Julius.

"Are we sure Alfred did this and not some unhinged member of the staff?" Julius asks. "That Danny chick is a little too devoted to the job, and the groundskeeper has a real Bundy energy, with the way he watches everyone. Not to mention his mullet."

"Alfred has his phone, so he must've had something to do with it," Zoe says.

"But he doesn't have his phone," Grace says. "We do." She pauses. "Why leave it behind?"

"We're wasting time with all this theorizing," TJ says. "I say we search for the phones room by room. Every closet, every guest room. Even our own."

Zoe's eyes widen. "Why our own?"

"What's a better hiding spot than right under our noses?" TJ asks. "They're the last places we'd think to check. Unless there's something in yours you don't want us to see?"

Zoe crosses her arms. "Fuck off." She tries to project an air of indifference, but TJ notices her sidelong glances at the door.

"Why don't you guys get started?" Grace suggests. "I'll finish rifling through Alfred's phone, then meet up with you."

TJ shakes his head. "I might be able to retrieve some of his deleted texts and emails. I've done it for my client a few times." A total lie. He has no more sophisticated an understanding of technology than the rest of them. His client has an IT whiz to help with digital security, but TJ's friends don't know that. "Go on. I'll let you know if I find anything."

Grace studies him. "Fine. I want the phone back when you're done." She leads Julius and Zoe out of Alfred's room. TJ waits until he hears them enter her room next door. Then, throat tight, he opens the Photos app.

He doesn't know what to expect. Nude photos of Grace? *Come on*, he chides himself. Grace finds Alfred repulsive. *Then why is she more fixated on checking his phone than on finding her own?* TJ scrolls through a cringe-worthy number of selfies—Alfred posing in front of a floor-length mirror in various outfits. He also finds lots of photos of the hotel, some of which he matches to posts from the Hitchcock Hotel's Instagram account. But there are no photos of Grace; there's nothing untoward at all. What is she hoping to find?

On the phone's home screen, TJ opens the Social folder and taps the first icon. He moves through app after app, checking every social media inbox for anything that might be relevant. When he's exhausted all the social apps, he tries a folder labeled Talk next. He looks through Whats-App, FaceTime, Contacts, Zoom, and Skype before landing on the final app in the folder. He always forgets about the Voice Memos app, has never used it himself. There's one recording, made yesterday. He clicks on it, presses play. He listens with alarm to the sounds of bedsheets rustling, skin sliding against skin, Grace's moans.

"I don't know, Teej," he hears her say, her voice muffled. *"I told you we shouldn't be doing this here. Someone could catch us."*

What is this?

"Have you given any more thought to telling Rob?" he hears himself ask.

"I don't want to talk about the future right now," she says.

"Isn't it nice having a whole weekend together?"

With every new sentence uttered, he wants to shout at both her and himself to shut up. He bows his head with guilt as they gossip about Zoe and her efforts to stop drinking. When the recording finishes, TJ sinks to the desk chair, shattered.

TJ was right—Alfred was eavesdropping. But he was doing more than that. Did Alfred show Grace the recording and threaten to send it to Rob? That would explain why she was such a pushover last night, why she didn't try to micromanage the search for the missing phones. Alfred had her right where he wanted her—under his thumb.

TJ's finger lingers over the delete button. He considers what might happen if this audio file found its way to Rob. The tears, the screaming matches, the cold shoulder. An overdue understanding that the marriage is beyond repair. Divorce, maybe. (TJ's heart races.) A fifty-fifty split, shared custody. Grace would need time, but also: a warm body, a sympathetic ear, a fresh start. TJ sees Grace and himself strolling through a park, coffee in hand, on Sunday mornings. There are so many public places they haven't been together. Beaches and museums and planes. He's sick to death of associating Grace with hotels and room service. He longs to come out from the shadows.

He swallows and emails the audio file to himself before he can chicken out. Then he deletes the recording and steps into the hallway.

THIRTY-THREE

Zoe

Zoe pulls a welcome packet and a notepad from the desk in Grace's room. Julius rifles through the dresser drawers. Grace rips the bedding off the mattress. They turn the room upside down.

"Whoa," TJ says from the doorway.

Grace lifts her chin. "We're shooting for speed, not tidiness."

"Fair enough," TJ says. "Seems like there's nothing here. About time we moved on to your room, Zo, don't you think?"

Zoe reddens and joins him in the hallway. "Shouldn't we do this closet first? It's closer."

TJ eyes the closet door next to Samira's room. "Why don't you want us in your room?"

"I don't give a shit," Zoe says. "I thought you wanted to go in order. Room by room, you said."

Julius comes out to the hallway too. "Where to next?"

"I'm going to change out of my pajamas, and then I'll join you." Grace closes her room door.

Zoe narrows her eyes at TJ. "Is there a reason you don't want us checking that closet?"

"Why would I care?" he says. "I've never been in there."

"Great. Let's check it out," Zoe says.

"Ladies first," TJ says.

"I hardly think Zoe qualifies," Julius quips.

Zoe steps on his foot, smudging his sparkling white sneaker. Julius shrieks. It feels good to be playful, to antagonize one another. For a second, Zoe pretends everything is normal, that she's back in college, without a care in the world. She marches to the closet door, grips the handle, and pauses. "Let's see what's behind door number three."

Julius crosses his fingers and chants, "Phones, phones, phones."

Zoe yanks open the door and screams.

Julius ducks under Zoe's shoulder, then clamps a hand over his mouth. TJ's knees wobble. The door to Grace's room flies open, and a fully dressed Grace emerges. She lets loose a cannonade of expletives when she joins them in the closet's entryway.

Samira comes rushing up the stairs and down the hallway.

"What's going on?" she cries. "Why are you shouting? Zoe, stop screaming!"

The group falls silent at once and stares over their shoulders at her. Zoe imagines how terrified the expressions on their faces must be, because Samira stops short. Her hand flies to her throat. She takes one slow, deliberate step at a time, as though she's moving through quicksand.

Turn back, Zoe wants to yell. *It's not too late.*

Then it is. Samira is by Zoe's side, seeing what Zoe is seeing.

The body is on its side, faced away from the closet door and tangled in the ladder, the left foot hooked on the bottom step. The shoe on that foot has fallen off. The right leg bends in a grotesque position. A small pool of blood has formed a halo around the head. The neck is fatally twisted.

The group stands at the closet doorway, frozen. Zoe forces her feet forward, like Samira did. She knows whose body that is, but she needs to confirm. She has to see the face with her own eyes.

"Zoe, don't," someone whispers. She keeps moving anyway.

When she reaches the body's side, she leans over it, careful not to touch the pressed trousers or the charcoal turtleneck. No matter how many times she blinks, the scene before her remains the same. Eyes closed, lips blue. Alfred is dead.

THIRTY-FOUR

Julius

Samira joins Zoe in the closet. Julius can't see Alfred's face, but he appears almost peaceful there, lying on his side. For a second Julius allows himself to believe he might be napping. Samira and Zoe crouch by Alfred's head. Samira turns him on his back.

"Should you be doing that?" Julius asks, dazed. Now that he can see Alfred's ashen coloring, pretending he's sleeping is a lot more difficult.

Samira ignores him. "Who knows CPR?"

Zoe puts her hand on Samira's arm and gently says, "He's gone."

Last night Alfred was walking, talking, apologizing for the missing phones. Julius tries to recall the last thing he said to him. Had he been kind? He can't remember.

Tears well in Samira's eyes. She puts two fingers to Alfred's wrist, waits, searches, waits, searches some more. "I can't find a pulse," she wails. "How did this happen?"

Julius struggles to form a coherent thought. He's seen dead people before, but only in coffins or on TV. Is it his imagination or can he already detect the odors of decomposition hanging over the group? Julius feels like he might vomit. He resists the urge to backpedal away from the closet and run down the hallway.

"He had to have fallen off the ladder," TJ murmurs.

"How did he cut his head?" Zoe asks.

Grace studies the hatch in the ceiling. "He must have banged it on the way down." She squints and points at a bloodstain on the lip of the trapdoor.

Samira gapes at Alfred, then cries, "He was a good man."

Julius bows his head along with the others. The moment of respect goes on and on until Julius can't take the silence anymore, until he can't bear to look at his dead friend another minute. Lately he's thought of little else but the precariousness of life, and now here's proof of it lying at his feet. When he was younger, he used to marvel at the strength of the human body, how hard it fights to continue living. Our skin repairs itself, bones heal, immune system battles intruders. He used to think dying was difficult. The older he gets, the less convinced he is of this belief. A spontaneous rupture in the brain. Monster cells ravaging the body. Death can eat away at you or take you in a flash. Human beings are too vulnerable, he's decided. All that separates us from our own end is one or two malfunctioning organs. It should be harder to die.

Julius clears his throat. His voice shakes when he speaks. "What was he doing in here in the middle of the night?"

Nobody answers. They all stare at Alfred in disbelief.

"Maybe he couldn't sleep," TJ says.

"Or he ran out of toilet paper?" Grace sounds far away.

"You guys think this was an accident?" Zoe mutters. They turn to gawk at her. "No one thinks he might've been pushed?"

"Who would do something like that?" Samira cries.

Zoe doesn't answer—she doesn't have to. *Any one of us.* Julius feels guilty for the thought, though he suspects he's not the only one thinking it.

"It had to be an accident," Samira says. "People fall down the stairs all the time. Accidents happen all the time."

"Or—" Zoe starts.

"Zoe, stop," Samira shouts. "We don't need your morbid imagination right now. Our friend died." She takes Alfred's limp hand in hers. Zoe hangs her head.

"Someone has to call nine-one-one," Grace mumbles.

"An ambulance?" Julius asks. Are they supposed to get up and function? Carry on with their day and the rest of their lives while Alfred lies there, dead? *Alfred is dead.* He repeats the three words to himself over and over, cannot make them make sense.

"Or a hearse?" Zoe says.

Samira moans. "I need to get out of here."

"We should call the police," TJ says, distracted. Julius follows his gaze to the hatch. "What do you think is up there?"

Zoe pulls herself to standing. "I'll go check." She climbs the ladder like she has weights attached to her feet, eventually disappearing from view.

The group waits in heavy silence. Julius hears nothing but Zoe's footsteps overhead, and the sounds of Samira's rapid breaths. *She's going to hyperventilate,* he thinks.

"Jesus Christ," Zoe says.

"What is it?" Grace calls. "What'd you find?"

"There's a bunch of weird stuff up here. Bags of old clothes, a stuffed crow, and this." Zoe reappears in the hatch with a glass of milk on a silver platter. Julius swallows.

"He was drinking milk in the attic?" TJ asks, confused.

"The milk isn't the weirdest thing," Zoe says.

"What's the weirdest thing?" TJ eyes Alfred's body.

"There are vents in the floor. Like, seven or eight," Zoe says. "You can see into each of our rooms through them." She pauses. "Alfred was spying on us."

THIRTY-FIVE

TJ

"I knew it," TJ mutters, the words tumbling out. The others peer at him. He regrets speaking up.

"You did?" Samira sniffles.

"You didn't think it might be worth telling the rest of us?" Julius asks.

"What the hell, dude?" Zoe says as she climbs down from the attic.

TJ steals a glance at Grace, who is staring at Alfred's body. TJ saw her sneak into this closet last night. Was Alfred already in here when she entered?

"What's all this hollering about?" someone calls from the other side of the hallway.

The group exits the closet to find the housekeeper scowling at them.

"There's been an accident," TJ says.

The old woman hurries toward them. "What sort of accident?"

Grace holds Danny by the arm. "Alfred had a fall, Danny."

TJ moves away from the closet doorway to reveal Alfred's body. Danny reels. "Oh my . . ." She steps into the closet and kneels by Alfred's side, checks his wrist for a pulse. Finding none, she cries out.

"His skin is already cool to the touch." Danny grips Alfred's hand in hers. "His body is stiffening." She glares at them through slitted eyes. "Why didn't you tell me he was like this? How long have you left him lying here on the floor?"

"I need to get out of here," Samira says for the second time.

"We only found him a minute ago," TJ says. "We were searching for our phones."

Danny wipes her nose with the back of her hand. "TJ, is that right?"

"Yes, ma'am."

"You threatened him yesterday. Upstairs in the hallway."

Everyone gapes at TJ, who flushes. "With all due respect, ma'am, you're wrong."

To no one in particular, Danny says, "Have you ever noticed that anytime someone says *with all due respect*, something disrespectful follows?"

"We had an argument," TJ says. "Not even. A disagreement. He was watch—" He stops himself. "It doesn't matter. I mean no insult to you, Danny, but I'm telling you I never threatened him."

Julius adds, "TJ wouldn't hurt a fly." TJ smiles, grateful for the backup despite his argument with Julius the first night here.

Danny focuses her ire on Julius. "And *you*." She spits the word like it's poison on her tongue. Julius blinks, confused. "Do you see the position his body is in?" Danny asks. They all gaze at Alfred. "Made to resemble a fall down a staircase. Is that ringing a bell?"

"The perfect-murder conversation Thursday night," Zoe says.

"Someone said you'd want to make it seem like an accident," TJ muses.

"Julius," Grace says.

Julius flushes. "You're not suggesting—"

"The rest of your friends heard it as clearly as I did," Danny says. The old woman is obviously lashing out, senseless with shock and grief.

"I can't believe I have to say this, but I did not murder Alfred," Julius squeaks.

"Can you prove it?" Danny stares at him.

"You can't prove a negative."

Samira climbs to her feet. "I have to go."

"You can if you have an alibi," Danny says.

"I was sleeping," Julius protests.

"So you say." Danny considers the circle. "None of you liked Alfred."

"That's not true," Julius says. "And I had nothing to do with his death."

"Me neither," says TJ.

"Obviously not," Zoe adds.

"We would never hurt him," Grace says.

Danny sneers. "You already had, over and over again. What was to stop you from doing it one more time?" Danny's expression turns melancholy. "All he wanted from you was an apology. But you couldn't even give him that, could you?"

"What did he tell you about Reville?" TJ asks.

She fixes him with a pointed stare. "Enough." TJ's spine tingles.

"I should have known you'd destroy him. You are not good people." Danny peeks back at Alfred in the closet. "My poor, poor boy." She stifles a sob.

They all stand there awkwardly, waiting for the housekeeper to collect herself. It takes a minute, but she finally wipes her eyes.

Samira heads for her guest room. "I'm going home."

"None of you go anywhere," Danny says. "Not until the police arrive. They'll see to it that justice is served. I'm calling them now." She moves down the hallway without a backward glance.

Samira stands at her door like a lost little girl. "I want my family," she says.

"Wait 'til the cops get here," TJ says. "You don't want to get in trouble for leaving too soon." Samira nods. He wonders if she actually heard him.

Julius looks like he might be sick. "I'm going to head outside for a minute, get some fresh air." He hurries down the hall after Danny.

He's going to leave the hotel. He's getting away, TJ thinks, but he's too drained to follow him, not sure there's any validity to the thought. TJ's mind feels fuzzy, unfocused. *Who put the boots and tie in my room? Could Alfred have done it before he died?* An even worse possibility occurs to him. *Could it have been the unsmiling man? Is he here?* The pain in TJ's chest burns bright. He massages his breastbone.

"What if Danny's right?" Samira says. "This is our fault."

Grace takes Samira in her arms. "She didn't mean that. She's in shock. We all are." But Grace doesn't appear shocked at all. In fact, she's remarkably poised, two inches taller than she was at breakfast.

She's always been good in a crisis, TJ reassures himself.

He hears the front door of the hotel creak open. Sneakers slap against tile. "Grace! Zoe! TJ! Samira!" Julius shouts from downstairs. "Get out here right now."

TJ exchanges a glance with Grace, then heads for the staircase. The others follow, close on his heels. Julius isn't in the lobby, but the front door is wide open. TJ sprints down the stairs, then hurries through the doorway. A dense fog hangs over the parking lot.

"Look, look," Julius is saying, pointing.

TJ gapes. There are seven vehicles in the lot. Every tire on every car has been slashed.

Today we tend to lump mysteries
and thrillers together, but directors
like Alfred Hitchcock saw them as
vastly different. He felt viewers watched
mysteries only to find out the ending. For this
reason, Hitchcock generally avoided whodunits,
calling them "intellectual puzzles" that
lacked emotional heft.

—Excerpt from Essay #214,
"Defining the Mystery vs. Thriller Genres in Film"

THIRTY-SIX

Julius

Grace kicks one of the deflated tires of Julius's Aston Martin and swears.

"Hey, watch it," Julius says.

"Like you don't have ten other cars?" she snaps.

Julius casts her a withering glare. "This one is special. It belonged to my grandpa."

Samira and Zoe run out of the hotel and scan the parking lot, mouths falling open like TJ's and Grace's did.

TJ fingers a tire. "The slashes are too big to repair with a plug kit. Whoever did this wanted to make sure we couldn't leave anytime soon."

Who would that be? Julius thinks, not liking the possibilities. "Did anyone come out here this morning?" They all shake their heads.

"I was the last one in the lobby last night," TJ says. "I checked the front and back of the hotel. Nothing was amiss."

Could Alfred have snuck downstairs and punctured the tires before he died? Did Danny do this as revenge for their past mistreatment of Alfred? Julius scans the windows. Danny paces in front of one of the rooms on the second floor, her cell phone pressed to her ear. She doesn't strike him as the tire-slashing type.

But that leaves only his old friends. He glances from Samira to Grace to Zoe to TJ, sees them performing the same mental calculus he is.

"Danny's calling the police," Grace says. "I say we keep searching for our phones while we wait for them."

"Might as well," Zoe agrees.

The fivesome heads back inside. Everyone appears disturbed, but Samira is approaching hysteria. She stops at the foot of the staircase, shaking from head to toe. "I can't go back up there." Her eyes shine with fear.

Julius has had the same thought. How are the others so collected and rational? Their friend is lying dead in a closet upstairs, for God's sake. Who gives a shit about the phones?

Then again, the sooner they find them, the faster they can get out of here.

Grace gestures at the computer on the reception desk. "Why don't you go online?" she says gently to Samira. "Find a tow truck company. See how soon they can be here."

Samira nods, walks mechanically around the desk, and sits in the chair. She wiggles the computer's mouse, then must sense all their eyes on her, because she says, "Go on. I'll be okay."

Grace nods and traipses up the steps. Despite his reservations, and out of habit more than reason, Julius follows Grace. How easily they fall into their old patterns. Grace always knew what to do during an emergency back in college. She would know what to do now.

A month ago, climbing two flights of stairs would have winded Julius, but since his diagnosis, he's been eating better and drinking less—except for occasional slipups, like this weekend. He goes on long walks every day now, sometimes around his cherished city. Other times he drives out to the Catskills or Adirondacks to dwell in their magnificence. He knows what a cliché he's become. He's turned into the guy he once made fun of, but he doesn't care. Maybe having your first brush with mortality at thirty-eight does that to you. Either way, he is no more out of breath than TJ by the time they reach the third floor. He tries to focus on gratitude instead of the closet at the end of the hallway.

"Should we check Samira's room next?" Zoe asks.

"We didn't search the closet," Grace says. Julius's eyes widen. "I don't want to go back either, but if that's where Alfred was, maybe our phones are in there too."

"What about the attic?" TJ suggests.

"Look if you want," Zoe says. "There's a bunch of old boxes and garbage bags up there."

Julius shivers.

Zoe heads for the closet. "I'll take the shelves on the back wall."

"I'll do the attic," Grace says.

Julius follows them inside the closet. He takes the shelves on the left side, as far away from Alfred's body as he can get.

"You going to help or what?" Zoe asks.

Julius glances over his shoulder to find TJ lingering outside the closet. TJ stares at Alfred, his complexion green. Julius is glad he's not the only one who's scared and struggling.

"I don't know if I can do this." TJ wrings his hands.

"Let's get it over with as fast as we can," Zoe says.

TJ shuffles into the closet, holds his breath, and leans over Alfred's body to search between the towels. Julius focuses on his own task, moving plastic bottles around on the bottom shelf to see if the phones are hidden behind them. His search is thorough, but he comes up empty. He moves on to the next shelf, a creeping sense of guilt tapping his shoulder.

Julius should come clean, tell the rest of them the truth. He's the one to blame for this entire weekend.

Julius could tell Alfred didn't like him the night they met. Where Alfred was chatty with everyone else in the group, he showed no interest in getting to know Julius, at some points even standing with his back to him. Julius shouldn't have cared—his father was always reminding him that he didn't need to win the hearts of unimportant people—but he couldn't help himself. He wanted to be liked. By everyone. So sue him. Is there a more human impulse than that?

As Alfred spent more and more time with the group, Julius made it his mission to figure out what Alfred's issue with him was. Julius's bold outfits? His constant wisecracking? His inherited wealth? Julius was used to people assuming the worst of him because of his money, though he found that a little unfair—like disliking someone for their freckles. He couldn't help the family he was born into. Wardrobe aside, he wasn't obnoxious about his affluence. *Screw 'em*, he decided.

"Casual enemies" were people Julius didn't much like but whose lives he wasn't trying to ruin. After weeks of getting nowhere with his campaign to befriend Alfred, Julius slotted him into this category. He antagonized Alfred little by little, made comments on his hairstyle and birthmark in front of the others. Did he feel bad? Occasionally, but despite Alfred's penchant for playing the victim, he wasn't a damsel in distress. He made plenty of digs about Julius's height, ruffling his hair and asking if he bought his clothes at the local Gymboree. This became their routine within the group: (thinly) masking passive-aggression as banter. They squabbled like an old married couple, pushing each other's buttons at every available opportunity, but neither crossed the line for fear of being booted from the crew.

Until senior year.

By then, all six of them were living in the blue house on Poplar Street. For the final parents' weekend of their college careers, they decided to throw a party for their parents and friends. Julius was shocked when his dad agreed to come. In the weeks leading up to the visit, he tried to downplay his excitement. Dad had never met Julius's friends; Julius was eager for him to make a good impression on them. Beer pong and flip cup weren't his father's idea of fun, but he knew how to turn on the charm when he wanted to. Julius hoped this would be one of those times.

On that Friday night in early October, the party was well underway when Julius and his father walked through the door. (Dad had insisted on taking the private jet, so Julius drove forty miles to pick him up from the regional airport. No way in hell was Julius going to let his dad roll up to his house party in a chauffeured Bentley.) Julius surveyed his dad's reaction to the scene before them. Twenty or thirty people were milling around, refilling their beers from the keg or munching on chips straight from the bag. Zoe and Samira were standing on the kitchen table, using hairbrushes as microphones, belting Third Eye Blind's "Motorcycle Drive By." Zoe's parents were laughing and clapping along. Samira's must have already gone to bed, or she wouldn't be up on the table, Julius knew.

To Julius's relief, Dad was on his best behavior. He spent the whole evening gamely sipping shitty whiskey from a red plastic cup, shooting the breeze with TJ, then Alfred, then the girls. He even played the drinking games, double high-fiving everyone around him, which Julius had never in his life seen him do. All in all, the night was a dream for Julius. *This,* he thought, *is what having a normal parent is like.* Julius had hoped this might be a turning point in their relationship. He should have known better.

At two in the morning, Julius walked his dad back to his hotel. He tried to play it cool but couldn't resist asking, "Tonight was fun, right?"

Dad nodded. "I didn't realize you were such an entrepreneur." Julius frowned in the dark. "Alfred told me about your little side business."

"What side business?"

His father's tone turned deadly. "If you ever, and I mean ever, sell cocaine to another student again, I will report you to the dean, and then I'll cut off access to your trust. Do you hear me? How could you risk the family reputation this way, you selfish, spoiled brat?"

Julius's blood ran cold. "Dad, I'm not selling drugs. I shared it with some friends." Technically, his friends had paid him back for the coke, but Julius wasn't a dealer. He gave it to a handful of people he hung out with on weekends. Super low-key. They would never say anything.

His father refused to listen. He wouldn't let Julius walk any farther with him, said he was ashamed to be seen with him. Dad told Julius to go back to the blue house and focus on his studies. He didn't speak to his son for months.

What was Alfred's reason for throwing Julius under the bus? Julius had made fun of Alfred in front of a girl he liked the weekend before. Said girl had ghosted Alfred after that, which Alfred blamed on Julius. Anyone with half a brain could see Alfred's retaliation was a huge over-reaction. Had he lost his mind?

The next day Julius made up an excuse for his father's absence, said that urgent business had necessitated his immediate return to New York. While everyone else passed the rest of the weekend making more memories with their parents, Julius spent his stewing and bloodthirsty. How dare Alfred come between him and his father? The anger hadn't dissipated as he sat through COM206 the following week, half listening to Dr. Scott's lecture about the symbolism of oranges in *The Godfather*. Seated between Zoe and TJ, Julius jiggled his leg the entire seventy-five minutes, restless, determined to one-up Alfred at his own game. As class was dismissed the solution presented itself, literally standing in front of him. *Alfred wants to rat me out for my "business"? Fine. Then more people need to know about his.*

Alfred was no longer a casual enemy.

Alfred thought his essay-writing business was top secret, but Julius knew all about it, had discussed it with Grace a few times. He had never used Alfred's services himself, not due to some moral code but because he loathed the idea of giving Alfred anything, including money. Julius knew Alfred had a good thing going, had supposedly produced papers for half the students in this classroom. He was raking in cash and using it to pay tuition, according to Grace. Julius had never had much reason to care.

By now Zoe had zipped her backpack and put on her coat. "Coming?" she asked him.

Julius shook his head. "I'll catch up with you later. I need to ask Dr. Scott a few questions."

Zoe goggled at him like he had three heads; never before had he stayed after class to chat up a teacher. She moved on, heading for TJ and the others. Julius avoided their gazes, occupied himself with jotting fake notes in his spiral. When only a few stragglers remained in the classroom, Julius rose from his chair.

Had his legs or voice shaken? Did he have misgivings, second thoughts? Honestly? No. He never even hesitated.

"Dr. Scott," he called, intercepting the professor as he headed for the door. "Can I discuss something with you in your office?"

Dr. Scott had glanced at his watch. "I have ten minutes before a faculty meeting." Julius nodded. He followed the older man to the elevator, watched him tap the 6 button, then stand back. "Julius, right?" Dr. Scott asked.

Julius was surprised that the professor knew his name, considering he never raised his hand or spoke in class, preferring to slouch in the back row and absorb maybe one or two of the forty-five points Dr. Scott brought up in any given lecture. He was remorseful for that now, in the elevator, though he supposed Dr. Scott was paid regardless of whether his students listened.

The professor led him to his office, a small but comfortable space crammed with books about movies. Julius wondered if he had read them all.

"Okay if I close this?" Julius asked, holding on to the door.

Dr. Scott seemed concerned but nodded as he sat behind his desk.

Julius took the chair opposite him. He surveyed the artwork on the wall behind Dr. Scott. "What's the deal with that print?"

Dr. Scott glanced over his shoulder. "It's a reimagined movie poster for the film *Suspicion*. Have you seen it?" Julius shook his head, and Dr. Scott mocked offense. "Hitchcock movie. Cary Grant, Joan Fontaine. Made in"—he stopped to think, gazing at the ceiling—"1941, if memory serves. A big if." He smiled.

"What's the significance of the milk?" Julius asked. The poster was black, save for a small glass of milk on a silver platter in the center.

"You'll have to watch the movie to find out." Dr. Scott winked, then straightened. "I suspect you didn't come here to chat about old movies, though."

Julius sensed Dr. Scott's gaze on him. "I hope this is the right thing to do." He picked up a stress ball from the desk, gave it a few good squeezes, then sighed. "There's massive cheating going on in our class."

Dr. Scott blinked a few times, the smile sliding off his face. Julius was sorry for him. He'd sometimes questioned whether professors turned a blind eye to cheating, for fear of retaliation or poor student ratings or pure indifference, but this man was stunned.

"Excuse me?" Dr. Scott removed his glasses. "How?"

"Do you promise not to reveal I was your source? I don't want my friends to hate me."

Dr. Scott nodded. "I promise." The professor kept his word. Julius's name was never mentioned.

"Someone started an essay-writing business." Julius chewed his lip. "It's taken off."

Dr. Scott's next question was the one Julius had expected, even anticipated. He flinched when the name rolled off his tongue—but only to fake hesitation in betraying a friend.

A rat for a rat.

After fifteen minutes of combing every inch of the closet and attic, Julius, Zoe, Grace, and TJ are no closer to finding their phones. Julius can't stand to be in that closet with Alfred any longer.

"They're not in here," he says. "Samira's room next?" She's still downstairs, calling the tow truck. What's taking her so long?

TJ sighs. "Guess so."

The foursome files out of the closet. Zoe closes the door behind them. Julius feels a little better now that he can't see Alfred anymore, but he's still nauseated. Grace holds up a key and moves to the door of room 301. Will this day never end?

"When did you get Samira's room key?" TJ says.

"I asked her for it before we came up here," Grace says. "She's not in a great place right now. I don't want to bother her more than we have to." Julius notes that Grace's mood is back to normal since—horrible to say it, but—Alfred died. She's cheerful, even. Grace inserts the key into the lock. Samira's door pops open.

"Should we split up?" Zoe asks. "Each take a room to make this go faster?"

"Let me guess which one you want to take," TJ says.

"I don't know what your problem is," Zoe says, "but I'm not hiding anything. I'll show you my room right now."

"Let's go," TJ says.

Zoe stomps over to 303. Grace and Julius stay where they are, but TJ follows her into the room. "Happy now?" Julius hears Zoe yell.

"Yikes," he says under his breath, picturing a dozen empty minibar bottles scattered around her room. No wonder Zoe doesn't want anyone in there.

Grace shakes her head and walks into Samira's room, which is bigger than the others. The room is disheveled—classic Samira. How does she manage her business so well when her surroundings are in constant disarray? Not that Julius is all that neat himself. Had he known the group would be field tripping to one another's rooms, he would've straightened up his own, made sure nothing is lying out that he doesn't want the others to see.

"You take the dresser," Julius says to Grace. "I'm not real eager to paw through Samira's underthings." He takes in the mess on the floor. "Though I question whether she's even opened a drawer. I think her room will look better after we ransack it."

Grace laughs and moves to the dresser, then yanks on the drawer knobs one by one. "God, I can't wait to get out of here."

Julius couldn't agree more, although the terror of surgery awaits him at home. He walks over to the desk.

"Um."

Julius stares at the handful of velvet pouches. One is deflated, obviously empty. He picks up a different pouch and opens it. "Um," he says again. Inside is a phone in a red silicone case. TJ's, maybe? The phone is turned off.

"I found them?" he says, the statement more of a question.

Grace whips her head around, sees the pouches, then steps into the hall. "Guys!" she yells. "They're in here." She rushes to Julius's side. Together they dig through each pouch. Julius unearths a white phone (Grace's). Grace pulls out a black one (Zoe's), then a phone with a neon orange case bright enough to land airplanes. Julius snatches it from her.

"I missed you," he says to the device as TJ and Zoe hurry into the room. Grace hands both of them their respective phones.

TJ blinks. "Where were they?"

"Right here on the desk." Julius points.

"Hidden?" Zoe asks.

Julius shakes his head. "Not at all. I stepped over here and saw them." He never gets to be the hero. He understands why people crave the feeling.

"Were there only four?" TJ asks.

"The fifth pouch was empty." Julius holds it up.

The room quiets as they all power their phones back on, waiting for the dark screens to illuminate.

"I'm gonna say what you guys won't." Zoe hesitates. "How the fuck did Samira not see these?"

THIRTY-SEVEN

Zoe

No one answers Zoe. She watches, one by one, as their phones boot up and ask for passwords, buzz with notifications, plead for attention. She notes that Grace's phone turns on fine—didn't Grace say last night that it must have died, that her battery was at only two percent?

"Are none of you going to say anything?" Zoe asks.

"There has to be a reasonable explanation," TJ says.

"Was Samira helping Alfred?" Julius says.

"Why would she?" Grace asks. She leaves Samira's room, the others on her heels. "More likely, he hid the phones in her room."

"Sitting out in the open?" TJ says. The group stands in a circle in the hallway.

"Not to mention the empty pouch," Zoe adds. "She clearly found the phones and took hers. Why didn't she tell us about them?"

"I don't care. I'm just glad to have my phone back. I need to call Rob," Grace says, already scrolling. "Does someone want to check with Danny how long until the police arrive?"

TJ is watching Grace with a furrowed brow. "I'll do it."

Grace doesn't acknowledge him. She walks toward her room, phone pressed to her ear. Why isn't she more disturbed?

"I want answers from Samira," Zoe calls.

"Then ask her yourself," Grace barks before closing her room's door behind her. Zoe pictures Grace in her office, using a charm offensive to get the plebs to do what she wants, and if that doesn't work, browbeating them.

"Ask me what?" Samira appears at the top of the stairs. Zoe rushes over, TJ and Julius not far behind. Samira still seems shaken but no longer stunned.

"What's the status on the tow truck?" Julius asks.

That's *his big question?* Zoe thinks. "Why were our phones in your room?" she blurts, pulling hers out of her pocket for proof. Julius and TJ do the same.

Samira flushes. "Oh my God. I'm so sorry, you guys. After we found Alfred, I came back to my room because I thought I was going to be sick. Our phones were sitting on the desk, but they weren't there this morning when I woke up. I meant to give them back to you, but I think I was in shock. They totally slipped my mind. I forgot." She starts to cry. "I forgot."

Zoe feels like an asshole and puts an arm around Samira's shoulders. "Any of us would've done the same," she soothes.

Still, something nags at Zoe. The hour since finding Alfred has been a blur, but did Samira go back to her room at any point? Wasn't Julius the only one who separated from the group, to get his "fresh air"? Didn't they all then run outside to the parking lot together? Who put the phones on Samira's desk if not Alfred? Zoe shakes her head. What does it matter?

Julius clears his throat. "The tow truck?"

"On its way." Samira wipes her eyes. "It should be here soon."

"I guess Alfred won't be paying for our replacement tires," Zoe mumbles.

"Zoe!" Samira scolds her. Zoe wants to snap back, *Am I supposed to feel sorry for the guy who was poisoning my food?*

For sixteen years, Alfred's actions have haunted Zoe. Every morning she wakes up to crushing, suffocating guilt. Addiction may run in her family, but Zoe's drinking never would have gotten out of hand if not for senior year. She knows from her recent stint in rehab that she has to take responsibility for her behavior, and she does. She also knows the guilt recedes only when she's buzzed.

How has she let it get this far? The GM at Saint Vincent all but forced her into a leave of absence. He said her alcohol use had made her work sloppy. If anyone else in the kitchen was this bad at their job, he said, Zoe would have told him to fire the person. Zoe had no rebuttal. The GM gently told her to get help, then return once she was feeling better.

Zoe had approached this weekend with magical—okay, delusional— thinking. She was never going to convince Alfred to confess. He was never going to turn himself in. Is his death enough to bring her closure, some semblance of peace? Or does she still owe it to herself to talk after all these years? She honestly doesn't see much point. Zoe's the only one who would get into trouble now. Because of her cowardice, he'll never face any consequences. Alfred Smettle gets to die a victim.

ACT
THREE

"What it boils down to is that
villains are not all black
and heroes are not all white.
There are grays everywhere."

—*Alfred Hitchcock*

THIRTY-EIGHT

Grace

Grace tells her husband and children she loves them, then ends the call. She stands there, in the middle of the hotel room, with her head bowed. Alone for the first time all day.

What has she done?

Grace has spent much of the past month operating from a place of fear, an emotion unknown to her prior to her becoming a parent. Motherhood has made her weak and vulnerable. When Grace is threatened, so is her entire family. To have her own life destroyed would also destroy the lives of her children. That she could not allow. Cannot allow.

The Hitchcock Hotel is surfacing memories Grace would rather leave buried. Take, for example, the day she met Alfred. They were both yawning through COM-whatever-it-was when he tapped her on the shoulder. She was drawn to him right away. He was tall and intense, handsome in an old-fashioned way. He wasn't embarrassed by his anachronistic passion, which was maybe what Grace liked most about him. Alfred had opinions—astute ones, perspectives she hadn't considered. Like Grace, he wasn't shy about sharing his beliefs. She has always been attracted to original thinkers. She can find herself curious about any topic, eager to learn more as long as the information comes from an enthusiastic source.

Alfred's magnetism was due to more than their shared love of Hitchcock. He had a darkness to him that intrigued Grace. That darkness didn't manifest in the boring, predictable ways it did in other guys their age: drugs and leather jackets and sleeping around and brushes with authority. No, Alfred's darkness was quiet, something he was intent on hiding until Grace pried it out of him, little by little. He confessed intrusive thoughts, brief fantasies of hurting himself and others. It wasn't the pain that fascinated him but the power. What was to stop him from jumping in front of a train? Pushing someone else in front of one? Maybe Grace should have been alarmed, but she'd had those same strange thoughts herself. She didn't want to act on them; the hypotheticals were what interested her. In Alfred she found a kindred spirit.

True crime didn't have a huge community back then. Alfred and Grace didn't know that a whole subset of people also delighted in the grisly. In 2004 they had only each other. They debated about cannibalism. Could they do it if they had to? They discussed blood oaths and serial killers and satanic rituals. Sometimes one of them would bring up the most bizarre topic they could think of, like bestiality, in an attempt to shock the other. It rarely worked. Grace and Alfred were both unshockable.

Maybe it was inevitable that their conversations turned carnal. Sex had so much depravity; or, given Grace's pesky virginity, movies and books at least hinted at its potential. BDSM, fetishes, caning. She discussed these things like she had a clue, annoyed that her lived experience came nowhere close to the wickedness of her talks with Alfred. The exchanges were intellectual at first but became flirtatious, until they got to the point where the sight of Alfred in class turned Grace on.

Grace thinks through almost every aspect of life before she acts, the exception being sex. The case with Alfred would set the precedent for a series of poor decisions that has continued all the way through her relationship with TJ. For all his darkness, Alfred was too polite to make the first move, so Grace straddled him one afternoon in the quad and kissed him. She hadn't intended a full-on make-out session, but it turned out she quite liked kissing him, so she kept doing it. The kiss went on for so long that multiple passing students whistled. Only when one yelled "Get a room" did Grace pull away. Alfred appeared dazed, had a dopey smile on his face. The next day, he texted to ask if she wanted to see *Rear Window* at the indie theater on Greet Street.

Grace and Alfred went to a matinee screening—one of the few times in college that either of them skipped class. They were alone in theater two and made it about thirty minutes keeping their hands to themselves before lust and hormones took over. There, with Jimmy Stewart and Grace Kelly bantering on the big screen behind her, Grace Liu finally had sex.

She could tell by Alfred's prowess that this was not his first time, which surprised her. So often he had described himself as having been an awkward loner in high school, though she now suspected that label had to do with how he'd felt more than how he was perceived. Wasn't everyone awkward in high school? Weren't they all lonely at one point or another? Alfred was a little nerdy, sure, but from Grace's observations, nerds were often the boys who fared best in high school. Nerds seemed safe and unthreatening to teenage girls, who had plenty of reasons to feel unsafe and threatened most of the time. If Alfred had kept the cannibal conversations to a minimum, he probably did fine.

Losing her virginity—a phrase she hated, because she hadn't lost anything—was not a watershed moment for Grace. Mostly she was relieved to have the event over with. Everyone had built it up so big in high school, yet she didn't know any girl who had enjoyed her first time. She'd been told that sex would hurt, that she might bleed a little afterward, but subsequent hookups would be better, more fun.

Grace tried not to talk much about Alfred with Samira and Zoe freshman year. She didn't want him to become a *thing*, but she must have mentioned him too often, because they insisted that she invite him to Samira's cousin's party one weekend. In the days leading up to the party,

Grace and Alfred had sex a second time, in his dorm room. For some reason he was living in a single, which was a little weird, but whatever. Her high school friends had been right. Sex got better after the first time, and Alfred made sure she got off—more than once. Even now, mortified as she is that their coupling happened, Grace still has to admit that Alfred was good in bed.

She was nervous the night he showed up at the house party, but Alfred got along well with the rest of the gang. The others tried giving him nicknames or calling him by his last name, but Grace always stuck with "Alfred," which meant the rest of them wound up calling him Alfred too.

During the two-week holiday break between fall and spring semesters, Grace went home to Albany while Alfred froze in the Chicago suburbs. He called or texted her nightly. She always answered, but she didn't like where these calls were headed. Grace had vowed to spend her four years in college hooking up with lots of guys, compensating for lost time. She was not going to pair off.

Alfred wanted the opposite experience. Grace would come to learn he had slept with two girls in high school, one of them many times though she had never wanted to be his girlfriend, for reasons he didn't share. Alfred had anticipated college as a turning point too. He wanted to have his first romantic relationship. He wanted to date Grace.

She put the kibosh on that idea real quick. Grace has never been known to sugarcoat, and this was no exception. "Nothing is wrong with you," she told Alfred. "I need time to myself." Movies always suggest that when you find the right person, you move mountains to make that relationship work. But Grace was in a season of life when she wouldn't settle down with the most eligible of bachelors, not even the models on the Abercrombie bag Samira had hung on their wall. Grace knew Alfred still had feelings for her, but she figured he would get over them. He did, for the most part. He said he'd rather be friends than nothing at all.

"Friends," she agreed. She should have run while she'd had the chance.

Grace leaves her hotel room, jogs down the steps, and finds TJ and Julius in the parlor. "What's going on?" she asks. They both stare out the window.

"Cops are here," TJ says.

Grace steps outside and takes in the police car with its flashing lights. The housekeeper is already standing in the parking lot, waiting for the officers to approach. Two cops climb out of the car. The driver is short and round, with a sunburn. The other wears aviators and a crew cut.

"Thank you so much for coming," Grace hears Danny say. The housekeeper squeezes their hands in hers.

Grace is not about to let this crone run the show. She walks over to the cops. The sunburned one speaks first, extending his hand and introducing himself. In her anxiety, Grace misses his name, but catches that the one with the crew cut is named Shaw.

"How many people are in the house?" Shaw asks, all business.

"I think, um, six, including me. Plus—plus Alfred," she stammers.

"That the name of the deceased?"

Grace nods. Danny butts in. "Alfred Warren Smettle."

"Anyone inside armed or otherwise dangerous?"

"I don't think so," Grace says. When Shaw tilts his head, she adds, "Not that I've seen."

"I wouldn't be so sure," Danny says. Grace grinds her teeth.

Shaw asks where the rest of the people are inside the hotel, then tells the sunburned cop to stay put while he sends them out. Grace, Danny, and his partner watch him go.

"What's the deal with the popped tires?" The remaining cop gestures with his chin at the cars around them.

"They were like that when we came outside this morning," Grace says. "Weird things have been happening all weekend."

The front door of the hotel creaks open. Grace turns to find TJ and

Julius standing on the porch, then descending the steps. Soon after, Samira and Zoe follow. Danny stands apart from the rest of them, her arms crossed against her chest. The short cop rocks back and forth on his heels just out of earshot.

Julius points at him. "What's Sunburn's deal? He fall asleep inside a tanning bed?" Zoe snickers.

Grace imagines Shaw alone in the house with Alfred. Will he put up the yellow caution tape like cops do on TV? Is the storage closet a crime scene now? Or will the police conclude that Alfred's death was an accident?

"Do you need us to make statements or something?" Grace asks Sunburn.

Sunburn shakes his head. "We're the first officers on the scene. A couple of detectives will be here soon. They're the ones who'll let you know how this is gonna go down."

Sure enough, a few minutes later, an unmarked vehicle drives up the lane. The car pulls into the lot, then parks in the spot farthest from the hotel. A man in his fifties climbs out of the passenger seat, one in his thirties out of the driver's side.

"How long do you think this'll take?" Grace asks as the group watches the detectives approach.

"Why?" Sunburn says. "You got somewhere to be?"

Grace then understands that she will not be leaving the Hitchcock Hotel anytime soon.

THIRTY-NINE

Zoe

Sunburn takes the detectives aside before they reach the group. Zoe can't make out everything he says, but he seems to be bringing them up to speed on the situation. When the detectives are satisfied, they nod and turn to the cluster of friends. They both wear khakis and black polo shirts with the precinct badge on the chest.

"Greetings," the older detective says. He has the hairiest arms Zoe has ever seen and is shaped like a gorilla. "I'm Sergeant Detective Agopian."

"And I'm Detective Gromowski," the younger one says. He smiles, revealing two rows of Invisalign braces. Zoe notes a wisp of a mustache and wonders how old the detective is.

"The third floor is off-limits while we process the scene," Agopian says. "For now, we need you folks to sit tight."

"I have to get home to my kids," Samira says.

"We'll move as quickly as we can, ma'am, but we'd appreciate your patience," Gromowski says. "We'll want to talk to each of you in due time."

Zoe and TJ share a grimace. Without warning, rain begins to fall fast and heavy. Julius squeals.

"Why don't we all go inside?" Danny says. "The screening room has enough seating for everyone."

Detective Agopian nods. "No conversations about the last twenty-four hours, please. Not until we've had a chance to speak with you."

The group runs toward shelter under the portico, then plods inside the house. Danny hangs back on the porch. "Can I talk to you a minute, detectives?"

Zoe doesn't like the sound of that. What ludicrous theories might the housekeeper try to plant in their minds? She's going to bias the investigation before the interviews have even begun. But Zoe can't think of an unsuspicious way to stop her from talking to them. Danny glares at Zoe until she files in after the others. The fivesome heads to the theater and slumps in the recliner chairs.

"I still can't believe he's dead," Grace murmurs. They all sit with the idea, waiting for it to sound less absurd. It never does.

"Should we tell his family?" Julius asks. It feels like his cancer confession happened three days ago.

"I don't think he has any," Zoe says.

"They've all died too," Grace says.

"What's going to happen to this place?" Samira asks.

"Plus all the birds?" TJ adds.

"He was so young."

"Too young."

"Should we plan a service?"

"Would he have wanted one?"

No one knows. They feel guilty for not knowing.

"I can't believe he was spying on us," Zoe says, though she easily can. She studies the room around them, searching for hiding spots and planted cameras.

The door to the movie room opens. Sunburn walks in, with Danny by his side. The housekeeper moves to the last row of seats and chooses the chair farthest from the rest of the group. She sits, then crosses both her arms and legs.

"What's the update?" TJ asks Sunburn.

"We're all going to hang out in here, per Ms. Danielson's suggestion." Zoe has no idea to whom the cop is referring until she follows Sunburn's gaze to Danny.

"So you're on babysitting duty?" Zoe asks.

Sunburn frowns. "Everyone has a role to play. The detectives are doing their thing upstairs. My partner is calling the funeral parlor." Samira lets out a soft whimper.

"The funeral parlor?" Grace says. "Meaning it was an accident?"

Sunburn cocks his head. "Not necessarily. We have an arrangement with the parlor owners. They take the deceased to the morgue for autopsies. You've gotta make do in a small town." He sucks his teeth. Zoe watches Grace recoil at the sound. "Do you have reason to believe his death wasn't an accident?"

Danny spews a bitter "Ha!" from the back row.

Didn't the detectives just say no talking about the last twenty-four hours? Sunburn is already failing at the job.

"I hope it was," Grace says. "Losing a friend is hard enough. I don't know what I'd do if his death turned out to be a violent one."

Why did you bring me here? Zoe wants to shout at her. *What do you want from me?*

"Sure is a tragic coincidence," Sunburn says. Zoe is about to ask what is, when the cop continues. "People keep falling to their deaths in this town."

Zoe glances at the others. They all look as surprised as she feels.

"Word gets around in a community this size," Sunburn says. "What else is there to do here besides gossip?"

Hours later, the two detectives make an appearance in the home theater. In all that time, the group has been allowed to leave only to use the bathroom in the game room. Even that was with Sunburn's supervision. Danny was given permission to go to the kitchen to make lunch for everyone after Sunburn locked the rest of them inside the theater; he accompanied her. Zoe feels the officer is enjoying his job a little too much. She bets this is the most interesting day of the small-town cop's career.

"Thanks again for your patience," Detective Agopian says. "We're ready to conduct the interviews."

"What about Alfred?" Samira blurts. "How much longer will he have to lie up there in the closet?" She wipes a tear before it dribbles down her cheek.

"The funeral home folks are on their way with the hearse. Your friend is in good hands," Agopian says softly. Then: "Who wants to go first?"

Zoe raises her hand—partly to get out of the room, partly because she figures the more she cooperates, the less suspicious she'll seem.

She follows the detectives into the parlor. Zoe sneaks a peek out the windows, but there's nothing to see except the parking lot full of cars with slashed tires. A streak of lightning illuminates the gray clouds. A clap of thunder follows. The detectives lead Zoe to the dining room, where they've pushed a couple of tables together. They sit side by side. Zoe half expected one of them to circle the table, use the intimidation tactics from TV shows.

They ask Zoe a number of questions about herself—first the standard stuff, like name and job and how she came to be at the Hitchcock Hotel this weekend. Next they want her to tell them what Alfred was like, to run them through the last few days in minute detail. Zoe is honest and forthcoming about almost everything—the missing phones, the slashed tires, the discovery of the attic and, most important, the vents. The detectives don't react to the vent revelation at all, so they must have been up to the attic already.

"How are you feeling about all of this?" Gromowski asks.

Zoe gapes at the detectives. "How am I feeling?" she says, incredulous. "Peachy, aside from the tragic death of my friend."

"Interesting choice of word," Agopian says to Gromowski.

"'Tragic'?" Zoe asks.

"'Friend,'" says Agopian.

"Not the one I would use to describe a person I suspected of poisoning me," Gromowski says.

They both study Zoe. She licks her lips. Who told them? It must have been Danny. Had she also mentioned Zoe's drinking problem? Zoe's cheeks burn.

"Force of habit," she says. "But while we're on the topic of poison, I found antifreeze in one of the cabinets." She gestures with her chin at the kitchen behind them. "You can go in there right now and find the bottle. I left it where it was."

"I think I'll do that." Gromowski rises from his seat and disappears into the kitchen. Zoe listens in tense silence as Gromowski bangs the pots and pans, searching. She feels Agopian's gaze on her, hunting for clues, waiting for her to give up something that will lead to his big break. Zoe resists the urge to air out her armpits. Beads of sweat form there, despite the chilly temperature outside.

A few minutes later, Gromowski's head pops out of the kitchen. "Can't find it. Maybe you can show me."

Zoe sighs but does as she's asked. Whereas the kitchen was airy and welcoming before, now that she shares the space with the detective it's claustrophobic, oppressive. Gromowski is wearing too much aftershave, the musk so strong that she almost runs from the room. Instead, she marches to the sink on the far wall. She runs her palm along the cool metal, bends down to open the cabinet, and moves a few jugs of dish soap out of the way. Haughtily, she says, "Right here."

She squints. The silver plastic bottle is gone.

Maybe she misremembers which cabinet the bottle was in. Zoe rummages around some more, her search getting sloppier as her desperation grows. Gromowski leans against the countertop opposite her, watching the spectacle with crossed arms. With each new cabinet door she opens, Zoe feels his skepticism solidifying.

"Where did he put it?" she mumbles, scrambling through the timeline. She found the bottle this morning. (Was that only this morning?) If Alfred was already dead by then, who moved the bottle?

Zoe takes Gromowski through this logic as they return to their seats in the dining room. "I made breakfast for the group at nine. That's when I found the bottle. I even showed it to everyone around the table—you can ask them. Like I told you before, we found Alfred's body around ten thirty."

Zoe's mind grabs at impossible solutions. What if Alfred isn't dead? What if he's hiding in the hotel walls right this minute? She knows this line of thinking is silly, but imagining that Alfred is alive is easier than the alternative—which is that one of her friends took the bottle. Or maybe it was Danny. But why? Why cover for a dead man? Maybe someone's planning to poison her again. Zoe vows not to eat or drink until she leaves this godforsaken place.

The detectives don't appear worried about the missing bottle of antifreeze. They probably don't believe her. Zoe is sick and tired of being discredited, of people thinking they know better than she does. Nobody ever listens to her.

"Do you remember Mr. Smettle sharing a story about the previous owners of the house? A couple you and your friends referred to as the Olds?" Agopian says.

The name sounds ridiculous coming out of the mouth of a fiftysomething man. Zoe nods. "Alfred said the old woman shoved grass down his throat until he died. Terrible way to go."

Ever since Alfred told them the story, Zoe hasn't been able to shake the scene from her head. She puts herself in the old man's place. Soiled bedsheets wet and stinking of urine. Gnawing hunger, a parched mouth. Her body turning on itself, feeding off itself. Did the old man die of suffocation or starvation in the end? Did Alfred say? Death must have been a relief.

Zoe much prefers to imagine herself as the old woman—with her simmering hostility and slowly forming plan. Her husband's cries, his pleas. The knowledge that she would never be subjected to his cruelty again. The power coursing through a body formerly invisible. The blades of grass between her fingers as she plucked them by the fistful. Did she want him to die fast or slow? What were her last words to the old man? Did she oink at him? Bellow, *I'll show you a pig*?

"Do you have any theories about who left the grass on your pillow yesterday morning?" Agopian asks.

Zoe's mouth falls open. "Who told you about that?"

"The housekeeper said she saw you drag Samira into your room, that you were yelling about grass on your pillow."

Zoe grits her teeth. "When I went to show Samira, the grass was gone. I couldn't have been out of my room more than a couple minutes."

"What was Samira's reaction?" Gromowski asks.

Zoe flushes. "I don't think she believed me."

"Why's that?" Agopian says.

For the thousandth time, Zoe swallows her pride, feeling about two feet tall. *I'm never drinking again,* she thinks. She hates herself for how often she's made that promise. *This time I mean it. This time I'm done.*

"She probably thought I was hungover and seeing things," she manages.

"Why didn't you report the incident to Alfred?" Gromowski asks.

Zoe stares at the men. "I assumed he was the one who put it there."

The detectives exchange a glance.

"Samira reported an intruder breaking into her room while she was in the shower yesterday afternoon," Gromowski says. "She told Alfred and the housekeeper that when she looked up and screamed, the person ran away."

Zoe's eyes bug out.

"Judging by your expression, I guess she hasn't told you about the incident?"

Zoe shakes her head. Why is Samira keeping things from her? Does she not trust Zoe? Did she tell everyone else?

"Samira has been off this weekend," Zoe says.

"How so?" Agopian asks.

"Sort of distant. Kinda snappy. Samira doesn't usually snap at people," Zoe explains.

Agopian scribbles something in his notebook. "Why do you think Mr. Smettle wished you harm, Zoe?"

Zoe tries to project surprise. "Who said I think that?"

"You don't believe he was putting antifreeze in your food for no reason, do you?"

Zoe's mind feels slow and thick. She knows she's being outmaneuvered, cannot keep up with these detectives. She's so tired of the lies, of trying to keep her story straight. Why not come clean once and for all? She's been keeping Alfred's secret long enough. He's dead now. He can't hurt her anymore. Zoe thinks of the missing antifreeze bottle. A cold blade of fear slices through her. She's not safe. Not yet.

"Alfred made a pass at me in college," Zoe lies. "I turned him down."

"Do you think someone would hold on to their anger over a sexual rejection for sixteen years?"

Zoe recoils at the use of the word "sexual" in reference to Alfred. She still judges Grace for her collegiate lapse in judgment. "You didn't know him."

"Ms. Allen, we need you to help us," Agopian says. "You do understand how this appears, don't you? The fact that the man you claim was poisoning you has turned up dead?"

Zoe takes a deep, shaky breath.

FORTY

Grace

In the home theater, Grace drums her fingers on the arm of her recliner. Maybe she should come clean about the affair and Alfred's threats right away. The last thing she wants is the police digging into her. People don't need much to turn on you. She witnessed that at Reville.

Julius told her what he'd done mere hours after he'd done it. Grace couldn't believe it at first. Julius wasn't the snitching type, and though he often acted rashly, he'd never acted *that* rashly. She demanded a blow-by-blow of his conversation with Dr. Scott, how the professor had ended their meeting.

"I don't know," Julius had cried, brushing his long blond curls out of his eyes. "He has a killer poker face. Promise me you won't tell Alfred. Please, Gracey, please."

Grace is not, by nature, a forgiving woman. She descends from a long line of proud grudge holders. Her father took a money dispute with his sister to his grave. Her mother still remembers every teacher and childhood friend who wronged Grace. Mercy was not highly valued in the Liu household.

Nevertheless, Grace promised—less out of a sense of duty to Julius and more because bending people to your will is easier when you've done them a favor. (Alfred liked to think this was a lesson he'd taught Grace, when, in fact, the opposite was true.) She was so furious with Julius for his betrayal, for his inability to think through the consequences of his actions, that she didn't speak to him for weeks. How could he do such a thing? She might've shown a tiny bit of sympathy if he'd ratted Alfred out because of moral compunction, but Julius had none. This was petty vengeance, plain and simple. Beef or no beef, there are lines you don't cross in a friendship. Alfred was also to blame—for getting Julius into trouble with his father. Grace thought less of them both after that day.

The blue house was strange that evening. Most of them were their normal selves. Zoe was blasting music, Samira was asking her to turn it down so she could study, TJ was reading a novel with his feet hanging over the back of the couch, and Alfred was typing away at his computer. Only she and Julius were off, anxious, he flashing her covert glances, she ignoring them. She resented Julius for pulling her into his secret keeping, for making her complicit. She too had done something wrong.

For one week, nothing out of the ordinary happened—one never-ending, torturous week of beer bonging and whisper-laughing in the library and waiting in line at two a.m. for a bagel sandwich. All the things Grace loved had been stripped of joy. She went through the motions, waiting for the other shoe to drop.

Then, on Tuesday morning, Dr. Scott asked Alfred to stay after class. Grace's throat ached so badly she couldn't swallow. She was responsible by association, because of the mere fact that she was seated next to Alfred in the first row. She had expected him to tense, to show some sign of fear, but he hadn't. Why would he? He had never been in trouble with a teacher before. He was the head of the film club. Dr. Scott was the club's advisor. This wouldn't be the first time their professor had asked to see Alfred in his office. Alfred probably thought he wanted to go over the next month of screenings or to discuss some administrative tasks. Grace capped her pen and put away her notebook. She allowed herself to pretend, for a moment, that that was all Dr. Scott wanted. She let herself believe their lives were not about to change forever. Grace picked up her backpack and walked out the door. She left Alfred there to face his fate alone.

Hours later he returned to the blue house. Grace was sitting on the couch, pretending to watch *Lost* with the others, when the door opened. There stood Alfred, stunned, face drained of color. Grace's pulse throbbed hard enough in her neck that she was sure Alfred would be able to see it clear across the room. He said nothing, kept blinking.

"What's wrong, Alfred?" she asked.

The others noticed him then too. Samira muted the show.

"Hey," Zoe yelped. "We're not recording this." (Ah, the days before streaming, when they'd watched TV live with the rest of the country.)

"Not feeling well," Alfred murmured as he shuffled to his room.

Grace rose from the beanbag chair. It had a basketball print on it— Grace had played the sport in high school. She'd brought the chair with her from Albany to Reville, wanting a touch of home in the mountains. All four years of college—from the dorms to an apartment to this house—she had made room for the beanbag, despite its bulk and weight. In that moment it struck her as juvenile, even tacky. She was not a child anymore.

"I'll go," she said. The others nodded, satisfied. Samira unmuted the show. How little it took for them to be convinced all would be okay. Most of them had never faced predicaments more serious than applying for college or getting told off by local cops for drinking in the park back in their hometowns. It wouldn't occur to them to be worried. They had done nothing wrong.

Besides Julius. He stared, wide-eyed, at the TV screen, faking enthrallment. Grace knew he was terrified. She also knew that since Alfred hadn't flown through the door and wrapped his hands around Julius's throat, Dr. Scott had kept his word. He had left Julius out of the conversation. This felt unfair to Grace. Somehow Julius's seemed the worse transgression. Maybe she *was* still a child, weighing loyalty and friendship above all else.

Grace walked to Alfred's room, knocked softly, then entered without waiting for permission she knew wouldn't come. Alfred was facedown on his bed, arms by his sides. She sat next to him on the mattress.

"What happened?" she asked.

For a while Alfred said nothing. Then, without lifting his face off the bed, he mumbled, "I'm done."

"Done with what?" Grace resented having to play dumb, something she never did but Julius had resigned her to. Another thing for which she would not soon forgive him.

"Scott knows," Alfred said. "He knows about Easy A."

Though Julius had already told her as much, Grace's breath still caught when she heard it confirmed. "Jesus, Alfred," she managed. "What did you say?"

He lifted his head. His cheeks were streaked with tears, voice thick with snot. Grace was moved by how young he seemed, how young they all were. "I denied it at first, but Scott had done his homework. He had all these essays on his desk. Highlighted the similarities in the language. Talked to some of the students too. They admitted to cheating, even if they didn't know who Easy A was."

Grace swallowed. "How did he know it was you, then?"

"One of the students told him. Scott wouldn't say which one." Alfred paused. "How would I even find out at this point? There have been hundreds of essays."

"Shit," Grace said.

Alfred continued. "He kept going on and on about how disappointed he was. I pointed out that I'm a first-time offender, so shouldn't I just get a warning? But Scott says there have to be consequences because of how widespread the cheating was. They have to deter anyone else from doing this. Everyone who bought an essay is going to fail the class." Grace thought of Zoe. "I have a meeting with Scott, the dean, and the provost next week to determine my punishment."

"Shit," Grace said again.

Alfred chewed his lip. "They said I can bring a support person to the meeting. The person doesn't have to say or do anything. They're there to be on my side."

Don't ask, don't ask, don't ask.

He looked up. "Will you be my person, Grace?"

She smiled, thinking of how to phrase a rejection without alienating him. "I so wish I could, Alfred." She squeezed his hand, then held on to it. His eyes shone. "I don't think I should be anywhere near this investigation. Do you? Maybe we can get Samira to go. She's better at this stuff than I am."

This stuff being basic human compassion. Grace felt like a lowlife, but she stood her ground.

Alfred nodded, then smothered his face in his pillow. Whatever he said next came out too muffled for Grace to understand. She pulled the pillow away from him. "Say again?"

"I don't want to tell Samira," he moaned. "Or the others. They're going to think I'm a bad person."

"They won't," Grace protested. "You were doing this to pay your tuition. People have done far worse. They'll understand. Samira will be there for you at the hearing."

Grace was wrong. Squeaky-clean Samira did not understand. She told Alfred she was sorry for what he was going through, but she wasn't okay with defending someone who had spent half of his college career running an organized-cheating ring. This was not a onetime lapse in judgment.

What Samira didn't say but Grace knew she was thinking, because Grace was thinking it too, was that she didn't want Alfred's hearing to somehow affect her job prospects. By then, the end of the fall semester was weeks away. Samira, like the rest of them, had five months to find a job. Her résumé had been perfected, interview answers memorized. Her list of potential employers was the length of her arm. Was it likely that these employers would even know she had attended one academic misconduct hearing? No, but who knew if such a thing would be recorded in her file? Samira was hoping to get a job as a therapist's assistant or in social work. Ethics mattered. She wasn't going to chance messing up her own future because Alfred had messed up his. Maybe she would have taken the risk for Grace or Zoe, but not for Alfred.

One by one, he begged each of them to attend the hearing with him. Zoe had to work a lunch shift that day. TJ would be in class. Julius was heading home to "spend time with his family" in New York. Alfred had never bothered to make friends outside their pod of six. He probably hadn't thought he would need to. On the morning of the hearing, Grace watched guiltily as Alfred trudged out of the blue house alone.

She was eating a peanut butter and jelly sandwich when he texted to say he'd been expelled.

FORTY-ONE

Julius

Julius joins the detectives at the dining table. He sits back in the chair and crosses his legs, resting his right foot on his left knee. "Let's do this," he says. His father would call him a dimwit for speaking to the police without legal representation present, but Julius knows what he's doing. He doesn't need a lawyer.

He answers their questions about his name and its spelling, where he lives, what he does for work. (Neither of them reacts, thankfully, when he says "philanthropist." At least that title is less humiliating than "socialite," which is more accurate in terms of hours devoted to a role.)

"We'd like to talk to you about the events of this weekend. Can you walk us through them? From the time you arrived at the hotel up until right now?"

Julius tries to focus, but he finds his attention wandering. Why isn't anyone sitting upstairs with Alfred? Is his body stiffening, like Danny said? Are his hands cold? Shouldn't the tow truck be here by now? Samira said she called ages ago. Maybe she sent it to the wrong address or, in her haze of shock, she thought she called but didn't. She wouldn't lie to them, would she? Say she'd called when she hadn't? Julius thinks of the phone pouches in her room.

He had planned to tell the detectives what Samira told the group—that her failure to mention the phones was an honest mistake—and leave it at that. Instead, he goes a step further. "Something about Samira's story doesn't add up for me," Julius says.

"What do you mean?" Agopian purses his lips.

"How did the phones get to her room in the first place? She said they weren't there when she woke up, which means Alfred would have put them there this morning. But he must've been . . ." Julius trails off. "By then. Maybe Danny was the one to do it? But why?"

"Do you think Samira could have been the one hiding the phones all along?" Gromowski asks.

Julius almost laughs. "She would have had to be in cahoots with Alfred. We found his phone in his room."

"Maybe she left it there to throw everyone off the scent," Agopian suggests.

Julius hasn't considered that, because the idea of Samira as a criminal mastermind is so preposterous. She doesn't appear to have changed much over the years—still the same earnest woman he knew in college. That doesn't mean she's not hiding something. Julius himself is, after all.

"Let's talk about the perfect-murder conversation at dinner Thursday night," Gromowski says.

Julius wonders if it was Danny or Zoe who told them about that. "What do you want to know?"

"We've been told that you proposed staging the murder as an accident. Making it seem like someone had fallen a great distance. Perhaps down a staircase."

Julius tries to keep his voice level. "What's your question?"

"Do you realize how closely your response matches the circumstances in which we found Mr. Smettle?"

Julius toys with the beads around his neck, then pulls his hand away when he sees Gromowski eyeing them. He wishes he hadn't worn the necklace today, but he can't take it off now. "Do you think I'm that big of an idiot? To tell future witnesses how I plan to murder our friend before committing said murder?"

"Some'd say idiotic. Others'd say bold," Agopian says.

"Why would I want Alfred dead in the first place?" Julius sputters.

"When we asked Zoe who in the group fought the most with Alfred, she said you," Gromowski says.

Julius's mouth falls open. "Sure, back in college. Alfred never liked me, so we fell into this one-upmanship. That was a show for the others. It meant nothing. I held no ill will toward him."

He's going to have to tell the detectives about his offer to invest. Zoe was there yesterday morning, eavesdropping. She might've already told them. "In fact, I asked Alfred if he would consider taking an investment from me as a way to bury the hatchet. Clean slate."

"Did he accept?"

Julius shakes his head. "He said he wanted to do this on his own. His days of going into business with a friend were over."

Gromowski rubs the back of his neck. "How do you mean?"

Julius hesitates. *Oh, what the hell? How could it make things worse?*

Alfred's expulsion took effect immediately. One day he was meeting with the provost; the next, he was packing his belongings. Julius had told Alfred the reason he couldn't go with him to the hearing was because he was going home to New York. Instead, he got on the highway, drove east for thirty miles, then sat in the parking lot of the first McDonald's he found. He couldn't bear to watch Alfred be punished, but he also couldn't bear to face his family. *(Pussy.)* The indifference of his mother, the silence of his father. His sister had decamped for the West Coast a long time ago. Julius had no one in New York. His friends at Reville had become his adopted family—yet look how he treated them.

Julius stayed overnight in a rinky-dink hotel, then returned to campus first thing the next morning with some contrived excuse about his mother falling ill and not wanting to get him sick. The others didn't push. They knew his parents sucked. He went straight to his bedroom and closed the door.

He spent most of the next two days like that, with the door closed, pretending to study, which no one believed he was doing but they left him to anyway, assuming he was licking family wounds in private. The truth was he couldn't bear to face Alfred. Julius was to blame for Alfred's getting kicked out of school one lousy semester before graduating. What Alfred had stirred up between Julius and his dad was shitty—no question. In terms of consequences, though, Julius's retaliation had been much worse. His dad would talk to him again in a few months, but Alfred's expulsion was permanent. Julius should've waited for his anger to subside, then talked the situation through with Alfred. Too late for that now.

Avoiding Alfred entirely wasn't possible; Julius had to eat. At dinnertime, Zoe, Grace, and Alfred sat at the dining table while Julius skulked in the kitchen.

"Where will you go?" Zoe asked.

"Home to Chicago, I guess," Alfred said. "I'll move in with my mom until I figure it out."

"Why don't you stay here?" Grace suggested. "You could get a job in town. Now that you don't have tuition, your expenses won't be bad."

Julius still remembers the way Alfred glowered at Grace. "I can't ever show my face in this town again. What if I run into the provost or the dean at the cafeteria? At the grocery store? All the professors will know soon if they don't already. I'm sure an article is being written for the *Reville* as we speak." (He was right. An article unmasking Easy A would be published in the student newspaper one week later.) "The entire student body is going to know I've been expelled. I'm supposed to watch the rest of you finish senior year, put on your robes, and throw your caps in the air while I stand around like a loser flunkie? No, thanks. I'll pass."

"It was just an idea," Grace mumbled.

"I've had about enough of your ideas, Grace," Alfred snapped. He rose from the dining table and shoved past Julius to throw his empty bowl in the sink. Grace and Zoe jumped when the porcelain hit the stainless steel. Grace chewed her lip, worried.

Julius was surprised Alfred didn't lay into Grace harder during those couple of days—or, if he did, Julius wasn't within earshot. After all, Easy A was Grace's brainchild, not Alfred's. She was the one who wrote the essays while he found the customers, secured payment, and delivered the goods. Julius was the only one in the house who knew of Grace's involvement—because he'd happened upon a Word document on her laptop with the name of one of their classmates at the top. The essay was titled "The Suspension of Disbelief in Film" and had two paragraphs written. Julius sat on Grace's bed, waiting. Upon finding Julius in her room, with her computer in his lap, Grace had rattled off an excuse, but she was flustered. When Julius threatened to share his theory with the rest of the group, Grace admitted what she and Alfred were up to.

That was why Grace was so furious with Julius when he told her about the talk with Dr. Scott. Grace was in an absolute panic that she would soon be found out too, that her fate would be the same as Alfred's. Grace had her entire future mapped out, and now Julius had ruined it. (Julius wanted to point out that she had ruined it herself by cheating, but he sensed that Grace might stab him with a kitchen knife if he spoke his mind.)

Instead of letting her go down for her sins, Alfred had saved Grace. He had sheltered her from the consequences of their scheme. He would go home to his mother while Grace would graduate and earn six figures at her first job out of college. Julius knew Alfred was in love with Grace, but he had a hard time imagining loving anyone enough to sacrifice himself like that. It made Julius like Alfred a teeny bit more.

Not enough to come clean, though. Alfred could be unpredictable. Most of Julius's quarrels with him were nothing more than feisty exchanges of words. A few times, though, Alfred had gotten physical. Once, he got in Julius's face, screaming until his cheeks turned red and spit stuck to his bottom lip. Another time, he chucked a mug at Julius's head from across the room. Julius had moved at the last minute and the mug bounced on the carpet at his feet. Yet another time, Alfred tackled Julius to the ground during a beer pong tournament in the backyard, though as soon as Julius was down, Alfred got up and walked away. That's not to say Julius stood by passively during these attacks. He couldn't beat Alfred on size or strength, but he devised his own ways to give as good as he got. Julius's combat highlights included smashing an ice-cream cone in Alfred's face, as well as leaving a used condom on Alfred's pillow. Since neither of them was ever seriously hurt by these shenanigans, the rest of the housemates took the violence in stride. They'd roll their eyes at the boys being boys. Julius walked away from that relationship with the understanding that, while Alfred typically had a long fuse, when the fuse was lit you'd better run for cover. Especially if you were the one who had lit it.

In the end, Julius decides to keep all this history from the detectives and leave the past in the past. He's embarrassed by how he behaved back then and isn't eager to relive those memories. Nor does he want to put Grace at risk again by bringing up Easy A. Nothing would happen to her—it's not like the school's going to revoke her degree—but what would be gained by divulging these stories? None of this is relevant to the investigation. If Grace wants to bring this stuff up to the cops, he'll let her do so. For perhaps the first time in his life, Julius keeps his mouth shut.

Detective Gromowski is still peering at him, waiting for Julius to explain his comment about Alfred starting a business with a friend.

"He founded our campus film club," Julius explains. Not a business, but whatever. They'll assume the spoiled rich kid doesn't know the difference. "We were all supposed to run the club together, but nobody else pulled their weight. Not the way Alfred did, anyway. I know he found that frustrating."

Alfred did complain about these things back then, but Julius always suspected he loved being in control. No one else picked better movies or led more riveting ("riveting") discussions than Alfred. The rest of them were slowing him down. "You're killing me," Alfred once yelled when they'd forgotten to reserve the screening room.

Little did you know, Julius thinks.

FORTY-TWO

TJ

When TJ sits down with the detectives, for the first time in months he's not thinking about his own problems. He's not thinking about the un-smiling man or the conversation with Julius that needs to happen urgently. He's not calculating how many years he'll spend behind bars if he doesn't fix the mess he created—and soon. He's thinking about Grace. Specifically, he's thinking about Grace sneaking into the closet last night.

What the hell was she doing in there, hours before Alfred's body was found?

Grace's whereabouts last night aren't the only issue. He's still shocked by what he learned from Julius and Zoe this morning. Grace was part of Easy A? She let Alfred take the fall while she stood by and did nothing? What kind of woman has he been carrying on with? What else is she keeping from him?

TJ puts his hand in his pocket and fingers his phone. He still hasn't told her about the audio file. He doesn't want to betray her, but if he hides the affair and Alfred's blackmail from the cops now, that will make him seem guilty later if the secrets come out.

Would Grace do the same for him? Risk an arrest and prison time to save his hide? She's been cold and distant toward him all day. It almost seemed as if the two of them really hadn't spoken in the past decade and a half. Maybe she was trying to be more discreet, like she said they needed to be. The thought does nothing to tame the burning in TJ's chest. He pops a TUMS into his mouth.

"You look worried," Agopian says.

TJ glances up. The detectives have been observing him. He coughs. "My friend just died. Of course I am."

"Can you think of anyone who might want to see Alfred dead?" Gromowski asks bluntly.

I can come up with one or two people.

TJ shakes his head. Already he's lied to the detectives, which is definitely a crime. One crime might be excused as poor judgment, but once you've committed two or more, does that make you a criminal? Why did this have to happen today of all days, now that he's worked up the guts to speak to Julius? He had a whole goddamn speech prepared too. How long does he have to wait? Until Alfred's been carted away? He can't stand peeking over his shoulder every day.

Agopian speaks up. "Do you always check out employee backgrounds before you check into a hotel?"

TJ squints at him. The detective must be referring to the questions TJ asked Danny about the chef at dinner last night, the ones about his wife and her job. Has Danny told them? Could it have been Zoe or Julius? Is the chef here somewhere? "I'm a Reville alum," TJ says. "I'm curious how the school has changed since I graduated."

Agopian scrutinizes him. TJ knows the look because he's given it a hundred times himself. *We're not so different, you and I,* TJ tries to communicate with a helpful smile. *We're both in the business of protection.*

He wants to tell them. He should tell them.

The detectives let an uncomfortable silence fall over the room. TJ struggles not to fidget. He doesn't want to appear guilty.

Finally, Gromowski says, "We appreciate your cooperation, TJ. Just a couple more questions."

TJ nods, relieved that this nightmare is almost over.

"Are you aware that the Hitchcock Hotel has security cameras?" Gromowski asks.

"No, but that doesn't surprise me, given the spying vents Alfred had installed," TJ says. "Have you seen them? Up in the attic?"

"We have," Gromowski says. "I'd like to focus on the cameras, though. There's one in each common room of the hotel. The parlor, the home theater, here in the dining room, the game room, the lobby."

TJ nods. What's his point?

"Mr. Smettle also had cameras on the exterior of the property. For example, one overlooks the parking lot."

TJ's heart stops.

Agopian clears his throat. "We've watched the footage, TJ. What we're wondering is: why did you slash all those tires?"

FORTY-THREE

Grace

At the dining table Grace sizes up the detectives while they do the same to her. She's not worried about the young one with the Invisalign braces, but the older one appears grizzled, seasoned—a man who could pull off a thick mustache and cowboy boots if he wanted, which he wouldn't. With his polished shoes, ironed shirt, and close haircut, he could be a veteran. Grace almost asks if he served, but she wants to avoid small talk.

Unlike Samira, Grace doesn't feel the need to fill a silence. Unlike Zoe, she doesn't run her mouth. There's no reason for her to speak first. They brought her here, so let them talk. She needs to even out the power dynamic at the table. She can wait.

"More than one of your friends here described you as the leader of the group in college," Agopian starts. "Would you say that's a fair characterization?"

Grace considers the question. "Yes." They wait for her to elaborate. She does not.

"Can you give us some examples?" Gromowski prods.

"I was the first named on the house lease senior year, the one who collected rent money," Grace says. "I organized spring break trips and

Friday night plans. I helped with their internship applications and final papers. I think I happened to be the most capable one in the group."

Grace does not mention her time as Easy A, the hundreds of essays she churned out night after sleepless night with nothing more than a mug of coffee to keep her awake. It still irks her that Alfred received all the credit for a business that was her idea. He was just a gopher and, later, a scapegoat. Without her, Alfred would have delivered easy B's. Yes, his short-term career prospects were ruined by the expulsion, but Grace knew he was thrilled to have something to hold over her, a way of forcing her to remain in his life. More than once, Grace had considered turning herself in, if only so she would never have to cater to one of Alfred Smettle's laborious whims again. But then she remembered the plan. Analyst for Goldman right after school, get poached by a hedge fund a few years later. She would keep her eye on the prize. Alfred was a nuisance. Nuisances she could tolerate. Failure she could not.

That's not to say she didn't grind her teeth when she found out about the Hitchcock Hotel. That too had been her idea, though she would never devote her life to such an asinine project. She and Alfred had been hanging out on the quad one afternoon freshman year when Grace told him about Hitchcock's infamous dinner parties. At one, Hitchcock gave each of his guests a shovel to dig up a human skull that was supposedly buried in his backyard. Alfred was floored by this anecdote, couldn't stop talking about its cheekiness, its fun. Thanks to his mom, he had a pretty deep repertoire of Hitchcock trivia, so Grace was always pleased when she taught him something new.

"Imagine attending a dinner party hosted by Hitch," Alfred had crowed.

"Imagine if he ran his own hotel," Grace had countered. "How creepy would that place be?"

Alfred's eyes had lit up, but he said no more, tucking away the idea for well over a decade. Grace scrutinizes the dining room. He had executed her vision satisfactorily, though she would have done it differently (better).

During her film studies classes in college, Grace sometimes wondered if Hitchcock's wife, Alma, ever watched his films and thought she could have done better. Alma had had a film career of her own, after all, before she met Hitchcock. By 1925 she had built enough of a name to be profiled in a London magazine. Being a wife and mother didn't slow her down either. A few years after the profile piece, a movie she wrote was one of the biggest hits at the UK box office. Much of her early work made it to the screen without any contributions whatsoever from Hitchcock. As her husband's fame grew in the fifties, though, she receded into the background. She began to focus on Hitchcock's career instead of her own. One Hitchcock biographer theorized that Alma understood how much harder it would be to climb to those same heights as a woman and decided to settle for a collaborator role instead. Over the decades, she worked on Hitchcock's films as a writer, casting producer, script supervisor, and editorial advisor—and those were just the professional roles. Hitchcock was a notoriously fragile and anxious man. Alma was the one who kept his head on straight. Her husband never hesitated to give Alma credit where credit was due, both privately and publicly, but still . . . How many moviegoers know Alma's name? How many understand that without her there would be no Master of Suspense? Grace believes that mastery is seldom achieved by a single person alone in a room. Maybe that's a womanly thought. Doesn't make it untrue.

Gromowski breaks the silence. "Just so you're aware, we know about the affair."

Grace blinks, trying to catch up, to keep the betrayal off her face. Did TJ tell them? How could he? He wouldn't. TJ is devoted to her. He would marry her tomorrow if she agreed—he told her as much last week. A small part of her thinks his dedication is sweet, but she also finds his inability to get a handle on his emotions pitiful. Grace was raised by parents who consider fits of passion a character flaw. The sharing of feelings is fine in small and controlled doses, but they take umbrage at the "oversensitivity" of American culture today. Grace's parents believe in meritocracy, scoff at the notion of participation trophies. They are about competence, responsibility, and logic. Grace has a hard time imagining either of them getting swept away by emotion or romance. When she was a teenager, she once asked her mom if she was happy in her marriage. "Happy?" her mother said as if it were a preposterous concept. "You make a commitment, you see it through." Grace is more scared to tell her parents than her husband about the affair.

Life has gotten simpler in the last few hours and is soon to get simpler still. Once she and TJ get away from this place, she will end the relationship. He's in too deep, while she intended only to wade around the shallow end. Grace knows what TJ thinks of her, though he's too spineless to say it to her face.

How can you live with yourself?

Here's what Grace has to say to that. TJ's longest relationship to date was two years. Two years is a honeymoon. Two years in, you still believe your partner's flaws are quirks. Quirks might be eliminated or improved. There's a reason marriage is sometimes referred to as being in the trenches. Long-term monogamy is not for the weak of heart. The adversary is also your comrade. It's the two of you against the world, but also you against him. TJ has no idea what that's like.

That's not to say Rob is a bad guy. On the contrary, he's a loving father and husband, an exceedingly decent man. He does his fair share of the parenting and housework. He doesn't make nearly as much money as Grace, but he pulls his weight. The battles between them are not serious cracks in the foundation but the little irritations and tiffs that build up over a decade spent side by side. For example, why is it okay for him to spend six hundred dollars on a watch but not for her to spend the same amount on hair and skin appointments? Or why do they have to keep the thermostat at a frosty sixty-five degrees overnight when he knows she can't sleep that cold? Why is it her job to teach their children respect, to do the bulk of the disciplining? Why won't he quit nagging her about getting a CPAP machine—the one her doctor has been recommending for months? "The snoring is enough to drive a man insane," he says.

These minor grievances mean nothing in the larger scheme of things.

Grace wasn't planning to have an affair. She had no ulterior motive when she ran into TJ while having lunch with a friend six months ago. There was never chemistry between the two of them in college, but TJ had gained about fifty pounds of muscle since then. She found herself flirting with him, buzzing when he flirted back. She went home that afternoon and kept the banter going via text. *We're just having a little fun*, she told herself. Then they were just having a drink in a hotel bar, then just kissing, and so on and so forth until she'd been sleeping with the guy for half a year.

Grace has told no one about the affair—keeping it secret is most of the fun—but she can imagine her girlfriends' reactions if she did. *You have everything, Grace. The career, the money, the guy, the kids. Why are you risking it all for something so meaningless?* The risk is the point, though. When you reach a certain stage of life, the predictability of your days becomes mind-numbing. Rise at half past four. Forty-five minutes on the Pilates reformer. Same bland breakfast every morning, followed by the same bland meetings in the afternoons. There are taxes and homework and soccer practice and dentist appointments and mammograms. The only variety in Grace's routine is the order in which these boxes are ticked. Her life is a series of administrative tasks. Even the yearly adults-only vacations for her and Rob have become a bore. Sex on the first and last nights, tacos or daiquiris every day in between, sunscreened noses buried in Kindles or, more likely, laptops. Before her liaison with TJ, Grace couldn't remember the last time her heart raced or her stomach fluttered. She had spent her twenties uncomfortable and hustling only to discover in her thirties that comfort was stifling. Sometimes she considers telling Rob about the affair just to see what would happen, then feels cruel for her cavalier attitude.

For the first few months, Grace found the relationship exciting. The affair was like being in college again—constant sex, jumping out of bed to brush her teeth before TJ woke in the morning. But any odd arrangement becomes mundane when recycled enough times. TJ was getting clingier. Grace knew when he proposed telling Rob about the two of them that it was time to end things. She's not going to break up her family over this guy.

Yesterday afternoon she allowed herself one more hookup. Now the relationship is over. She doesn't deny that it's mean that only one of them knew they were having breakup sex, but Grace has never been known for her kindness. Kindness is for people without talent.

"The affair with TJ," Agopian clarifies, as if she might be conducting simultaneous relationships. Grace has an urge to slap the smirk off his face. "We're also aware the deceased was blackmailing you."

"W-what are you t-talking about?" Grace stammers. All Alfred did was verbally threaten her. Did he threaten TJ too? Did TJ tell the detectives? Maybe he turned on her after all. He has always been too by-the-book for her taste, puts too much faith in law and order.

Agopian pulls his phone from his pocket. For a horrifying moment Grace thinks he has photos. Her mind zips back to the attic, to the spying vents. Alfred wouldn't have . . . would he?

When the detective sets the phone on the table, Grace glances at the screen. He's pulled up the Voice Memos app and pressed play on a seven-minute clip. Grace waits, hand at her throat.

The sounds of sex fill the room. Kissing, giggling, moaning that she recognizes as her own. Grace's cheeks burn. She focuses her gaze on the phone, but she feels both detectives watching her.

Alfred recorded me.

Little that Alfred does—did—surprises Grace anymore, yet he managed to pull one over on her one last time. Alfred and his childish schoolboy crush, his megalomaniacal need for power over her. Grace could kill him again.

"Where'd you get this?" Grace demands.

"We can't tell you that," Gromowski says.

"Were you aware the deceased knew about the affair?" Agopian asks.

Grace thinks about lying, but TJ has already blown their cover. "Yes." She tries to keep her voice light but doesn't quite succeed. Why didn't he tell her about the clip?

"Were you worried Mr. Smettle was going to tell your husband?"

"No," Grace says.

"I would be. I'd be real worried," Agopian says.

"Your friends told us about Alfred's feelings for you," Gromowski says.

"That was a long time ago," Grace says.

Agopian turns to his partner. "You know what I find interesting?"

"What's that?" Gromowski asks. Grace clenches her jaw at their stupid gee-whiz routine.

"Hours after recording this audio, Mr. Smettle turned up dead."

FORTY-FOUR

Zoe

Zoe sits in the home theater, biting her fingernails to the quick. Grace has been with the detectives for a while. What's taking so long? Were the rest of them in there this long? Zoe checks her watch, but the time is useless since she didn't note when Grace's interview began.

She steals glances at everyone else in the theater. Sunburn, who was so energized at the beginning of the day, has grown bored of his job and is now scrolling through his phone. TJ beats out a nervous rhythm on his thigh while Samira pinches the bridge of her nose in between long bouts of texting. After his third attempt at a joke at which no one laughed, Julius jumped out of his seat and perused the library shelves. He returned to his chair with the book he pronounced "the least boring" and is now flipping through the pages faster than he could possibly be reading them. In the back corner of the room the housekeeper, with her deep frown, might well have turned to stone. Danny has not shifted from her position—legs crossed at the ankles, hands folded and resting in her lap—since she served lunch hours ago. Zoe might have thought the old woman was in shock, but her beady eyes roam the room, tracking each and every one of their movements.

When Zoe has no nails left to bite, she moves on to her hair. She tugs at the strands at the nape of her neck. The door to the theater opens. The other cop, Officer Shaw, walks in.

He clears his throat. "The folks from the funeral home are here. They're going to load up the deceased and take him to the morgue. Thought you all would want to know."

"I need to see him before you take him away." Danny stands on shaky legs. "He'll want to wear his favorite turtleneck, the burgundy one. It complemented his coloring."

Shaw's eyes soften. "There'll be time for that later, ma'am. I'm afraid he's got to get to the morgue before we do any outfit changes."

"Can I send Binky with him at least?" she asks. Zoe and the others stare at her. "He mentioned once that he'd never had a blanket to sleep with as a child. His mother never made him one. Isn't that terrible? I said I would knit one myself, and it's almost finished. I can fetch it from my room right now."

A knitted blanket for a man approaching forty? What else does Danny have for him? A rubber ducky for bath time? Jesus Christ.

"I need to get up to that closet too." Danny pulls her shawl tighter around her shoulders. "Alfred won't be happy about a bloodstain on the floor. He's so conscientious, you know. Fastidious about maintaining the hotel for his guests."

"Why don't you take a seat, ma'am? You won't be able to get into the closet today, but we'll work as fast as we can." Shaw gives Danny a warm smile, then leaves.

Danny mutters something about idle hands and shrinks back into the recliner. TJ paces the second row of seats, then walks circles around the room. Zoe wants to yell at him to stand still, that his anxiety is aggravating hers. She closes her eyes instead.

When will this day be over?

The door opens. Gromowski enters, with Grace behind him. She seems worried and ruffled, eyes her seat but remains in the doorway.

"I can't take this anymore," she says. "I'm going crazy in here. Can we go outside for a bit? Please?"

Sunburn and Gromowski exchange a guarded look. Gromowski tips his chin. "Yeah, all right," Sunburn says. "Anyone else want to come?"

The others shake their heads. This is the first room in the hotel where Zoe has felt safe, and that's mostly because Alfred is dead and a uniformed officer with a gun in his holster is standing guard at the door. She doesn't want him to leave.

"Can't you wait, Grace?" she says.

"I won't be long," Grace promises.

She and Sunburn leave the movie theater. Zoe listens to the two sets of feet padding away. Behind her, Julius sighs and turns a page. TJ buries his nose in his phone. Danny sits stock-still, staring straight ahead.

Detective Gromowski regards Samira and says, "I believe you're the only one we haven't spoken to, Ms. Reddy."

Samira nods, then rises from her recliner. Zoe watches from behind as Samira fixes her sweater and sets her shoulders. "I'm ready," she tells the detective.

As the two of them are about to exit the room, Danny speaks up. "Be sure to ask Samira what she was doing in the third-floor closet at one o'clock this morning."

Samira's mouth falls open, but no words come out.

Danny adds, "She ran out of there like she'd seen a ghost."

FORTY-FIVE

Samira

In the dining room, standing before the detectives, Samira feels a wave of nausea and fights the urge to tuck her head between her knees. How will she ever look her children in the eye again? How can she meet her own gaze in the mirror?

Survival over truth. All day long she has been repeating these three little words to herself, an improvised mantra she's not even sure she believes in. Lying to her friends is one thing. Lying to the police is a different beast altogether. *Would I do it? Could I?* she had wondered. The question is irrelevant now. The housekeeper has made that decision for her.

"Samira Reddy, right?" Agopian asks.

She nods and pulls out a chair across from them, her hands shaking so hard that she misses the chair the first time she goes to grab it. She sits, then clocks a small black recording device on the table. Samira stares at the glowing red light.

"I can't imagine how tough today has been on you," Agopian says. "I'm sorry for the loss of your friend."

"Thank you," Samira says. When the detectives ask her for the details of the weekend, she leaves nothing out. She tells them about the perfect-murder conversation at dinner the first night. She shares the story of the house's previous occupants, the pile of grass clippings supposedly left on Zoe's pillow. She explains the shower intruder, how unsafe she's felt in the hotel ever since.

"Let's talk about Danny's comment," Gromowski says. "She said she saw you leaving the third-floor closet around one a.m. today. Is that true? Were you in the closet?"

Samira nods, winding dark strands of hair around her fingers.

"Tell us how you ended up there. Everything you can remember about last night."

Samira inhales deeply and opens her mouth. In the space between the inhale and the exhale hangs her freedom, normal lives for her children. She hasn't yet confessed anything, and already she feels like she's made a mistake. She speaks anyway. "I got in bed at eleven," she begins, "but I couldn't fall asleep."

Sleep was a laughable goal. Samira couldn't stop thinking about the shower creeper. First she'd imagined him lurking outside her door. Then a worse possibility presented itself—what if he was hiding somewhere inside her room? She jumped out of bed and flicked on the nightstand lamp, then the room lights. She held her breath as she ripped open her closet door, clawed the shower curtain back, squinted into the dark space beneath the desk. She was alone in room 301, but that did little to ease her mind. Suppose someone broke into her room. She had no way of calling for help, with her own cell phone missing and no in-room phones at this glorified bed-and-breakfast. Samira hated to acknowledge her dependence on technology, but—*Oh, screw it*—she'd feel safer knowing emergency services and her family were one call away. She would never fall asleep this wired, so she decided to search the hotel.

Samira slipped on a sweatshirt over her sleep shirt. She put her room key in her pocket, crept into the hallway, and peered in both directions, unsure where to look. In hindsight she wishes, more than anything, that she had snuck down to the first floor and started with the kitchen or parlor, combing room after room. She would have come up empty, true. She wouldn't have found the missing phones, but Samira would have gladly lived out the rest of her life without a cell phone if it meant preventing what happened last night.

The fact of the matter, she admitted to herself, was that she didn't trust Alfred. She did not believe the concierge had taken their phones home by mistake. Instead, she suspected that Alfred had stolen them and hidden them somewhere on the hotel property. One weekend together was not enough to know the man he'd grown into, but too many unsettling things had happened on Alfred's watch to believe him innocent.

Samira paused outside the storage closet next to her room. She tried the handle, opened the door, entered, then closed it behind her and breathed unevenly in the dark space, waiting for her heartbeat to slow. She tapped the flashlight button on her watch, used its beam to find the light switch and flip it on. She flinched when the closet flooded with light. She didn't want to leave the light on any longer than necessary, lest someone see it under the closet door and find her snooping. Samira glanced around the room, desperate for clues.

Why her gaze flicked upward she'll never know; the phones wouldn't be taped to the ceiling. What she does know is that she noted the outline of the hatch door and thought *attic*. What better hiding place could there be? In short order she found the metal rod leaning against the wall, unlatched the hatch door, and eased the ladder down. Nervous about how long she'd kept the closet light on, she turned it off before stepping onto the ladder. Once again, she relied on her watch to light the way.

When Samira's head came even with the attic floor, she noted the glass of milk on the platter right away. Before she could process its strangeness, though, she squeaked and almost fell off the ladder, stubbing her toe hard in the process. In a corner a woman was watching her, unmoving. Samira shined her watch flashlight toward the woman.

It was a mannequin wearing a wig and a frumpy dress.

"Oh, thank God." Samira exhaled.

The rest of the stuff in the attic was more run-of-the-mill—cardboard boxes, old furniture, and storage tubs. The crow perched on the antique dresser, wings spread, disturbed her. Like the owl in the bar, it seemed so real. Samira began pulling the dresser drawers open one at a time. All were empty—except the last one. There, in the bottom left drawer, were the velvet pouches.

She bit the inside of her cheek as she opened one and pulled out her cell phone. "Bastard," she breathed.

What she found next made her forget the phones altogether.

Samira heard a snore. She froze. She and Grace had been roommates, then housemates, for four years of college. She would recognize that heavy, open-mouthed breathing anywhere. It used to keep her up at night freshman year. She studied the floor and felt metal under her slippers. She was standing on a vent. Samira knelt and waited for her eyes to adjust to the darkness.

I'm looking into a guest room. Samira sucked in a breath.

A dark shape shifted in the bed below. Grace. She was looking at Grace's room. Room 302, the one across from her own. Samira glanced down the length of the attic, saw the gleams of more vents. She licked her lips.

Samira did not trust her feet to carry her. On hands and knees she crawled from vent to vent, gazing at her friends as they slept—save for TJ, whose vent was covered by a magazine page. Had he known about the vents, then? Samira kept crawling until she'd reached the end of the attic. What the hell was this? Was Alfred a Peeping Tom? How many people had he spied on? Was this his reason for opening the Hitchcock Hotel? She sat there on her knees, palms flat against the floor, unable to move. She thought she might vomit.

What other conclusion was there? The attic setup couldn't be one of his employees' doing; Alfred would have found it by now. The other day she'd seen him slink into the closet. He had claimed he was replacing toilet paper in the guest rooms. Alfred had promised he would find the intruder who watched her shower. All along, that intruder was him.

By now the detectives are hanging on her every word. "Then what?" Agopian asks.

Samira hesitates. She's already explained her presence in the closet, answered Danny's accusation. (Where was Danny hiding last night? Why didn't she say anything to Samira?) Does she need to continue?

"You seem like a good person, Samira," Agopian says.

"One who would want peace for her friend," Gromowski adds.

"Help us help Alfred," Agopian finishes.

Samira's knee bounces under the table. She forces it to still. For a moment, Samira believes she can hold in what she knows. When she imagines her children, the new baby, growing up without her, her resolve strengthens. Then she imagines the truth eating away at her, bit by bit, year after year, driving her toward madness. Samira wants to be tough but knows she can't do this. The secret will destroy her.

"I was so disturbed by the vents," she says, "that I didn't hear him coming until he was already in the attic."

One step. Another. A soft click as the light bulb's pull chain was tugged and the space lit up.

Exposed, Samira had frozen on hands and knees. After the longest few seconds of her life, she clambered to her feet and spun around. She saw an arm raised overhead, the shine of a blade. She had no time for logic or reason. She acted, too terrified to scream.

Samira lunged at Alfred and shoved him as hard as she could with both hands. He squeaked in surprise—a sound she will never forget for the rest of her life. She watched as the Swiss Army knife slipped from his hand as he windmilled his arms to stay upright. She heard a thud when he hit his head on the lip of the hatch frame. Then he was gone from view.

She stood there, frozen yet shaking, listening to his strangled cries. He was stuck on something—the ladder, maybe. He sounded like a kitten mewling for help. She held her breath and waited for the sickening crash of his body hitting the floor. Then: silence.

Samira had inched toward the ladder until she could peer through the hatch into the closet below. Alfred's body lay in a crumpled heap. His face was tucked out of view under his arm, and he didn't stir. *Maybe he's unconscious,* she thought. *This might be my one chance to escape.*

As fast as she could, Samira grabbed the phone pouches and raced down the ladder. She had one hand on the doorknob when she heard a loud moan behind her. She didn't look back, just got the hell out of the closet, darted to her room, and dead bolted the door. She sat with her back against it, shoulders heaving. An inhuman whine leaked from her mouth. Samira waited and waited for Alfred to bang his fist on her door, to yank her down the hallway by her hair, to hurt her in unspeakable ways. For hours she sat, dread caking her throat and belly.

"But Alfred never came," Samira tells the detectives. A single tear runs down her face. "Because I'd killed him."

FORTY-SIX

Grace

Grace and the sunburned cop step out onto the portico. The rain has stopped. The air outside is dank, has that post-downpour smell.

"Is it okay if we take a walk?" Grace asks. Sunburn nods, and they head toward the parking lot. "How'd you get a sunburn in New England in October?"

"I was in Fort Myers last week," the cop says. "Drove down with my family to see my in-laws."

"How long of a drive is that?"

"Twenty-five hours," Sunburn says. Grace whistles. "Cheaper than flying my wife and three kids down there."

Grace takes in the view of the valley and mountains from the parking lot. Normally she loves the fall colors, but today they're menacing. The bloodred trees, others as orange as fire. Fog has settled atop their canopies, threatening to push down and smother them all. Grace is surrounded by nature's warnings, but she can't leave now. She doesn't have a choice.

Sunburn heads around the side of the hotel. Grace follows him. "Are you from here?" she asks the cop.

Sunburn nods. "Townie through and through." He says it with a hint of amusement, no bitterness. "Born and raised."

"Did you go to Reville?" Grace asks. The cop appears to be a few years older than she is, but maybe they were in school at the same time.

Sunburn smirks. "I'm not the college type." Grace feels like an ass for assuming.

She'd thought a blast of fresh air on her face would improve her mood, but it hasn't. Her pulse drums against her neck and wrists. She detects threats all around her. The snap of a twig, the call of a bird, the unassuming shed. Grace isn't used to feeling unsafe—not until recently, anyway.

The backyard has a patio with three seating areas, each of which has comfy chairs and tables with umbrellas. Fairy lights are strung across the patio. Beyond the backyard is a firepit with more outdoor furniture. The cushions and throw pillows are soaked from the rain. A stone path off the patio leads in two directions. To the left are the woods, and to the right is the pond. Grace and the cop head for the forest.

Tall trees creak and groan as they sway in the wind. Grace hears the crack of a branch breaking in the distance. Her pulse picks up speed. She takes a deep breath to soothe herself, nostrils filled with the scents of rotting wood and decomposing leaves. Branches scrape her arms and legs as she and Sunburn make their way through an unkempt passage on the trail. Moisture from the damp forest floor seeps into her sneakers. She wishes she had packed a pair of boots.

Grace tries to keep the tone of her voice casual. "Have you heard about the people who lived in this place before Alfred?"

Sunburn raises his eyebrows. In a low voice, he says, "My partner has a connection to this house."

"What kind of connection?" Grace slaps away an insect when she feels the prick of its bite.

"You've gotta stick around a lot longer than a weekend to be privy to that information."

Grace is about to press him when she hears the high-pitched screeches of dozens of birds. She glances back at the aviary but can barely see it through the trees. From here the crows resemble a single monster of giant proportions. She imagines the dark swarm hovering over her, then attacking all at once. What are they squawking at? Grace's mouth is so dry she can't swallow.

She focuses on her five senses, searching for signs of movement besides the fluttering of leaves. A squirrel climbs a tree. A sparrow lands on a branch. More than once she's sure she sees eyes shining in a tree hollow. She walks straight into a cobweb, then bats it away from her face.

"Maybe we should go back to the hotel," she says.

Sunburn chuckles. His laughter infuriates Grace. *Silly woman*, she hears him thinking.

"I wouldn't mind a walk around the pond first," the cop says. Grace can't tell if there's a touch of malice in his voice or if she's imagining it. She eyes the revolver on his hip and acquiesces.

They retrace their steps through the woods until they reach the fork again. Now they take the path on the right. The pond comes quickly into view. Grace has to admit that Alfred did a nice job with the landscaping. Reeds and long grasses poke out of the water. In the pond's center are lily pads with colorful flowers. Benches and chaise lounges are scattered between bunches of dandelions and cattails around the pond's edges. In different circumstances the pond would be peaceful, a good place to get lost in a book.

The detectives didn't ask Grace why she was alone in Alfred's room yesterday afternoon. TJ must not have told them he saw her. Maybe he's still on her side after all. Grace won't tell the detectives the real reason if they do ask. She already has a plausible excuse at the ready. The truth? She went to Alfred's room, and later, the attic, to search for a pair of eyeglasses. Finding them would have loosened his choke hold on her. She doesn't need to worry about that anymore.

She never found the glasses in Alfred's room, but she did chance upon a deck of white index cards with notes in his careful handwriting. *Samira's children,* said one. *Zoe's drink of choice. TJ's job title. Julius's non-profit. Grace's kids' school.* She flipped that card over. *Trinity School* was written on the other side, the address beneath it. Without thinking, Grace had ripped that last card into tiny pieces, then shoved them into her pocket—as if that would make Alfred forget the information he'd spent weeks, maybe months, memorizing. She had hurried from the room, courage run cold.

Grace snaps out of her trance when she spots something bobbing in the rushes near the edge of the water. "What is that?" she asks, jogging ahead.

"Wait up," Sunburn yells, but Grace doesn't listen.

When she's twenty feet away from the bobbing thing, she stops. She's close enough to see, though now she wishes she weren't. A body is floating facedown in Alfred's pond.

FORTY-SEVEN

Julius

The minutes tick by more slowly than seems possible. Samira hasn't re-turned from her interview with the detectives, and Grace is still out for a walk with Sunburn. Julius, TJ, Zoe, and Danny are locked in the screen-ing room—all lost in their own worlds, judging by the blank expression on each face.

Was Samira in the closet last night like Danny said? What could that mean other than her involvement in Alfred's death? Maybe they tussled over the phones. Julius has a hard time imagining Samira in a physical altercation. How else to explain Danny's allegation, though?

A ringing phone breaks his trance. TJ's. From the back row Julius watches his old friend glance at the screen. Will TJ answer this time? He's avoided talking to the mysterious caller all weekend. Julius doesn't know who the caller is, but he's pretty sure he's figured out the nature of the call. TJ's near-constant heartburn, the regular snacking on TUMS, the paranoid glances over his shoulder. Julius has known for days why TJ keeps trying to pull him aside for a private chat. He has been on the re-ceiving end of these pleas more times than he cares to count.

When TJ hits the ignore button, Julius speaks up. "Is that your booty call? She sure is desperate to get ahold of you."

TJ makes a face. "Business associate."

Julius laughs. "Why don't we get this over with, Teej?" TJ feigns confusion. "What did you want to talk to me about?" When TJ doesn't answer, Julius finds himself getting angry. "You need money, right?"

Zoe glances up from her phone. Danny doesn't react to the accusation. She keeps knitting Alfred's blanket. Officer Shaw brought the knitting basket down from her room.

"No." TJ's eyes bulge. "Not exactly." He pauses. "Can you come down here so we can talk privately?"

Julius snaps closed the book he was pretending to read. He shimmies past Zoe, then follows TJ to the front of the room. Julius stands there with his arms crossed. "What did you do?"

TJ resettles his baseball cap, avoiding eye contact with Julius.

"Come on. Let's hear it," Julius says. "Gambling addiction? High-class hookers? Tell me it's not heroin."

"I didn't know I was doing anything wrong at first," TJ mutters. "It started with free Ravens tickets."

"I assume that's a sports team and not a cockfighting ring?" Julius says.

TJ doesn't laugh. "I thought my boss was being nice, showing his appreciation for the overtime I was working. Then he offered me a free round of golf at his country club."

"Who do you work for, again?" Julius asks, irritated by the pace of the story.

"A member of Maryland's house of delegates," TJ whispers. "This guy is wealthy. He sold his company for hundreds of millions, then got into politics. When I began working for him I wasn't sure why he'd hired me, other than paranoia and an overinflated sense of importance. State representatives aren't go-to targets for people mad at the government, you know? Most Americans don't even know who their state reps are."

Julius taps his foot on the carpet.

"Some of my client's colleagues in the House are working on this real estate bill. They're trying to limit exclusive listing contracts between homeowners and Realtors. These contracts prey on unwitting buyers, so you'd think most House members would support the bill, right? Protect the little guy? My client was in favor initially. I remember being proud that I worked for someone actually serving the public's interest. Then, one day, he announces he's changed his mind. He wants to kill the bill."

Julius feels a headache brewing near his temples.

"My job is to hang around my client all day, to log who's coming and going. I noticed this one guy in particular had been coming to the office every week for months. I did some digging and learned that he owns a lobbying firm in New York called Clayton Capital. One of his clients is Blue Sky Realty. They've been working to convince my guy to vote against the bill."

"Are we talking about kickbacks?" Julius asks.

TJ grimaces. "I should've reported them as soon as I figured out what was going on."

"What did you do instead?" Julius isn't sure he wants to know. He peeps over his shoulder and sees Zoe watching them. He turns his back to her so she can't see their mouths moving.

TJ swallows. "Accepted a bonus of sixty thousand dollars."

Julius's jaw drops. "You're joking."

"I used it to pay off my student loans." TJ hangs his head.

Julius half groans, half moans. "How could someone so smart be so stupid?" he hisses.

TJ is talking so quietly now that Julius has to strain to hear him. "I freaked out almost as soon as I spent the money. I had, like, ten seconds of relief to have this giant loan off my back, followed by this crushing guilt over what I'd done. What if I was found out? What if I went to prison? I talked to a friend in security about finding a lawyer. The next day, I get a call."

Julius closes his eyes. "A fixer for the lobbying firm?"

He opens them in time to catch TJ nodding. "This guy calls me ten times a day. He follows me in his car. He lurks outside my apartment. He wants to make sure I don't talk."

"That's why you came here," Julius realizes. "To get away from the guy."

TJ's head bobs. "I needed to lay low for a while. Until I could come up with a solution." He eyes Julius uncertainly.

"Until you could talk to me," Julius finishes for him.

"I've been trying all weekend, but the moment was never right," TJ says. "I couldn't get you alone, and I didn't want the others to know." They both glance at Zoe, who averts her gaze. "I almost did it last night, but then the phones went missing, and . . ." TJ throws up his hands. "You weren't in the mood for a discussion. Then, at dinner, you kept trying to convince everyone to go home. I panicked. I had to keep you here long enough to talk to you."

TJ was the last one to head upstairs to his room last night. TJ was left alone in the lobby, so no one would have noticed if he went out to the parking lot. TJ didn't want anyone leaving the Hitchcock Hotel.

"Please, for the love of God, tell me it wasn't you who slashed every tire in the lot," Julius says.

TJ flushes. "I didn't want you all to know I did it. I figured everyone would assume Alfred was behind the tires. So much weird shit has happened here this weekend."

Julius mumbles a bunch of expletives. He's relieved that Alfred isn't haunting them from beyond the grave but furious with TJ for being such a dumbass.

"I have to come clean." TJ's voice cracks on the last word. "I looked it up. Since the lobbying firm is based in New York, these were interstate transactions. Meaning I could be facing federal charges. Bribery, money laundering, tax evasion. I don't know what else." He winces. "The fixer is the least of my worries. I'm way more scared of the FBI banging down my door."

"Where do I come in?" Julius asks.

"I need good lawyers." TJ hesitates. "Which I can't afford. When I take this to the authorities, I'm going to lose my job. I don't know whether I'll be expected to pay the sixty thousand back or what."

"Let me see if I have this right," Julius says. "You need sixty thousand dollars, a monthly living stipend, and the free use of my lawyers' time?"

TJ stares at his shoes, then moves his head so minutely that it can barely be interpreted as a nod.

"And you thought the best way to go about persuading me was to accuse me of planting mentions of myself in *Page Six*?"

"Sorry again about that," TJ mumbles.

Julius observes his friend, the quiet guy who once believed all the answers to life's conundrums could be found in books. In college people often found Julius and TJ's friendship baffling. *You're such opposites*, they were told time and again, but the traits Julius lacked that TJ had in spades were what he loved about his friend. Composure, sincerity, depth. Being around TJ used to make Julius feel better about himself. He misses being surrounded by warm people, especially now. Julius is tired of facing cancer alone.

"I'll help you on one condition," Julius says.

TJ glances up.

"You come live with me in the city while we sort this mess out," Julius says.

"Like housemates?" TJ asks with a small smile.

"Like housemates," Julius agrees. Before he can make a snarky joke, TJ grabs him in a bear hug.

FORTY-EIGHT

Grace

From the side of the pond, Grace watches Sunburn wade into the water toward the dead body. Its floral-patterned dress is soaked through, long locks of hair tangled in the reeds. Grace is reminded of *Vertigo*—Kim Novak dropping flowers in the bay beneath the Golden Gate Bridge before jumping into the water herself.

Gingerly, Sunburn flips the body over. "It's a mannequin," he calls.

Grace is weak-kneed with relief, so much so that she sinks to the grass. Sunburn drags the dummy up the embankment. Grace recognizes the dress and wig when he sets the dummy next to her—the same mannequin she saw while searching the attic last night.

"Can we go back to the hotel now?" Grace asks.

The cop nods and hoists the mannequin under his arm. Side by side, they walk along the path to the backyard, not speaking. Why did Alfred save such a grotesquerie? Who put it here in the water? Alfred, before he died? Danny, following Alfred's orders? One of her friends? What message was the person trying to send, and for whom?

Despite having seen his lifeless body with her own two eyes, Grace feels Alfred lurking nearby. Haunting the grounds, haunting her. Even in death, he will not let her rest.

In the days after Alfred's expulsion from Reville, Grace could tell he was pissed at all of them, but especially her. He met the others' questions with curt, perfunctory answers. Grace he ignored altogether, as though she no longer existed.

This shouldn't have bothered her as much as it did. Grace prided herself on her ability to put reason before emotion. Why should they both go down for the "crime"? Why should two future careers be ruined? Though Grace was sure the hour-long meeting with the provost was a harrowing experience to go through alone, surely Alfred could understand why she'd kept her distance. Grace wanted to keep her name as far away from this mess as possible.

She's not heartless. She tried to make it up to Alfred. First Grace suggested dinner on her at the lone white-tablecloth restaurant on campus. This invitation Alfred ignored. A Hitchcock-movie-marathon proposal was met with similar stony silence. She even tried to pull some strings with the university's film professors (besides Dr. Scott) to get Alfred a job as a TA or a plain old personal assistant. But what Alfred had said was true. They had all heard about the expulsion. No one wanted to affiliate with the cheater. The editor in chief of the school newspaper was insulted when Grace pitched Alfred for a film-review column—he delivered a long self-righteous speech about the importance of ethics in journalism. Grace told him to screw off before she stormed out of his office.

As regarded the employment of Alfred Smettle, the one taker she found that was film adjacent was for a cashier job at the indie theater— the same one where she'd had sex for the first time. When Grace presented the opportunity to Alfred, he glared at her with a hatred so venomous that she felt afraid. Alfred's lack of options confirmed that Grace had been right to conceal her involvement in Easy A. Alfred would be okay someday, but to Reville and this town, right now he was poison.

Seventy-two hours after being expelled, Alfred loaded his grimy station wagon. He would have to make the thousand-mile drive home to Chicago alone. His mother had fallen into another depressive episode.

That night, Grace stood in the driveway of the blue house, arms wrapped around her waist as she watched Alfred pack the car. She thought about offering to make the drive with him but worried he'd say yes. She had class the next day, was on track to graduate summa cum laude.

"I'm sorry," she said when Alfred closed the trunk. Grace trembled in her cashmere sweater. She should have put on a coat before coming outside.

"I wish you didn't have to go through this," she added. "It must be a terrible feeling."

Alfred moved around the side of the car. To Grace's surprise, he embraced her. She forced her shoulders to relax into whatever this was. She pushed her face into his chest. Alfred petted her hair. "You might know how it feels soon enough," he whispered.

A hot, pulsing fear ran up and down Grace's body. She gaped at Alfred. "How so?"

He shrugged and winked, but this wasn't cute or funny.

"Alfred?" she prompted.

He dropped his arms and stepped back, made his way toward the driver's-side door. "I should get going."

Only then did Grace clock how dark it was outside, that it had been so for hours. Who began a seventeen-hour drive at ten o'clock at night?

Someone who didn't intend to go.

Grace followed Alfred around the car. When she gazed up at him, she saw what he wanted. The answer was right there in his eyes, in the way he pursed his lips. Even after two years of nothing but friendship, he still wanted what he always had.

Grace didn't hesitate. She threw her arms around his neck, thought about squeezing with all her might. Instead she said, "Come inside. Let's talk."

"I don't know, Grace."

"We'll go to my room," Grace promised, without so much as a flinch.

He hesitated, considering. Grace would have done anything for the information that Alfred had. If the administration was coming after her next, she wanted to be prepared. Grace put her lips on Alfred's and bit the bottom one softly.

"Say yes," she murmured. Even with her eyes closed, she could sense him smiling. He let her lead him back into the house and up the stairs. On that Friday night in mid-October, midterms were over. Everyone had gone out to celebrate. TJ, Julius, Samira, and Zoe had said their goodbyes to Alfred hours earlier. Grace and Alfred had the house to themselves.

With every step up toward her room, Grace's palms dampened a little more. She would do as little as she had to to get what she wanted. But she would get what she wanted. Grace always did. This time was no exception.

FORTY-NINE

Samira

Samira isn't finished with her confession. Now that she's talking to the detectives, she feels like she'll never stop. She tries not to worry about the recording device on the table.

"I didn't know how close Alfred was to the ladder. I swear I didn't mean to shove him down it," she pants. "All I could think about was getting away from him."

The memory of last night looms large, still frightening despite Alfred's death. Her breaths are coming too fast. She feels like she's having heart palpitations.

"Did you find the knife?" she gasps.

Gromowski nods. "Tell us what happened after you descended the ladder."

Samira assumed Alfred had broken a leg or sustained a concussion. She had no idea he was fatally injured. In that moment, she was too concerned with her baby's survival to worry about Alfred's welfare. Samira had one thought only: *Run*. She doesn't recall deciding to rise to her feet, sprint to her room, or slide the key into the door lock. Nor does she remember consciously choosing to pull her dead cell phone from its pouch and plug it in to charge. Only once there was a locked door between her and Alfred did she stop to think. She wanted to get out of the building but had no clue where he might be lurking, whether he had traps in place. What if her room door creaked when she opened it? What if Alfred heard her trying to flee and came after her with the knife? She could hide on the property, but he knew the grounds much better than she did. She pictured herself crouched alone behind a tree, hearing footsteps coming closer and closer and closer. She bit down hard on her knuckles to stop herself from wailing.

What about the others? She should have gone to someone else's room, not her own. Safety in numbers. But Alfred might have been right behind her. Zoe or TJ or Grace may not have woken up in time. She could've died pounding on a friend's door, Alfred's knife sinking into her back. At least she knew she could access her own room—and quickly. She'd made a split-second decision and didn't regret it.

Now, though, Samira questioned whether she should try to wake her friends. The last thing she wanted was to sit alone all night. She thought again about what Danny had said earlier: *There are things they've done that they're not telling you.* Grace's insistence that they all come to this reunion. The persistent phone calls TJ refused to answer. Zoe's claim of knowing something sinister about Alfred. Julius's strange mood swings and new morbid perspective. Samira wasn't sure she trusted any of them, or that they would wake to her knocking before Alfred did. He could be in the hallway right now. She imagined swinging open the door and a blade aiming straight for her belly. This time she bit her tongue to hold back the shriek.

The safest place to wait was here. Samira triple-checked the window locks, reclosed the curtains, then sat against the dead-bolted door. On second thought, given the vents she'd found in the attic, did she trust that any of the locks in this place actually worked? She stuck the back of her desk chair under the doorknob, then pushed the desk across the room to barricade the doorway. Better. She listened and listened and listened. The hallway floors were made of old wood. A board would give Alfred away if he tiptoed out of the closet.

The third floor was quiet, though. She detected no movement behind any of the guest room doors. *How are any of you sleeping?* she wanted to shout.

Samira peered at the nightstand, where her phone was now lit up like a beacon. She dialed 911, then paused with her finger over the call button. *Where is he? Why hasn't he come after me yet?* Samira wondered if Alfred had a concussion after all. Maybe he was knocked out cold in the closet. Should she check? Some instinct for self-preservation switched on. *Not so fast,* an age-old voice said from deep within her. Samira felt a kick in her abdomen. She knew it was not possible, that the fetus didn't even have legs yet, but the reminder of its existence was enough to root her in place.

One hour turned to two, then three. What if Alfred had died in there? What would the charge against her be? Involuntary manslaughter? That carried jail time, didn't it? She had no idea how much, but she couldn't give birth to this child in a prison cell. She couldn't be separated from a newborn, not to mention her daughter and son.

But it was an accident. The police would understand. Plus, Alfred had a weapon. He'd been holding a knife. That's why she'd screamed and shoved him in the first place. He had startled her.

On the floor of her hotel room, Samira clenched her molars so hard she could've broken a tooth. Alfred was no innocent. The mere existence of the vents in the attic proved that. She had no doubt now as to who the shower creeper was. Maybe she had done the world a favor by putting an end to his perversion. Maybe the vents and the break-in and the knife would bring the police to her side.

Even if she was cleared of wrongdoing, though, wouldn't there still be an arrest? Her name splashed across every major news site? She could see the headline now: STARTUP WHIZ & WOMEN'S RIGHTS ADVOCATE SLAYS COLLEGE FRIEND. How would that impact her company? Who would want to buy a vibrator from a woman who had killed her friend? If her business suffered, how would she support her family? How would she provide for this new baby? Who would give her a second chance? Was she willing to take the risk of having her life ruined by this freak?

She was not. She put her phone back on the nightstand.

Samira closed her eyes and pictured Alfred's body as she'd run past it. Hopefully the others would interpret his fall as an accident, but if not, at least one of them would remember yesterday's dinner conversation. Julius had been the one to suggest pushing someone down the stairs. Samira felt evil for the thought, but if anyone had to be arrested for the crime, Julius was the best option. He had no partner or children; plus, he had more money than God. He could afford the lawyers to get him out of this situation. She couldn't imagine him serving time. She would never let it go that far.

Would she?

Samira crawled under the desk and leaned her head against the door, the adrenaline draining from her. It had been a long time since someone Samira knew had died. Sixteen years, to be exact. One week after Alfred drove home to Chicago, post-expulsion, tragedy struck Reville's campus. The film club's beloved Dr. Scott had died. In the confusion that followed, in the search for answers, it came out that the professor had stage 4 lung cancer, terminal. His oncologist had told him he had months to live. He died one week later. Samira remembers how shocked she had been, how hard she'd cried over a man she didn't know all that well. This was worse. So much worse. Her eyelids and limbs were heavy. She allowed her eyes to close for a minute. She did not remember dozing off.

There on the carpet, Samira swore the hallway floorboards had creaked once, twice, three times, but when she pulled herself to standing, she heard nothing. Half-asleep, she dropped the phone pouches on the desk, then crawled into bed. Mere hours before, she had been sure she would never again enjoy a night of good sleep, but she passed out as soon as her head hit the pillow. She slept soundly, deeply, dreamlessly.

When Samira woke this morning, she tells the detectives, she was too frightened even to shift on the mattress. She convinced herself that Alfred had somehow stolen into her room overnight, that he was waiting under the bed like a child's boogeyman. She lay there, breathing and straining, until she summoned enough courage to lift the bed skirt. What if he was somewhere inside the hotel, waiting for the right moment to strike? She saw his knife gleam in the moonlight again.

Around seven thirty Samira heard voices in the hallway. She pressed her ear to the door to listen. Julius and Grace were heading down to the dining room. She almost ran out the door then to catch up with them, tell them what had happened. But what if Alfred was dead? If Samira wanted to stay out of trouble, she shouldn't tell anyone, shouldn't call 911. A flush crept up her neck. She went to the bathroom and turned on the shower. Samira would clear her head. She would go down to breakfast. She would act as perplexed as the rest of them. She would protect herself so she could protect her children.

"That was the plan, anyway." Samira lets out a low and long moan. The sound surprises her, is not of her. The detectives give away nothing. "Say something, please," she begs. "How much trouble am I in? How long will I go to prison for?"

Saying the word aloud makes Samira dizzy. Has she made a huge mistake? Sacrificed her children's welfare to assuage her own guilt? No, this is the right thing to do. If you mess up, you have to own up to it. A basic lesson she has been instilling in Aditi and Shivam for years.

Had she really thought the issue of Henry and the pregnancy was unsolvable? In the face of Alfred's death, the solution seems laughably simple now: Henry would move back in for the first months after their child was born. Once the baby was sleeping through the night, they'd find homes near each other, no more than a ten-minute drive apart. Samira would have to move her family out of the city, but she's known for a while that that day was coming. She wants to give her kids a backyard and a big dog. She wants them to wander the neighborhood on their bikes. She and Henry would raise their children together but apart.

That plan would've worked fine had she not pushed Alfred to his death.

Samira wonders what's going to happen to the hotel now that he's gone. She knows both Alfred's mother and father have died, that he has no siblings. Who will take care of his funeral arrangements? Who will deliver his eulogy? What if no one offers? What if no one attends? Despite what she now knows about his proclivities, Samira doesn't like the idea of anyone dying alone. Even the worst of the worst should be remembered by someone. A mother if no one else. She can't think of anything her children could do that would stop her from loving them—including murder.

"Am I going to prison?" Samira asks, picking at a chip in the wooden table.

Agopian clears his throat. "In the future I wouldn't make a habit of withholding information from the police. You should have come to us right away."

Samira bows her head. "I know. I'm sorry."

"That said, I wouldn't worry."

She gazes up at the detective. "What do you mean?"

Gromowski turns off the recorder. "We don't think the fall is what killed Alfred Smettle."

"But his neck was all twisted. His head was bleeding."

"The fall may have paralyzed him," Agopian says, "but there's something you all missed when you rushed into the closet." Samira squints at him. He pulls his phone out of his pocket and taps a few buttons. "The turtleneck. You didn't check under his turtleneck."

The sergeant slides his phone across the table. On its screen is a photo, a close-up of a neck. The side of the neck has a big purple birthmark, the one Alfred had always tried to hide. But that isn't why Agopian is showing Samira the picture. Slashed across Alfred's throat, like a signature with a flourish, is an angry red rope mark.

FIFTY

TJ

People keep falling to their deaths in this town.

Now that TJ has Julius on his side, now that he's able to see a (narrow) tunnel out of the mess he's made of his life, now that he can stop taking his gun everywhere he goes, he's able to focus on the last few hours. He replays Sunburn's words in his head. *What else is there to do here besides gossip?*

The cop had to be referring to Dr. Scott, right?

TJ couldn't believe it when he found out that his professor had died. He hadn't been the type in college to befriend teachers or even talk much in class, but Dr. Scott was his favorite professor. TJ liked that he treated the students as equals, that the class involved more discussion than lecture. Though TJ may not have contributed often, he enjoyed listening to the other students debate. It amused him to watch Dr. Scott change their green minds.

TJ believed classes like Dr. Scott's exemplified the point of a liberal arts education. College wasn't only about teaching you the practical skills required to do your job. It taught you how to think. It made you a more well-rounded person. No one in TJ's family ever sat around dissecting movies for the fun of it when he was growing up. Their discussions at the dinner table were never about art or music; they revolved around money and work and school, the logistics of managing two jobs while raising two children. TJ didn't resent his parents for his upbringing, not by a long shot. Still, he loved being surrounded by people who didn't find conversations about movies frivolous. People who, on the contrary, believed these conversations were vital. The films TJ and his peers watched in class reflected their own humanity back at them, tried to answer the unanswerable question: why are we here?

For a week straight after hearing the news, TJ could not stop picturing the *how* of Dr. Scott's death. He knew the professor liked to take his lunch breaks on the roof of Carroll Hall. He'd told them as much back in sophomore year. Dr. Scott said he loved the view of the White Mountains. *Not a lot of tall buildings in this town. If there's a better vantage point to watch the seasons change, I haven't found it yet.* TJ imagined him lining his toes up with the edge of the roof, feeling his stomach drop six stories to the waiting concrete. The professor would have watched the students on the sidewalk below mingling without a care in the world. He would have been jealous of their freedom, their youthful bodies that had yet to turn on themselves. TJ wondered if Dr. Scott sensed the cancer taking over, if this was the lone way he could regain control of what little life he had left.

Did he have second thoughts? Take a step back from the edge, tilt his face to the sun, and exhale? TJ pictured him squeezing balled-up wax paper in his right hand, oil-slick from the Italian sub he had just finished. With his tongue he dug out a sesame seed lodged between two teeth. His mouth still tasted of red onion. He focused on the birds chirping, the sun's rays on his cheeks. A breeze goosed the back of his neck. He should have worn a scarf. Dr. Scott pushed his glasses up his nose, squinted at the Victorian house on the hill, and shivered. He should have worn a scarf.

What was the last thing that ran through his mind? TJ hopes that he thought of his wife, that he wasn't scared. After his death, TJ had heard rumblings that the professor's wife had demanded an investigation, but TJ wasn't sure the rumor held any truth.

Had Dr. Scott's entire life story whizzed through his mind? Or had he thought of nothing at all? For a split second, maybe he'd felt powerful and free, in flight. At the end, perhaps he had understood that it wasn't falling he feared. It was landing.

FIFTY-ONE

Zoe

The local police force had interviewed all of Dr. Scott's students about the day he died. They'd taken special interest in those who had failed the class because of the recent Easy A cheating debacle, which included Zoe. Ironically, she had bought her essays from Easy A in an effort to get out from under Alfred's thumb. She didn't like the way he implied that she owed him big-time. She sensed his feeling of power over her. Little did she know Alfred was still behind her papers, this time with an alias.

A theory spread across the student body. If foul play was involved in Dr. Scott's death, the assailant must have been someone who was pissed that he'd failed them. The enrollment for COM206 was mostly seniors, students who had finished the coursework for their majors and wanted a stress-free elective that wouldn't put them to sleep twice a week. These were students trying to lock in goal GPAs, students who hoped to graduate with distinction. Now the cheaters would all have a scarlet letter on their transcripts, proof of their morally anemic character. It didn't matter to Zoe's peers that they were in the wrong. Most of them summoned the outrage of victimhood. Zoe took her failing grade quietly, knowing she deserved worse given how much cheating she'd done in the past two years. She worried what her parents would say when they found out, devised ways to hide the transcript from them. They would ask to see it upon her graduation—not because they suspected her of bad behavior but because they were bursting-at-the-seams proud. "Our family's first college graduate," Mom had said more than once. "I'm going to frame your diploma and put it in the living room." Zoe felt a spike of regret for the hundredth time.

When the police asked Zoe if she knew of anyone with a grudge against Dr. Scott, she thought of Alfred. The cops weren't even looking in his direction. As far as they knew, he was a thousand miles away, in the suburbs of Chicago, when Dr. Scott fell to his death. No one had seen him on campus since he'd taken off in his station wagon a week earlier.

Except for Zoe.

While a crowd was gathering around Dr. Scott's body in front of Carroll Hall, Zoe had been in the alley behind the building, with no idea what had happened on the other side. Her class had just let out in the lecture hall next door, and though the campus had been smoke-free for two years, Zoe still sometimes snuck into the alley and crouched between two dumpsters to have a cigarette. She was sitting on her haunches there, smoking, when the emergency-exit door of Carroll Hall bounced open. A man wearing a baseball cap and sunglasses strolled out of the building, blond hair sticking out beneath the hat. He was tall and gangly, squinted over his shoulder once as he walked away. Zoe would have recognized that loping gait anywhere.

"Alfred?" she had said, incredulous.

He stopped in his tracks, clocked her, and hesitated, as if debating whether to take off in a run.

Zoe stubbed out her cigarette and stood. "What are you doing here? What's with the wig?"

Alfred pulled the cap down more tightly around his head. "I'm reinventing myself," he said, scanning the alley. "I've got to get going, Zo."

Zoe narrowed her eyes. "What did you do?"

"Nothing." He shifted from foot to foot. "I don't want anyone to know I was here. I don't want my name in the school paper again."

Zoe remembers almost laughing. Who did he think he was—a celebrity? She almost made a joke about the paparazzi waiting around the corner, but the graveness in his expression stopped her.

"I mean it, Zo. You haven't seen me since I left last week." Alfred stepped toward her until they were nose to nose. Nose to chest, with his height. Calmly, he said, "If the school were to find out the extent of your cheating the past two years, you'd be heading home to Boston sooner than planned. Dear old Mom and Dad wouldn't get to hang your diploma on the wall after all."

Zoe swallowed, wishing she'd never told him about that. "What have you done, Alfred?"

"I forgot a few things—that's all." Alfred's hands were empty. He carried nothing on his person. "Don't worry about it." He clapped Zoe on the back. "Let's keep this meeting between us, okay? We don't want Marco and Lisa finding out about their baby girl's lack of morals. Lord knows I have enough of *your* papers on my computer to shock them."

Zoe ground her teeth. Alfred stuck his hands into his pockets and took off down the alley. "Have a good life, Zoe Allen," he called over his shoulder.

She stood there, shaking, until he disappeared. What could Alfred have done that warranted threats of blackmail? What did he want her to hide? She hadn't seen him do anything besides walk out of a building in a weird disguise. Maybe he wasn't allowed on campus after the expulsion. But no, that was absurd. Zoe lit another cigarette. She paced the alley for who knew how long, trying to piece the puzzle together.

Her answer came with the whine of sirens. Bile rose in Zoe's throat. *Fire,* she thought. *He set the building on fire.* She rounded the side of the lecture hall, and stopped when she turned the second corner and saw the crowd. Zoe couldn't see what they were gathered around, but some of them were crying, others wailing. One student shoved his way out of the mix with a hand over his mouth, as if he were about to puke.

Zoe elbowed the kid next to her. "What's going on?"

"A professor jumped from the roof."

Zoe had a sinking feeling, like all her organs were making their way toward her toes. Her lungs constricted. She almost asked which professor, but only one took his lunch breaks on the roof. Only one had dared to cross Alfred.

Zoe's gaze traveled six stories to the top of Carroll Hall. For a second she swore she saw Alfred there, grinning demonically in his blond wig, waving down at her like a mascot from Disney World. Later she would recognize that her brain had been playing tricks on her, that Alfred was nowhere to be found. By the time Zoe realized what he had done, he was already out of town.

FIFTY-TWO

Grace

Grace and Sunburn return to the home theater, where Zoe, TJ, Julius, and Danny wait with worried expressions. Julius raises an eyebrow at the waterlogged mannequin tucked under Sunburn's arm.

"Don't ask," Grace mutters as she settles onto the same recliner as before. "Is Samira still with the detectives?"

TJ nods.

What's taking so long? Grace wonders. *What does she know that I don't?*

She wants to rest her head on her knees, to jam the butts of her palms into her eye sockets. Signs of distress wouldn't necessarily be suspicious to everyone else in the room—she has, after all, lost a longtime friend.

To think that all of this began with an email. Two emails, really. The first one the entire group received, inviting them to a reunion at the Hitchcock Hotel. Alfred's tone in the missive was jovial and welcoming. No trace of residual bitterness built over the course of sixteen years. Grace had been surprised. She was in the middle of concocting a polite no when the second email arrived.

This one was for her alone. Message and tone were less breezy. Grace, it said. Making sure the rest of them say yes is in your best interest. If anyone doesn't attend, I might have to take a walk down Memory Lane with the Reville police.

As she sat in her glass-walled office, with a view of the Hudson that she never had time to enjoy, Grace's foot jittered against the floor. She put down the fork in her salad bowl, appetite gone. For a long while, she drummed her fingers on the keyboard. She couldn't respond with questions or demands of her own—she didn't want a paper trail. The thought of calling Alfred made her skin crawl, but it had to be done. Grace took the elevator forty floors down and stepped into the hustle of the Financial District. She searched for somewhere private and decided on an alley where only a few rats would overhear the conversation.

Grace dialed the phone number listed in the signature of Alfred's email. He answered after one ring.

"Grace Liu," he said cheerily. How had he known? She had never called or texted him from this number. They hadn't been in touch in years.

"Hi, Alfred." Grace hesitated.

"I assume you're calling about the email," he continued. "I hate to resort to threats, but I didn't want you dashing off some excuse about why you couldn't make it."

"Have you . . . told anyone? About senior year?" Grace asked.

"Haven't told a soul," Alfred said. "Our secret's safe with me."

His use of the word "our" grated on Grace, brought some fire back into her. "You know if you turn me in, you'll go down too, right?"

She could hear the eagerness in his voice. "Maybe. Although no one can place me on campus that day. I like my odds better than yours."

Grace needed to gain the upper hand. "I could just as easily turn you in. Sounds like you have a lot more to lose, what with your new business venture."

"No need for nastiness," Alfred said. "If the other four show up, you have nothing to worry about." He ended the call.

Grace stood there in the alley, staring at the black screen while an empty Pepsi can blew past her feet. Alfred had never hung up on her before, had never been the one to push her away. He had always savored every scrap of attention she gave him. In college, he had wanted her affection more than anything else. What if he no longer did? How would she keep him in line? Moreover, how would she get the others to attend against their will? Who besides Samira would want to go?

She plodded back toward her building. By the time she'd reached her corner office, she had already sent an email to Zoe. Next came Samira, whom she told she could use a break from work and family; plus, she'd love to see everyone. Could Samira help convince the others? Her sincerity and popularity would go a lot further than Grace's hectoring. One by one, they responded to Alfred's email with feigned enthusiasm. When the last reply came, a week later than everyone else's (Zoe's, naturally), Grace closed her eyes and sat back in her desk chair. She had done what he asked. She had delivered.

There are a lot of things Grace wishes she had done differently in college. Not running Easy A, for one. Alfred cheated to make tuition money, but Grace's tuition was taken care of—she had a partial academic scholarship, and her parents were paying for the rest. Grace wanted the money so she could put it in the stock market. She had learned about compounding interest in her finance classes and understood that the sooner she started investing, the sooner she'd get rich. Plus, she liked pushing boundaries. College became so predictable after a few semesters. Go to class, get drunk, lather, rinse, repeat. She needed a new challenge, something more entrepreneurial in spirit. She watched, underwhelmed, while Zoe and TJ worked their asses off bartending and waiting tables to make paltry sums.

Mistake number two was letting Alfred join the operation. She should've flown solo and kept all the profits for herself, but Grace had stupidly begun trusting Alfred again junior year. She missed his friendship, was stressed about keeping this project a secret. Grace had told herself Alfred was the best possible partner—she could control him if need be. Back then, he had never shown what he was capable of.

Mistake number three was not coming clean to the Reville

administration about her involvement in Easy A. Grace sees now that she could have recovered from an expulsion. She could have applied to another school, finished senior year somewhere more prestigious. One of her colleagues doesn't have a bachelor's degree. She would have found her way to this career, this life, even without a diploma from Reville.

Funny how narrow your understanding of the world is when you're young. Nothing is more important than the current semester's exams, than your GPA, than your extracurriculars and awards and all the other things you work so hard to achieve to distinguish yourself as an entry-level jobseeker who no employer gives a shit about. She hadn't known then that those were only boxes to check. What matters is who you know. Grace was brought up to value her education, to get good grades, to be the best. At twenty-two, she could not imagine a fate worse than being expelled from college. Her fear of failure is not an excuse for what she did. Only an explanation. How easy to get wrapped up in one's little dramas, to lose the forest for the trees.

That night senior year when Alfred was supposed to be driving home to Chicago, the two of them lay in her bed instead. With his arms wrapped around her, her face buried in his chest, Grace summoned the guts to ask again what Alfred knew. What had Dr. Scott said about Grace?

"He's looking into you," Alfred had told her. "He's suspicious."

"But how?" Grace had never been more scared in her entire life. "Did you say something?"

Alfred had lifted her chin to face him. "I would never, Grace. One of our customers must have."

Grace extricated herself from Alfred and ran her hands through her disheveled hair. "We have to do something."

Alfred propped himself up on one elbow. "What do you have in mind?"

Their actions weren't as maniacal as they sound. No stroking of the chin, no prayer-steepled fingers, no villainous laugh. Neither of them ever said *Let's kill him.* Not at first, anyway.

They ran through other options. They considered bribing him, scaring him off the investigation, running him out of town. Each proposal, one or both of them dismissed. The ideas were too risky. What if Dr. Scott told the cops, and they got into even more trouble? As long as the professor was around, Grace was at risk.

She noted that the longer they talked, the more excited Alfred got. Whereas Grace dreaded the direction the conversation was headed, Alfred reveled in it. She could tell by the way he spit Dr. Scott's name, by the gleam in his eyes, that Alfred wanted an excuse for violence. Dr. Scott had ruined Alfred's senior year, his job prospects, his reputation, his future. He would never work in academia now. Why should the professor get off so easy?

Neither of them slept that night. They stayed up talking, making sure to leave the house before the others stumbled home at three in the morning. They parked at the local Walmart and got serious about a plan. Alfred would drive home to Chicago. He would borrow his mom's car to return to Reville, leave it in the Walmart parking lot with the license plates removed, then ride a bike to campus. He and Grace would meet in Carroll Hall around lunchtime. She would let him in through the back door, the one by the alley. They'd wait in the emergency-exit stairwell, the one no one used because the building had multiple elevators and the doors to the stairs had big red EMERGENCY EXIT ONLY signs on them. People probably assumed that if they opened the doors, an alarm would sound. Grace always had.

She can't remember whose idea the push was, but she does know Alfred volunteered for the job. Grace was supposed to stand guard in the stairwell while Alfred followed Dr. Scott up to the roof. Alfred would be out there no more than forty-five seconds.

They crouched on the fifth-floor landing, waiting with breath held. Grace was overcome by a dizzying delirium. She hadn't slept much the past week, was having a hard time applying reason to any of the choices she was making. She knew only that she had to act. She had to win.

At twelve thirty, Dr. Scott still hadn't come, and Grace worried that something in his schedule had changed. She found herself not wanting him to show. Maybe this was a sign that she had gone too far. But Grace didn't believe in signs. She believed in strength. And strategy.

At twelve forty, the door to floor six creaked open. Grace craned her neck to see Dr. Scott with his usual Italian sub wrapped in greasy paper. He bought one from the sandwich shop on Greet Street every day. He wasn't whistling that day, which was unusual, because he whistled everywhere he went—a trait Grace would have found annoying in anyone but him.

She listened to the professor climb the stairs to the roof and had misgivings. *I can still stop this,* she thought. What if she left Dr. Scott to his investigation? What if she let the administration expel her? She saw herself packing her belongings under the cloak of night like Alfred had. The provost wagging his finger at her. Mom with her face in her hands. Dad avoiding her eyes. Now she was wiping down a table at her hometown Applebee's. Standing at the altar with her loser high school boyfriend because no one else would have her. Kids crawling all over her, as lazy as their father. A cheap coffin. A poorly attended funeral. A shitty headstone in the cemetery next to the highway. An afterlife spent watching better people go places and do things. When the door to the roof banged closed and Alfred rose to his feet, Grace could have stopped him. She did not.

Her heart beat in time with Alfred's steps up the two flights of stairs. The door to the roof opened a second time. His footsteps disappeared. Grace checked her watch and counted the seconds. Would she hear a scream from inside this concrete stairwell? She hoped not.

Grace made it to forty-five, then sixty, then seventy-five. Alfred did not come. At one hundred, she could wait no longer. She crept up the stairs toward the roof, opened the door a crack, and peered out.

Alfred had Dr. Scott backed up to the edge of the roof. The professor had his hands raised in surrender, eyes wide with alarm. His glasses had fallen off, the frame bent, lying a few feet away from where he stood.

"I idolized you," Alfred was shouting. "You ruined my life over one error in judgment."

With horror, Grace saw that Alfred's shoulders were shaking. He was crying. Grace crossed the roof until she reached both of them. "What's going on, Alfred?" she said mildly. The professor pressed his palms together in prayer, begging for her help.

Alfred hung his head. "I can't do it, Grace. I'm sorry."

Of course he couldn't. He didn't have the mettle. In less than a second, Grace weighed her options. Expulsion would be a cakewalk compared to imprisonment for attempted murder. If Dr. Scott walked away from this rooftop, her life was over. She had no choice.

"I'm sorry too," she said as she shoved Dr. Scott with both hands.

For an awful moment the professor wheeled his arms through the air, trying to catch his balance. Then, without a shriek or plea or any sound at all, he was gone. Grace and Alfred stood for a moment or two, staring at the empty space that Dr. Scott had occupied.

"We have to go," Grace said. She dragged Alfred by the arm toward the stairwell.

"Wait." He pulled away and picked up Dr. Scott's glasses, then slid them into his coat pocket.

"Leave them," Grace hissed. "What if the cops figure out they're missing?"

But the small-town cops never did. Nor did anyone else.

"A souvenir," Alfred said with a wry grin. Every nerve in Grace's body told her to get away from him. Sixteen years later, as she sat in her corner office questioning how to resolve the issue of Alfred, she thought of Dr. Scott's eyeglasses. Might Alfred have kept the souvenir all these years? Grace never went anywhere without a plan, and the Hitchcock Hotel was no exception. She vowed to search every room in the building until she found evidence that would place Alfred at the scene of the crime. Once Alfred had been arrested, her life could return to normal. She would be in charge again. Grace had ransacked the hotel this weekend, but there had been no sign of the eyeglasses anywhere—not even in Alfred's room or the attic.

On that day atop Carroll Hall, though, she had no clue Alfred would turn on her. The idea was for him to leave the building via the back exit while she would go to the third floor and sit in the cubicle designated for the film club. Grace would flee the building when the masses did, would spill into and blend with the shocked crowd. Meanwhile, Alfred's bike was stashed in a rack nearby. He would ride to the Walmart, then drive his mother's car back to Chicago with as few stops as possible, putting the license plates back in place once he was out of town.

Grace and Alfred scrambled down the concrete stairwell. On the third-floor landing, they paused. Alfred locked eyes with Grace and squeezed her hand. "I made it up."

Grace's blood ran cold. "Made what up?"

"Now we're linked for life." He grinned.

She ripped her hand from his. "Made *what* up, Alfred?"

He was already skipping down the steps. Without a backward glance he said, "Scott had no idea you were involved."

FIFTY-THREE

Zoe

In the days after Zoe's encounter with Alfred outside Carroll Hall, she told no one what he'd said. Maybe she was being silly, but she had an uncanny feeling that he was watching her, that he had somehow bugged the blue house and would know if she betrayed him. Zoe found herself running her fingers atop picture frames, dropping to her knees to search under her bed, racking her brain for other nooks and crannies where Alfred might've hidden a camera or recording device. She was going crazy, being paranoid—but was she? She coped by drinking until she passed out.

One week after Dr. Scott's fall, even booze couldn't keep the guilt away. There were rumblings around campus that the police were going to rule his death a suicide. Zoe kept waiting for someone else to speak up. Alfred couldn't have covered his tracks that well. Someone would have seen him in the building, or at least around campus. The burden couldn't rest on Zoe's shoulders alone. She liked to think she wasn't a bad person, but she was self-aware enough to admit that she was no hero.

No one else came forward.

When Zoe could stand the secret no more, she decided on a

compromise. She wouldn't go to the police, but she would confide in one of her friends. To be able to tell one other person the load she was bearing—that would take off some of the pressure, wouldn't it? After careful consideration, she decided on Grace. Out of everyone in the group, Grace was the closest with Alfred. He'd been snappy with her recently, but that was just because of misplaced anger about his expulsion. Alfred valued Grace's opinion, listened to her more than he listened to the others. He would never hurt her. If anyone could convince him to turn himself in, it would be Grace. She would know what to do.

Zoe knocked on Grace's door one Tuesday night in early November.

"Come in," Grace said. She was sitting pretzel-style on her bed, a pencil tucked behind her ear as she tapped at her laptop's keyboard. Without looking away from the screen, she said, "What's up, Zo?"

Zoe stood in the doorway. Grace's room hadn't changed much from her and Samira's freshman-year dorm. She still had the Third Eye Blind poster and the bougie Eiffel Tower bedding. These things seemed too young for Grace now. She was only twenty-two, but Zoe could already envision her friend's future home: a sleek penthouse with harsh lines and uncomfortable furniture. A lot of beige. "I have to tell you something."

Grace was half paying attention, typing away. "Shoot."

Zoe swallowed. This was the point of no return. "Let's go out back."

Grace glanced up, brow furrowed. "What's going on?"

Zoe didn't answer. She headed down the hall, through the kitchen, and out the back door without waiting for Grace. The porch light clicked on as she paced the yard, trying to drum up some courage. Zoe still remembers that the night was unseasonably cold—she could see her breath when she exhaled. Grace joined her after a minute, serious now.

Breathless, Zoe told Grace everything that had happened on the afternoon of Dr. Scott's death, from the moment she left class all the way to watching Alfred retreat from the alley. When the entirety of the story was out there between them, Zoe was lighter. Grace would confront Alfred. Zoe wasn't in this alone.

Grace was quiet, possibly in shock. Zoe expected her to say something, to spring into action, but she stood there, fingering the cuff of her sweater.

"What should we do?" Zoe prodded. "We have to get him to talk to the police, right?"

Grace chose her words carefully. "Alfred's been through enough with the expulsion, hasn't he?"

Zoe tilted her head. "But he killed someone."

"We don't know that for sure," Grace said. "He could've been referring to something else altogether. This might be a big coincidence."

Zoe didn't know if Grace was naïve enough to believe that or if she only wanted to see the best in their supposed friend. She clicked her tongue in disgust and headed back into the house, leaving Grace alone on the porch.

Twice more Zoe brought up the topic with Grace, sure each time that she would change her mind, that she would call Alfred to demand that he do the right thing. But Grace never wavered. She told Zoe to let it go. The last time Zoe brought it up, Grace snapped, "If you believe Alfred is capable of murder, do you think crossing him is wise? What's to stop him from hurting us?" Zoe was surprised by the heat in Grace's voice.

Maybe she had something to hide too.

Zoe should've consulted someone with more scruples next, not fewer. But Samira would have gone straight to an authority figure, with or without Zoe's agreement. TJ might have too. Instead, Zoe went to Julius. He was on the couch one night, watching *The O.C.*, when she approached him. The others were home but in their rooms. Zoe glanced upstairs. Grace's door was closed.

"How come you never bought an essay from Easy A?" Zoe murmured.

Julius did a double take. "I didn't want to give Alfred my money when he was such a dick to me all the time."

"But Alfred wasn't running it alone," Zoe countered. She had a hunch, no more than an educated guess. Zoe's friends thought she was too much of a mess lately to pick up anything besides her next shot, but she'd caught the clues over the past year and a half. Grace's encyclopedic knowledge of American filmmakers. Grace slipping Alfred flash drives—more than once. Julius staying after class a few weeks ago to talk to Dr. Scott. Grace and Julius whispering in Grace's room. Junior year, Alfred had written the majority of Zoe's essays for her. They were solid but derivative (not that Zoe was complaining), regurgitated topics and theses that everyone in class used. Easy A's essays were different. The thoughts may not have seemed original to film-industry insiders, but they did to the Reville student body. Zoe was impressed when she read the first essay. It had a certain, well, grace to it.

"You know?" Julius whispered. Zoe nodded. "Grace swore me to secrecy. How'd you find out?"

Zoe stammered a bullshit explanation about a drunken admission as she worked through her suspicions. Grace didn't want Alfred to turn himself in because the Easy A scheme would be dragged back into the spotlight. Officials might then discover Grace's involvement. She'd be expelled too.

Had Grace known about Alfred's plans for the professor? Did she try to stop him?

Zoe didn't discuss her theory with Julius, instead left him to the rest of his *O.C.* episode. She trod up the stairs to her room, gripped by the knowledge that the more people she shared the secret with, the bigger the hole she dug for herself. A few days before, she thought the worst thing that could happen was her own expulsion from Reville. Now she was worried about what Alfred and Grace might be willing to do to protect their secret.

She soon got a glimpse at the answer. One night, at three in the morning, she clambered back to the blue house having finished a double bartending shift. She wanted nothing more than to land facedown on her pillow and sleep for fourteen hours.

When she got to her room, the door was closed. As an unspoken rule, no one in the house closed their bedroom doors unless they were inside and wanted privacy. Zoe never ever closed her door before she left the house. Nervously, she turned the handle and walked in.

A wave of nausea swept over Zoe. On her bed was a dead baby bird.

FIFTY-FOUR

Zoe

For the rest of senior year, Zoe kept her distance from Grace and the others. She never found out who left the bird on her bed. Alfred seemed most likely, but Zoe could see from the photos he was posting on Facebook that he was home in Chicago. First he was watching Hitchcock movies with his mom; then he was starting his first day of work at the La Quinta near his childhood house. She considered deleting him as a friend but thought better of it. This way she could keep track of him.

If Alfred hadn't planted the bird, Grace must have. Who else could it have been? Zoe didn't have any enemies, and she didn't know any other secrets. Such an act seemed out of character for Grace, but increasingly Zoe questioned whether she knew Grace as well as she'd thought. Zoe hoped Grace hadn't killed the bird, that she had instead found it abandoned in a nest somewhere and scooped it up to use for her own sick devices. Whatever the case, Zoe got the message loud and clear. She kept her mouth shut. Both Alfred and Grace knew Zoe's parents and brother, had met them several times during campus visits. Zoe wasn't going to chance putting her family or herself in danger. The risk wasn't worth it.

Grace didn't behave any differently toward Zoe. Never once did she bring up their conversations about Dr. Scott's death. Nor did she mention the bird, which Zoe had put in a plastic bag, then taken outside to the trash can and buried under the rest of the garbage. She was terrified that she might run into one of her housemates along the way—how would she explain the dead bird?—but needn't have worried. By then the time was four a.m. Everyone else was asleep.

Zoe asked for more shifts at work. She spent more time at the bars and at house parties, invented as many excuses as she could to be away from the blue house, went home to Boston more times than she had the previous three years of school combined. She thought about moving out for spring semester but didn't want to cause trouble. Samira, TJ, and Julius would have questions that she couldn't answer. She stayed the course for four months, walked the graduation stage, then got the hell out of Reville. Zoe never talked to any of them again, save for Samira, and that was only because Samira was relentless about keeping in touch.

In the back row of the Hitchcock Hotel's theater, Zoe rocks in her recliner, replaying her interview with the detectives. Did she say enough? Did she say too much?

Officer Shaw is standing guard at the door while Sunburn takes a break. The new cop hasn't said a word to any of them. He stands there with his arms loose, watching, scanning, equal parts interested and uninterested. Zoe glances past Julius, who's chewing his fingernails, to the housekeeper in the corner. In Danny's lap is a pile of yarn. Her fingers work the needles, lips pressed together. Alfred's almost-finished blanket is spread across multiple seats. Zoe wonders if Danny is going to insist that he be buried with it. Who could stop her?

The silence grows and grows, save for the clicking of Danny's needles and Julius's clearing phlegm from his throat. Zoe is desperate for something, anything, to break the tension. She glances at TJ, who also seems restless. Earlier she tried to eavesdrop on his and Julius's conversation, but all she could make out was that TJ needed money and Julius agreed to give it to him. Maybe Julius will tell her later what kind of trouble TJ is in if she can get him alone.

"Officer Shaw, right?" Grace suddenly asks the cop. Shaw nods. "Can I ask you a personal question?"

Shaw looks suspicious. He opens his mouth to respond, but then the door to the theater opens. Zoe holds her breath. Samira walks in, dazed. She dumps herself back into her recliner. Zoe trades a nervous glance with Julius.

"That depends on the nature of the question," Officer Shaw says.

Grace crosses her arms. "Your partner said you're related to the previous owners of this house."

Shaw appears annoyed by this revelation. "They were my parents."

What the actual fuck?

Julius gasps. TJ's eyes widen. Even Samira snaps out of it.

For a second, Zoe quits worrying over everything that's about to happen and focuses on the fact that she is sitting before a man who found his father dead in his bed, starved by his own mother. Impulse control has never been a strength of Zoe's. Without thinking, she blurts, "Is the grass thing true?"

Shaw squints at her. "Excuse me?"

Zoe regrets speaking up, but now she can't stop. "Alfred told us—"

"Zoe, shut up," Samira whispers.

Shaw seems irritated but gestures for Zoe to continue.

"He said your mom . . . fed your dad . . . grass," Zoe manages. "That that's how he died."

"Disgusted" is the only word to describe the expression on Shaw's face. "My parents loved each other. Their life together was ordinary and peaceful. Their behavior was odd at times because they both had dementia. My pop's memory got so bad that my ma had to move him to a full-time care facility. When the house's upkeep became too much for her to manage alone, she signed the deed over to my sister and me." He bows his head. "They both died in hospice."

"I'm sorry for your loss," Zoe murmurs, feeling about two feet tall, "and for the mix-up. Alfred said the Realtor told him—"

"Our Realtor let us know the prospective buyer was a weird guy,"

Shaw interrupts. "Prodding for some grisly history of the house. She told him the truth, which is what I just told you. Whatever this grass story is that you're referring to came from his imagination."

Danny speaks for the first time in hours. The needles in her hands never quit moving. "Alfred meant no harm. He was trying to create a mood. To evoke the Hitchcockian spirit."

The cop raises an eyebrow. "That's the reason we sold him the place. Our parents were huge Hitchcock fans. We thought they would've gotten a kick out of their retirement home being turned into a themed hotel."

"Thank God they had a happy ending," Samira breathes.

Shaw stares her down. "You call that a happy ending? Instead of spending their golden years reflecting with fondness on lives well lived, two decent people lost bits and pieces of themselves until they didn't recognize their own children. Until they couldn't swallow their food."

"I'm sorry. I didn't mean—"

Once again, the conversation stops when the door thumps open. The two detectives enter and ask to speak to Shaw. The younger detective is holding under his arm a clear evidence bag with what appears to be a coiled rope inside. All three men step outside the screening room. Zoe strains to listen but can't hear a word they're saying.

Officer Shaw reenters, pulling handcuffs from his belt. Sweat drips from Zoe's armpits. Has she done the right thing? She'd told the detectives everything she'd been hiding the past sixteen years. The Easy A scandal, Dr. Scott's death, catching Alfred coming out of Carroll Hall, his and Grace's threats, Grace's insistence that Zoe attend this reunion. Zoe told the detectives that if they searched Grace's email they'd probably find a warning from Alfred, blackmailing her into coming, demanding that she convince the others as well. Maybe, Zoe theorized, Alfred threatened to give Grace up one too many times. Maybe she couldn't take life as his puppet anymore. Maybe she snapped.

Zoe's confession came a decade and a half late, but she finally came clean. Perhaps now she could meet her own eyes in the mirror. She could quit self-sabotaging and rewrite the narrative that she doesn't deserve happiness because she's a bad person. She feels a thousand pounds lighter. She should have done this years ago. Why is honesty the obvious solution only in retrospect?

Shaw opens the handcuffs and steps across the room to the second row. Zoe wants to look away but can't. Her hands and feet are numb. For a moment she worries that she's having a heart attack, a panic attack, an attack of some sort. She watches the cop glare down his nose at Grace and her disdainful expression. Then, as if in a Hitchcock movie, he says words that bring Zoe both dread and relief. "Grace Liu, you're under arrest for the murder of Alfred Smettle."

FIFTY-FIVE

Danny

It amuses me to watch Grace Liu sputter and blink like a malfunctioning doll. She is unused to facing consequences.

"What the hell are you talking about?" she demands.

"Put your hands behind your back, please," Officer Shaw says.

"I didn't do this," Grace protests. "It wasn't me."

"Ma'am, please do as I say, and put your hands behind your back."

"I want to call my husband and my lawyer," Grace growls, but she obeys him. How long I have waited for the sound of the metal cuffs locking in place. Finally, she will be held accountable for her actions.

The rest of the group watches with their maws hanging open as Grace is escorted out of the screening room. I study TJ in particular. His face is ghost white; his hands grip the arms of his chair. He had no idea who he was sleeping with. I have wondered about that, how complicit he was or wasn't.

The air carries a lethal silence. Even the loathsome Julius Thénardier has stopped his fidgeting. The only sound is the dutiful clicking of my needles. Zoe scowls at my hands, but I'm hardly going to worry about the opinion of a wino like her.

Detective Gromowski leaves but soon returns. "The tow truck is here."

Sergeant Agopian adds, "You're all free to go. If you'd like to gather your belongings from your rooms, Detective Gromowski or I will accompany you."

I scan the room without moving my head or neck even an inch. No one rises; no one moves. They flick expressions of concern at one another. They think they're better people than they are.

"Should we . . ." Samira trails off. "Should we call Rob?"

No one answers. How many of them even have Grace's husband's phone number?

"How do you know Grace is behind this?" TJ demands of the detectives.

His question is easily answered. The detectives have her on motive because I shared the audio clip from Alfred's phone with them. They have her on opportunity because she cannot prove that she was asleep in bed at the time Alfred died. Lastly, they have her on means. The rope used to strangle Alfred was found tucked inside a pocket of Grace's suitcase.

"We're not at liberty to discuss an ongoing investigation," Detective Gromowski says.

TJ throws up his hands and heads for the door. "I'm getting out of here." The detective follows him from the room. Now that the mooch has what he came for, there's no need for him to stick around.

Zoe is next to leave. I can tell by the lightness in her step that she has shared her troubled past with the detectives. She has unburdened herself and therefore believes she's on the right side of history. She is wrong— she's as immoral as the rest. For fifteen years, eleven months, and twenty days, she let their beloved Dr. Scott toss and turn in his grave. For nearly sixteen years, she refused to give my husband the peace he deserves.

FIFTY-SIX

Danny

You cannot trust the police when it comes to the pursuit of the truth, a lesson I learned soon after Jerome's death. Never for a moment did I believe my dear husband would jump off a six-story building. Jerome had a joie de vivre the rest of us can channel only sporadically. He went skydiving for the first time at fifty-five. He brought home a new foster dog monthly, though we already had Buster and Charlie to rear. Every summer he planned a trip for the two of us to a destination where one of his favorite films took place. In 1999 we went to Nice (*To Catch a Thief*). In 2002 we visited Morocco (*Casablanca*). The year 2006 took us to Egypt, Greece, and Nepal (*Raiders of the Lost Ark*).

"Nepal?" I'd said. "That's nowhere near Egypt!"

He merely grinned and winked. When Jerome put his mind to something, no one could talk him out of it.

That included his battle with cancer. His doctor had pronounced him terminal, true, but that made Jerome only more determined to use his remaining time wisely. Weeks before his death, he'd been toying with the idea of whisking me away to Italy. We could live out his final days among the lemon trees of Amalfi, he said. A romantic to the end.

I told the police that he had plans for the final months of his life, that he was not a desperate man on that October day. Initially they listened to me. But when their search continued to yield nothing, they decided I, not the missing killer, was the problem. They wrote me off and ignored my pleas.

Fuming, I returned to my work running a bed-and-breakfast in Portland, Maine. I had opened the B and B twenty years prior, when a midlife crisis at forty prompted me to quit my job in sales and start the small business I'd always dreamt about. At that time Jerome was a film studies professor at a university in Portland. I wish he'd never taken the job at Reville.

I buried my husband. Afterward I tried to move on, to shake the nagging suspicion that something wasn't right. When that didn't work, I investigated on my own. The project became so consuming that it interfered with my business. I shut down the inn and focused my efforts fulltime on Jerome's case. I had his handsome Reville pension to support me. Every week when I visited his grave site, I promised I would not rest until his killer had paid for what they'd done to him.

The most obvious person to look into was the student who had been expelled for running a cheating ring in Jerome's classes. Alfred Smettle was his name, and Jerome had told me all about him. A weaselly kid he never liked much, for reasons he couldn't put his finger on. I had chastised my husband—chastised him!—for wanting to say no when Smettle asked him to be his club's advisor. I encouraged him to give Smettle a chance. Maybe the boy would grow on him.

I am as responsible for my husband's death as anyone else.

Jerome never did take to Smettle, but he liked some of the other members of the film club. He thought Grace Liu was sharp as a tack, TJ Stewart quiet but insightful. He commended Samira Reddy's enthusiasm, even if she could be a bit of a brownnoser. Jerome saw the potential in Zoe Allen, though he never got to hear her speak unless he called on her, which he was not in the habit of doing. He didn't subscribe to methods of forcing students to participate. He believed even those who appeared unengaged might soak up some of what he was saying by listening. Julius Thénardier, for example, whose father had paid for the renovation of the business school's three buildings. Jerome suspected that was the sole reason the boy had been granted admission to Reville. Julius wasn't much of a student.

I hired a private investigator to keep an eye on Smettle. The young woman was good with computers too, eventually breaking into Smettle's email and cloud storage. All we learned from that endeavor was that Smettle had not operated the cheating ring on his own. Grace was his accomplice, though she had somehow escaped notice by the administration. Jerome had never mentioned her involvement either. Perhaps she had let her friend Smettle take the fall.

In exchange for what? I mused.

The PI dug and dug, but everything she found about Alfred Smettle discouraged me further. On the day of Jerome's death, Smettle had tagged himself in various establishments near his childhood home in the Chicago suburbs. His cell phone records showed that he had remained there all week. I was frustrated but unconvinced. The PI taught me that one doesn't have to physically be in a place to tag oneself there on social media, and Smettle could have left his cell phone at home during his trip back to Reville.

We searched Smettle's credit card statements for an airline ticket purchased or car rented, a hotel booked. Nothing. Nor had he conducted a single transaction in the Reville area since his expulsion. The PI made a visit to campus and had discreet conversations with students. Even when she located those who had first stumbled upon Jerome's body, none of them could recall seeing a man on the roof or anyone fleeing the building. We hit one dead end after another.

I shifted focus to Grace Liu. The PI found even less to work with there. The Liu girl was clever enough to empty her inboxes regularly. Her cloud storage was encrypted, and my investigator was unable to hack it. After multiple years of working together, we were no closer to an answer. I admitted to myself that I was wasting Jerome's pension on a wild-goose chase. I ended the relationship with the PI, then didn't leave the house for weeks. I stewed; I fumed; I cried.

Once again, I tried to move on.

For the next decade, though, I kept my eye on Smettle—where he was living, what he was up to. Then came a bombshell from a local newspaper.

FORMER REVILLE STUDENT PLANS TO OPEN THEMED HOTEL

According to the article, Smettle had purchased a three-story house not far from campus. Before long, he created an Instagram account with the username @hitchcockhotel. I watched from afar as he gutted the old Victorian and renovated it. He would need employees, I realized. For the first time in a long time, I had a glimmer of hope, a sense of control. I promised Jerome I would not fail him again.

Getting the job was easy. Before the renovations were finished, I emailed Smettle at the general hotel account and professed my love for Hitchcock. I dropped bits of trivia that only true fans would know— thanks to Jerome's educating me all those years—and said I would be honored to play any role in the hotel's rise to glory. Smettle invited me for an interview the following week. I could tell he was disappointed when I showed up (ageist prick), but I demonstrated my dexterity and acuity before either of us had to partake in an awkward letdown. I volunteered to help Smettle with the makeover. The sooner I embedded myself in his life, the sooner he would tell me something worthwhile.

I wasn't worried about being recognized by Reville staff or townspeople. I had lived and worked ninety minutes away, in Portland, the entire time Jerome was a faculty member at the university. He kept an apartment on campus that he slept in Monday through Wednesday. After class on Thursday, he headed home to me. All our friends were in Portland, people we'd known for decades, so we didn't spend any of our free time on campus. Plus, getting away from my work at the B and B was hard. When Jerome had holiday soirees or end-of-semester parties to attend, he went alone. I wouldn't have recognized any of the faculty members, and I doubt they would have known my face either. I had no plans to spend time on campus anyway.

Initially I never stayed the night at Smettle's hotel, but once the rooms were set up and the beds installed, he invited me to sleep there when I liked. He was under the impression that my home was thirty minutes away, a drive he deemed too long for a woman of my age and with my eyesight to make in the dark. I took him up on the offer with increasing frequency. I find people tend to let their guard down more in the evenings.

Smettle wasn't the sort to open up easily. It took well over six months to get him to share anything personal. When at last he did, he spoke about his mother and where his love of Hitchcock derived from. I pretended to find such admissions fascinating, waiting with gritted teeth for the day the conversation would turn to Reville. I managed to wring a confession from him about the cheating ring by admitting to some bogus cheating of my own, but he never went further than that, no matter how I probed. "Aren't you furious with that professor?" I asked. "He ruined your career over one lousy mistake."

These questions succeeded in ingratiating me to Smettle, but he wasn't giving up the goods. Nor did he like to talk about his friends from school. He was still angry that none of them had come to his disciplinary meeting with the provost. He had been alone when the expulsion was handed down. Some friends.

In a stroke of genius, while scrubbing toilets and making beds, I realized his peers could be the key. If I could get them all to the hotel and stir up old trouble, maybe someone would say something that would lead me to more evidence. Smettle would be more likely to trip up when his emotions were already flying high, but I couldn't bring up the idea of a reunion out of the blue. I had to let Smettle think this was his brainchild.

I waited and waited for the right moment to present itself. The closer we came to the first anniversary of the hotel's opening, the more preoccupied Smettle was with its lack of business. He claimed to have tried everything. He'd offered potential and past guests exclusive discounts. He had procured listings with local travel websites and the chamber of commerce. He'd improved the hotel's booking process and SEO results. These changes moved the needle incrementally. Most weekends, more than half the rooms were empty. Smettle said we needed to build a buzz around this place, to get a big publicity hit that would put us on the map. Two months ago, he took me aside in the parlor.

"I've got it," he said, twitching with excitement. "The solution came to me from a novel, of all places. Have you heard of *The Shining*?"

Everyone had, but I let him spell his idea out for me anyway. The Stephen King novel was set in the fictitious Overlook Hotel, he said, which was based on the real-life Stanley Hotel in Estes Park, Colorado. King stayed there with his wife for one night during the offseason in 1973. They were the lone guests in the place, and the experience unnerved him so much that he wrote a book about his night in room 217.

"Guess what the Stanley Hotel's most requested room is fifty-one years later." Smettle grinned.

"Number 217," I said.

"Bingo." Throngs of people travel from all over the country to stay in the infamous haunted hotel, Smettle said, just like they visit Salem, Massachusetts, or Pearl Harbor.

By now he was pacing the parlor, tugging his hair like he always did when agitated. "Why do we slow down when we drive past a car wreck? Why do stories of suspicious deaths fascinate us? What is it about human beings that makes us want to stand in the place where tragedy has occurred?" He gazed at me. "We don't need to answer these questions. We need to capitalize on the intrigue behind them."

"So we make up a horror story about the hotel, like King did?" I asked.

Smettle nodded, awaiting my reaction, seeking my approval. The lightbulb went on.

"That's a good idea," I said slowly, "but it's a little *been there, done that*, isn't it?" Smettle frowned. "Too bad you can't create a real horror story."

"You mean an actual murder?" he asked. I smiled. Smettle shifted from foot to foot. "I couldn't hurt an innocent person."

You already did, I thought.

"What about a guilty one?" I pushed.

"Like who?" He tugged at the collar of his turtleneck.

"What about those friends of yours you're always ranting about?" I suggested. "The ones who betrayed you all those years ago."

Smettle demurred, but I knew he was intrigued. Here was his chance to bring art to life. He could step into Hitchcock's shoes, gain publicity for his hotel, and show his college friends what happened to traitors. In his darkest of hours, they had deserted him. Smettle believed that the provost might have been more lenient in his sentencing if he'd had a friend or two to defend him at the hearing. He'd needed someone to vouch for his character, to tell the disciplinary board they had it all wrong. More than once, he told me he never would have been expelled if his friends had shown up for him. He blamed them for his decade of hard labor at La Quinta. His future was full of potential until they'd dashed it to pieces. He would have been a professor, a journalist, maybe even a director like his idol, but because of his so-called friends, he'd wound up cleaning toilets instead. I waited patiently as he convinced himself they needed to pay for their actions.

"Why risk your own freedom to help me?" he asked once. "If something goes wrong, you could wind up in prison."

"I'm not going to help you commit the act," I said, "but I won't stand in your way either. I know what it feels like to have your world flipped upside down with no one there to pick you back up. I never got closure when my life fell to pieces. Maybe you can." I gazed at him. "Besides, if things go topsy-turvy, I'm sure you'll insist I wasn't involved."

Smettle nodded dutifully, though I'm sure he wouldn't have hesitated to take me down with him.

One month ago he announced that he'd finalized the plans. He would invite his former friends here and give himself two days to decide who would be the victim and who would be the killer, then frame one of them for his crime. As far as Smettle was concerned, they were all guilty. Every single one of them refused their support when he needed them most. The question was, who was the guiltiest? Who was most deserving of prison without parole? Who deserved to pay with their life?

Part of me hadn't expected Smettle to actually agree to my suggestion. Once he did, I had my own decision to make. If I didn't report him to the police—and soon—blood would be on my hands too. In the end, I decided that justice for Jerome was more important than saving a stranger. I would turn Smettle in after he committed his heinous crime. He might never go down for the murder of my husband, but he would spend the rest of his days on earth in a cell.

Another part of me wasn't convinced Smettle would actually go through with it. Shoving an acquaintance to his death was one thing, but killing one of his friends at close range, betrayal or not, was another. He was no longer the brash twenty-two-year-old he'd been in college. He was older now, had the hotel to lose. I saw the way he longed to impress his friends, how he craved easy camaraderie. I reasoned that even if he backed down, I could tell the police he'd been poisoning Zoe. Attempted murder carries a hefty sentence too.

I couldn't chance the Reville six's hitting it off and burying the hatchet. I needed them against Smettle, Smettle against them. Much was achieved by listening. At dinner in the private dining room that first night, Smettle told his outlandish story about the previous tenants. While Smettle and his guests all ate breakfast the next morning, I snuck outside to pull some grass from the backyard and left it on Zoe's pillow. I had noted her snappy comment at dinner when Julius suggested pushing someone from a great height. *Isn't that what you did?* she'd said to Smettle. Oh, how my heart pounded. *She knows,* I thought. *She's known all this time and said nothing.*

She deserved a few doses of antifreeze for that.

(Once Zoe found the bottle in the kitchen, I moved it back to the shed, where it belonged. I didn't want the detectives thinking her poisoning claim had merit.)

Then came Samira, who made such a big stink about the intruder in her room. I wasn't trying to sneak a peek at her nude body—I was hoping to search her cell phone for any useful texts or emails. After that, I'd learned my lesson and snooped only while they were all dining together on the first floor.

Some of my stunts were simply meant to scare them. The boots under TJ's curtain and the mannequin in the pond, for example. Smettle had one thing right—power over the wicked is addictive.

He came running straight to my maternal embrace when he discovered that Grace had nearly told TJ about a secret she and Smettle had shared for years. He played the audio recording for me, said he was being betrayed all over again. Smettle had made veiled references in the past to Grace owing him one. Now that he'd learned of her unfaithfulness, he was desperate to degrade her name in an inconsequential way, by which I mean confiding in me.

"The essay business was her idea, you know," he sneered, striding around the home theater as I fluffed the recliner pillows in advance of the *Rope* screening. "I put my neck out for her, and this is the thanks I get?"

I moved to straighten the books on the shelves. "She sounds horrid," I agreed, with my back to him.

"Worse than you know," Smettle mumbled.

I was getting nowhere. I needed something concrete. I tried baiting him for the hundredth time. "Young people aren't known for their good decision-making, though. You were practically teenagers, after all," I said. "How bad could she be?"

Smettle didn't respond for a while. I sensed his eyes boring into my shoulder blades. His voice was soft when he spoke. "That depends on your opinion of murder."

My hand stilled on an old leather-bound book. I turned slowly. "I'm sorry—did you say *murder?*"

Smettle backed off. "Forget I said anything. I'm being emotional."

"Alfred," I said, because I never called him Smettle to his face, "what has she done?"

He appeared uncertain then, still questioning whether he could trust me, even after all our board game nights and movie marathons. I stepped closer to him and put a palm on his arm. A risk, to be sure. Sometimes he craved physical contact; other times he pushed it away. Discerning which mood he was in and what he wanted from me was often difficult. He stared at my hand. "I was exaggerating," he said. "But she did hurt a former teacher of ours."

"Why didn't you tell anyone?" I asked.

He studied me. "Because I hurt him too."

Over and over, for sixteen years, I'd had to summon the resolve to keep hunting for clues, to get vengeance for Jerome. Yet nothing required more willpower than the simple act of keeping my palm on the arm of the man who had murdered my love.

Once I trusted my voice not to shake, I said, "Hurt how?"

Smettle smiled sadly. "All I can say is, he deserved it." I could have killed him right then and there.

Twelve hours later, I got the chance.

FIFTY-SEVEN

Danny

The guests file out of the theater—TJ, then Zoe, then Samira, then Julius—until I'm alone in the room. I pull myself to my feet. Most days I don't feel my age, but in this moment every joint aches; every bone is weary. At last my work here is done. I shuffle through the lobby and up the stairs to collect my things. The detectives do not shadow me like they do the others. I am too old to be a threat. Plus, by now they trust me.

Eager to be pronounced an ally, I gave the detectives those all-important initial leads: Zoe's poison suspicions, Julius's remarks during the perfect-murder conversation, TJ's questions for me about Chef's background, Grace's role as ringleader, her and TJ's affair, and, of course, Samira's visit to the storage closet. Agopian and Gromowski wanted to know why I'd been poking around in the middle of the night, why I hadn't checked what Samira was up to in the closet. I told them I had strict orders from my boss not to disturb his friends, so I'd had to settle for observing them from afar. Someone like me couldn't afford to lose her job; after all, I was on my own financially since my husband's pension had run out, and I was unlikely to secure another employment offer at my age. I said I worried for my boss but reassured myself that he knew his friends better than I did. I had no idea his life was in danger, or I would've stepped in.

In reality, I haunted those halls with little fear of repercussions. On the first night I saw and heard nothing out of the ordinary. I continued my watch Friday evening, the night Smettle had designated for murder. He had told me before going to bed that evening that he'd finally assigned roles to his unwitting guests. Zoe would be the victim and Grace her killer. Why those two? Zoe knew too much, he said, and Grace needed to face the consequences of her actions sixteen years ago. Grace hadn't crawled off campus with her tail between her legs like Smettle had. She didn't suffer any humiliation senior year. Now she would. Smettle declined to share the specifics of the plan but assured me he had worked it all out. He told me to stay in bed and not leave my room until the following morning.

As you already know, I ignored that order.

Minutes before one a.m., I was climbing the final stairs to the third floor when I caught Samira stealing into the storage closet. What was she up to? I moved down a few steps so as to escape notice, and waited. Ten minutes later, Smettle emerged from his room and also headed to the closet. Was Samira in on Smettle's plan, or was she an unforeseen complication? Were they in the attic together?

I had discovered the attic early on in my employment. My housekeeping duties brought me into the storage closet often. For the first month or so, I didn't think much of the hatch door built into the ceiling. Lots of old houses have similar hatches. Smettle had explained that he kept his mother's belongings up there, sentimental items he couldn't bear to part with but had no use for in his daily life. I assumed the attic housed nothing but dusty cardboard boxes filled with scrapbooks and framed photos.

As I tracked my boss's whereabouts, however, I saw that he was spending odd amounts of time in that closet. I reasoned that he must be going up to the attic—what could he be doing in a small closet for hours at a time otherwise? My curiosity grew. What was in the attic that drew him to it? My image of boring old boxes shifted to something spookier. A shrine to his dead mother. Her skeleton in a rocking chair, wearing a housedress like poor Norma Bates.

One afternoon Smettle had to run an errand that would keep him out of the house for hours. I took a desk chair from a guest room, barricaded the closet door from the inside, then pulled down the steps. I was so worried about being caught that I didn't have time to fear what I'd find in the attic until I was already up there. The mannequin and stuffed crow were odd, but I pushed on, searching every drawer in the dresser. In the top right one, I found something that made my breath catch. Jerome's eyeglasses, coated in dust, the wire frame bent out of shape on one side. The black chain was still attached to them. Tears welled in my eyes. I had bought him that chain from a market in Istanbul. Could this be the evidence I needed to take Smettle down?

After some consideration, I doubted the glasses would be enough. They were too circumstantial. I couldn't prove that Smettle hid them in this dresser, even that he knew of their existence. Nor could I prove that Jerome was wearing his glasses the day he died, or that this pair had belonged to him. A DNA swab might confirm the latter, but Smettle would make quick work of such flimsy evidence. The glasses would be his word against mine. I wanted ironclad confirmation, proof the police couldn't ignore.

I told myself to leave the glasses where they were, lest Smettle come searching for them someday. Emotion won out over logic. I pocketed the frames and kept them in my nightstand, removing them from time to time when I needed strength. Occasionally I worried that Smettle would find me out, but based on the amount of dust on Jerome's glasses, he hadn't touched them in years.

While I was reeling from my discovery, from the proof of Alfred Smettle's involvement in my husband's death, a conversation caught my ear in the attic. I could hear, drifting up through a vent in the floor, a discussion between two of our guests. The hair on my arms stood on end once I understood what I had in front of me. A spying station. Smettle had opened his hotel in the hope of watching decent people do indecent things.

I was sickened, as anyone would be. I considered going straight to the police and turning him in. Selfishly, I didn't. I let innocent strangers check into his hotel week after week, though I knew full well that their privacy would be invaded. I sacrificed them in order to keep fighting for Jerome. I was finally making inroads with Smettle and wasn't about to stop now.

Such satisfaction it brought me to give him a dose of his own medicine. Planting the platter and the glass of milk in the attic was no trouble at all. I did it while Smettle was settling his friends in the dining room for supper last night. I wasn't sure whether Smettle would understand the symbolism, whether he'd remember the poster from my husband's office. Jerome owned a lot of movie posters, but that one was his favorite. He loved how, without context, the image was innocuous. But if you'd seen *Suspicion* and understood that Joan Fontaine believed Cary Grant was poisoning her; if you remembered Grant's long climb up the staircase in the dark, carrying a glass of milk on a platter to his beloved with the grimmest of expressions on his face, you would understand the object to be anything but innocuous. That was what fascinated Jerome about movies—the way an image could have a hundred interpretations. A glass of milk can be wholesome, evoke the Midwest, cows grazing in a field, children with strong bones. Or it can represent a man trying to kill his rich wife for her life insurance.

I hoped Smettle would interpret the milk as a threat, a warning from the grave. Someone knew what he'd done to his professor. Someone wanted him to pay. Even if he'd long forgotten about the poster, even if he didn't connect it with Jerome, at least Smettle would know someone had discovered his precious spying station. He'd assume it had been one of his friends. Grace, most likely. She was the only other major Hitchcock fan among them, and the only one with intimate knowledge of Alfred's past crimes. He had threatened to expose her affair, and now she was threatening to expose his spy vents. If Smettle had been having second thoughts about his "publicity stunt," the glass of milk would strengthen his resolve. Maybe he would make a last-minute role change, choose Grace as his victim instead. Though I'm no fan of Zoe Allen's, I preferred that death knock on the door of the woman who helped kill my husband. At the very least, Smettle would now understand the vulnerability of the watched.

Huddled on the staircase, I waited for something to happen in the closet. Either Smettle, Samira, or both would come charging out of the space. Or perhaps they wouldn't. For the first time, I was worried. How well did I know any of these people? I was already aware of how dangerous Smettle was—what if the others were as bad? Maybe I'd been a fool to pursue vigilantism. Maybe I was a mindless old woman pretending to be a superhero.

A distinct thump shook me from my thoughts. The sound had come from the closet. I craned my neck, waiting, but heard nothing else. A minute or so later, the closet door opened again. Moving so fast that I could hardly make her out, Samira fled the closet and stumbled back inside her guest room, all but slamming the door behind her.

What had Smettle done to her?

I waited for him to exit the closet too, but after twenty minutes, he still hadn't shown. What could he be watching them all do through the vents at this hour? Most of them were asleep, weren't they?

Quiet as a cockroach, I tiptoed down the hallway, avoiding the floorboards that creaked. I put my ear to Samira's door and heard her crying. I continued on to the closet and cracked the door open, inch by inch. There I found Smettle, lying on his side with blood dripping from his head.

I ran to him and checked his pulse. Faint and flickering. He was unconscious, eyes closed. I glanced at his right leg, tangled in a painful position on the pull-down ladder. Shock made me slow, but I managed to identify three courses of action. Save him. Leave him. Kill him.

I backed out of the closet and pulled my ring of housekeeping keys from my flannel pajama pants, tripping over my feet like there were shoe-boxes on them rather than slippers. I fumbled with the keys until I found the one labeled 304. Smettle's room.

How many times had I searched his room? How many times had I memorized its contents? I pulled on a pair of leather gloves from his ar-moire, then moved over to the desk. I knew where he kept his prop weapons. I pulled out the rope, a replica from the prop used in the movie Smettle and his friends had watched hours earlier. I rushed out of the room and back to the closet. The hallway was quiet, undisturbed.

I'll say this much: strangling a man to death is fairly straightforward when he's unconscious. It took longer than I would have liked, but I won't lie and say I didn't relish the task. For so many years I had left the job to the authorities, and where had that gotten me? No one loved Je-rome like I did. Nobody was going to give me the resolution I needed. I would have to grab it for myself.

The body fought back, but only a little, reflexes meant to keep it alive. They weren't enough. I would have sat there all night with my foot on his chest, pulling both ends of the rope as hard as I could. When Jerome died, I began taking kickboxing classes as a way to protect myself. For so long, my husband had been my safety net. From kickboxing I learned I was capable of a strength entirely my own. I was more than equipped to get the job done.

Afterward, I pulled up his turtleneck to cover the red ring around his neck. Smettle was small and pitiable there on the floor, a broken baby bird. He wasn't such a mighty man after all. Just a vicious one.

In his room I found his phone and remembered the recording of Grace and TJ. That was when I came up with the idea to take down my husband's other murderer as well.

Later I would tell the detectives about the clip Smettle had played for me. Later, while the group was helping themselves to breakfast down-stairs, I would move the rope from Smettle's room to Grace's, scrub it with her toothbrush to ensure ample DNA transfer, then hide the rope in her suitcase. I have no way of knowing whether Smettle or Grace gave

Jerome the final shove, but now I don't need to. Both of their lives have been ruined the way they ruined ours.

At some point the detectives will dig up the cold case of Dr. Jerome Scott. Sooner or later, they'll connect the dots that I'm his wife and come knocking. I will tell them fate brought dear Alfred and me together. He reached out to me years ago, I will say, mourning the death of his favorite professor and mentor. We spent hours reminiscing about my husband, forming a friendship of sorts. Months later, dear Alfred shared the news that he was opening a hotel in the professor's honor. I begged to be a part of it, to join the staff. I was a lonely old woman, you see, eager for companionship and a tie to my dead husband. Over our year of working together, Alfred and I became close, almost like mother and son. I had no idea the man who had hired me was, in fact, my husband's killer. Cue histrionics. Cue awkward glances between the detectives. Cue my being sent home with reassurances and a pat on the back. Grace will rot in prison, and Alfred will rot in the ground. A fitting end for two killers.

It takes me no more than ten minutes to pack my things. I will donate my three uniforms—unlike Alfred Smettle, I want no mementos. I only want to return to my home in Portland, to sip a warm cup of coffee on the porch and read a book under a heavy blanket. We have a few weekends yet before the sun's rays weaken.

I sit in the lobby, waiting for Sergeant Agopian to come bustling down the stairs. When he does, he offers me a ride to the auto garage. The cars have already been towed.

"Thank you for your help today," he says. "Mr. Smettle was lucky to have you in his corner."

I peer at my shoes to tuck my smile out of view. We wait for the others to join us, hauling their duffel bags and suitcases. When all are accounted for, Samira, TJ, and I ride in Agopian's car to the garage, while Julius and Zoe ride in Gromowski's. I have to put up with the insufferable lot of them for another hour while we wait for our tires to be repaired, but an hour is not so long. An hour is a blink when you've been counting time by the years. I am in no hurry.

Tomorrow I will take a bouquet of dahlias, Jerome's favorite, to his grave. I will go through my usual routine. Set up the camping chair, arrange the flowers just so, put one hand on the cold stone and pretend the slab is his strong, sturdy back. I will tell him all I've done. I will say I hope he isn't mad at me. Were he alive, I know he would've persuaded me years ago to drop this quest. Jerome wasn't one for grudges.

That's why they're called our better halves.

When at last the mechanic hands me my keys, I lower myself into the driver's seat of the Camry. Jerome bought this car twenty years ago. The vehicle is beat-up and ornery, and I should replace it, but I can still remember us driving it out of the lot together, stopping for burgers and fries on the way home.

Samira, Julius, Zoe, and TJ stare at me wearily. They have aged several years in forty-eight hours. If Zoe knew how close she came to dying last night . . . If Samira knew that by hurting one friend she'd saved another . . . I like to think I played my own role in saving Zoe, given that I killed her would-be killer. I hope she devotes the next chapter of her life to pursuits worthwhile and honorable. I hope they've all learned something about themselves this weekend.

Perhaps someday, like the detectives, these people will learn my identity as the wife of their former professor. I won't be around to catch their reactions when they do.

"So long," I say to the four of them. I leave the lot without waiting for a reply.

FIFTY-EIGHT

Zoe

Zoe and the others watch the old housekeeper drive down the road. After a minute, her car disappears around a bend. *She left as quietly as she worked,* Zoe thinks.

"What an oddball," she says.

"She gave me the heebie-jeebies," Julius agrees.

The four of them stand in a small circle in the parking lot, glancing at the garage every so often. Zoe hopes her car is finished soon too. She's ready to get out of this town.

"I still can't believe Alfred is dead," Samira says.

"Do you really think Grace killed him?" TJ asks, pale-faced.

No one answers. The sun is trying to burn through the clouds. The odors of oil and gasoline waft through the air. A cold wind gooses the back of Zoe's neck. She should have packed a scarf.

Samira speaks up. "I have to tell you guys something." She describes her late-night trip to the attic, how Alfred startled her, which resulted in her shoving him to the closet below. She shares her confession to the detectives and their reveal of the rope marks around Alfred's neck. By the time she's finished speaking, TJ's eyes are popping and Julius's mouth hangs open.

Zoe's head spins. "Why didn't you tell us earlier?" she demands.

"I was scared of going to prison. I couldn't ask you to keep something like that hush-hush. I thought I killed him." Samira lets out a sob.

Zoe pulls Samira in for a hug. Julius mouths *Oh my God* behind Samira's back.

"What I don't get is why," Samira says. "Why would Grace kill Alfred?"

The four don't speak while Samira cries into Zoe's shoulder. TJ stares at his feet and mumbles, "We were having an affair. Alfred found out about it."

"You and Grace?" Zoe says.

TJ nods.

"Holy shit," Julius says.

"Since when?" Samira asks.

"How did it start?" Julius prods.

Zoe can't resist a jab. "You call *my* life a mess?" She feels a stab of anger at both TJ and Grace, then feels juvenile for being angry. Grace knew Zoe had a thing for TJ back in college, but Zoe doesn't anymore. Why should she care if two friends she hardly speaks to were sneaking around?

TJ doesn't answer any of these questions. Instead, he says, "I think Alfred threatened to tell Grace's husband."

"So she killed him?" Julius cries.

Zoe isn't so sure. She thinks back to what she told the detectives about senior year at Reville. Alfred had kept Grace's involvement in the essay scheme a secret, but that secret was too low stakes to warrant such drastic behavior. The murder of Dr. Scott, on the other hand, was not. All this time, Zoe thought Alfred had acted alone, that Grace knew what he'd done but kept quiet for fear of getting herself expelled too. What if Grace took a more active role, though? Maybe Alfred and Grace killed their professor together. Maybe Alfred threatened to go to the police if

Grace didn't comply with his demands. Is that why Grace insisted that they all come to the reunion this weekend? Zoe rubs her forehead.

TJ peers at her. "What?"

She shakes her head. Zoe now feels painfully aware of her body—its too-rapid breaths, the beating of her heart, the sweat on her palms. She has wasted years stuck in the past. No more.

A mechanic in coveralls walks over to the group. "Cars are ready when you folks are."

Zoe studies the face of each of her friends, these people who once knew her better than her own parents. She feels a surprising reluctance to leave.

"We're going to drop off TJ's rental car at the airport," Julius says, "and then he's going to come back to New York with me. Do you all maybe want to—I don't know—join us for breakfast in the city tomorrow morning?"

Julius's tone is casual, but Zoe detects hope there too. Zoe wants to ask why he and TJ are buddies all of a sudden, but when she glances at the latter, his cheeks are aflame. Maybe he's in bigger trouble than she thought.

"We could have an informal memorial for Alfred afterward," Julius adds.

"I'd love to." Samira smiles for the first time all day. "I'll have some news to share."

The three of them turn to Zoe. She pictures their foursome on a patio, eating huevos rancheros or French toast. That might not be so bad. Other future scenes dance around in her head. Her friends dining at Saint Vincent, with Zoe reinstated as head chef. All of them crowded around Julius's hospital bed postsurgery. Babysitting Samira's kids. Giving TJ pep talks. Celebrating Zoe's first month of sobriety. Maybe she wrote them off too early. There might be something here worth salvaging now that they've cut out the rot of Alfred and Grace.

"Count me in too," Zoe says. Zero percent chance she's participating in the memorial, though. Alfred can burn in hell as far as she's concerned. None of them know what he did to their professor. She will tell them soon. Her stomach churns, still uneasy.

Julius claps with delight. They climb into their cars and, like Danny before them, pull out of the parking lot one by one. Zoe is the last to go. She speeds down the single-lane road. In her rearview mirror she spots the house on the hill. Zoe presses harder on the accelerator until the Hitchcock Hotel is no longer in sight.

FIFTY-NINE

Months later

The crows recognize the housekeeper as soon as she enters the courtyard. She has always hated them, hissing whenever she passes the aviary. A while back she went so far as to let loose one of their own. The murder wonders what happened to him. What fate has he succumbed to?

The old woman has brought with her a man, smartly dressed, official-looking. The birds scream at the housekeeper as she circles their cage with her hands behind her back.

"I don't have to keep them, do I?" she asks, gesturing at the crows with her chin.

"Mr. Smettle's will doesn't indicate any care plans for the birds," the man says with a shudder. "I can see why you'd want to get rid of them. Nasty little things."

The housekeeper smirks at the crows. They pick up their cries, in mourning. What happened to the tall, lanky man? He was the lone person who loved the birds. He spoke and sang to them often, confided his problems and plans. Where has he gone? What has she done to him?

"You and Alfred must have been quite close," the man says. The housekeeper bows her head. "What will you do with the hotel now, Ms. Danielson?"

The housekeeper shrugs. "I haven't thought that far ahead."

The man nods and heads back inside the building. "I'm sure you'll come up with something."

The housekeeper watches him go, then turns to the crows. "Burn it to the ground," she whispers with a smile.

ACKNOWLEDGMENTS

I'll begin where the dedication ended: with my best friend, Ali, whom I met my freshman year of college. At eighteen, I was quiet and awkward around new people (some things never change), but Ali scooped me up and changed the trajectory of my life. When she gave a speech at my wedding, she told the roomful of guests that I was *her person*, taking the words right out of my mouth. Twenty years of pep talks and snort-laughs and vent sessions and love, so much freaking love. I can't believe my luck. This one's for you.

Like Alfred, I too lived with my friends in a blue house off campus during college. Unlike Alfred's friends, mine had my back no matter the quandary. To Kelsey, Rachel, and Caty: you made college all it was. Thank you for letting me borrow (steal) from our memories. I hope this story takes you back.

Dr. Scott from the book is named after a real-life Dr. Scott who was a professor of mine at Miami University. I took his film studies course as an elective and loved it so much I took a second class with him. He almost certainly doesn't remember me, as I was not the kind of student to speak much, but he's the one who introduced me to Hitchcock, via *North by Northwest*. To him I owe a boatload of gratitude.

Three texts were instrumental in teaching me about Hitchcock the man— *The Twelve Lives of Alfred Hitchcock: An Anatomy of the Master of Suspense* by Edward White; *Hitchcock/Truffaut* by François Truffaut; and *Alfred Hitchcock: A Life in Darkness and Light* by Patrick McGilligan. For those craving a deeper dive into the director, I highly recommend all of these books.

My agent, Maddy Milburn, continues to enable me to do what I love most. Thank you for your vision, your determination, and your unwavering optimism. To the rest of the MMLA team, especially Saskia Arthur, Hannah Kettles, Hannah Ladds, Giles Milburn, Valentina Paulmichl, Georgina Simmonds, and Rachel Yeoh: thank you. It takes a village, and you all are one brilliant village.

My incisive editors, Amanda Bergeron in the US and Max Hitchcock in the UK, helped me shape this idea into a book as quickly and painlessly as possible.

Thanks to Sareer Khader and Emma Plater as well for their sharp (but gentle!) pens. All four of you made this book immeasurably better. Much appreciation to my copy editor, Zach Vigna, for his careful attention. Sorry again for all the unclear antecedents.

To the Berkley team: Loren Jaggers, Danielle Keir, Hannah Engler, Emily Osborne, Claire Zion, Craig Burke, Jeanne-Marie Hudson, Christine Ball, and Ivan Held. To the Penguin Michael Joseph team: Courtney Barclay, Sriya Varadharajan, Christina Ellicott, Lauren Wakefield, Vicky Photiou, Elizabeth Smith, Hannah Padgham, Richard Rowlands, Akua Akowuah, and James Keyte. And to the Simon & Schuster Canada team: Adrienne Kerr, Shara Alexa, Jeremy Cammy, Lisa Wray, Jasmine Elliott, Mackenzie Croft, and Nicole Winstanley. Thank you all for your creativity and passion, for lifting up my work and sharing it with the world.

Shout-out to the design team at Cover Kitchen for the iconic US cover.

More than once, Andrej Zukov Gregoric patiently explained the career paths available to hedge-fund analysts, which made Grace Liu's career path more realistic. Thank you for your expertise.

To reader Lily Agopian Gromowski, who generously donated to the Authors for Voices of Color fundraiser and lent both of her last names to the detectives in this story.

To my family: Vicki, Ryan, Jackie, Matt, Cadence, Logan, Sheila, Taylor, and Paul. You celebrate my wins and explain away my losses. I don't know what I'd do without you.

My parents, Ron and Kathy Wrobel, give the best advice and attempt to sell my books to every unsuspecting stranger they encounter. Long have I joked they should be on Penguin Random House's payroll. You sure know how to make a girl feel loved.

To my inimitable husband, Matt. When I told him my idea for this book, he suggested I come up with something else. I still adore you anyway. Very, very much.

Last but certainly not least, to the esteemed director himself and his creative partner/wife, Alma Reville. I suspect Hitchcock would publicly pooh-pooh (but privately crave) a tribute, so I'll keep mine brief. I can think of few storytellers who have taught me more about my craft than the two of you. Thank you for the lessons you continue to impart and for the mountain of art you left behind. We owe you one. A big one.

P.S. Sorry for turning this book into a whodunit halfway through, Hitch—I know how you felt about them.